HE TURNED TO
TREMBLING W...

Frank clipped a maga... ...he rifle, passing her the handgun. "I'm going up front. We can't sit here and wait for Saburov to get lucky with one of those bombs. Anything happens to me, take the pack and head back, as far as you can, into the cave."

"I'm coming with you."

Frank shook his head. "No point in you—"

"Frank—"

He paused. "Stay here," he said softly.

There was another explosion to the south, farther along the cliffs toward the pinnacle. "What'll I do?" she shouted frantically. "If you don't come back? Frank!" She took his arm, clinging to him.

There was more debris falling over the cave's entrance, then a bomb exploding nearby. Soon it was several minutes since the last bomb had detonated. Then the dirt stopped falling. Silence. Had they given up? Minutes were ticking away.

Think, he told himself. Think like that bastard, Saburov.

STORM

IAN SLATER

W✦RLDWIDE ®

TORONTO • NEW YORK • LONDON • PARIS
AMSTERDAM • STOCKHOLM • HAMBURG
ATHENS • MILAN • TOKYO • SYDNEY

For Marian,
Serena and Blair

STORM

A Worldwide Library Book/June 1988

ISBN 0-373-97073-0

ACKNOWLEDGMENT

I would like to thank Dr. Noel Boston, a friend from my oceanographic days who is now Director of TEC in Vancouver. I also extend my gratitude to my friend, Professor Charles Slonecker, for his help, and to Mr. Cy White, whose assistance in the preparation of the manuscript was greatly appreciated. Most of all I am indebted to my wife, Marian, whose patience, typing and editorial skills continue to give me invaluable support in my work. Many thanks.

Chapter One
November 1, 3:50 a.m., Northeast Pacific

"MAYDAY, MAYDAY..."

The radio operator of the M.V. *Lvov*, a twelve-hundred-ton Polish trawler of the RT-800 type, out of Gdansk and now seventy miles off the United States west coast, tapped out the SOS calmly, bracing himself against the heavy swells. The other ship's lights, seen earlier in the pitch-darkness, were only seven miles to the east and the ship should be receiving the *Lvov*'s call for help despite the sea clutter caused by the approaching storm.

"*Czy macie odpowiedz?* Any response?" shouted the *Lvov*'s first mate.

"No," answered the operator. "Not a— Hang on...yes! They hear us. They're coming!"

"Thank God," said the mate, quickly turning and taking the steps up into the wheelhouse two at a time. "Keep her into the wind," he shouted. "Steady as you can."

ABOARD THE OTHER SHIP, the M.V. *Swiftsure*, a United States trawler of more modern vintage, the captain took up his Zeiss binoculars, scanning the blackness. He could see nothing, even though the Mayday had given the Polish trawler's exact position. He glanced down at the National Ocean Service's chart 18007, covering the seas off Cape Flattery from the northernmost point of Washington State to San Francisco in the south, then looked at the compass, steady within the crazy motion of its gimbals mounting.

"Hard aport," he ordered. "Steer zero-four-one."

"Zero-four-one," came the confirmation.

Lowering the glasses, the captain switched on the bridge-to-radio room intercom. "Signal to M.V. *Lvov*. Am approximately five miles southwest of your position and closing but unable to see you. Repeat. Unable to see you."

"Yes, sir."

"Where the hell are her lights?" asked the captain as he flicked off the intercom.

"There she is!" called the helmsman. "Off the port quarter."

The captain swung the glasses around toward a red speckle dancing between the distant swells. "She's afire! Light circuits must have blown." He glanced at the compass again. "Steer zero-three-niner."

"Zero-three-niner."

Pistons straining, making twelve knots even against the southward-bound Californian current, *Swiftsure* was only twenty minutes from the *Lvov*, but the American captain could now see the fire more clearly in his binoculars. A few toy-size black figures were frantically fighting it on the well deck, as flames leaped between the trawler's wheelhouse and its bow. She rose and fell in the undulating glow, lumps of fishing nets faintly visible near a forward winch. The fire's reflections on the swells were repeatedly speared by the trawler's mast as it disappeared and reappeared, dipping between the waves. Now and then thick shadows, wafting smoke, obscured the fire. The American captain spotted one of the trawler's lifeboats swinging wildly out of control, its bowline still attached to a davit, its stern bumping and scraping alongside as *Lvov* bucked and rolled in the troughs.

"Lifeboat wouldn't do 'em any good anyway," said another of *Swiftsure*'s lookouts. "Not if this weather gets any worse."

The captain heard the remark but it didn't register, his eyes intent on the direction and size of the swells, his heartbeat steady but faster, worried about reaching *Lvov* in time. Even in summer it was only a matter of minutes in these cold northern waters before hypothermia set in. In November, and in pitch-darkness, the Polish seamen wouldn't stand a chance.

Chapter Two

IT WAS FIFTEEN MINUTES later and farther west, aboard the 150-foot, 550-ton United States oceanographic vessel M.V. *Petrel* when Captain Tate's voice crackled from the bridge into the oceanographer's cabin. "Mr. Hall. Mr. Hall... please report to the bridge."

Frank Hall could smell the perfume enveloping him as Mary Crane bent her head coyly, almost childlike, her long, golden-blond hair swinging effortlessly like wind coral against his face, her deep blue eyes fixed on his. His arms enfolded her, pulling her closer. Suddenly the captain's voice invaded the darkness again, and they were separated, he dropping her hand guiltily as her late husband, his onetime boss, suddenly appeared. Now Mary tossed her hair back unabashed, her breasts firm in tropic sun, coconut-scented breezes blowing her hair lazily against a sun-glinting cobalt sea. Palm trees swayed high above them, bent in obeisance to the trade winds' caress, and all around them hibiscus bloomed, vivid reds splashed against the ice-cream Hawaiian sky. Tate's voice sounded again. Frank was sitting up in the bunk, still feeling vaguely guilty, the pitching and rattling of the vessel replacing the tranquillity of his dream.

"Mr. Hall... please report to the bridge. Please report..."

Frank Hall swung his feet over the edge of the bunk, his stomach rolling with the ship as it yawed between the swells that had traveled unimpeded thousands of miles across the Pacific. He had been to sea a hundred times, working first for Joe Crane as senior marine geology technician in Canada, and then, after receiving his science degree from Oregon State, as geologist in a never-ending search for the elusive, mineral-rich deposits of the seabed known as sea gold. He had spent more time in the Pacific than most of the seamen aboard *Petrel*, but still, the first twelve hours or so were always the same. His senses of balance, taste and smell had to reacquaint themselves with the odors and the constantly moving world of the ship. High up on the starboard side, his cabin, the chief scientist's, was cold, its blackness heavy with the clamminess of recycled air and diesel fumes, its portholes, like all the others on *Petrel*, sealed to preserve what the designers had been pleased to call "the integrity of the ship's air-conditioning." As Frank's muscular, five-foot-ten-inch frame swung down from the bunk, feet slapping the hard steel deck, his normally alert blue eyes looked back tiredly at him from the wall mirror, and the rugged, sunburned cheeks beneath the bushy shock of light brown hair seemed paler than usual. He wondered whether the designers of the *Petrel* had ever been aboard their latest oceanographic vessel on her test runs. She wasn't a bad ship and she had every modern scientific convenience, from the latest bottom-sounding sonar to the highly accurate loran navigation system. But her aluminum superstructure, housing a wet and a dry lab on the main deck and the scientists' and officers' cabins above, was unusually high for her 150-foot length. As the sailors liked to say, she would roll on a morning dew. In anything over force four, with little more than ten-to-sixteen-knot winds, Frank's cabin would rise and fall in gut-wrenching gyrations, and in force ten, the crew of twenty called her the Scream Machine. Still Frank, as Mary Crane's partner in what was now her company, Sea

Gold Inc., gladly put up with the ship's eccentricities, grateful for the chance to have bid on and won six days of scarce ship time on such a well-equipped government research ship.

Captain Tate's voice came over again, and a shape, barely visible in the lower bunk, groaned and rolled closer to the bulkhead as an empty can of Foster's Lager rolled aimlessly across the cabin floor. "Tell 'im to put a sock in it!"

Frank ignored his new assistant's advice, steadying himself against the metal desk near the bunk and depressing the intercom button. "Oceanographer to bridge. Be right up."

"What time is it?" asked the shape.

Though still only half-awake himself, Frank braced himself against the next roll and began to pull on his khaki shirt, faded jeans and standard-issue, bright canary-yellow oilskins. Spray from the bow splattered and smeared the cabin's forward porthole as Frank glanced at his leather-covered watch. "It's 0400," he said to the shape. "Four o'clock to a landlubber like you."

"In the *morning*?"

"Yes, but don't worry. We're not due on station for another hour."

"Then what's the panic?"

"Don't know. Old man wants to see me."

"Geez, it stinks in here."

"You should wash more often."

"Cheeky Yank!"

Frank flicked on the desk lamp. The shape withdrew from the soft peach light like a sea slug snuggling closer in to the bulkhead. "Does this happen often?" came the flat Australian drawl.

"What?"

"Being woken up in the middle of the bloody night."

"I told you. Every few hours there's a sampling station. You'll get used to it, Aussie."

"No, I won't."

"Why'd you come to sea then?"

"Same as you. I need the loot and I'm soft in the bloody head. Geez, I feel a bit crook, Frank."

"Don't feel great myself. But you'll be all right. Stay in the sack till we're on station."

"Thanks."

Frank zipped up the oilskin jacket, snapped down the metal buttons, donned his favorite old navy-blue toque and was gone. Before heading up the stairwell to the bridge he opened the forward bulkhead door under the projecting lip of the bridge. A blast of icy air instantly returned the color to his cheeks, bringing him fully awake.

The moment he entered the soft blackness of the bridge, tiny islands of colored lights winked at him, attended by men he could not yet make out. He also sensed a somber mood, which was soon explained to him by *Lvov*'s continuing call for help, now a fading, crackling SOS, all but lost in an increasing rush of static. As his eyes became accustomed to the darkness he could make out Captain Tate, his thin, tall frame hunched over the green glow of the radar. Multiple beeps and amber spots on the screen marked the position of *Lvov* and the rest of the Polish fleet, which were all too far south to help their sister ship.

"Mayday, Frank," said Tate tersely. "Have to cancel your stations, I'm afraid."

"Of course."

Tate nodded toward the small chart room, a step down, immediately aft of the steering console. "First mate has plotted a new sea gold search line for you from the Mayday position. Don't know how much time we'll have left after the rescue, if we reach them in time for a rescue. There's another ship approaching her but she's not as fast as we are—the *Swiftsure*."

"What's she?" asked Frank.

"Trawler, out of Astoria. In any case we have to reduce the number of sampling stations you'll time for. Can

you mark out a series of priority stations from your pro-
jected search pattern?"

"That's no problem," replied Frank, hiding his disappointment. Since the death of Joe Crane, Frank and Mary
Crane had tried hard to get an allocation of vital ship time
in order to determine the exact locations of the hot springs
that yielded the sea gold. He and Crane, through dredg-
ing, taking cores and grab samples and dropping seismic
charges, had confirmed the general existence of the rich
muds on the vast ocean floor off the Pacific Northwest,
but the sampling covered such wide areas that precise locations had not yet been found. To be delayed further in
finding out whether there were untold riches here, off Oregon and farther south from their earlier search patterns,
was an understandable blow. But Frank knew, too, what
it would be like to be aboard the stricken Polish trawler at
this moment, your vessel ablaze, a vast, angry sea all about
you. Out here, he reflected, there was only one national-
ity—seaman. The ocean was a common love and a common enemy. You dropped whatever you were doing and
helped one another no matter what. There was no other
code. They would do the same for him.

Stepping down into the redded-out chart room he saw
Mary Crane. The blood-red glow, used to ensure easier
adaptation to night vision, had the effect of softening the
lines on her face while giving a lurid sheen to her lips and
long hair. Mary Crane's deep blue eyes seemed even more
mysterious than they usually did.

"You have the list with you, Frank?" she asked.

"No. It's on the computer disk in my cabin," he answered. "I can double-check later but I think I can remember most of the locations on the first leg. Let's have a
look at the chart."

With the pullout desk top fully extended to accommodate the 18007 map, *Petrel*'s small chart room shrank even
more.

"Bit cramped in here," Frank announced good-humoredly as he picked up the parallel rule.

"Yes," she said, her thigh pressing his as the ship shifted hard to starboard and back again.

He tried steadying the rule as *Petrel* climbed, momentarily suspended, before crashing into the next wave, throwing him full against her.

"Sorry," he said, embarrassed.

"What for?" she said softly. "Can't help it. Can we?"

It was now 0428. *Petrel* and *Swiftsure* were still receiving the failing *Lvov*'s Mayday but, as radio and radar signals became more scrambled, bouncing crazily off the growing seas, the radar dots that were once *Lvov* and her sister trawlers soon became indistinguishable from the general clutter. It was as if someone had sprinkled iridescent pepper all over the radar screen.

"My God!" Captain Tate was watching the radar set. One of the myriad dots had suddenly swelled from the size of a pinpoint to that of a quarter. As everyone on the bridge looked on helplessly, the blip became intensely bright, almost white, then quickly faded, instantly replaced by hundreds of tinier, less luminous dots. Then from outside, over the howling of the wind, came a sound like rolling thunder from the explosion.

"Jesus!" said *Petrel*'s first mate. "She's gone! Must have been her boiler that blew."

"Or her fuel tanks," Tate said grimly, immediately instructing Sparks to call the American trawler, *Swiftsure*, for any additional information she might have on the explosion.

"I have been calling her, sir," said Sparks, a short, dapper man with an immaculate mustache. "No answer yet. Radio traffic's gone to hell."

"Nothing?"

"No, sir. Not a word."

"Hell," said the first mate, "you don't think *Swiftsure* reached her just as she went up?"

"Went down," said the lookout gloomily.

"No," said Tate. "There was only one blip—not two. How about you, Frank? With all the army and seismic charges you've used you're the explosives expert around here."

"It's possible there were two explosions if *Swiftsure* was in close when the other trawler blew. Won't know for sure, though, till this weather eases so we can get a clear count of the number of ships on the radar."

"Yeah," added the mate. "This friggin' sea clutter's..." He checked himself. "Sorry, Mrs. Crane."

"That's all right." She turned to Tate. "Captain, if *Swiftsure* had been that close, wouldn't we have heard a Mayday from her?"

"Not if she went down fast," answered Frank.

"But wouldn't her radio operator have been right by his set in that situation?"

"Should have been," Tate conceded, "in a rescue op. Then again the atmospherics are so bad he could be radioing us now, but as Sparks says, we wouldn't hear him in this static."

"Never know," the first mate interjected optimistically. "Forecast said there's a long storm line coming up from the south but lulls in between. Might be able to see the radar and hear radio traffic then."

"Well," began Mary Crane, "we might as well resume the grab stations."

"Right!" Frank said eagerly. "I'll start rigging the—"

"If you don't mind," the captain cut in chillingly, facing both of them. "I'd like to go in and look for possible survivors from *Lvov*."

"Of course," Mary said. "I just assumed that if you thought the American trawler was still there and afloat that she could—"

"We aren't sure, Mrs. Crane," said Tate, turning his back on her to face the steering console. Mary was about to apologize, but he was already giving the helmsman a new course toward the point of the explosion.

AS FRANK MADE HIS WAY back to the cabin to check his list of stations on the floppy disk, the dawn was graying sullenly. He slumped into the heavy wooden chair by the scientist's desk, looking despondently at the salt-crusted porthole as spray spit at it every few seconds. For a moment on the bridge he had shared Mary's willingness to get on quickly with the new line of stations, and it made him feel ashamed. At first he told himself that after such an explosion on a trawler, no one would even think of survivors, not in these waters and certainly not at this time of year. But then he began wondering why he hadn't thought of at least going to search in the area. Had his and Mary Crane's search for the sea gold become so all-consuming that it had willfully pushed the possibility of any survivors out of his mind? It was true that all he and Mary had talked of lately was finding the hot spots that signaled sea gold deposits. They had spent night after night studying the charts and Joe Crane's logs of past cruises, looking for the most likely places for the fissures, wherever the water temperature taken in sampling bottles was sixty degrees Fahrenheit, six times the normal bottom temperature for these parts. In such places, boiling seawater, after traveling thousands of miles through subterranean rock aquifers and leaching out minerals, blew up from the hot suboceanic crust into the ice-cold water of the deep ocean, depositing burnished hills of golden-colored deposits fantastically rich in everything from iron to manganese, cobalt, silver and gold. So rich was the prospect of sea gold, that nation was fighting nation in the international courts for the rights to mine the ocean resources, particularly those countries that needed scarce minerals for their defense-related industries.

Aboard *Petrel* Frank had carried out a search on the dry lab's computer of all the old bottom samples taken on oceanographic cruises off the northwest coast during the past ten years, plotting possible locations of the vents wherever higher than normal temperatures were reported and wherever gelatinous green ooze and the rotten egg smell of hydrogen sulfide had been found in bottom samples—indicating a lack of oxygenated water and possible deposits. His completed list, plotted on the Mercator projection map of the Northeast Pacific, formed a long, L-shaped area off Oregon's northern coast, south of the main Juan de Fuca Ridge system and running along the seams of the oceanic plates that ground against one another at depths of one thousand fathoms and more. But now in the predawn gloom, he made a mental note not to let his desire for sea gold smother common decency and hoped that if anyone had somehow managed to survive the explosion on the Polish trawler, *Petrel* would reach them in time.

The intercom spluttered, ''Bridge to scientist.''

''Go ahead,'' answered Frank.

''We've received a Morse message from *Swiftsure*,'' said Tate gruffly. ''They'll pick up whatever survivors there might be, so we're back on line.''

''Thanks, Captain.''

''What? What's going on?'' The questions came from the bundle on the lower bunk.

''Five o'clock,'' said Frank. ''Time you were up, Aussie.''

''My mouth tastes like a shit house.''

''You always so eloquent?''

''When's the station?''

Frank glanced at his watch. ''Thirty minutes. A thousand fathoms.''

''How long'll that take?''

Frank usually did the calculation mentally, but turned to the computer instead, punching out the monochrome figures on the green screen.

"Twenty-four minutes down, an hour and twenty up," said Frank.

"Listen, sport." The bundle sat up, ginger hair sprouting from a tepee-shaped blanket. "How about you do this station and I'll take the next one. What d'you say?"

"Off your butt!"

"I don't feel so hot, Frank. Dinkum." He rubbed his stomach delicately. "The old gut's a little fragile."

"The old rotgut," Frank answered. "You'd better lay off the sauce, Aussie. You'll be woozy enough your first time out, without booze on top of it." Frank kicked the wastebasket; an empty whiskey bottle rattled forlornly amid a bevy of empty beer cans.

"Ah, yeah—well, it's not the beer, mate. It's the home brand whiskey, Torio. Tasmanian Oil Refineries Number Ten, we call it. Use it for jet fuel."

"Then why do you drink it?"

"Cheap, mate. 'Round the world for a dollar.'"

Frank shook his head, taking the Australian's repartee in good humor, but he didn't like boozing on a cruise, especially before the very first station. "Listen, Digger, I'm serious. If you don't go easy you'll be in trouble."

"Ah, c'mon, Frank. Don't read the bloody riot act. I'll be okay. Right as rain. All I need is a bit of time for a shit, shave and shampoo, and we're off to the races. A bit of tucker in me and a cup of char and it'll be Errol Flynn out there. Fair enough?"

Frank swiveled the computer head into the lock position, looking dubiously across at the bedraggled shape. The cabin atmosphere was still thick with body odor and recycled air.

"Listen, sport," pressed the Australian. "You put this bloody grab down or whatever and bring it up, and I'll do *two* stations for you later on. Fair enough?"

Frank nodded. "Okay, but from now on it's off the hooch or off the ship."

"Going to toss me overboard?" asked the Australian cheekily.

"Off the payroll when we get back. Tell you the truth, I wouldn't have hired you if I hadn't been shorthanded and on short notice. And I sure as hell wouldn't have taken you on if I'd known you hit the sauce so much!"

"Ah, don't come the raw prawn—"

"Look!" said Frank, "I don't mind you feeding me a line about having worked on ships before, but drinking is something else. If you're smashed on deck you're a menace to everyone, not only yourself. The equipment that'll be swinging about out there is heavy stuff, and once that storm line clobbers us it's going to get worse."

"Storm line?" The Australian's tone betrayed alarm.

"Yes. Storms blowing up from down south—Panama. There'll be a lull here and there but we'll get most of it."

"Christ! It's a bloody gale out there now!"

Frank grinned. He couldn't help liking the Australian. "Are you kidding? These swells? Compared to what you're going to see, sport, this is plain sailing. The warning's for a force twelve. *That's* a storm. Hell, this is just a bit of fresh air."

The Australian's head jerked farther from the blanket into the semidarkness, freckled face florid, brushlike hair sticking up like the frayed ends of a mop. "Fresh air, my arse! Look at that spray. It's splashing all over the front!"

"The *bow*," said Frank. "Anyway, they're just piddling waves. It's the depth of swell and the frequency that matters. Don't sweat it. You'll find your sea legs quickly enough. Most people feel a bit queer the first few days out."

"Right!" said the Australian skeptically.

Frank watched him glaring out through the porthole at the giant, thousand-pound Petersen grab, its huge steel jaws spread wide apart, ready to spring and clang shut, trapping anything in its bite with a viselike grip. Aussie slumped back down on the bunk, and even in the dim light

Frank could see he looked a bit green around the gills. It struck Frank then that it wasn't so much the weather as the new job that was worrying the Australian, a kind of delayed stage fright after he'd talked his way into the position, pretending he knew more about oceanography than he really did. Once he and Mary had unexpectedly been granted sea time aboard *Petrel*, Frank had had only enough time to take the newcomer at his word. Perhaps taking people at their word was something he did too often.

"Look, Aussie," Frank assured him, "you'll be all right. Remember how we ran through it ashore over the training tank. When you swing the grab out you have to keep it clear of the ship, but the winch man and pike man will look after that. And when it's coming up from the bottom, keep watching the meter wheel. At ten fathoms tell the winch man to stop and wind it in slowly. The moment the grab breaks surface, cut the winch immediately, otherwise the grab'll come crashing into the ship and send the old man into apoplexy. Puts a big dent in the side. So whatever you do, don't let go of the grab's cable during a roll, or she'll swing out wild then come in like a wrecking ball."

"Sounds terrific. I can hardly bloody wait."

"I'll come out and give you a hand."

"Thanks, Frank. That's nice of you."

Frank shrugged and checked out the floppy disk that contained the secret locations he'd chosen as promising sites for future sea gold claims. He put it away in the small safe that was welded to the deck and bulkhead beside the chief scientist's bunk, and spun the combination lock. "You better get as much sleep as you can now," he told the Aussie. "I'll give you a shake about a half an hour before the second station."

"Thanks, mate. Your blood's worth bottling."

"I'm off to breakfast," said Frank.

"Don't tell me," the Aussie moaned.

"Yes," continued Frank, bracing himself against a roll. "Think I'll have a couple of nice fried eggs. Then some greasy bacon and—"

"You bastard."

IN FIFTEEN MINUTES they'd be on station so Frank hadn't bothered taking off his wet gear and heavy boots. He stood nursing a cup of coffee, wedging himself in the nook between the after starboard winch and the bulkhead of the wet lab, where fresh samples from grabs and corer barrels were labeled and stored for analysis. Swilling the dregs of the coffee, he tossed them leeward into the bubbling S of the ship's wake, which was becoming increasingly visible in the predawn light.

It was at that moment, up forward on the bridge, that the lookout thought he spotted something off on the starboard quarter, about a mile away. He lowered the binoculars and used his shirt cuff to clean the salt specks off the lens. He knew that on watch a person's eyes can play a hundred tricks: confusing stars for shore lights, interpreting the misbegotten shapes of clouds as land or seeing a salt particle on the lens, backlighted by dawn, as the dot of a ship. Now through the cleaner lens he saw nothing in the magnified circle of metallic gray, only a heaving, foam-streaked sea. But then, just for a fraction of a second, he was sure he saw something blur between massive swells. Just as suddenly it was gone.

Chapter Three

THE ROTUND AND BALDING fishing commissioner sat in his chair overlooking the huge, spidery gantries around the port of Gdansk, and watched the snow fall, mesmerized by the countless flakes. When the phone rang, his hand reached out, robotlike, his gaze still captive to the snow; his voice and arm also seemed detached. "Hello."

"Commissioner?"

"Yes."

"We have a relay, sir, via Baltic station from the Third Fishing Fleet."

The commissioner's gaze shifted around slowly, reluctantly, toward the large wall map of the world's oceans, the different fleets identified by red, white and green pins. He exhaled lethargically. "Northeast Pacific?" he asked.

"Correct, sir. Canadian and U.S. west coast."

"Proceed."

"There's been a mechanical problem."

He forgot about the snow. "Problem?" It was a word that told the commissioner that something much more serious than a simple mechanical breakdown or ripped trawls and nets had occurred—something that the mother ship had felt she had to relay immediately to higher authority. Perhaps one of the trawlers had ventured too far into the United States coastal fishing zone and had been arrested by either the American or Canadian coast guard. All he knew was that the fishing fleet was under his ministry and it would be his neck if anything had gone wrong.

"Who's responsible?" he asked. It was always a good question. If the phone call was tapped then it was better to start recording other names, preferably senior people, so as to spread the blame if it became necessary later. At least get in a captain or two.

"Beg your pardon, sir?"

"Who's responsible?"

"The weather."

"*Nie bądź głupi!* Don't be a cretin!" snapped the minister.

"I'm sorry, sir, but it *was* the weather. There's a storm line approaching, a lot of sea clutter. It snowed out the radars, otherwise the situation would have been much clearer earlier on."

"No one's been arrested, then?" This was code for "no one's in trouble?"

"No, sir. They've recovered now but, uh, the mother ship thought you should know."

"Fine. What's the main catch?"

"Cod. No Flounder."

Cod meant that everything was all right now, despite an interruption, but Flounder would have meant there was the possibility of recurrence.

"The U.S. Met Office," the caller continued, "is forecasting a big storm, force twelve. I wouldn't want to be aboard."

"You're not," the commissioner replied tartly and hung up. He got up to stretch his legs, reassuring himself. There was no reason to panic. In fact, the approaching storm, though it might well have caused the trouble, might yet prove useful. In any event, the main thing was that everything now seemed back under control. When he sat down, he turned back to face the window. The phone rang again.

"Yes, what is it?"

"Moscow," said the operator.

The commissioner sat upright, his grip on the phone increasing. "Commissioner here."

"Hello, Commissioner. Comrade Kornon."

"Yes, Comrade." It was a practiced cheerfulness. "What can I do for you?"

"We've had a report that the fishing isn't so good?"

The commissioner's jaw tightened. The Russian bosses hadn't even had the decency to wait five minutes, to pretend, at least, they had not heard the news before him. "Ah, yes, Comrade. Bad weather drives the top fish down. But the fleet'll be all right. It can ride out the storm, then continue trawling."

"Really?"

The commissioner shifted forward in his seat, the fingers of his left hand drumming on the blotter. "Yes, I believe everything's under control, Comrade."

"You *believe*?"

"Yes, Comrade."

"I *believe* it's snowing in Gdansk right now. Is it?"

"Yes, Comrade." The commissioner glanced out the window just to make sure. "It's coming down a ton."

"And what will happen when the snow stops? Will you be able to see things much clearer?"

The commissioner began to sweat. What was Kornon up to? Their Moscow arrogance was unbelievable. Always talking down to you as if you were forever the pupils and they the masters. Which they were.

"When it clears we'll all be able to see better, yes, Comrade," answered the Pole.

"And so will radar," Kornon replied.

The Polish commissioner's throat felt dry. Yet the more he tried to determine precisely what the question meant, the more confused and flustered he became. "I don't understand."

"That's obvious, Comrade. When the weather clears there will be no clutter on radar screens. If certain people think you have lost a ship, don't you think they'll investigate? Check out what ships are in the area?"

Mother of Christ! thought the commissioner. Why hadn't he seen it before? He scrambled for an answer. "Ah—well—of course our fishing fleet will be, ah...much farther south by then, Comrade."

"I see. You think the Americans turn their radar sets off when you fish farther south?"

The commissioner stopped drumming on the blotter; now he was curling its edges back, flattening them so they would never be the same again. "No sir. But I expect our trawler captains know what to do."

"I hope so, Comrade. But you didn't think ahead, did you?"

What was the use? "No, sir," confessed the commissioner.

"You should have," chided Kornon. "Fortunately we did, but what if it had been a situation we had not anticipated—one we hadn't instructed them about? We would be relying solely on you to direct them, Comrade—to use your brains."

The commissioner felt as if he was in a sauna. "I apologize, Comrade."

"Very gratifying, Commissioner. But fishing quotas are my responsibility, also. We must share in the catch, Comrade, and apologies won't save me if anything else goes wrong. And remember, Comrade, if a mother ship sinks in rough weather the little ones are lost. You take my meaning?"

"Yes, sir."

"Good day."

When the commissioner put down the phone his hand was shaking, the palm glistening with perspiration. Why did Moscow have to involve him at all? If Kornon was so worried why didn't he run it directly himself? Because they needed a front, the commissioner answered himself, that was why. If anything went wrong the Poles would take the crap, not them. Opening his desk drawer, the commissioner reached in and poured himself a large glass of plum brandy, then called for his secretary. "Advise the mother ship—Fishing Fleet Three—to take the following precautions..."

"In code, sir?"

"Yes, yes. Code. For God's sake—" He held up his hand. "I'm sorry, Nina." Composing himself, he offered her an American cigarette, and, leaning over the desk, lit it for her. Their eyes met and she knew what he would want after dictating the message. When the commissioner needed to let off steam he did it in a very traditional way. She didn't mind. After all, that's how she got the job, and besides, in order to assuage his latent bourgeois conscience afterward, he never failed to issue her "luxury" coupons for the party specialty shops, which were hidden from public view.

"My message," instructed the commissioner, "will have been sent two hours ago. You understand?"

"Of course, sir."

He sat back, drawing heavily on the filter tip, relaxed by his cunning. By having the message recorded as if it had been sent two hours before, any subsequent party investigation would show that he had acted promptly *before* the call from Moscow. He would instruct the mother ship likewise to record receipt of his radio instruction two hours earlier.

"Are you free for dinner, Nina?" he asked his secretary.

"If you wish."

"I do."

"Then I'm free." She smiled. The commissioner nodded, satisfied. Everything was under control.

Chapter Four

"WHAT DO YOU THINK of the plan, Minister?" Kornon had asked Borgach six months ago in his office in the Kremlin. "As a member of the Politburo?"

Nikolai Borgach, short, stocky and slightly drunk, had smiled knowingly at the younger, more junior general, who at fifty-one was one of the eight first deputy ministers of defense and the one who handled liaison with the Department of Fisheries and Ocean Resources. "You mean," asked Borgach, "what do I think of your plan as minister for the Committee of State Security?"

"As you like," replied Kornon, his tall, lean frame and immaculately tailored civilian-blue suit and tie in stark contrast to the general's khaki and rows of colorful decorations from the Great Patriotic War of '41-45.

Looking past Borgach's sycophantic aide, Colonel Ustenko, and through the thick grayish-blue smoke that was filling his office, swirling around the electric candelabra, Kornon could see the Kremlin's spires and snow-dusted cupolas, the onion domes tinted pink in the fading winter light. He hoped the older general would give him a simple yes or no, so that he could air his office and get on with it. Borgach poured another vodka; it left a scummy film on the small, thick glass. He sniffed the liquor then tipped the glass toward the shaded light. "Where did you get this?"

"In the German Democratic Republic—Potsdam," answered Kornon.

"You should have left it there." Colonel Ustenko smiled dutifully. Borgach tossed back the vodka anyway. "Your plan?" Borgach said finally, shaking his head from side to side with bemused condescension, the weak candelabra light reflecting off the gold braid on his red shoulder boards. "Kornon, I'm sixty-four. I was born on the eve of the revolution, thirty when Stalin's purges began. A lieutenant in the people's commissariat of state security—the NKVD then."

"Yes, I know, sir, but the plan. What do you—"

"Let me finish."

Borgach took another drink. "I survived *yezhovshchina*, the worst of the purges in '37-38. You cannot possibly know what they were like. We started at the top,

Kornon. First Zinovyev and Kamenev. At the top! Do I make myself clear?''

''Yes, Minister,'' said Kornon patiently.

''The October Hall in Trade Union House.'' Borgach waved the empty glass. ''Cameras, flashbulbs, foreign press everywhere.'' His voice slowed, a little slurred. ''Then after the top of the grain was gone we started chopping down the stalks. In one week, more than four thousand comrades shot. In secret. If you failed to get your quota convicted at the public trials...'' Borgach drew a finger across his beef-red throat, then walked toward the window, shaking his head in pained remembrance. ''I tell you, Kornon, they were jumping out of the insurance building like...like people from a burning house.''

Kornon nodded somberly out of respect; many of the older party members like Borgach still referred to Lubyanka Jail as the insurance building it used to be before the revolution.

''We were eating one another alive,'' continued Borgach. ''It was you or someone else. Nobody was safe—least of all Stalin's old 'friends.' Oh, they tried to fight back in the Ukraine.'' Pausing, Borgach looked out of the lead-paned window as night enfolded Lenin's mausoleum. ''Well, I can tell you, Comrade, Molotov and Khrushchev soon fixed that. The purge spread to the army.'' He turned back to Kornon. ''*Marshals*, Comrade—*marshals* tried secretly and shot. Thirty thousand officers liquidated for 'treason.'''

Borgach threw up his hands. ''So who did we have when the Nazis attacked? The cream was gone. No wonder they waltzed through our defenses.'' His earlier half-drunken smile had now vanished. ''More than eighty percent of all generals gone. Not eight, Comrade—*eighty* percent!'' His voice dropped. ''Then came Beria.... Well by then, who knows—six million...maybe seven—we lost count in the gulags. Then in '53 Beria himself was shot and the KGB was born.''

Borgach now cocked his head like some rare bird to look admiringly, contentedly at his raised gold epaulets. "That's when I got these." He was smiling again, his voice rising and falling, out of the past but never far from it. "So, you ask me, Kornon, what do I think of your plan? I *don't.*" He indicated the bottle and Colonel Ustenko hastened to refill the glass. "I don't think of your plan at all. Six months and I'll be retired. You want to do it. You do it. I don't think of it at all. I've done my duty." He saw Kornon about to speak but cut him short. "No, I don't sign anything. I want to feed the pigeons...." Borgach's hands went out in happy anticipation of the retirement almost in his grasp. "Watch a few funny movies down at the Illuzion—Charlie Chaplin, eh—a little skating with the grandchildren perhaps. A little chess."

"I need authorization, Minister," pressed Kornon.

"Get it from Ustenko here. He's young. He *has* to think, otherwise he'll stay a colonel the rest of his life—eh, Ustenko?" Borgach didn't wait for an answer. It was meant as a joke. Ustenko had no power to authorize any such plan but Borgach enjoyed teasing his efficient but somber junior. Borgach pulled on his heavy military greatcoat, digging out his gloves. "Regimental garrison duty in the GDR with rotten vodka. That's where Ustenko'll end up if he doesn't exhibit initiative. Right, Ustenko?"

Ustenko tried a smile but it came out a thin grimace. "I suppose so, General."

"Go on!" Borgach pushed Kornon. "Ask Ustenko what he thinks of your scheme."

"Well, Ustenko?" Kornon snapped. As a first deputy minister with *blat*, good personal connections with Borgach's KGB, Kornon far outranked the colonel.

Still, Ustenko was unafraid. He knew that as Borgach's chief aide he would be given a major promotion before Borgach retired—providing Borgach didn't foul up before the happy day. Ustenko glanced out at the late-evening snow, which had not lost its whiteness and was beginning to take on a cold blue aura. "I think it is..." He hesitated, at once conciliatory yet guarded. "I think it is speculative."

Borgach roared with laughter. "You'll go far, Ustenko," he said, slapping the colonel jovially on the back. "Get the car."

Pouring another glass of the East German vodka he had disparaged, Borgach waited until he could hear Ustenko's footsteps receding down the long corridor outside Kornon's office. He downed the vodka, smacking the glass smartly down on the table, then studied Kornon while he put on the wide, red-banded cap of the Soviet officer elite and did up two heavy brass buttons of his military greatcoat. "Kornon."

"General?"

"It is dangerous," said Borgach. "Your plan is fraught with danger. It is devious as a Georgian plot. Like a mad Tartar's ax." He tugged at his gloves. "But—" he paused, leaning forward, his right hand spreading, now rocking gently side to side like a lifeboat "—it has a certain glint to it. A brilliant edge. This much I admit. It shows balls. And to win big stakes you must roll dice, eh?"

Kornon was delighted. "Then you will..."

Borgach held up his hands. "I told you, I will do nothing. I will sign nothing. No approval. No support." He had walked to the door, gripping the huge, lavishly engraved knob firmly with his gloved hand, then turned. "I will sign it if you are successful. I will predate it." He pointed his finger directly at Kornon. "Only if you are successful. But—" The gloved hand suddenly fell to his side as if chopped from his body. "If you fail, I've heard nothing."

"I understand. But it has merit?"

"Ah!" said Borgach. "The car's arrived. Good night."

It was then that Kornon, hungry for promotion to the inner sanctum of the Politburo before he got too old to enjoy it, carefully, secretly, had set the final phase of his plan in motion so that by November 1, the M.V. *Lvov* and the rest of the Polish fleet would be four thousand miles away from Gdansk in the northeastern Pacific.

Chapter Five

ON THE MORNING *Lvov* sent its SOS, it was already 6:00 p.m. on an unseasonably warm autumn day in Zurich. An evening shower that had swept in from Germany had passed, leaving the trees about the lake in front of the Burkliplatz a sparkling, polished green. Herr Klaus, a man whom Kornon's Zurich office was watching closely, made his way across the gray span of the Quai Bridge then, as he did this time each day, turned right, heading toward the open-air café of the Bauschantzli. Tall and lean, he walked with an aura of command and unpretentious prosperity, immaculately dressed in a dark pin-striped blue suit with white shirt and maroon-and-navy-blue-striped tie. He had the build of a runner though he only ever walked—running would have seemed to him undignified, if not slightly vulgar. His self-possessed air was reinforced by the dexterity he demonstrated in lighting a thin Dutch cigar with a gold Dunhill lighter without a pause in his step or deigning to look at either article.

The verve and sheer nerve Klaus had displayed in expanding his massive Swiss Rhine Petrochemicals empire into "high risk" investment areas was known to only a few of the other powerful men in Zurich. Like them he was anonymous to the world at large, despite the fact that Swiss Rhine Petrochemicals was now the fourth most influential multinational in Europe after Royal Dutch Shell, British Petroleum and Unilever, with employable assets of

27.8 billion dollars. It helped that when other multinationals and their subsidiaries all over the world couldn't get their "black blood," oil, to keep their vital industries running, Klaus never had a problem. He had what the few big bankers in the know referred to as a "personal arrangement" with Colonel Khaddafi—a Libyan tanker always en route to Hamburg, Rotterdam or Cherbourg, wherever Klaus's insatiable industries needed it. But what Klaus really wanted now, with South Africa's stability as prime supplier of strategic minerals to the United States and Europe always an open question, was to secure a monopoly for Swiss Rhine Petrochemicals as the major supplier for the huge North American metals market.

That desire was much on his mind this evening, though no one would have known anything was causing him the slightest concern as he made his way into the open-air section of the Bauschantzli Café where colored paper lanterns were lit, suspended like fireflies among the greenery. As usual, he took a table by one of the thick, vine-covered stone walls of the island restaurant, which overlooked the junction of the river with the lake. No sooner had he sat down than the headwaiter appeared at his side. A German family who had been waiting for some time at a nearby table stared across resentfully.

"The usual?" the waiter asked, though he had already placed the order for a slice of *Rübelikuchen*—the local carrot cake—and a beer. Klaus astonished him this evening, however, by ordering milk instead of beer. Klaus saw the man's surprise but ignored him as one would a rude peasant; his pride would not countenance the idea of explaining anything, or even talking, to someone worth less than ten million in Swiss francs. Money was the only measure for Klaus—everything else was dependent upon that. Even one's health could be prolonged if you had enough money. Yet the truth was that Klaus's sense of achievement, indeed his sense of order and control in the world, had been secretly and badly shaken of late. His ordering milk rather than beer was testimony to what his doctor, who attended him privately at his huge, brooding mansion on the Tobystrasse, had the temerity to call an upset stomach. It was, in fact, as Klaus's computer had quickly informed him, a 1.2 million-Swiss-franc upset stomach, caused by frustrations in his latest and most ambitious venture. He had recently established a Canadian/U.S. company, called CANUS Ore—a "front" through which he hoped to plunder the enormous mineral wealth of hot springs off the North American west coast. These hot springs, unfortunately for SRP, lay within the two-hundred-mile American and Canadian economic zones. Unable to put his own company's ship into North American waters, he had instead used CANUS Ore in Portland, Oregon, and its subsidiaries to try to beat the Canadians and Americans to the sea gold.

What had caused his "upset stomach" to act up this evening was the same thing that had been eating at him for the past three weeks, since his operatives in Portland had telexed that an oceanographer by the name of Frank Hall would be setting out in *Petrel* again on November 1 in an attempt to pin down the exact location of sea gold deposits off Oregon. It was then that his ulcer had begun in earnest, for Klaus and Hall, though they had never met, were old enemies, so much so that the mere mention of the American's name was enough to trigger a terrible burning sensation in the pit of his stomach. Against his will, Klaus found himself thinking about how one of his spy ships, a North Sea trawler flying under various flags of convenience, had managed on one cruise to shadow *Petrel* so closely that there had been a race to the mainland between *Petrel* and Klaus's ship to file a "sea bed exploration" claim. The race became so close that Klaus's crew had been authorized by him to use what he had euphemistically called "unorthodox methods." But in the final stages of the race it had been this Hall who had outwitted Klaus's crew.

The waiter brought the milk, but already Klaus's stomach was turning sour, causing an upwelling, not unlike a hot vent, he thought, threatening to surge up into his esophagus, its contents not nearly as pleasant to contemplate as sea gold deposits.

It wasn't only the memory of the money he had invested and lost in the trawler that was interfering so drastically with Klaus's digestion this evening, it was the unbearable, insufferable and constant knowledge that he, Herr Klaus, had been beaten—and by an American upstart at that—someone no one else had ever heard of. The sea gold claims this Hall had presented covered large areas and were yet to be fully explored, so Swiss Rhine Petrochemicals still had a chance. But what continued to gall Klaus was that he had *never* been defeated in a business venture before this Hall had come along, and the mere thought of losing a second time to the American was so hateful to him that his gastric mucosa had been thrown into a constant state of tension and aggravation. Adding insult to injury, apparently this lout Hall, his operatives reported, wasn't even from an important American family.

Thinking quickly about what more he must do to beat Hall this time, Klaus unconsciously hurried his carrot cake and immediately regretted it. He closed his eyes briefly, breathing deeply, exhaling slowly, trying to relax his stomach muscles as best he could. The only way to contain an incipient ulcer, he knew, was to neither overeat, nor starve it but, through moderation, to feed it small amounts at more frequent intervals. He drew from this an analogy for the new action he must now take against Hall. This time he would be more patient, only committing his forces in full when absolutely necessary.

Klaus rose from the table, leaving the usual five-franc tip, and proceeded toward the Bahnhofstrasse. Perhaps a little window-shopping would calm him before he sent his message to Portland. He would walk back down past the

Fraumünster Kirche, rest awhile, go in and look at the vibrant colors of Chagall's window, then he would call CANUS Ore's office. The time difference did not concern him, for the telex line was staffed twenty-four hours a day.

His message read: Is our cousin on schedule? He signed it, Uncle.

The answer came back within five minutes: Cousin delayed by bad weather in Cascade Mountains but is back on the road again Stop Will send air traffic report.

Klaus folded the message into a neat, tiny rectangle. He was dissatisfied yet hopeful, for while the prearranged phrase "Cascade Mountains," to mean northeast Pacific, told him there had been a delay of some kind due to bad weather, *Petrel* was apparently now back on course, resuming its search for sea gold off the United States coast. The message also told him that within the next hour, SRP's aircraft, a Beechcraft ostensibly owned by CANUS Ore, would be taking off from Clatsop Airfield, across from Astoria near the mouth of the Columbia River, to find out whether *Petrel* was already sampling and where.

Chapter Six

"WRECKAGE!" shouted *Petrel*'s lookout. "Starboard quarter!"

This time he was sure he'd seen something more than just a blur between the swells. Captain Tate took up his glasses to confirm the report. In the circle of wind-whipped ocean, deep blue reflected the clear sky of the lull in the approaching storm line, and the captain spotted what looked like a lumpy red-and-white sheet up and over the swells about two miles away, and beyond it a flotsam of what appeared to be planks, and glints of some kind of lightweight metal on wood, which he guessed were the remains of splintered decking and superstructure ripped apart and scattered by the trawler's explosion. He looked carefully for any bodies as the crest of the swells came into closer view but could see none, nor for that matter any other wreckage. The explosion must have been so sudden and violent that *Lvov* had gone down fast and with all hands, releasing only the red-and-white-rubber life rafts that, packed in drums, were preset to burst open once a rip cord was pulled or the drums became submerged. Tate altered course for the windward side of the wreckage, to let *Petrel* drift downwind and retrieve whatever it could in the heavy chop.

As *Petrel* heeled hard astarboard, lost for a moment in a burst of spray, Frank Hall braced himself, countering the high pitching of the bow as the shock of a head-on collision with the cross swell punched the vessel amidships. He could hear the lashed cargo groaning against the acrylic rope that held it in place, its bright yellow web moving against the white of the ship and blue sky. In an instant Frank's wet gear was drenched with spray and foam, running off him in rivulets onto the rust-red deck and into the scuppers, pouring over the starboard side. Down below, lockers were flung open under the big wave's impact.

Frank knew instantly from the speed of the unannounced turn that something extraordinary was up. The last time he could remember the ship heeling so fast and hard was in the final stages of the home run to port as Klaus's trawler sought to stop *Petrel* as she raced to reach port ahead of her rival.

Though the rolling almost ceased after the turn was completed, the pitching became steeper and more dangerous, as *Petrel* quickly cut across massive swells to get to the wreckage. By now several crew members were crowding the rail, craning to see what was up. The bosun appeared with a long aluminum pike, ready to try gaffing the deflated life raft, and asked Frank to take the ship's camera and snap some shots of the wreckage for the ship's log. Frank glanced at the deceptively clearing sky that gave the sea below it the sharp, cold cerulean-blue, and set the Hasselblad's aperture, hoping to catch pictures of what little debris there was without blurring or distortion. The ship's cook was gripping the rail, eyes watering in the wind as he stared at the flotsam. His tall white hat, fluttering furiously, threatened to take off, while obstructing Frank's field of view.

"Chunky, can you move toward the stern?"

The cook heard only a garbled sentence, the slipstream whipping away the sound so that Frank had to yell.

"Right," said Cook. "This far enough?" He was almost at the stern.

"Bit farther."

The cook, cupping his hands and turning with his back toward the already gale-force-eight winds, shouted, "Would you like me to jump overboard?"

"Fine!" Frank shouted. *"Muchas gracias."*

"Yeah, and your ass, too!"

Frank grinned, shook his head, his hair a brown frenzy in the wind, in marked contrast to his cool, matter-of-fact preparation. In fact they were all preparing themselves against the unexpected—the appearance of at least a few dead Polish seamen. There were none, confirming Tate's view that even as the American trawler, *Swiftsure*, had been drawing close to the rescue, *Lvov* had gone down so quickly that the Poles would have had no chance to get to the lifeboats.

Several of *Petrel*'s crewmen were casting out an array of fishing gaffs and pole nets, trying to retrieve what debris they could from the elusive swells.

"Waste of time," moaned Aussie, looking out at the undulating red-and-white sheet of the partially inflated life raft, nearby flotsam of decking and what looked like red cabbage and assorted garbage including some disintegrating cardboard boxes and paper. He handed Frank an eight-foot aluminum pike.

"Not going to help 'em now, is it, bringing in all that crap?"

"Old man has to give it to the coast guard when we get back to port."

"If you can get it aboard," Aussie chimed in, still looking drawn and whey-faced, trying to ignore the heaving swells that were changing color under cloud-shaded sun, their hues moving from deep blue to bottle green. "Two bucks you miss it," said the Aussie.

"All right," replied Frank, buckling on the canvas safety line and clipping it to the starboard side ocean-ographer's platform, a four-foot-square sheet of metal that dropped from the side of the ship, suspended by chains like a tiny drawbridge. "Why don't you make it five?" challenged Frank.

"Big spender! Okay, mate."

Frank held the pike close to his oilskins as *Petrel* slammed into the swells. The spray enveloped the ship, running down the well deck in torrents that swirled about the crew's feet and streaming off the ship through the scuppers and the stern A-frame in a roar of dazzling foam.

In a lull before the next swell, as the deflated life raft came into view sliding up and down a cresting wave, Tate reduced speed and Frank stood full against the thin pipe rail of the work platform, raising the long pike like a whaler's harpoon. The dead raft appeared on the starboard quarter.

On the bridge, Tate could see it would be too far out. Accordingly, he hit the jet bow thruster, pushing the ship hard to starboard. The raft rose on the next swell. Frank, leaning forward, his body almost forty degrees to the platform, thrust the pike. The yellow rope streaked out like an angry snake before the pike struck the raft as *Petrel*'s bow dropped, crashing into the next wave, throwing Frank upright, back hard against the rail. Next time Mary Crane looked, Frank was gone from the platform, then she saw one hand grasping its edge, Frank's safety line taut. Forgetting his seasickness, Aussie dashed out from the dry lab, dropped to the deck and extended his right hand. Soon Scotty, the second mate, was by his side, grasping Frank's oilskins, helping to drag him aboard as the ship dipped then took a long roll to port.

INSIDE THE WET LAB, after peeling off his oilskins, Frank leaned back on the cold bulkhead to catch his breath.

"Bit wet, mate?" Aussie grinned.

Frank exhaled slowly, as he pulled off his sodden T-shirt. Mary looked on worriedly. Aussie handed his cabin mate a mug of coffee.

"Thanks," said Frank.

"You owe me five bucks."

Everyone in the wet lab started to laugh.

Through the portholes, Mary could see nothing but dark gray sea sweeping by as a cloud completely covered the sun. Crew members laboriously fought the roll as they dragged the wreckage they'd managed to gaff along with the deflated lifeboat up for'ard to the open area of the well deck, as *Petrel* resumed course toward its first sampling station.

Going out and bracing himself against the A-frame, Frank took one last zoom shot of the receding debris for the record. Though he couldn't see Mary behind him, he could smell her perfume; it excited him in spite of his preoccupation with the camera. She leaned closer. "Come to my cabin when you're finished out here."

As they walked together from the stern deck toward the lab, another wave hit the ship's side with a long, whooshing sound, casting a gossamerlike spray over the entire length of the ship, sunlight breaking out of the cloud, reflected in a golden halo.

"What's the matter?" Frank asked Mary.

"My cabin," she said quickly.

Frank glanced up at the lab's clock; it would be fifteen minutes at least before they got *Petrel* back on direct line for the station using the sounder to put them exactly over a suitable sampling area.

"Okay," he said, then, hesitating before the door leading to the ship's main passageway, he waited for her to go first. She smiled at him. Yet it made him feel uncomfortable. There was an air of condescension about her, like all those women, he thought, who view traditional manners as nothing more than a quaint absurdity, confusing a man's old-fashioned respect for women with male chauvinism. With the door open they could first feel, then hear the heavy pounding of each of four General Motors 170 HP engines directly below as the ship drew on more power against the growing gale.

"I'll come down in a minute," he said. "But first I have to put these Polaroids away. Coast guard will want to have them for the record."

"Well, hurry," she said. "It's important."

On the bridge, Tate was remarking on how the lull had improved visibility threefold and had cleared up some, but not all, of the sea clutter. Frank handed him the Polaroid prints, checked the loran position and noted the depth from the bridge sounder. It was becoming shallower, five hundred fathoms, but still too rugged a mountain range to risk snagging either a dredge or the giant grab. It was tough enough in calm weather, but buffeted by gale-force seas it was doubly dangerous. The slightest error could suddenly shift the ship, change the wire angle dramatically, and before anyone knew it they could be winching themselves under a heavy swell, capsizing, sinking in minutes. It had happened at least twice before, once in Australian waters near the Great Barrier Reef and the other on Georges Banks off the east coast of Massachusetts. They would have to wait for the mountains three thousand feet below to drop abruptly to the vast abyssal plain of mud.

Glancing at the radar as he passed, Frank noticed how the clutter had lessened. How easy it was to forget that each dot—eleven of them, he counted—represented not only a ship but much more—hundreds of lives, sailors, loved ones and families half a world away. With the improved visibility, the first mate switched off the radar, the dots fading, then finally disappearing.

Frank made his way down to Mary's cabin and knocked softly. The door opened as a steward walked by with what Frank thought was a bigger grin than necessary. Or was Frank merely imagining it, only too aware that once you were at sea the immediate divorce from shore routines and entertainment and the onset of the boredom of long watches invariably brought out the voyeur among the crew, who relieved the boredom mainly by talk of sex, drink and more sex.

Mary clicked the door shut behind him. "Someone's been through my things," she said without preamble, pointing to one of the drawers below her bunk.

"You sure?"

"Yes. Ever since that last cruise when you told me that you thought another ship was shadowing us, trying to get information about where we were going, et cetera, I've followed your advice." She picked up a piece of thin cotton thread from the highly polished dresser by the entrance to the tiny bathroom. "It wasn't in the drawer when I came back from the bridge early this morning."

The ship shook as its bow dived into the crest of two waves in rapid succession, giving off a staccato, ramming sound that reverberated throughout the ship as if someone was attacking it, battering down its watertight doors.

"You put the thread in the drawer before the steward made up your room?" asked Frank.

"The steward doesn't make up my room. I told the third mate when we left Astoria that I'd do my own bed. Last cruise they had a habit of barging in after two short taps on the door, just as I—we were getting dressed. *Remember?*"

Frank ignored her question, which she had phrased so that it sounded like a suggestion. "Anything missing?" he asked her.

"Can't say for sure, but everything's been gone through. In the dresser as well as below the bunk."

"Could be the movement of the ship. Shifts things around a lot."

"Possibly," conceded Mary, "but the thread—broken like that?"

"You'd best ask the mate if you think anyone's been in," Frank suggested.

"Why not ask the stewards outright?"

"No," Frank countered, his tone definite. "If any of the crew think they're suspected of pilfering or something it'll sour everything for the rest of the cruise. We need all the help we can get. A quiet word with the mate is the best way to go."

"All right." She paused. "It's not that I care if anything's missing, really, but it's the thought of someone just walking in and invading—" She hugged herself as if feeling a sudden chill, a tremor passing through her. "Hold me," she said. He held her gently, her perfume engulfing him once more, and the next moment he was kissing her. There was a knock on the door.

"Mrs. Crane?"

"Y-yes?"

"Five minutes to station."

FRANK UNLASHED the giant grab's trip mechanism, which would dangle twenty feet beneath the grab, hit bottom first, releasing the thousand-pound Big Bess, as she was called, allowing her free-fall, driving her open jaws into the bottom. He signaled the winch man to take up the slack so as not to have the cable whipping about the deck.

Mary went to see the third mate while they were waiting for the ship's engine to change tone, telling them they were in the final turn downwind. The mate had just woken up, readying himself for the eight-to-noon watch. His cabin emitted a sour odor of unwashed clothing, overhung by the heavier and stronger smell of stale cigarettes. His breath was no better as he stared blankly at her, his stubble a dark shadow above an ash-stained T-shirt and track-suit pants. She asked the question again—whether or not the stewards had been told by the mate, as she had requested, to keep out of her cabin. He blinked, looking about the cabin as if the answer was lurking somewhere behind him, his eyes widening like an owl for whom daylight was an eternal mystery.

"Two minutes to station!" the intercom blared.

While the mate gathered his wits, outside on the stern deck Frank checked the trip weight as the ship cut across several waves before coming about. Big Bess had slid a few feet in the turn, and Frank, moving his canvas glove in circles, signaled the winch man to take up the slack, then held up his hand for him to stop. There was a loud clunk as the winch brake engaged the plates. Now Frank, his body easing to accommodate the ship's change in direction as if his legs were on independent suspension, reached up and grabbed one of the ladder rungs on the inside of the stern's A-frame. He then climbed up to reset the meter needle to zero on the block through which the cable would pass, down over the stern roller once the cable railings were undone, the A-frame reclining seaward in order to suspend the grab clear of the twin props.

Mary had returned to the deck. The hood of her yellow rain top was flapping so fast it became a blur of color as she stood by the port winch in anticipation of watching Frank do what he did best—next to making love. A minute later when "On station" sounded over the ship's PA system, *Petrel* had come fully about to run with the wind. Suddenly it was a different world. The waves were just as high, the troughs as deep, the wind as fierce as before, but now the different elements ran together in a fierce harmony that, though powerful, was no longer in an all-out war with the ship, buffeting it from side to side. Though she still rolled, it was not anywhere near as violent as before, and there was a new, stabilizing surge of power as sea and props worked in concert.

While Frank waited for the half dozen or so crewmen to take their positions, Mary moved closer to him. "The mate *forgot* to tell the steward not to bother making up my cabin," she told Frank. "I felt stupid," she added.

"Well," said Frank, relieved by the news that no one had been rifling her cabin after all, "we all make mistakes."

"Even oceanographers," she said jocularly, in self-admonishment.

"They're the worst." He laughed, then quickly turned his attention to the business at hand, instructing the winch man, "Okay, Spence, take her up slowly." The winch came to life with a reluctant groan and the five-eighths-inch cable, already taut, became more so. Some of the dry wire made a splitting sound like green timber, sending off little puffs of dried salt into the air.

Three other crewmen came on deck, heads inclined against the wind and spray rushing them from the stern. Each held a long pole to keep the trip weight pushed out from the stern so that it could be lowered quickly before a wave could smash it against the stern brace, causing a pre-trip of the giant thousand-pound grab, now suspended fifteen feet above Frank's head. As the cable flexed farther, jerking the needle of the tension meter above the winch, Frank heard a further splitting sound. He watched the meter wheel, the advancing swells, the inclinometer, which showed the angle of the deck against the horizon. Once the pre-trip weight, a two-hundred-pound tear-shaped lead block, was clear of the stern roller, he gave the signal, winding his hand clockwise, for the gear to be lowered as quickly as possible. The winch's groan moved into a higher whine, then the cable rapidly became a blur, the meter wheel spinning, twenty fathoms, forty fathoms, eighty fathoms. Now the winch's whine became a howl as Big Bess, jaws open, drove down toward the sea bottom, a hill-dotted plain more than two miles below. Seeing the white luminescent numbers about the spinning needle, Frank was reminded of the slower spinning of the radar arm before the explosion. He had watched the coin-size blips amid the pinpoints of sea clutter that were the Polish fishing fleet and *Swiftsure*, and out of habit, he'd noted the number—eleven blips representing eleven ships.

It wasn't until the meter wheel showed him the grab was at 650 fathoms that he realized what was bothering him. The American trawler, Sparks had told them on the bridge, had acknowledged it was okay—so obviously only the Polish trawler had gone down. But why, after the explosion, were there still eleven dots, and not ten as there should have been? Having to watch the tension meter closely as the meter wheel bucked violently, indicating sudden strain on the cable, Frank dismissed the question of the blips for the time being, after one last speculation. Had one of the blips he had counted been some kind of giant sea clutter?

Chapter Seven

THE BEECHCRAFT ROSE through the stratus that hung like a dark canopy over Astoria, turning the cobalt-blue of the Columbia's estuary into a wide, dark slate, wrinkled at the edges where it spread out to join the sea. Sixty miles out, the cloud cover became suffused with more light filtering through, until the plane broke through a big hole in the stratus into a cold, clear patch of sky, a lull in an otherwise unbroken line of towering cumulonimbus.

The plane's pilot, Shirley Waites of Portland, Oregon, banked the Beechcraft, putting it into a shallow dive, taking it down to three thousand feet. The breaking waves below were no more than creamy scribbles on furrowed blue. Down to her left, to the south, through the sun-slashed blur of the port prop she glimpsed a white peak, the lone, guano-encrusted rock at the southern end of Eagle Island—a long, thin, grass-covered haven for the millions of seabirds that filled the air off the cloud-shrouded cliffs like falling pepper and salt. Beneath the folding edge of low stratus, the northern part of the "exclamation mark," as some mariners called the island, lay hidden. Shirley Waites then spotted the gray flecks of the Polish fishing fleet, the big factory or mother ship closest to her, partly visible just a mile or so westward of the island, the trawlers mere dots far to the south.

Above the sharp, rocky peak designated the Pinnacle on the charts, which lay at the southern tip and was bereft of the giant species of sedge grass peculiar to the island, she saw swarms of gulls, just dots, waiting their turn to land on the rocky crag. Distracted by the birds, Waites didn't spot another white speck until five minutes later, this one longer and thirty miles or so farther west of the Polish factory ship, barely moving against the dull horizon. She was sure it must be M.V. *Petrel*, given the vessel's time of departure from Astoria, and she swung the Beechcraft toward it. As the ship raced in her direction she was busy flicking through her copy of the coast guard's K-4 chart of silhouettes and rigging, noting the details of the 150-foot research ship. Up forward, twenty feet below the slanting glass-faced bridge, there should be two orange forward winches bolted to the dark red well deck, one a heavy-duty Swann, its drum of five-eighths-inch cable squatting on the forward port side, the lighter five-thirty-seconds-inch hy-

drographic winch situated on the starboard forward side.
Banking the plane, to make the sea run uphill and thus reduce the glare, Shirley Waites looked down toward the afterdeck where there should be, among other things, a
telescopic Austin-Western hydraulic arm, a twin of the one
on the starboard side of the fo'c'sle. She saw it—the arm
fully retracted. There was no doubt. It was *Petrel.*

FRANK DIDN'T SEE the Beechcraft approaching until it was
almost on top of them; he was too busy watching the
needle on the meter wheel move slowly counterclockwise
as the starboard winch strained to pull up the giant grab
from the plain of ooze.

"Coast guard?" asked Mary.

"Not unless they're hiring private planes," he said,
watching the plane roar over, its shadow warping as he
tried to read the lettering on the fuselage. All I could
make out was AN.

"Competition?" Mary held the rail, her other hand
shading her eyes as they followed the Beechcraft.

"Well," said Frank, "if it is competition it won't do
them any good. Our grab's not up yet. Even we don't
know what's in it."

"No, but they'll have our position."

"Yes," replied Frank. "Still, it isn't accurate enough
taken from a plane. Our sonar's a heck of a lot more exact than that. No use guessing to the nearest mile in this
business. You're either right on top of something or you
might as well be a hundred miles off."

"They could drop a sonar buoy." Mary recalled their
first search for sea gold and all the trouble they had. "As
a marker," she added. "Wouldn't that give them exact
depth and bottom contour? Show them where to dredge?
Its radio signal would be beeping out the information all
the time, wouldn't it? All they'd have to do is beam onto
it."

"Tricky things," Frank shouted above the wind.

"What do you mean?"

"Sonar buoys," said Frank, still watching the meter wheel but standing relaxed, arms folded, his body leaning back against the winch, at one with the motion of the ship.

"What's so tricky about them?" she pressed.

"They're likely to get rammed by a ship."

It was difficult to tell whether he was smiling or squinting in the sun. "Then they're no use at all," he went on. "You'd never find the place again."

She moved closer to him to be heard over the howl of the winch and just to be near him, her perfume a fleeting presence in the salty air.

"Same thing could happen to us, couldn't it? If we found sea gold and marked it."

Arms still folded, Frank was looking up at the black dot of the plane as it was turning. "You mean if we put out a buoy someone could sink it from the air?" Frank asked. "You have any idea how tricky that is from a commercial plane? Even trained bomber pilots would miss on nine out of ten runs. Didn't see any bombs, did you?" Before she could answer he added, "Anyway, we won't use a buoy. We'll mark it on our bottom chart and use sonar to locate the exact spot again if we find anything. Don't worry, if we find sea gold we'll be the only ones who know the exact position. I'll put the coordinates in our safe." He patted her arm. "You're worrying too much, Mrs. Crane."

"What if they see what we bring up in the grab? They could radio a ship to keep us in sight. Like last time."

"Then we won't bring the grab up until the plane clears off," said Frank easily. "Besides I can't see any ship bearing down on us. Can you?"

"No," she said, visibly relaxed, grateful for his reassurance.

The Beechcraft came in low and buzzed them again. Glancing up at it, Frank waved jovially to the pilot. "Just want to make sure we're out here," he said. "Report back. Reconnaissance probably—that's all. Any close-in stuff is bound to be done at night. And then we can pick them up on the radar, anyway.''

''How will we know it isn't one of the Polish trawlers?''

Frank shifted his gaze from the meter wheel to the southeast where the Polish fleet was strung out south of Eagle Island. He frowned in the glare. ''Goddammit!''

''What?''

''I definitely counted eleven dots on our radar.''

''So?''

''There should have been ten if that trawler, the *Lvov*, went down . . .''

Mary was way ahead of him. ''You mean the extra blip could be another ship in the area, one that looks like a trawler.''

''Yes.''

They were wrong, said Mike, the first mate, when they asked him. He explained that the eleventh blip was probably the radar reflection of Eagle Island, now a faint smudge on the eastern horizon. He showed them by drawing in the line on the chart from their loran position to the island—the line to the island and the radar vector from the eleventh blip exactly coincided. ''So you see,'' he told them, ''there are only ten ships in our immediate area—not eleven. Everything's roses!''

SHIRLEY WAITES WAS en route back to Astoria to confirm for Klaus that Frank Hall and Mary Crane were venturing out, risking the approaching storm line to be the first to find sea gold off Oregon. She saw the stratus cloud thinning in the lull, though the seas were just as rough as before, forming a creamy white ring around Eagle Island as breakers smashed against the base of chocolate-dark cliffs. With a little more of the island visible now as she headed toward the long blue scratch of the mainland seventy miles due east, the big Polish mother ship was clearly visible. Flicking through the coast guard chart, impressed by the

mother ship's enormous size compared with that of its
trawlers, she matched it up as a Pioniersk class, B-64 series; 543 feet long, 70 feet across the beam, three sets of
giant cranes spaced along the massive foredeck, dead-
weight ten thousand tons, carrying two thousand tons of
fuel, a crew of more than 250, speed fifteen and one half
knots and a helicopter hangar mounted high astern to ferry
seamen and supplies back and forth to the trawlers,
weather permitting. With an endurance of seventy-five
days the mother ship could process, including light salt-
ing, two hundred tons of herring a day, another hundred
tons of fish from the trawlers, and manufacture fish meal
on the spot.

The clear patch in the stratus was widening, and now
Shirley saw one of the trawlers, a dot on the horizon south
of Eagle Island, as she marked the approximate position
of *Petrel* with a circle to send to the Swiss address—Zurich Helm 104—as soon as she landed at Astoria. Glancing again at the factory ship she tried to imagine what 150
tons of fish meal must look like—a small hill probably.
And what an unbelievable stink! Everything must have to
be frozen. The big ship, she noted from the coast guard
chart, also produced twenty tons of ice a day. As she swept
the ship with her binoculars to pass the time she wondered idly whether the Poles watched porno movies or
whether there were women aboard. Shifting the binoculars northward again, on a line straight ahead, she saw the
mother ship's helicopter rising slowly into the sky like a
dragonfly, obscured at first by layers of low stratus, then
in the clear again, then just as quickly swallowed as it went
higher into the thicker stratus at the edge of the clear patch
of sky.

Her binoculars moved east toward the vague grayness of
the mainland, now forty miles away. She caught a fleeting
glint of sunlight from the copter's blades before it disappeared into cloud again. Her attention moved back to the
mother ship, its stern chute, a great black hole that could

haul in a trawler's entire catch, staring up at her like some great prehistoric mouth. For a moment she thought she caught a shadow of a school of fish, porpoises perhaps, swiftly changing direction, but it was a cloud racing high overhead darkening the water. Then she thought she saw sharks, or perhaps it was a small school of killer whales, common to these waters, swimming parallel to the creamy line of surf smashing against the guano-splattered rocks at the base of the great towering slabs of rock that rose straight up from the sea to form the jagged rim of the island. For a moment it looked as if the whales or sharks were dead, one of those mysterious mass suicides that baffle marine biologists. She banked the Beechcraft and went down for a closer look. The helicopter still opposite her, across the other side of the island, reappeared and, again like a dragonfly, came to a halt in midair, about a thousand feet above the sea and about five-eighths of a mile from the big ship. She saw a wink of light from the copter's belly and a wisp of smoke.

Shirley Waites died the next instant.

AWAY TO THE WEST Frank Hall saw the burst of light, an orange-black ball curling over and over into itself against the turquoise sky, and not until several seconds later did he hear the muffled bang of the Beechcraft's explosion.

"Jesus!" said the winch man, his foot instinctively hitting the brake. "What was that?"

The helicopter, a mere speck in the eastern sky, was hovering over the spot, and though from *Petrel*'s bridge Tate couldn't see the pencil-thin lifeline descending from the chopper's belly, his binoculars could make out a twirling red-and-yellow blur at the end of the wire, a rescue harness, he presumed, swiveling in the wind like a noose as it was quickly lowered to the sea. But through his binoculars Tate saw there was no one left to rescue, only big scraps of aluminum fuselage floating, occasionally shining as the sun pierced the cloud hanging over the island.

"Son of a bitch," said the port lookout. "It was that plane—went up like a bloody bomb."

Immediately the Polish mother ship was on the air, already making its way toward the crash site. Still on station, seven miles off, *Petrel* nevertheless offered to help recover wreckage, though it wouldn't be able to move until the giant grab was aboard—at least another hour.

The Polish captain of the mother ship radioed his thanks to *Petrel*, saying he was, as required by United States and international maritime law, dispatching a tender to collect the debris, some of which was being washed toward Eagle Island. The Polish captain's English was not the best but ironically conveyed a succinct description of the situation, telling *Petrel*'s captain of his "sincere intention" not to rest until he had done all possible to convey "the bits and pieces of broken body if any can be found—uneaten by sharks" to the United States Coast Guard "with all possibly hurry."

"WHAT'S GOING ON?"

Frank and Mary turned around. It was the Australian, bleary-eyed, having fallen asleep while watching the endless transit of the stylus burning out the trace on the bottom sounder in the stern lab. He was unkempt as usual, unsteady, hugging the port winch like a crutch. "Can't a man get any rest around here?"

Mary said nothing, in no mood for banter; the thought of the pilot's death, even if the plane had been snooping on them, made her shiver, and an overwhelming rush approaching panic made her realize what it was to be alive, how short a step it was to sudden death.

"Frank," she said, her voice tremulous. "Can Aussie take over?"

Frank glanced at the meter wheel moving slowly and saw the tension meter needle quivering with strain. There was something in the grab. He didn't want to leave but Mary was shaking.

"Think you can handle it, Aussie?"

The Australian looked unenthused. "All right," he said. "Seeing I'm up anyway."

"Fine," replied Frank. "Any trouble—hit the brake and call me."

"She'll be right," said Aussie. "Not to worry."

INSIDE HER CABIN Mary swung around as Frank asked her irritably, "Why did you want to leave? This could be the station we've been looking—"

"Hold me," she said, her tone frantic. "Frank—hold me." She was already unbuttoning her blouse, fingers trembling. Frank felt a surge of blood shooting through him. She told him she was scared—terrified from seeing the plane go down, from the sinking of the trawler, of the approaching storm, of being a widow, of death, of not having lived before... "Please," she implored. There was no need. His oilskin came undone in one ripping movement, his sea boots and toque flung aside. Above him he could hear the groaning of the winch, all about him feel the deep throbbing of the ship, and all he could smell was her, her breasts pushing full and luxuriously against him, her lips yielding to his. Bracing her, one arm around her naked waist, his other hand gripping the top edge of the steel bunk, he lowered her and they made love as the ship pitched, yawed hard aport, then momentarily seemed suspended in space and time before plunging, its whole being shuddering through the oncoming wave.

AT PEACE, FRANK STOOD by the winch, watching the meter wheel's progress as the Australian, a yellow-clad torso draped over the rail, saw a furious greenish-white circle of boiling water. "The bugger's coming up!" he shouted excitedly.

"You're supposed to say, 'In sight,'" Frank called out good-naturedly. "So there's no confusion on—"

"Okay—the bugger's in sight!"

The winch man shook his head, stamped on the brake, putting the Swann into low gear for the final and most dangerous pull of all.

THE POLISH PILOT saw his helicopter safely lashed and secured in the mother ship's hangar and reported to the bridge of the huge ship. Captain Ilya Novisk, a man of medium height and build in worn blue corduroys and a coarse gray polo neck sweater that matched his eyes, asked the pilot if he thought the pilot of the Beechcraft had seen anything.

The chopper pilot shrugged. "I'm not sure, sir, but anyway," he said, grinning, "now we've made sure."

Novisk frowned. He couldn't afford the pilot's easy optimism. As captain of the fishing fleet's mother ship he was the one who would have to answer to Gdansk, which in effect meant he'd be answering to Moscow. "Radio officer?"

"Yes, captain?"

"Are you positive the plane didn't get an SOS off?"

"Absolutely, sir. We would have picked it up. She didn't have time, Captain."

Novisk looked surprised. "How do you know it was a woman?"

The second officer on the eight-to-noon watch stepped in. "We've been monitoring her, sir, ever since she left Astoria, asking the tower there for takeoff permission. She reported nothing, Captain. No one knows. We're safe." The radio officer nodded his agreement.

Novisk's face slackened a little but the worry lines were still evident. He would remain tense until this business was over. Why, he was asking himself, couldn't the damned Russians do it themselves?

WHEN KLAUS WAS TOLD that his Beechcraft had blown up in midair off the coast of Oregon he dismissed the possibility of accident. In his world there was no such thing—there was only intent. Somehow the aircraft must have been sabotaged in Astoria. Time bomb probably. Very well, if Mr. Hall wanted to play rough, SRP would up the ante. He swallowed another antacid pill instead of chewing it, as his secretary came in, middle-aged, bifocals and no-nonsense. She was giving Klaus the gist of the report even as she handed it to him. "The CANUS office in Portland say they don't know how Hall could possibly have found out Ms Waites."

"Who?" asked Klaus.

"Waites—the pilot."

Klaus waved the information and the secretary out of his office. He wasn't interested in pilots' names, especially pilots who were of no further use. What he wanted now was action. Drawing out one of his favorite Dutch cigars from his platinum case he gave his full attention to the problem as the traffic murmured far below him on the Bahnhofstrasse. Of course it was obvious that Hall wanted him to react—to have him break out of cover before any rich deposits of sea gold were found. No, Klaus told himself, he must resist the temptation to even the score. For now, he must show patience. He would continue the surveillance, wait for Hall to do all the work, until the moment the American hit "pay dirt" as they called it in America. Then, and only then, would he strike.

Convinced now that he had made the right tactical decision, Klaus reclined in the plush leather chair, luxuriating in the taste of his cigar, blowing the blue-gray smoke in a near-perfect cone toward the sparkling chandelier high above. Then he paused and sat up abruptly. What if meanwhile Hall discovered SRP's other operatives as he had this pilot— Way, or whatever her name was? Klaus stubbed out the cigar and began chewing more antacid tablets. If SRP's other operatives were blown he would have no alternative but to act immediately and stop *Petrel* dead in the water rather than allow Hall to continue the search unopposed. He rose from the plush leather chair, leaving the office early for his daily stroll to the Bauschantzli. It was as he was crossing the bridge, as the colored lights sprinkled around the restaurant came on, blinking at him through the trees, that the idea of a suitable interim action struck him. The force of his revelation was so great that when he sat down at his usual table and the waiter appeared, smiling, ready with a glass of milk, at room temperature, Klaus sent him away, ordering instead a beer. Ice-cold. It was time, Klaus decided, to send birthday greetings to the M.V. *Petrel*.

Chapter Eight

BY NOW, *Petrel* was completing her second station. The sediment from the first haul was too low in metalliferous deposits. With seawater cascading from her as she broke surface, watery brown mud bleeding through her clasped jaws, the huge grab began swinging pendulously.

Frank could see Tate watching anxiously from high on the starboard wing of the bridge. It was a familiar scene for Frank, as every skipper he'd ever known paced the bridge until Big Bess was safely aboard. But this time Frank knew he'd timed it just right. As the ship started lunging to starboard, they had the grab over the rail, everyone straining to hold her as steady as possible for the split second it took the winch man to bring her down onto the deck where she rolled awkwardly to one side, then sat there like some prehistoric beast stranded upon an alien shore. Frank handed the crank handle to Aussie.

"Unwind her, Sport. Let's see what we've got."

"Phew, it stinks! Smells like a bloody dunny."

"A what?"

"Lavatory. Toilet."

"Wish you Aussies would learn to speak English."

"Cheeky bloody Yank."

The two kept up the banter as Aussie wound open the monstrous jaws that had slammed shut fifteen hundred yards below in one of the twenty-mile-long valleys between mountain ranges. In the air of expectancy, crew materialized from all parts of the ship as news that the grab wasn't empty, hadn't struck just plain old boring rock but something else, quickly spread. As the jaws began to open, a massive excretion of green mud oozed out on deck. "Bloody lovely!" said Aussie.

While the crew made the usual obscene observations, Frank whipped a trowel from the tool board inside the stern lab, took a sample of the gelatinous mud, put it in a plastic bag, tagged it as number 2 and wrote in his notebook its exact position and depth. Then he looked around for Mary, whose job it was to stand by with the saltwater hose to flush the unwanted ooze from the deck so the rest of the sample could be seen. Instead, Frank saw her talking animatedly with the third officer up forward on the well deck immediately below the bridge. Aussie straightened from the hunched-over position. "Time for smoko."

"What?" asked one of the crewmen, an oiler, his long, thin face and nose giving him the appearance, especially in his gray-toned boiler suit, of some great undernourished bird waiting for his next meal.

"Time for a rest," explained Aussie. "This is hard yakka, mate."

"C'mon," called Frank. "Keep cranking."

Aussie bent back over the grab. "Flamin' slave driver. Two to one there's no sea gold in this stuff." Suddenly his head shot up and back. "For Christ's sake!"

Several of the crewmen laughed. "What's the matter, Aussie? You see a snake?"

"It's that pong. Like rotten eggs."

As he continued cranking, another crewman, one of the lookouts from the earlier four-to-dawn watch, offered to take Aussie up on his prediction. "I'll bet you ten bucks there's sea gold inside there, Aussie."

"You're on, mate." He was almost done unwinding the spring mechanism that held the jaws together, and in the dark gut of the grab he could see what looked like lumps of brown coal.

Unknown to the Australian, the crewman, as Frank guessed, had made a shrewd wager, because the repulsive odor of rotten eggs, hydrogen sulfide, signaled the absence of oxygen in the mud. The wager also reminded Frank of how Aussie had pretended to know much more about marine geology than he did.

"Frank!" It was Mary, holding fast to the rail.

One look at her face and he knew something was wrong. Before he could ask what it was he saw Aussie jumping down off the grab.

"Watch out!" yelled Frank, but it was too late. The grab vomited a rushing stream of ooze and chocolaty basalt and swirled about the crewmen, knocking Aussie down on the deck, where, as the ship pitched, he slithered toward the A-frame, bashing his head on the roller. Blood spurted from the Australian's head, and as the ship pitched again, heeling hard in a rogue cross swell, its bow dipping then rising sharply, Aussie slid farther back over the roller. One arm reached for the cable rail above the roller but missed.

"Man overboard!" yelled Frank, pressing the white emergency button by the winch, rushing to the bulkhead, snatching a life tube and tossing it astern. But as the churning wake passed over Aussie, Frank could see the Australian facedown, unconscious.

His right hand jerking down hard on his life vest's lanyard, Frank dived off the stern. *Petrel* was heeling hard astarboard, already turning as he hit the ice-cold sea, the ship's wake sucking him down. The suction increased in a trough, dragging him under while he kicked as hard as the cumbersome oilskins would permit, trying to hold what breath remained after the shock of the dive. The next swell helped, lifting him, pushing him farther away from the vortex high on a wave's crest, where he caught a glimpse of Aussie, now conscious, thrashing about, a hundred feet away deep in a trough running between fourteen-foot swells. Then he disappeared and the next thing Frank saw was the white outline of *Petrel* parallel to him three hundred yards to his left, its normally high superstructure sinking in a trough, the figures crowded about its Austin-Western boom on the forward deck looking ridiculously small.

When he was fifty feet from Aussie and could see him again, he yelled to him to stop fighting, to float, but the noise of the gale-force winds and seas drowned his call. The Australian, arms flapping, gulping frantically for air, started to go under for what Frank knew would be the last time. Cantering over its own wake, *Petrel*'s bow threw up curtains of spray, obscuring Frank's vision so that he lost sight of the Australian again.

It was only when *Petrel* slowed to use her bow thrusters that the flailing arms slipped in and out of sight in a long wave that had caught Frank from behind, surfing him to within fifteen feet of his drowning companion. By then Frank had managed to kick off his sea boots and swim forward, giving his crawl everything he had, reaching for the other man's collar. He missed but got a handful of hair and pulled the sacklike body, now facedown, toward him. He rolled onto his back in a kind of half backstroke and turned the Australian over, shouting over the howl of the gale and noise of the ship, "Hang on, Aussie!" He kept repeating it, not knowing whether the Australian was alive or dead, only that he was near the end of his own strength, his vision blurring as he glimpsed through the noise and chaos of the sea the long extension arm of the Austin-Western boom jerking, sliding, then swinging gracefully out over the angry waves, which to Frank seemed to be growing more threatening with every second. His limbs, heavy with cold and fatigue, had lost all their power, becoming deadweights, dragging him under as successive swells sloshed over him with an infuriating indifference.

"Get out of the way!" ordered the bosun angrily, trying desperately to see through the throng of seamen clustering at the rail, some supposed to be there under the orders of the third mate, others merely gawking. The bosun knew that if he misplaced the hook dangling from the extension arm he would either miss them altogether or kill them with it.

"Get out of the goddamn way!" the third mate shouted, leaning outboard, hooking a pike's collar around the hydraulic arm's cable, keeping it closer to the ship's side until they were near enough to the two men so he could guide it down. Hall looked all right to him but the Australian seemed done for, all his energy expended in the shock of the head injury and in fighting against the sea instead of having let himself go with it as much as possible in hopes of holding out longer.

Frank caught the edge of the hook's canvas sling on the fourth pass and looped it around Aussie's body. The Austin-Western's whine joined the cacophony of gale winds, the roaring of sea and the truncated phrases of the fifteen-man crew as they called instructions to one another in the urgent and dangerous job of pulling up the two men from the surges of foaming sea every time a swell coursed beneath the ship, lifting her high then dumping her into the bowel-wrenching void above a trough.

CLUTCHING A MUG of steaming soup, teeth chattering despite the thick blue woolen blankets around him, Frank watched as the Australian was carried into the dry lab. One of the seamen, the tall bird-face, was already bent over him, giving mouth-to-mouth resuscitation, pausing only long enough to clear some vomit, until Aussie's head gave a violent start and his chest heaved with dry retching as he slowly began to recover full consciousness. Immediately the tension in the lab began to ebb. Aussie finally raised himself on one elbow only to collapse again, his eyes still glassy, exclaiming to the ring of faces above him, "Can't bloody swim."

"Son of a—" began the third mate. "How the hell did you stay afloat?"

"Dog-paddled." The Australian's eyes went around the haze of grins until he saw the bird-face. "Thanks, mate." He weakly put out his hand.

Mary didn't waste any time, as she had Tate resume course for the next station. The sample from the grab hadn't been analyzed yet, but to hang around after a grab had been brought up was a certain giveaway that you had found something. Best to keep any opposition guessing.

Once the new course was set with enough jags in it to reveal whether or not anyone was shadowing them, Mary felt that what she had been about to tell Frank just before Aussie's accident couldn't wait much longer. At the moment only she, the captain and the bosun, whose job it was to supervise clearing and cleaning the deck after any station, knew. She waited until Tate had finished bawling out the third mate for not having enforced the hard hat and life jacket rule either on deck during Aussie's accident or after, when Aussie had been carried up to his cabin by stretcher, where, once the gash in his head had been stitched by the cook, who also served as ship's medic, he had fallen fast asleep.

"AREN'T YOU GLAD to see me?" Frank joked when he saw the frown.

Mary was slumped on the bunk. "I thought you'd be killed."

There was a long silence; he could see something else was on her mind, something that she didn't want to bother him with so soon after his ordeal but that was too urgent to wait.

"Tate wants to see you," she said. "As soon as you're up to it." She was looking at his fresh khaki shirt and jeans, which she thought fitted him as well as she'd ever seen clothes fit a man, and noting how his tanned complexion, though he'd be the last to know it, highlighted the cool blue of his eyes.

"I'm up to it," he said gamely. "Let's go."

She had seen it before, how the close brush with death invigorated him.

A few minutes later, like figures in slow motion, Tate and his two companions walked slowly, holding the storm lines now strung along the well deck, making their way forward beneath the fo'c'sle. The captain unlocked the main hatch as they passed into the dark and oppressive air of the ship's ten-by-four-foot paint locker. In there *Petrel*'s motion was markedly worse than amidships, and in the high pitches Frank felt his stomach had been left behind, the violence of the yaw and pitch threatening to bring up what was left of breakfast. Mary, too, looked uncomfortable, swallowing a lot and perspiring in the clammy and claustrophobic atmosphere. In the middle of the locker between boarded-up rows of paint cans there was a paint-splattered canvas drop cloth, and off to one side assorted scrapers and brushes clattering around in a large tea chest.

"Take a corner," Tate instructed Frank, lifting up one side of the drop cloth, about six feet square, bringing it back as if unfolding a tent. Underneath the cloth Frank saw the deflated red-and-white-striped life raft that they had hauled in among other wreckage from the *Lvov*.

"So?" he asked the captain.

"It's a life raft," said Tate ingenuously.

Despite the headache he was starting to get from the thick fumes, Frank was grinning across at the other two. "I know it's a life raft. I gaffed it. Mind you, I almost fell—"

Mary was looking nervous, unsteady.

"Come over here," said Tate, kneeling down, lifting one of the still-wet and flattened edges of what had been the raft's inflatable side tubes. "'Course a lot of it was ripped away and lost, but on this side you can see pretty well what it looked like." With that he drew six or seven pieces of the lacerated rubber together. "Parts of it, I guess, were torn by wind and shards from the explosion, but you can still make it out. Bosun was first to see it, everyone else was busy clearing the well deck. Almost missed it himself. I've told him to say nothing—not a word."

The ship pitched high, throwing them off balance, and Frank had to hold a stanchion in order to concentrate and make out the letters on the base tube: WIF URE.

"Jesus!" he said, looking up at Mary, then Tate.

"Yes," confirmed Tate. "It's from *Swiftsure*."

At that moment all Frank could hear was the banshee howling of the wind. Everything seemed to be rattling, coming undone, as if an impossibility had visited them but one so undeniable that it had to be faced. "Then why?" he began. "Why the hell didn't we see nine blips on the radar after the explosion instead of ten? Two from eleven leaves nine, right? One for *Lvov*, one for *Swiftsure*? Nine!"

"But what about *Swiftsure*?" said Mary. "That message from her saying she was all right?"

Frank turned to Tate. "It was a Morse transmission we received, right, Captain? No voice."

"Right," confirmed Tate. "Definitely Morse."

Frank still saw the problem posed by Mary's question, that the message had been sent *after* the explosion, but just as quickly he saw a possible answer. "Another ship!" he said. "Could have slipped into the area during the clutter, milling with the others in the dark and used *Swiftsure*'s call sign. Using *Swiftsure*'s name as a cover."

"But who?" began Mary. "I mean why would—" She stopped; she was turning pale. "Oh, my God—you mean one of Klaus's?"

Frank shrugged, unsure, but his face grim with the possibility.

"As well as checking us out with the plane?" she said.

"Why not?" said Frank. "I told you that a plane can spot us, but beyond that it's almost impossible to tell whether we've found sea gold or not, unless we hang around a station too long after the grab's up. Klaus knows that, too. So his blip on our screen fronts as *Swiftsure*. Very neat. Who would know?"

"Frank Hall," she answered.

"If I'm right."

ALONE IN THE DRY LAB, while Mary was trying to get some sleep before the next station, Frank found himself besieged by questions as he made preparations for the testing of the grab sample from the second station. If *Swiftsure* had sunk, why hadn't they seen any bodies as well as the life raft and the other debris? And what if *Swiftsure* was all right, her Morse message genuine, the life raft having simply come adrift in the heavy seas and washed overboard? He looked out the porthole at the gray blob that was the big Polish mother ship seven miles away. That was another thing. Why hadn't the mother ship wanted *Petrel* to help search for wreckage from the plane? And what about the poor bastards from *Lvov*? What the hell was going on?

Chapter Nine

TWENTY MILES TO THE SOUTH, wreathed in mist where the colder northern waters off Oregon meet the warmer air masses coming up from the south, a Polish trawler lay rolling in the swells, her Marconi II radar having to be stripped for repairs. Impatient though he was to get under way, her captain wasn't about to charge ahead through the mist for fear of colliding with any of the other trawlers in the fleet. And so while his technician was up in the wheelhouse checking the electronics, the captain decided it would be as good a time as any to watch the video his first officer had made, or, more accurately, that the Milnik Mark I ship console had made, during and after the Milnik's brief flight of 1.2 seconds, hitting its target 1100 yards away at a speed of 2500 feet a second.

"No wonder," said the captain, "there were no bodies, eh, Pod?"

Podborsky, the first mate or *oficer elektronik*, electronics warfare officer, as he was designated in Gdansk's "special" fleet files, shrugged nonchalantly. He was secretly very proud of the East German-made missile he was in charge of, but part of his mystique aboard the ship was maintained by his pretense that it was all old hat to him. In fact he'd fired only two of them before being assigned by Gdansk, through Moscow's request, and both of those had been in practice at Peenemünde, the Baltic's offshore range that had once been used by the Nazis to test their flying bombs. On the ship's video the flight of the ship-to-ship missile was so fast, so short that it was nothing more than an orange streak on the film. Then it hit the M.V. *Swiftsure* just below the wheelhouse. Podborsky had first picked up the American trawler on his hull-mounted sonar, getting a reasonable scan of the American's profile, but it wasn't until he got a readout on *Swiftsure*'s mast arrays that he recognized that *Swiftsure* was a U.S. ELINT or electronic intelligence ship. It was then that the mother ship ordered *Lvov* to go into her well-practiced distress mode, blacking out all lights, navigational as well as interior, simulating the propane—with color additive—fire on the well deck. When the American spy ship was at effective point-blank range, with a safety moat of at least three hundred meters around *Lvov*, he'd been ordered to fire the Milnik, then change *Lvov*'s name on bow and stern plates and maintain radio silence before heading south out of the area during storm line activity.

Watching the video, *Lvov*'s captain was impressed by the weight-to-explosion ratio. The instant the Milnik hit *Swiftsure* beam-on, there was a boiling pall of crimson fire shot through with blues and greens, as the American ship's aluminum superstructure and her volatile plastics, from Formica tabletops to the crew's synthetic clothes, instantly melted then caught fire. Flames flew skyward in the vacuum following the rocket's impact, infusing the low fibrous clouds with ballooning fireballs burning fiercely and throwing off a glowing rain of debris that at times illuminated the longer, duller glow of the bisected hull, all that remained of the ship. It sank in less than four minutes, making a noise, *Lvov*'s captain thought, like a drainpipe emptying, going down in huge, oily bubbles of variegated color.

Only four of the Americans were left on the surface, waving their arms desperately, two of them making for a lifeboat, but it had been badly holed by the hail of white-hot aluminum chips and Formica shards from what the *Lvov*'s captain could only guess had once been parts of the galley. One American sailor managed to reach the boat but he was so badly burned he could not hold on. In any case, the boat soon sank. Of the other three Americans, one dropped out of sight, caught in a treacly brown lump of burning bunker oil. The remaining two made it to *Lvov* where the political officer from Moscow escorted them one at a time to the sick bay. Afterward, he explained that both men had *zaputalsya*, stumbled on the stairwell, falling headfirst all the way down to the steel deck.

"Both of them?" asked the captain.

"Yes."

They weighted the two of them with half-inch chain and threw them overboard.

Now, her radar repaired, *Lvov* emerged from the fog, no longer the M.V. *Lvov* out of Gdansk but *Neeska*. Podborsky leaned forward, watching the rotating arm of the surface radar, as suspicious of *Petrel*'s whereabouts as he had been about *Swiftsure*'s. *Petrel* was listed by the Americans as a civilian oceanographic vessel, which, Podborsky thought, could be as good a cover as a trawler. The orders from Moscow, via Gdansk, were unequivocal—if any foreign ship or aircraft of any kind got too close to the mother ship it was to have an "accident"— with no survivors.

Chapter Ten

JOHN D. HORNBY, Portland chief of CANUS Ore, was lying in his cocoon, a rectangular, three-sided, hospital-white metal box, seven feet long by four wide with a single neon tube giving off a low-intensity white light. It had been designed to brighten depression-prone spirits in the northwest states where almost continual rainfall at times drove the inhabitants to brooding about life under perpetual overcast. Hornby was wearing a plush white terry robe and rose-tinted sunglasses that gave his hazel eyes a mousy gray appearance. His short, stubby fingers, quite out of proportion to his heavy six-foot frame, were busily exploring the delicate fold of skin beneath his secretary's skirt. She didn't like it but the money was very good, and as an unskilled single mother she had to either put up with it or join the legions of the unemployed. There were worse ways of surviving. She squirmed as he thrust his finger deep into her. "You like that, honey?"

She tried to smile but couldn't.

"Hurt you?" he asked.

"Sort of, Mr. Hornby."

"Good," he said excitedly. "It's gonna hurt a lot more, honey. And no more Mr. Hornby shit, eh? Call me Johnny...." He undid his robe. "You ever see one that big, baby?"

"No...I..."

"Knock you right over?"

"Could I have another drink...Johnny?"

Hornby's wide lips pursed, his laughter more a stifled snort. Never seen a broad so dumbfounded. He felt great and in a few minutes he was going to feel even better. The neon box helped too—made him feel warm. Maybe he wouldn't rush it after all. Hell, there was no hurry with this pussy...no twenty-minute sprint...just a fucking slow boat to China. "China!" He liked her because she was half squaw, her old man a full-blooded Indian. "Hey, you hear about the Indian? Went to the supermarket. Manager said, 'Can I help you?' Indian guy says, 'Yeah, I'm lookin' for some toilet paper.' So the manager says, 'Well, we got some Cashmere here. That's a good seller.' Shows him all the brand names, right, then shows 'im the 'no name' brand on special. The Indian takes four rolls of it—comes back next week. Manager sees him and says, 'How'd that toilet paper work out?' Indian says, 'No good. Down on the reserve they're callin' it John Wayne paper.' 'John Wayne paper?' says the manager. 'What do you mean, John Wayne paper?' 'Well,' says the Indian, 'it's rough, tough and it doesn't take crap from Indians.'" Hornby was so busy guffawing he barely heard the telephone.

"The phone's ringing," May said coldly.

He lumbered to his feet. "Shit! I should've taken the fucker off the hook. You wait there, sugar. When I come back I'm really gonna come. Right." He said it looking down, admiring his erection. "Hornby," he barked into the receiver. Suddenly a transition took place. No longer were his words clipped, irreverent, his arrogance deflated as quickly as his erection. "Yes, sir...yes, sir. No, right away. Yes, sir... Half hour at the most. Yes, sir. Just 'Happy Birthday and many more.' Yes, sir. No, sir, I understand, no one else. I'll attend to it personally. Yes, sir...and...thank you for calling, sir." When he put down the phone his face was a pink to match his eyeglasses, which he now took off. There were creases in his face where before it had looked like baby fat. She knew it had to be a call from the boss in Switzerland.

"From the big chief?" she asked, but he was too agitated to get her irony.

"Jesus!" said Hornby, doing up his robe, pulling the tie tightly.

"What's the matter, Johnny?"

"The shit's hit the fan. I've got to send a message to a guy. Shit!"

"What's the problem?" she inquired solicitously, enjoying his discomfort more and more.

"Never mind," he said, glancing down at her. "C'mon, move your ass. We have to go down to the office."

She took her time putting on her blouse, asking him to do her up at the back. As he did up the buttons she pressed her buttocks into his groin. "Gee, what happened to it, Johnny? It's gone all flat."

"Christ!" he said. "I hope I don't have to go out."

"Where?"

"To sea. Christ, I hate boats." He looked down at her for sympathy. "It churns me all up. Get sick as a dog."

"Gee, Johnny, I hope you don't have to go."

"You're a good kid, May, you know that? I always thought Indians were a bunch of fuckin' drunks till I met you."

"Gee thanks, Johnny."

"That's all right, sweetheart. But listen, when we're in the office, better call me— I mean, better not call me Johnny. Okay?"

"You mean the other guys might get jealous you've got me?"

"Yeah...you know, something like that."

"All right, Johnny."

He put on his jacket, a corduroy check—the only one in all Portland, he said. She believed him.

When he got into his black TransAm she asked him if he really thought he would have to go to sea. He said he didn't know; they'd have to take a run down the coast to Astoria. It all depended on whether he could get out a message on the normal channels in this weather or not. Besides, even if he did get it sent, with all the usual messages from wives, sweethearts and family to their men at sea, even then he might have to go if things didn't work out.

"To lend a helping hand," he said. "Just have to wait and see."

"Gee," said May, "I hope you don't have to go. Weather report last night was lousy. Marine forecast is a storm warning. Waves up to thirty feet in a day or two."

"Oh Christ!" Hornby moaned, sliding farther into his bucket seat, pushing hard on the wheel. "I can't do anything when I'm seasick. Honest to God, it fucking ruins me."

"That's a shame," said May. "Maybe you could take some pills or something. Anyway, maybe you won't have to go."

"That's right." He perked up. "Dammit, you're right, May. If everything clicks according to plan I won't even have to get my feet wet." Hornby slipped his hand up her thigh. "You'd miss me, wouldn't you, baby?"

"Yes, Johnny."

Chapter Eleven

IN THE WET LAB, Frank spun the wheel locks on the watertight doors so that no one could watch him sticking a thermometer into the sample of green ooze, which smelled even more strongly now of hydrogen sulfide. While he waited for the temperature reading he took one of the pieces of reddish-brown encrusted rock, the size of a baseball, which had come up in the second station's grab. He chipped a piece off with the geology hammer, placed the marble-size chunk into a mortar and, while bracing himself against a series of high pitches and gut-drop rolls, began to methodically grind up the crusty sample until it was the consistency of finely grained brown sugar. After cutting off a finger-length of platinum wire, he placed the wire next to the mortar and pestle and lit a Bunsen burner. He adjusted the sleeve valve until a wide, soft saffron flame rose up, soon roaring into a small spear-shaped purple flame within a larger onion-dome-shaped flame of vibrant turquoise. Taking a few milligrams of flux from a glass phial, he added this to the ground-up sample.

Below him he could feel the deep, rhythmic pulsing of the G.M. engines as *Petrel* engaged the heavier seas of the advancing storm line. He knew that if they were to retrace the line of stations in order to put down cameras and survey the extent of the stations that had tested most positive, the work of lowering the specially designed Edgerton cameras would prove hair-raising, especially for Aussie who knew as little about photography as he did about any other oceanographic work.

Slipping on a big white protective asbestos glove, Frank braced himself against the counter's antispill rail, waiting for the precise moment at which *Petrel* reached the apogee of her pitch. He then quickly, but adroitly, touched the fine tip of the platinum wire to the tip of the purple flame and waited thirty seconds, holding the wire steady in the flame's tip until it glowed plum-red. Next he took it from the flame and deftly touched it to the mixture of crushed sample and flux. A small bead of the mixture adhered to the end of the wire, which Frank passed back and forth through the turquoise flame until the bead became a molten droplet. At that point he removed it from the flame and waited for the result of a thousand hours spent in calm and crazy seas, of nights where the stations had been so long that he had fallen asleep against the winches as they waited for ice-cold grabs, corers and other instruments of the search to break through the surface. Outside, the wind was a persistent howl now, decks constantly awash, wind and water so powerful they could knock a man down, sweeping him over unseen into the turbulent blackness.

Frank watched the tiny bead, catching his breath in anticipation as it lost its redness and its mystery and turned, not into a dark ball of ash or the hardened gray of failure, but into the singular beauty of robin's-egg-blue, confirming the presence of manganese, the sign that undersea precipitation was occurring. Sea gold was here! Off Oregon, on the abyssal plains south of the Juan de Fuca Ridge. A camera station at some future date, perhaps on the return to Astoria, was now mandatory. Yet despite his excitement, he knew that any celebration would have to wait until the cameras told them whether they had discovered a few hundred meters of manganese deposits down there or more extensive sources of sea gold in the form of thermal vents spewing out the kinds of strategically important metals like cobalt and nickel so vital to everything from teaspoons to the Stealth bomber—metals that the United States could not produce enough of and so had to import, placing itself at the mercy of often politically unstable regimes.

Taking out the large map showing the jagged edge of the Oregon coastline at the easternmost part of the Juan de Fuca Ridge system, where the Pacific Plate rubbed against the Continental Plate, Frank carefully checked the satellite loran position of the station, which only he and the officer on watch were permitted to know. Careful this time, after the experience of an earlier cruise, not to press too hard on the marker pen lest he leave an imprint on the map that would show, if traced, the exact latitude and longitude of the loran fix, he wrote down the coordinates on a paper towel, put it in the top pocket of his lab coveralls, cleaned up, then made his way in a growing mood of deep satisfaction against the bucking and roll of the ship up to the scientist's cabin. In the shaft of light from the hall he saw Aussie, blanket pulled up high around him as usual. He closed the door softly, went to the low safe, one hand out, feeling for the cool bulkhead as his eyes grew accustomed to the semidarkness and then turning the tumblers through the combination that only he knew. Once the safe was opened he reached inside and switched on the small rechargeable flashlight in the sheath that was attached to the right inside of the safe and that he had often used so as not to have to wake anyone sharing the cabin.

Suddenly his hand froze. He had always made it a point to have the flashlight in its sheath so that the bulb was facing toward the safe door and not the rear of the safe as one would normally expect—a security precaution only he knew about. The flashlight bulb was now facing *away* from him. Someone had been in the safe.

He looked again to be sure. It was facing away. Angrily he swung around, switched on the main light. No one would have dared try to rifle the safe for the secret station positions knowing that someone was sleeping in the cabin. Besides, how would they know whether the cabin's occupant was asleep or awake? Now everything started rushing into place...the Australian's pretense of knowing more oceanography than he did to get hired...all his noise about wanting to sleep in...but being on deck just when they happened to be about to work the station...his unexpected eagerness in wanting to uncrank the grab...to be the first to see what was inside...

Frank wrenched the heavy blanket off him. "All right, you son of a—"

Aussie's head rolled over, the scrapes and scratches he had received from being swept over the stern still weeping moisture. But the Australian was dead, his blue eyes fixed, staring at nothing, mouth agape, lips leathery and blue, the chest still.

CAPTAIN TATE'S VOICE was slow, heavy with the long experience of a man who had seen it all. "Died in his sleep," he said, looking up at Frank. Tate had never really liked Aussie's cockiness, the very thing that Mary had told Frank she found most engaging, for all his faults. For her, the young, happy-go-lucky Australian had been a welcome counterpoint to the often stern if competent solidity of the captain and the Scottish mate.

"My God," she said. "I realized he was battered about by the time we got him back on board...." She stopped, unable to bear the eyes looking at her anymore. "Can't you do something about that?" she said to no one in particular.

Frank drew the eyelids down as the captain, almost losing his footing, steadied himself against the bunk and handed Frank two quarters.

"We'll need some tape," said Frank, his voice noticeably subdued. After fastening the tape over the coins on the dead man's eyelids, he pulled up the woollen blanket.

"It was the cold," said the first mate authoritatively. "And that belt he got on the head when he hit the roller."

The captain, to Mary's relief and surprise, told them there was nothing to be gained by trying to run back to Astoria against the storm until there was a lull. Going by the barometer alone, that wouldn't be for at least forty-eight hours, so they might as well continue, and do as many stations as possible.

No matter how reluctant he now felt about going on, Frank knew the old man was right, was simply being practical under the circumstances. "All right," said Frank. "But we can't leave him here."

"I've already thought of that," replied Tate. "Don't mean to sound hard, but unfortunately he's not the first man I've seen die at sea. Disease regulations mean I'll have to keep him in one of the freezers until we get back."

"My God!" said Mary. "That's a bit grim, isn't it?"

"It's what they do at a morgue, Mrs. Crane," explained the captain as gently as he could. "Just another name for it. It's not going to make any difference to him."

Frank was silent. The immediate decision of whether or not to go on had momentarily taken his mind off the fact that someone had been in the safe and had seen the secret list of station positions that *Petrel* was heading for. Or— and the prospect depressed him as much as the Australian's death—perhaps Aussie had rifled the safe.

"We'd better search his effects for next of kin," said Frank, offering to do it himself.

"Right," answered Tate. "If you find an address, give it to Sparks."

Frank nodded as the captain and the mate shuffled noisily out of the cabin.

"You want me to help?" she asked solicitously.

"No, thanks. Maybe you can keep an eye on the dry lab sounder for me."

She touched his arm, glanced down at the Australian's corpse with a fleeting, morbid curiosity and left, feeling the ship changing course under her as if somehow Aussie's death had signaled a turn into the most dangerous seas so far.

In the Australian's wallet there were fifty-three dollars and six dollars in light red Canadian two-dollar bills. There was also a Blue Shield insurance card; a Washington state driver's licence; Visa and American Express cards—preferred status, at which Frank raised an eyebrow; four lot-

tery tickets; one unclaimed scratch lottery win for ten
dollars; a social security card; half a dozen receipts from
7-Eleven convenience stores, the blue ink
almost faded to nothing; and two Visa receipts from
Domino's Pizza. No pictures, no next-of-kin addresses. It
was a single man's wallet. There was certainly no list of
stations in either Aussie's wallet or his clothes—which
Frank felt bad about searching but searched nevertheless—and no list in the drawers beneath his bunk or in his
suitcase. Next Frank gingerly rolled the corpse over and
had a look beneath the bed linen and in the pillow covers.
Nothing but a few specks of foam stuffing. Suddenly the
Australian groaned.

"Jesus!" Frank jumped back before realizing the sound
had just been the escape of residual air in the corpse's
lungs. One of the coins had slid despite the tape, leaving
Aussie staring at him with part of one eye.

Averting his gaze, Frank sat by the scientist's desk and
tried to work through the problem. As there were no signs
of force used on the safe, Aussie would have had to know
how to listen for the tumblers to get the combination. It
wasn't a very sophisticated safe, but you would still have
to know what you were about to open it without blowing
it. Unless, of course, you knew the combination. Frank
knew he was the only one with that information, and it was
in his head.

Sitting there, his body going back and forth with the
motion of the ship, his gaze avoiding the corpse as if by
merely looking at Aussie he was accusing him, Frank noticed a line of dust beneath the edge of the bunk. It was the
concentration of the dust that held his attention. Leaning
over, he discovered it was made up of particles of dry,
crumbling foam rubber from the pillow. Then, looking
more closely, he noticed much more of it on and around
the body, especially in the chest hair.

Suddenly he started as someone knocked at the door.
Frank got up, still preoccupied with the crumbling foam

rubber that couldn't have accumulated on the floor for more than a day without being swept up. He opened the door. It was the scruffy, young third officer with a folded stretcher. "Give you a hand, Frank?"

"What?"

"Take him below. Easier to stuff him in a bag down there than trying to carry him down in it. Bastard of a job."

"Oh, yes. Sorry. I was thinking."

"What about?"

"Why all this stuffing from the pillow?"

"Probably making love to it," said the mate callowly. "Guys get lonely at sea, right?"

"Guys get lonely anywhere."

The mate shrugged, lifting Aussie's body by the shoulders, leaning against the roll. Frank took the feet.

"Well, at sea they get specially lonely," the mate went on. "Nothing else to think about." Then, as an afterthought, "Those goddamn videos only make you hornier. Rub it in."

Carrying the corpse out through the doorway was an awkward business, for it seemed to Frank to weigh twice as much as it should. But that wasn't what was worrying him. After they had put the body in the freezer he went back to the cabin and took the pillow from its cover, examining the foam filler. Both ends looked as if they had been savagely clawed. Either Aussie had been passionately lonely as the third mate had crudely suggested, or in the darkness he had been fighting for his life, desperately trying to prevent someone from suffocating him, before or after they had rifled the safe.

"On station in five minutes. On station..." It was the first mate on the PA, his voice echoing between the deserted and now, to Frank, eerie spaces between decks. Eerie, for even if he was wrong about Aussie's death, there was still the matter of the safe that had been broken into. Or had he, just once, in a hurry, put the flashlight back in its holder as you were supposed to—and not reversed it as a trap for an intruder?

It was like leaving home, then wondering whether or not you had left the stove on. The more you thought about it, the less sure you were.

Chapter Twelve

ABOARD THE MOTHER SHIP, anchored off Eagle Island, Captain Novisk ran his stubby, tobacco-stained fingers around his dark brown polo-neck sweater as if a sudden rash had assaulted him. "Why the devil didn't you see them before?" he asked the helicopter pilot. "You told me it was clear. 'Eagle Island is deserted—just as it says on the map.' That's what you told me, isn't it?"

"Yes, sir," began the pilot, "but the problem was—"

"The problem, Lieutenant, is that you're too cocky. You think just because you're on loan to us poor Poles you have to teach us what hotshots you are in...where is it?"

The lieutenant knew very well that Novisk knew where he was from. This was a little Polish humiliation you had to put up with whenever you were assigned to the fishing fleet. "Kiev, sir," he answered.

"Yes, Kiev. That's near Chernobyl, isn't it?"

The lieutenant's tone was as chilled as the currents swirling about the island. "That's right, sir. My mother was one of the first victims."

There was silence on the bridge of the mother ship as Novisk realized he had taunted the Ukrainian too far. "All right, my apologies, Lieutenant. But that doesn't alter the fact that you were mistaken. We could have walked into a monumental foul-up. When we arrived twenty-four hours ago all we had to do was complete the project—little more than tidying up—and now we have these bird lovers roaming the island.''

"Ornithologists, I think," said the lieutenant.

Novisk ignored the distinction. "What went wrong?" he asked irritably.

"The weather, sir. One minute it was clear over part of the island—the next you couldn't see a thing. On our first flight, before that Beechcraft got too close to the ship, we flew over and didn't see a thing besides the high sword grass that covers the island and a few streams that run right to the cliffs. And of course we saw the birds—thousands of them. Only other thing we spotted was the old survival hut that the report had already told us about. It's a hundred meters above a rocky ledge on the northwestern side. The only thing marked on the map that we didn't see were eagles. Apparently there aren't many of them. They gather about the peak of the Pinnacle—big rock at the southern tip or..."

"Or atop the cliffs on the eastern side," added Novisk, to make it clear that he, too, was familiar with the report prepared by Moscow. "I even remember that some of the cliffs are rust-red." He paused. "Why is that, by the way, that some are red deposits while..."

"Color of the party, I guess," said the lieutenant gamely. There was a polite ripple of laughter on the huge bridge. Even the tall, stern political officer, Colonel Saburov, joined in. It would help ease the tension.

"According to our geologists," Saburov explained, "the redness comes from the iron oxides in the rock. Very valuable if you can mine it—and economical for the state if you have something big enough to transport it."

"Yes, yes," Novisk said. "But that doesn't help us deal with the situation at hand." It would be his neck if anything went wrong, and he wanted the political officer in on the decision as well. He looked across at Saburov, who was

in military khaki and whose eyes were as gray as his ship.
"Have you any ideas, Colonel?"

"How many are there?" Saburov asked the lieutenant.

"Three . . . so far as we can tell. We only flew over once
so as not to—"

"What are they doing?"

"Chasing birds, it looks like, sir."

"Been at sea too long," said one of the Polish officers.
A lookout guffawed.

Captain Novisk ignored the buffoonery. "Any sign of a
boat?"

"Yes, sir, but only a fiberglass dinghy with an outboard. The boat's on the rock ledge, a hundred meters or
so below the shack. Outboard's outside the survival shack.
They probably use it to go from one end of the island to
the other when the sea's calm. Whenever that is, around
here."

The lieutenant knew what the old man was worried
about and sought to allay his fears. "It's certainly not big
enough to cross the seventy-odd miles to the mainland. I'd
say it's a runaround for them when they're banding the
birds. There has to be a bigger vessel that brings them out
once a year from the U.S. coast, then returns maybe a
month later to pick them up. In bad weather they can hole
up in the shack. I think that's why we missed them on the
first reconnaissance."

"But dammit," said Novisk, "the island's supposed to
be deserted. Nothing but tall grass and bird droppings."

"It is," Saburov retorted, defending the party's report,
"for most of the year. This is clearly an aberration." He
made the bird banders' presence sound like nothing more
than a temporary anomaly in the inevitability of Marxist
dialectic.

"Well, this 'aberration,' Comrade," Novisk countered, "has to be confronted. We've got to complete the
job and go home. So the only question now is how it's to
be done."

"Accident, Comrade," said Saburov, the dense, bluish-gray Turkish tobacco smoke rising and curling about him. "Don't you know that a storm line plays havoc all up and down the American coast? Fishermen have one of the highest death rates in the world. And not only in American waters, let me tell you. It's even worse in—"

"These people aren't fishermen," growled Novisk, looking down again at the black-and-white stills that the lieutenant had taken from a couple of hundred feet with an East German zoom. There were two men—one middle-aged, the other young—and a woman. Novisk didn't like East Germans or any Germans, but by God, they made good cameras. The young woman looked to be in her mid-twenties, about the same age as his niece in Warsaw. His heart went out to her. "They may not get too close," he ventured.

Saburov was unmoved. "We cannot afford the risk, Comrade."

"Well then," the political officer pressed, "how will you do it?"

"You mean," interjected Saburov, "how will *we* do it?" He paused, glancing around the bridge at the assembled officers. He wanted it recorded as a unanimous decision, at least among all the officers on watch. There were murmurs of assent. He waited a little longer until all the Poles agreed. The Poles, he noticed, displayed a peculiar squeamishness when it came to dealing with Americans. He was convinced that in some cases it had less to do with many Poles having American relatives than with all the God mumbo jumbo the two countries had in common. But in the end they would usually cooperate, because even if they didn't like the fact that you were a Russian, they understood simple arithmetic: Moscow has more divisions than the Pope. And then, of course, there were their families still in Poland.

"When do we do it?" Captain Novisk asked unenthusiastically.

"Oh, no point in waiting, is there?"

He ordered the helicopter ready in thirty minutes.

Chapter Thirteen

THOUGH THE SKY WAS still overcast, the wind had blown away the low stratus and Eagle Island could be seen in its entirety, the two-mile-long, half-mile-wide exclamation mark running roughly north-south and parallel to the Oregon coast seventy miles over the horizon to the east. The lone rock, or Pinnacle, a monolith of reddish-stained basalt jutting more than two hundred feet above the smashing sea and forming the island's southernmost extremity, was really another island separated from the longer by a funnel-shaped channel, its wider, western entrance about thirty feet across, the eastern or narrower end of the funnel twenty feet in width. Parts of the rocky weld binding the two parts of Eagle Island were visible only at low tide.

On the longer part of Eagle Island, apart from a small whaler's survival shack built during one unusually calm day in 1905, the only signs that man had been anywhere near the place were an old, abandoned, guano-encrusted cement barracks and the overgrown foundations of what had once been an Army radar station, hastily erected and manned by a lonely contingent of twelve men in the panicky days immediately following Pearl Harbor. Seven men had died getting the building materials ashore.

Beneath the cave-pocked face of the towering cliffs that rose precipitously on both coasts of the island, colonies of sea lions, seals and occasionally sea otters cavorted and snorted in the creamy surf, while millions of birds, mostly gulls and cormorants, filled the gray sky above, waiting and often fighting for every piece of available land or rock. Offshore, cormorants and more gulls glided in the high winds and dived, the cormorants, in their spectacular swept-back-wings formations, wreaking havoc with the schools of fish that the trawlers were chasing down the Californian Current over the Cascadia Basin and Blanco fracture zone that, 1.8 miles below, formed the southern-most extent of the Juan de Fuca Ridge system.

JULIO SUAREZ'S ANGER had been on the boil for weeks, and now he watched Gloria Bernardi, his fellow graduate student from Oregon State, with ill-disguised disgust and jealousy. There was little doubt in his mind that the beautiful and petite brunette he'd fallen hopelessly in love with was flirting shamelessly with her boss, graduate adviser Professor Locke from the Oregon Institute of Ornithologists, blinking her brown eyes at him in a way that would have marked her as a whore anywhere in Julio's native Mexico. What Julio either would or could not see was that Gloria Bernardi was genuinely attracted to the "old" man, as Julio despairingly called the fifty-year-old Locke, nor could he see that Locke was equally taken with her.

She was a vivacious twenty-four-year-old from the East Coast, eager to learn as much as possible about the flora and fauna of the Pacific Northwest for her master of science degree in biology. As an amateur photographer she had already won several awards in Boston for her still life studies. She had brought a lot of fast film with her, nothing less than 400 ASA, but it wasn't the speed of the birds she found was her biggest challenge on the island but the unrelenting weather. Charles Locke had assured her that there was good weather to be had this time of year and that there wasn't always a storm line blanketing the Northwest, but it had been raining on and off ever since they'd landed on the island, so that now she jokingly pretended not to believe anything Locke said on the subject.

Charles Locke delighted in her gently teasing manner, and each time she smiled at him he had visions of sleeping with her, of doing things with her that he had longed to do with his ex-wife but that she had been too prudish to try. Making love to Gloria, he was sure, would not be the quick, joyless affair, done more from a sense of marital duty, that it had been with his ex. It would take time, so he welcomed the bad weather, knowing they would have to be on the island together for as long as it took the storm line to pass before the charter boat could return for them. Till then, bedding down in the crude but cozily intimate survival shack with Gloria next to him would be no hardship. He had worked out every detail. He would reach out for her in the dark across the moist, earthen floor, over the backpack that acted as the divider between them and unzip her sleeping bag. Then, aching to be consumed by her, aching for her to reach over for him in the darkness, he would pull her unprotestingly toward him and enter her, loving her slowly, then faster and finally uncontrollably until they would lie happy and exhausted, the velvet darkness enfolding them. Outside, the wind would moan its soulful dirge, and then softly, gently, he would kiss her again, feel her again, make love again until utter exhaustion carried them to blissful sleep.

"Can you give me a hand, Professor?" It was Julio, wrecking Charles's fantasy, asking for assistance in banding a recalcitrant giant albatross chick. For perfectly good reasons, it was objecting to having the Mexican student throw an oilskin over its head then falling on it, while either the professor or Gloria took one of the chick's legs. Providing they could hold it steady, they had to fit the stamped aluminum band around the white, hairless leg, and squeeze the band shut, making sure it was not so tight that it impeded the bird's circulation, or so loose that it could be shucked free.

As Gloria bent to help hold the chick's leg, her down jacket and windblown hair inadvertently swept across Ju-

lio's arm and he was sure he felt the full swell of her bosom
brushing against him and that she was doing it on purpose. She tried to brush her hair back out of her eyes but
no matter what she did, because she was on the windward
side, the long, dark, silken strands kept softly whipping
Julio's face. He held the chick tightly around the neck
while the professor took an aluminum band from the
string of rings he had around his neck, like some ancient
warrior, and reached for his pliers.

"Easy with that chick, Julio. You'll strangle him to
death if you're not careful."

"Well, then, you two do it!"

With that, Julio thrust the terrified bird not at Locke but
at the astonished Gloria. There was an explosion of feathers, Gloria falling backward into a tall clump of sword
grass that released a powder cloud of dry seed dust from
its dead interior.

"What the—" began Charles, reaching over to Gloria
to help her up. "What the devil's got into him?"

"I...I don't know," answered Gloria, knowing full well
what the matter was with Julio but not wanting to embar-
rass him any more than he had himself, and wary of the
delicate relationship between graduate students and their
advisers. Everyone tried to pretend that personalities
shouldn't enter decisions about who should or should not
be granted postgraduate degrees, but Gloria Bernardi had
seen and experienced enough of the world to know differ-
ently. A tantrum like the one Julio had just pulled could
cost you a year.

"Maybe," she proffered weakly, "the weather's getting
him down. To a Mexican this climate must be the pits.
Gray sky most of the day. Not to mention the cold."

"But where's he going?" asked the professor, watching
the Mexican student striding off angrily southward, at
times stumbling. "Young fool! Looks like he's heading
toward the Pinnacle. I told him that none of us was to take
that on alone."

"Oh, he won't try to cross the gap until low tide. He's not that silly."

"No, but even then with only a foot or so of water going through, it's still tricky. I've only done it once and that was with a banding team nine years ago." The moment he said it, Locke wished he hadn't. Next to his slight baldness, his age was the thing that struck his vanity hardest, particularly in the company of a beautiful woman. Gloria had undone her down jacket to shake out some of the finely powdered grass that had slipped down her collar when she had fallen back. Watching her intently, Locke was reminded again of how sexy she was, a loose blue woolen sweater emphasizing the fullness of her breasts swelled with each breath she took. The professor decided to take a chance. "He's jealous. Is that it?"

"What..." she began, flustered. "I..."

"Of course you know, Gloria. He's been drooling over you ever since you arrived at college." He turned her around and began dusting her off. "And so have I." He felt her tensing beneath his touch. "Don't worry. I'm not going to take advantage of the situation." He paused. "Though I'd be an awful liar if I said I wouldn't like to." He felt her relax a little and watched her hair blowing in the wind. "You're very beautiful," he said, then stooping toward the clump of grass, careful of the swordlike edges, he retrieved his fallen backpack. "C'mon, let's go and get Julio before he tries something stupid."

She hesitated. "I don't think that's a good idea." As she said it, she tried to look Charles straight in the eye but his compliments to her made it impossible for the moment.

"What do you mean?" he inquired easily. "He should've cooled off enough by now." He smiled. "With all this wet grass he should be more than cooled off, he should be damn near frozen."

It was a weak joke, but it got her smiling. "Maybe he is," she said. "But he's very proud. He's blown his stack a few times before in the grad office.... Not this badly but . . . I really think the best thing to do is let him walk it off. He'll be back soon. If we go after him we might hurt his pride more than if . . ."

"You should be doing your master's in psychology," said Locke good-naturedly. "A study of the Mexican Spotted Sulk of the Pacific Northwest!"

They both laughed easily and finished banding the last several albatross chicks of the day. On the way back to the survival shack they talked easily, with a newfound familiarity, about the unexpected in their work—how, for example, you would think a frightened chick would up and fly immediately anyone approached to band it, yet even if the wind was more than the minimum fifteen miles per hour required to get their big bodies airborne, chicks on such remote islands as this never thought to flee, never having seen human beings before and so having no specific fear of them.

"It's amazing, really," said Locke, walking with a renewed vigor. "If you wanted to you could set out to kill all of them and they wouldn't suspect a thing."

"Oh, I don't know," Gloria challenged happily. "I think they'd sense something was up if you had murder on your mind. No different from us as far as that goes. Anyway, if the chicks have no memory to run from, surely the older ones do. You'd think somehow they'd pass on the sense of approaching danger to their young."

"Yes," Locke said, noticing—or was he imagining it—that she seemed to be walking much closer to him than she'd ever done before. Perhaps, he thought, it was a case of his biologist's acute sense of "comfortable" or "safe" space between individuals of the species becoming distorted through a very unscientific bit of wishful thinking.

JULIO KNEW he should not keep on walking toward the rock. In a few hours it would start to get dark and with the overcast and rain he could see sweeping toward him in great towers of pumice-gray, darkness would come earlier than usual. He knew that it was only temper and pride that kept him walking. He knew how childish, how stupid and how damaging it was to his career, this habit of suddenly flaring up, stalking off, fuming and brooding for hours, reason only ever winning the battle by passion's default. He knew all this and still he could not help himself as he trudged doggedly through the windblown grass to the cliff, toward the solitude of the big rock.

It was childish to want to make them sorry, pretending one second that he merely wanted time away from her to think, the next instant admitting to himself the truth, that it was a kind of self-pity driving him on, a pity for which he despised himself but that simultaneously gave him a sense of purpose and revenge in a life too often ignored by others.

All the stupid "Mexican" jokes he'd heard at Oregon State, about *señoritas*, tequila, Montezuma's revenge... kept going through his head like a discordant choir of *burlones*, scoffers. Didn't the fools realize what he was really capable of, that he wasn't from some barrio in Mexico City where they were forced to eat shit, that he was a descendant of one of Montezuma's most famous lieutenants and was bright enough to win a *beca estudiantil nacional*, a coveted student scholarship to study up here in this perpetual rain, that he wasn't a "Yanqui" Care package—"Here you are, you poor little Mexican peasant. We'll give you some dollars to find out what it's like to live in God's country."

No, that was being unfair. The Americans had treated him well. Whatever their faults they were truly generous. What was really hurting was Gloria, her milk-white skin that he had dreamed of every night since he met her four months before. They had driven with Professor Locke to visit Seaside and to see the great mouth of the Columbia River where so many ships and men had perished and where the small fishing boats riding hard at anchor, halyards flapping metallically in the wind, reminded him of the little villages near Puerto Vallarta.

They had walked along the wonderful Prom, as the Americans called it, and he had smelled the sea again, the first time since leaving Mexico, and had watched the girls in tight shorts roller-skating all the way from the Avenue U to 12th Avenue. He recalled the pleasure he took walking with Gloria as the professor droned on, explaining how the promenade had been built to replace a boardwalk ripped apart by big winter storms.

On the island his memories of those early days tortured him, especially at night when the work of the day was done and left nothing but memories to crowd in on him, and the professor sleeping next to her—so close. In the first years of college he had told himself there could be no hope of love for one could not expect much, it was too early, and he could tell himself that he must give her time to like him more than a friend, more than just another grad student. Then he had begun noticing the way Locke looked at her in the laboratory when she wasn't aware of it, the way the professor managed to be around whenever it was coffee break and how he could talk to her about other things than work. Julio couldn't always hear what they were chatting and laughing about—only that every time she laughed it seemed that somehow they were laughing at him. At such times he would become so angry that he had to leave the lab.

Somehow he had thought it would be different on the island, that away from the university he could impress her with his manly skills as someone who knew about survival beyond the comforts of American life, that he might somehow shame the professor, who was getting on in his fifties, and who carried too much around his belly. Julio knew how much Gloria admired physical fitness; her jogging every day was a glorious thing for him to watch as she ran about the perimeter of the campus. He would show her, cross the channel at low tide in a half hour or so and

climb to the top of the two-hundred-foot rock, and once
on top he would hood and band the half dozen or so of the
chicks that were supposed to be nesting there. Then he
would head down and still be in time to be back at the
survival shack at dusk, or maybe a little later. He smiled to
himself, unable to resist the temptation of worrying them
a little after dark.

Reaching the bottom of the cliff he saw there was still
about five feet of water racing through the channel with a
force that looked a lot more dangerous up close. He hesitated. He still wanted to show them what he could do, that
he didn't need anyone, but he kept recalling a line from
one of his undergraduate courses, from Sophocles, something to the effect that an angry man is not a safe man. He
would wait for the lowest ebb of the tide before wading
across to the base of the Pinnacle, its pyramid of rock
towering darkly above him.

Soon Julio saw the tide was at its lowest, washing against
the purplish stains of algae and crustaceans not normally
seen. As he started across the channel he glimpsed the huge
stern of the Polish mother ship swinging into view through
the eastern end of the gap. She was about two miles from
the rock but during the next surge she passed from his line
of sight. He had chosen the narrowest part of the channel
at the eastern end of the funnel, because while there was
less rock showing there he could see the rush of water
starting from the western side and could better time his
dash. He thought about turning back but now it had become *pundoner*, a matter of honor. He leaned forward in
anticipation, waiting for the next rush of white water to
pass and exhaust itself.

Chapter Fourteen

PETREL'S WINCH WAS in high gear, water droplets jumping from the streaming cable as it fed the howitzer-shaped corer down into the Cascadia Basin six thousand feet below. The depth sounder showed compact oozes and muds possibly as deep as a hundred yards or more below the basin floor. Frank watched the crewmen as nonchalantly as he could, trying to detect anything suspicious, but saw nothing. Perhaps he was mistaken about having replaced the safe's flashlight in the telltale position. Even if there *had* been someone in the room with the Australian, any signs of the crumbled foam rubber would now have been scattered. There had been ample time, also, for anyone involved to have noticed the clingy stuff on their clothes, or if they hadn't, then the timing of the station was still to their advantage for wet-weather gear covered the regular work clothes they wore inside the ship.

As she watched the sounder, Mary advised that the trip weight was visible, well below the subsurface turbulence of the approaching storm.

"Slow the winch!" Frank called out, allowing the trip weight and the corer to become more perpendicular to the bottom so that in the free-fall the corer would plunge straight down rather than at an angle. If the penetration wasn't head-on Frank knew he would have to abandon this station altogether, or take hours to repeat the operation and so necessitate cutting out one of the later stations, which could turn out to be the richest deposit of all. It was then, while waiting for the trip weight to slow and steady itself before touching the bottom, that Frank saw the bosun's mate, Jamie, otherwise known as Jack Daniel's, come out from the dry lab, ruddy faced, cheery as usual, propping himself directly behind the unused winch on the port side of the stern deck, away from the full blast of the

gale-force winds. Wedging himself comfortably between
the bulkhead and winch he put a boot against the tarpau-
lin and unsteadily began rolling a cigarette. The deep cleats
of the boot were filled with wet foam rubber and, for some
reason Frank couldn't make out, there was a strong smell
of sickly-sweet deodorant coming from him, an odor like
that of an industrial cleanser.

Jamie saw Frank glancing over at him and smiled.
"How ya doin', Frank?"

Frank, smiling, waved at him. "Okay, Jamie. How
'bout yourself?"

"Never better."

I'll bet, Frank thought. It was beautiful, really, when
you thought about it. The ship's boozer. Who would suspect Swiss Rhine Petrochemicals, or whoever had owned
the Beechcraft, of using the ship's resident drunk? On the
other hand, it was the perfect cover for an informer—or a
murderer. Jolly Jamie, right? All he cared about was how
to get enough money to keep him in hooch. An easy buy-
off. Perhaps too easy?

The cable, winding in now at about a yard a second,
would take another ninety minutes before the corer broke
surface. Frank leaned back on the rail, letting a brief show
of sunlight wash over him, warming him inside. The
warmth and the steady roll of the ship lulled him into a
moment or two of relaxation. But it only lasted until he
thought of Aussie again, how he had been quick to suspect him, how he now regretted it, and how if Jamie was
the plant, why had he gone into the cabin after the first
station instead of waiting until all the stations were finished? One answer that presented itself was that the un-
foreseen explosion aboard the Beechcraft meant the only
way SRP had of knowing where *Petrel* was headed was to
activate whoever was the plant aboard the ship. The trouble with this answer, however, was that anyone could find
out the ship's change in course merely by visiting the
bridge. Then again, maybe Jamie was *only* a plant and

nothing more—a decoy? Then how about the foam rubber? If he asked Jamie outright, though, Frank would show his hand.

Another thing bothering Frank was how had Jamie, if he was a plant at all, received his instructions to act when he did? Equally important, how was he to contact his boss ashore? There were only two real possibilities. One was by Aldis lamp, a trick that Frank had quite literally run into once on an earlier cruise, nearly losing his head for his trouble; the other possible way was a radio message of some kind, though in bad weather neither of these methods was reliable. Besides, the only ships in the area right now were the Polish mother ship, about twelve miles to the northeast, and a few of her trawlers scattered over a hundred miles or more of ocean. Besides, what would a big capitalist outfit like Swiss Rhine Petrochemicals have in common with Communists?

Frank felt tired. There had been the constant battle against the sea, the Beechcraft crashing as though in a self-destruct, the Polish trawler going down so fast, or was it the American trawler that had gone down and *Lvov* that had been resurrected? If so, what had *Lvov* become? And what for? The sheer number of questions to consider was weighing him down. It was as bad as taking out a mortgage, he thought, except that at least with a bank you already knew the damage.

Mary came on deck then, looking fresher than anyone had a right to in the continuous blow, and she disagreed with Frank's entire estimate of the situation.

"First of all," she pointed out, "since you've been out here the head steward ordered your cabin fumigated... some health rule going back to the days of sail, and one of those who volunteered to do it was Jamie. That's why he smells of Lysol."

Frank was tired, but he wasn't as sleepy as he thought perhaps Jamie wanted him to be. "Wait a minute," he interrupted Mary. "You said he volunteered?"

She thought for a second. "You think he might have done that to cover himself?"

"Right. I mean, he doesn't exactly like working. So why volunteer?"

She shrugged. "Maybe, but your analogy about mortgages doesn't fit."

"Why?"

"There are always hidden costs. You don't know about them till they hit you." She paused. "It could be the same here."

The third mate appeared on the bridge's starboard wing, bellowing through an electric megaphone, "Squall approaching!" The PA system was apparently not working. He was so loud, his voice traveling with the wind, that in the huddle of seamen spilling reluctantly out of the lab to help get the big corer inboard before the squall struck, someone began mumbling about shoving megaphones in various parts of the mate's anatomy.

"Christ," said Jamie, "he's so goddamn loud they'll hear him on the island."

"What?" asked Frank as the winch began howling in protest. Already Tate was maneuvering *Petrel* as fast as his unnatural anchor of the corer would allow, intending to take the squall's assault bow-on if he could and avoid the full force of the maelstrom of wind and water that was rushing at him and was capable of capsizing bigger ships than his.

"How do you know there's someone on the island?" Frank asked Jamie, at the same time the third mate was ordering Mary off deck.

"Saw 'em through the binoculars. Two of 'em," answered Jamie. "Looked like there was three for a while. Dunno, mighta been penguins." He laughed, exuding a breath of Jack Daniel's. Changing the subject he pointed to the fast-approaching squall. "Gonna be a bastard, this one!"

Frank agreed, and was watching the tension meter, strained to breaking point, its needle in the red.

"Watch the wire!" he warned everybody. "She could go any second."

Smoke was starting to pour from the winch.

Fifteen miles wide, traveling at ninety-six miles per hour, the squall showed no favorites as it tore through the scattered Polish fleet south of *Petrel*. Some of the trawlers had already turned to face it; others were slower to respond depending on whether or not trawls were out. Catching two boats in tandem, their gear out, the squall, with the sudden fury that is its trademark, punched one trawler over so far that it teetered on the brink of capsizing, only to roll frantically aright when its skipper ordered all trawl lines cut.

Frank saw the squall speeding toward *Petrel*, appearing at first to be little more than a heavy rain shower on the horizon, scuttling across the rolling gray of ocean. It was only when he fixed his eye on it, using one of the Polish trawlers far to the south as a reference point, that any estimate of its true speed could be made. Willing the meter needle to move faster, he watched helplessly as the squall swallowed up another trawler in seconds in its advance toward *Petrel*. If he failed to get the corer aboard, or at least alongside, beneath the water level, before the squall hit them, then the cable would shoot out from the rail as the squall pushed the ship downwind away from the ascending corer. A savage tug-of-war would result, the cable stretched beyond its limit. To cut it then would be to invite disaster as its tail came whipping back like a scythe.

JULIO SAW IT coming but did not know what it was, the purple hue caused by the curdling maelstrom of hailstones and, ironically for such a gray day, by shafts of glorious silvery rays of light descending from a sunburst in the overcast. All Julio was sure of was that the edge of whatever it was, probably rain, would pass over the island.

It was too late for him to climb back up the cliff he had descended. Besides, the Pinnacle's more rugged outcrops held the promise of greater protection from the elements. Tense, he saw a rush of water coming down the channel, waited until the suck-back wave had passed him, and immediately set out for the honeycombed base of the Pinnacle.

ABOARD THE MOTHER SHIP, final preparations were in progress, chocks pulled out on their long lanyards, the helicopter's blades a whir, their chopping of the heavy sea air passing from a steady thudding now to a deafening rattling sound, the blades' angle to the deck decreasing, engines screaming to full power. Then the noise fell back to a steady chopping sound again, the rotors' arc sloping toward the deck. Before the rotors stopped, four crouching crewmen went in under the blades with the chocks, kicking them back into place. Inside the chopper's cabin the political officer looked across at the pilot. "What's wrong?"

"It's called off, Comrade," said the lieutenant, looking relieved. "Squall heading our way." With that the lieutenant told two marines from the Spetsnaz, or Special Purposes Forces detachment, that they could disembark and go back inside the hangar.

"Can't you operate it in any weather?" asked Saburov.

One thing the pilot had to give Saburov, the bastard had guts. He'd go anywhere in any conditions for the party.

"Yes," said the lieutenant, "you can go up in bad weather, but you can't see anything in a squall, Comrade. It's like pea soup. Crashing into the rock won't help us get the job done."

"Neither will waiting around, Comrade," said Saburov. "For all we know their pickup ship could be on the way."

The lieutenant took off his helmet, flicking up its thin intercom mike. "Well, our bird enthusiasts wouldn't be seeing much in the storm, Comrade. There is also another problem. Landing."

"On the island? You've done it many times before."

"Not in weather like this...not in a squall. Anyway, Comrade, I didn't mean the island, I meant landing back here on the mother ship. When the squall hits it will be *shivorot-navyvorot*, topsy-turvy, for a while."

"How long must we wait?"

The lieutenant shrugged. "Depends how long the squall lasts. Could be over in an hour. Maybe two." He could see Saburov trying to think of another way. He was too impatient. "Don't worry, Comrade, the revolution wasn't built in a day."

"Don't give me the revolution, Lieutenant. You were still soiling your pants when I was a boy in the Great Patriotic War. We didn't wait for weather. Neither did the fascists. You realize the chance we have here?" It was a statement rather than a question. "We...you, Lieutenant, have the opportunity to do something in your lifetime that is more important than..." Saburov paused for a second, not wanting to denigrate any of the motherland's great feats of the past in front of a subordinate but wishing to convey the magnitude of what was being done.

The lieutenant opened the cockpit door for the political officer. "I understand its importance, Comrade," he said in a conciliatory gesture. He knew that he was one of the best chopper pilots in all the Soviet republics, and he wanted his record to keep showing that...not that he was uncooperative. He loved flying and the very thought of being downgraded to a possible desk job in Kiev HQ made him suddenly acquiescent toward Saburov. "Colonel, if you wish to overrule Captain Novisk on this matter— which I know is your right—I'll gladly support you, but may I point out one other consideration?"

"What is it?"

"This is the only helicopter we have. The trawlers can only give us so much help, and besides, for them to stay out here any longer would be certain to arouse suspicion. If we go up in this weather, Comrade, and I'll gladly go— and something went wrong and the helicopter was damaged landing on the island or back here on the mother ship, we'd have to waste precious time working on her. How would we explain the delay to Gdansk?" Saburov knew the lieutenant meant "Moscow" and the lieutenant knew Saburov knew. But it got the message through and saved face.

"Very well," agreed Saburov, looking up at the enormous bruised area of sky, now only five miles off their starboard quarter and closing fast. "Yes, of course..." Saburov didn't finish. There was no need—both had a very clear idea of what postings to Siberia were like. "But," Saburov insisted, "the instant this..."

"Squall," the lieutenant reminded him.

"Yes. Once it's passed us, then we go straight to the island. It has to be done."

"No question about it, Comrade."

Meanwhile, inside the cavernous stern deck hangar two marines from the ten-man Special Purposes Forces detachment, who knew no more than they were on the ship to follow the political officer's orders, stood about, cradling their rifles, watching the chopper wheeled in, the flex of the automatic roll-down door rumbling like thunder, sealing them off from the deck in the oily smelling semidarkness of the hangar. "What's going on?" one asked the other after the lieutenant and Saburov had walked away, still talking, up the ladder leading to the bridge.

"Don't ask me," replied the other soldier. "We're just the fucking workers."

"CORER IN SIGHT!" Frank called, slipping the long pike's hook around the cable, pulling on it with all his strength, trying to reduce the sixty-degree angle between cable and ship as *Petrel* continued turning to get between the cable and the squall, which was now less than three miles, two minutes, away. Frank knew they needed an angle of less than thirty degrees, that there was no way they could get the corer aboard in time, given such a wide angle. The ship kept turning and the angle kept dropping... fifty-one degrees... forty... thirty-four... holding at thirty-three... Then the squall hit, a breath-stealing scream of wind making it impossible to breathe unless, as Frank and the winch man did, you turned your back to the squall. The next second Frank heard a thud. The winch stopped as the dead man's pedal sprang up, shutting off the winch the moment its operator was torn from his seat, flying, hitting the well deck, sliding across to the opposite scuppers. The first gigantic wave lifted him up like a broken log, his body a moment in the white wall of water crashing over the port side but his safety line holding.

Clinging to the cable, frayed strands lacerating his hands, Frank was smacked off the deck until he was parallel to the well deck, the lower half of his wet gear whipped from him, his legs sucked out toward the port side like a torn pennant. He looked up, choking with saltwater, eyes searching for the winch man, but the next second he felt the entire vessel shaking in trauma as the second big wave, or what was really a massive bunching of waves, struck *Petrel* full on, lifting her bow so high that on the bridge the captain, his hands gripping the engine room override panel, his legs dangling in space, stopped all engines lest the downward stroke of the props drive the ship under. The moment Tate threw the steering lever to Stop All Engines, Mary Crane in the stern lab screamed, seeing the cable snap at the block and Frank disappear in the boiling white that was surging down the ship's starboard side.

LIKE A MAN ON HOT COALS, Julio walked fast yet as cautiously as haste would allow, fearing unseen holes that might be hidden beneath the backward suck of the low tide coursing through the gap between the towering Pinnacle's

cliffs coming toward him and the more gradual but less
protective cliffs of the island behind him. He stumbled on
a barnacle-encrusted rock but quickly righted himself,
hands out sensibly like a high-wire artist, glancing almost
furtively now and then at the purplish blob heading his
way, the wind already twenty to thirty miles an hour
stronger than before.

Once he was across the gap he felt an enormous relief
and began to feel renewed confidence, until a minute later
he realized he'd made a mistake. The base of the rock that
stretched above into the morbid grayness was honeycombed all right, offering more protection from wind and
rain, but watching the squall, which he guessed was about
five miles from the big Polish ship anchored a mile from
the Pinnacle, he realized that the sea, whipped into high
waves by the force of the wind, would soon come rushing
through the funnel-shaped gap in a massive wall of water.
In the few seconds it had taken him to see this he also saw
that the purplish waterspout, or whatever it was, was
turning black and that the mother ship had changed from
light to dark gray as it became enwreathed in a curtain of
rain. He would have to climb higher whether he liked it or
not, or else he would be swept from the base of the cliff.

His rising panic subsided momentarily when he discovered how the honeycombed rock provided any number of
footholds and handholds, and he found a second to joke
with himself, to boost his courage like an exhausted runner at the end of a long race, telling himself that there were
only 160 feet to go to get to the top. Then he saw that the
mother ship had vanished. He felt the hailstones striking
the rock like an avalanche of broken glass, so loud that
they drowned out the screams of the seabird colonies and
the low mournful barking of sea lions and seals, which,
like Julio, were seeking refuge from the onslaught. Craning his neck, he looked up to find the next crevice in the
rock but could see nothing. He pulled his head down into
the collar of his parka like a tortoise. His eyes stung from

the hailstones, small at first but then the size of golf balls, and his other hand felt desperately for a handhold, while his legs cramped on an inch-wide ledge beneath him. Saying a Hail Mary, he saw a swirling caldron of hail-churned sea below him. Then he began swearing in the foulest language he had used for years, telling himself that now was not the time to be *un cobarde quejumbroso*, a whimpering coward, but to be strong, to take a deep breath, to be resolute, to hang on with everything he had. To imagine the Virgin Mary watching him, seeing his courage.

SWEPT FORWARD by the force of the wave, Frank never once let go of the pike, its hook becoming entangled in the spiderweb lashing of the stacked core barrels, breaking his momentum so that when his feet hit the port rail he was swept no farther. But as the wave passed, and he tried to crawl toward the stern, past the forward port side scuppers, to escape the main force of the next wave, the side wash of the first wave was so powerful that a crewman could barely spin open the wheel of the port stern door and drag him in. Frank's lungs were so full of saltwater that, retching violently and gulping for air, he blacked out.

AS JULIO CROSSED the gap, Gloria Bernardi and Charles Locke, oblivious of the squall, which was hidden from view by the Pinnacle, reached the survival shack. The professor decided he was right, Gloria had been walking a lot closer to him on the way back, as if now that he had told her the way he felt about her she was loosening up, not so much the female student, afraid she would say or do the wrong thing in front of her prof, but a woman, more confident, relaxed. For Locke it made her more desirable than ever.

Inside the small twelve-by-ten shack made of odd-size planking and whatever else old mariners had managed to bring ashore on that calm day almost a century ago when it was first built, it was dark and musty. Yet neither of them felt any sense of gloom or foreignness in this place on the lonely, windswept island; rather they shared a sense of coziness quite apart from their sexual attraction. Ordinarily they would have been more worried about Julio, but once they were back in the windowless shack for a good half hour, the danger Julio was in was still unknown to them. They were agreed that it was best to let him work off steam in his own good time, resolving not to interfere with his therapeutic sulk other than to go out to hurry him along if he had not returned by dusk.

While Charles started pumping the Coleman stove and Gloria was being particular about adding the correct quantity of water to the freeze-dried packet of beef stew, Charles was busy forming strategy, aware that if he didn't have her before Julio returned then the opportunity would probably not present itself again until they were back ashore in five days' time. Amid familiar surroundings, his university duties, more people, more students would all conspire against their ever having such an ideal opportunity again. Secretly, a little ashamed, but only a little, he hoped young Julio *would* stay out till dusk. He pumped the stove faster until it started emitting a steady, comforting roar that added to the coziness, completed by the kerosene lamp, its silk wick turning from a dull red to an incandescent white, casting a warm glow in the tiny shack. He looked across at her and she at him, a shy but unafraid "yes" in her smile. They said nothing, sharing their meal in an air of suspended expectation. Finishing his stew in ill-disguised haste, which made her laugh and had her wondering how long he had been without a woman, he turned to her, indicating the Coleman burner turned low but hissing steadily. "Like some coffee?"

"Not right now," she answered softly, adding, "I think we should save fuel. Don't you?"

"Absolutely."

He tried to contain his impatience, taking her slowly, gently in his arms, but the moment their lips met, her tongue seeking his, he was almost out of control. "Oh God..."

Unprotestingly, invitingly, she let him reach beneath her sweater, and as he squeezed her breast hungrily she lay back on the sleeping bag, reveling in the rush of excitement as his thigh pressed in hard against hers. She arched her back, pushing her breasts into him.

"Jesus...sweet Jesus..." he murmured, his left hand cradling the back of her head, his right sliding down behind her, unclipping her bra, pulling off her sweater roughly while trying to be gentle, his face collapsing onto her milk-white bosom, his mouth savoring her nipples, his tongue darting almost uncontrollably from one to the other, unable to choose as each hardened and darkened to a deep cherry-red. He had assumed she was a virgin, but now the thought that she might have made love before only heightened his excitement. If he didn't do it soon...

Above the smooth purr of her zipper he could hear the wind growing in intensity and felt the shack groaning under the first onslaught of the squall. She arched again as he pulled off her jeans. "Oh, God." He gasped playfully. "Don't do that again."

"Why?" she asked gently, perplexed.

"I love it. Can't stand it." She arched again.

"Oh, God," he said, and then the hail crashed into the hut in such a crescendo that Gloria started in fright. "What—"

He tried to calm her, alarmed himself at first, but then hearing the rain and wind.

"Hailstorm," he told her quickly. "Don't worry...it's all right. It'll pass in a minute," he whispered, stroking her hair gently as one would a frightened pet. "Shh..."

But the sudden, harsh fury of the squall had broken the spell, and she thought immediately of Julio. She sat up. "I'm sorry, Charles..."

As she began to dress hurriedly Charles Locke snatched his clothes from beside the sleeping bag, put on his pants and zipped up his jacket so violently that the zipper tore clean off its track. Seeing his fury, like none she'd witnessed before, Gloria laced up her parka hood and, bracing herself, headed out into the squall. A moment later Charles appeared, his face red, his eyes already watering from the high wind, his body, like Gloria's, bent over against the force of the blow, his mouth moving, the sound of his voice snatched away.

"What?" she asked, her words too instantly gone in the wind.

"Goddamn...damn...damn...goddamn! When I find that Mexican son of a..."

Gloria moved on ahead, pretending she couldn't hear. Poor Julio was going to get it.

LIKE A KNIFE rending a dirty sheet the squall cut through the overcast at sunset along a jagged north-south axis, leaving the sharp white line of *Petrel* a speck on a silver sea. The calm was deceptive, though, for while the sky directly above was clear, it was only temporary before the two sheets rejoined, and in any case the winds were still force eight, the storm line still advancing from as far south as Baja.

For Julio Suarez and the Polish mother ship riding at anchor off the island ten miles northeast of *Petrel*, the sun was invisible, the squall swirling around them, its fury unabated, its rain torrential. The shrapnel of hail whistled through the air in a cacophony of sound made more frightening by terrified screams of tens of thousands of chicks and other seabirds caught in the open or unable to find refuge on the rain-shrouded cliffs. Far below Julio, at the edge of what was now the hidden sea, the unbroken bellowing of the sea lions and barking seals as they rushed en masse for the misty water added to the general terror and confusion.

Julio tried to breathe slowly, not to panic. His body was pressed to the dripping rock face, one arm shielding his head from the enfilade of hailstones, his only other protection being his backpack. Soon his arm began to ache but he dared not try to raise his other hand from the grip it had on the rock. Soon both arms were cramping so badly he began to lose normal feeling in his fingers and instead was conscious of a pins-and-needles sensation creeping up from his hands, going deep into his shoulder blades. "Hold on!" he told himself. "Hold on...."

"GODDAMMIT!" said Charles, the hail flailing him and Gloria as they ran blindly to an overhang of grass midway down the island, the roots exposed where birds' nests had eroded the earth beneath the humps of tall, razor-sharp grass. Huddling for shelter, Charles was still thinking about sex, despite the trouble he knew Julio must be in.

"You okay?" he asked Gloria, slipping his arm around her.

"No," she said. "I'm worried about Julio. He must be trapped somewhere." She peered out at the rain and hail swirling around them in great swaths as if in a fight for supremacy over the island. "Why isn't he back? I..." she began.

Charles squeezed her reassuringly. "Oh, don't worry, he'll be okay. Just a bit scared, that's all. Probably holed up same as we are, waiting for the worst to pass."

"I hope so," she said anxiously.

"'Course he is. Now don't you fret, little girl."

Her look told him she didn't like his patronizing tone. "Well, you're not," she said.

"What?"

"Worried."

"Look," he said, taking his arm from around her, "it was his doing, right? He's the idiot who stalked off, not me, *Miss* Bernardi!"

She turned away from him, staring angrily into the rain.

"Well, wasn't he?" Charles pressed.

"Wasn't he what?" she replied without turning to look at him.

"Wasn't he the idiot who stalked off?"

"He did it because he was jealous," she said softly. "He wanted more than just sex."

"What did you say?" His voice was rising with each question, hers becoming softer.

"Nothing," she said, looking back at him. *"Professor."*

Cheeky bitch. It made him want her even more.

Chapter Fifteen

THE HAIL WAS GONE, then the rain eased, and Julio knew the squall was passing. He dared to glance up, seeing a gull, then another and another hovering over him like angels of the Immaculate Conception and, amid the myriad of waterfalls cascading about him, he silently thanked God for his deliverance. Then, as if in answer, the sun, through the break in the clouds, began suffusing the grayness with saffron light, even as it sank lower toward an indeterminate horizon.

THE PROFESSOR AND GLORIA, several yards apart, resumed their hike toward the Pinnacle, the tall grass soaking them, the strange pale sunlight stealing low over the island so they knew that in another half hour the island would be thrown back into a primeval darkness of night and storm cloud. In her effort to reach Julio before darkness fell, Gloria was walking as fast as the sodden clumps of grass would allow, while her professor, in a lather of perspiration and indignation, tried valiantly to keep up with her. It seemed that every time he got close to her she would start off again, leaving him more breathless and humiliated by his age and in no doubt that her concern for Julio outstripped any for him.

For her part, Gloria was convinced that her thesis would now take much longer than a year to complete. Or, perhaps Locke would want to get rid of her as quickly as possible now that there had been a rift between them, now that she had shown that she cared about Julio more than anyone, including herself, had suspected. Maybe, she thought, she had unconsciously been playing off one against the other as the best way not to be forced into having to make any decision. In the distance she could see the sharp pyramid of the two-hundred-foot Pinnacle rising through mist that was being whipped away by gale-force winds as soon as it escaped from the honeycombed rocks like the smoke from thermal vents. She estimated that she and Locke, if he could keep up, would reach the top of the cliffs above the gap in twenty minutes or so. The three of them would have to wind their way back in the darkness, but at least they would not have to put up with hail, though the coming storm clouds held a threat of more rain. She glanced around for Charles. He was nowhere in sight. She looked over to her left, toward the eastern flank of the island, thinking he might have found it easier going.

"Charles?"

He appeared, exhausted and grimacing, from a spongy depression where he'd slipped, sprawling in a mud patch between the dripping clumps of grass. When he looked up at her his face was like a clown's, smeared with mud that he had only spread farther in an attempt to wipe it off. She went back and handed him a bunch of tissues.

"Thanks. I slipped."

"Yes."

They both tried not to laugh but it happened, and Gloria knew that she would not be deliberately forestalled in getting her degree on bird life on the remote islands, but that it would be a while before the professor tried to make love to her again. But she felt now that she might want him, too—she had a weakness for men who could laugh at themselves, no matter what their other foibles. Charles, too, felt better, now that the tension between them was abating, even feeling more charitable toward Julio. After all, it was only masculine pride; hadn't he demonstrated himself just how silly a man can be in his quest for a beautiful woman? He no longer wanted to chew Julio out for what he had done, only to reestablish the strong sense of camaraderie the three had shared coming to the starkly beautiful, if godforsaken, island. Once again the air was peppered with thousands of birds, dots against a turquoise streak of open sky.

ON THE PINNACLE, Julio inched carefully along the narrow ledge, willing caution to buffer the exhilaration he felt after having managed to hang on against the squall's worst. With dusk rapidly descending, common sense prevailed, however, and he knew that although he would now make his way down to a point above the high tide mark, he would have to spend the night at the base of the Pinnacle. Very soon it would be pitch-dark and to try the descent across the rising tide in the funnel would be suicidal. But every step had to be thought out before he dared give it his full weight, for the runoff from the top of the Pinnacle was increasing from the melting of the hail that had been amassed in a basinlike depression near the summit of the monolith. Now dozens of instant waterfalls leaped and streamed down the two-hundred-foot drop to the sea, cutting the route he had wanted to retrace. His progress was steady but painfully slow as he felt his way like a blind man, and sought to circumvent the most powerful waterfalls.

WITH THE LAYERS OF MIST rising faster in the last warm rays of the sun, Gloria and Charles could see the top half of the Pinnacle, but in the crazy pattern of black shadows on chocolate- and rust-colored granite it was impossible for them to see Julio, even had they been looking in his direction.

"Should have brought the field glasses," said Charles. "That was dumb."

"No," said Gloria. "I thought of them but I didn't think we'd be seeing much in a hailstorm. I still can't get over how changeable this island climate is."

"Like the people," he added ruefully.

She smiled and, reaching out, took his hand. "It wasn't your fault," she said graciously in a voice much older than her years.

He realized he really didn't know much about her at all. It was another reason for his continuing to find her exciting, appealing to his need for a more mature companion as well as his need for sex, though watching her as she broached a hillock, her figure momentarily etched against the darkening sky, he had to admit it wasn't only simple companionship that had been on his mind when he had first seen her.

Gloria was pointing out to sea, eastward from the rock, at the sloping, squarish stern of the Polish mother ship. A helicopter, probably the one they had seen passing over the island the day before, was lumbering up from the high after-deck pad while the big ship held its bow steady into the southern wind. Gloria had yet to see a helicopter that didn't remind her of some sort of flying insect, and this one, with a set of double rotors, looked for all the world like a dragonfly complete with huge, bulbous eyes. This impression was reinforced by the buglike appearance of bubble Plexiglas windows up front and atop its wide, thick head, and slightly behind the cockpit, another set of eyes, engine intakes, adding to the all-round ugliness of its thick body. Yet it elicited from her, as ugly bugs did, not the repulsion that most people felt but an appreciation that just as with so many natural things from the primeval swamps and seas, this man-made thing was perfectly adapted for its purposes, among them, she assumed, air-sea rescue.

BRUISED BUT RECOVERED from the squall's attack, Frank attached the cable to the shackle of the new corer. He, also, saw the helicopter, although from where *Petrel* was, nine miles west sou'west of the island, the chopper was a mere dot in the twilight visible for only a few seconds before its head drooped, its long tail turning and lifting as it moved forward from its hovering position above the mother ship, disappearing behind the jagged silhouette of the Pinnacle. They were going the wrong way to be delivering any supplies to the trawlers, which were scattered to the south, but perhaps, he mused, they had something to do with whomever Jamie had reportedly seen on the island.

Turning back to his work, Frank lugged a three-quarter-moon-shaped weight to attach to the corer's top stem, joining the weight to the next one in the stack by manhandling it so that the two steel lugs beneath it, each the size of a man's thumb, dropped into the female receptors drilled into the top of the weight beneath. This would prevent the weights from sliding on one another, causing a sudden shift in the corer as it hung suspended above the deck. He resented the extra time, several hours at least, that redoing the station would cost him, but without the sample, lost in the squall, there was no other way of knowing the chemical composition of the sediments two miles below.

As a few of the crewmen, Jamie among them, helped him load up the new corer, he found himself going over Aussie's death again, trying to put the pieces together. Had it been murder or had Aussie succumbed to the blow he had had on the head when he was swept overboard?

In any case, Frank resolved to play it safe, and smart. Whatever the analysis of the sample showed, he would keep the real results somewhere known only to himself, substituting a dummy set of results and station coordinates in the cabin safe.

"What the hell's that chopper doing?" asked Jamie.

Frank glanced over at where the dot had been. "Maybe they're going to lower a fish buoy somewhere," he replied.

"What's that?"

"Well, they let out a sonar buoy that can pick up undersea noise . . . like a big school of fish. Then the trawlers hone in."

"No kiddin'?"

"Ever been to the zoo—heard a killer whale?"

"Yeah."

"It's like that. Sea's alive with noise. Usually high-pitched stuff that we can't hear. Like a dog whistle."

"Yeah?" Jamie asked with some amazement.

"Sure," said Frank, tightening up the nut on the square plate that held the stack of weights in place. "You go even deeper you'll pick up sounds of big mud slides coming down the continental shelf toward the continental slope. Sounds like a dozen locomotives out of control."

"Yeah?"

Yeah, Frank thought, and how come you're so surprised? Was it because Jamie, like most sailors, really only talked about sex and booze—at least while they were at sea—or was the bosun's mate trying to create the impression that he knew zip-all about oceanography, to cover up what he did know about, especially how to knock off a ship's safe? He looked innocent enough; you wouldn't even know he was a drinker when he was on watch; all you could detect now was the nice fresh smell of Certs.

AS THE TACTICAL HIP E V-8 helicopter gained height above the mother ship, its pilot, the young Ukrainian from Kiev, was looking decidedly pale.

"You all right?" asked Colonel Saburov.

"I will be," answered the Ukrainian, "the farther we get away from that damn ship."

As the helicopter rose he saw that curtains of rain had fallen westward of the island, so that he could no longer see the American oceanographic ship.

"I nearly brought up my dinner," said the pilot.

Saburov smiled. "Thought you would be used to ships by now, Comrade."

"I am—but it's the stink of all that fish. And the squall didn't help."

"The squall helped a great deal, my friend. It's what some of our Polish comrades would call a blessing in disguise."

"I don't understand."

"You speak English?" asked Saburov.

"Only what we learned in school. Why?"

"Give me the megaphone," he said to one of the four marines. One of them passed it over as Saburov slid back the six-foot-square side hatch. "And don't look so glum," he told the pilot. "Just keep her steady."

"How low do you want me to go?"

"Can you land by the survival shack?"

"Bit tricky with all that grass. Looks smooth but it's uneven humps. Besides, after all that rain we could bog down."

"All right, then go as low as is safe."

"Comrade Saburov!" It was one of the four marines, pointing down at two tiny figures crossing the tussocks, about five hundred yards from the cliffs at the south end of the island. They seemed to be heading in the direction of the big rock.

"Where's the other one?" the pilot asked no one in particular.

"Can't see him."

"All right," said Saburov, "let's go down before it's dark."

Moving back into the HIP's cabin, Saburov clipped his safety wire to the overhead runners and reached for the handhold on the port side of the rear door hatch, holding the megaphone firmly in his right hand.

GLORIA AND CHARLES withdrew to the outer limit of the rotors' down-wash, trying to look up despite their bodies' intuitive reaction of backing away from the tremendous roar created by the twin Isotov turboshafts, the trailing edges of the five main rotor blades forming a shimmering gold quadrant as they reflected the sun's last rays. Charles and Gloria were waving up at the HIP, about fifty feet above them, when they saw someone in an olive-green flying suit waving back and speaking into a megaphone. But they could only hear occasional words or rather sounds garbled in the down draft and roar of engines. The copter rose slightly, then fell, buffeted by erratic gusts coming in from the sea up over the nearby cliffs. The smaller tail rotor was describing a hypnotic blur that even amid the turmoil of engine noise, winds, and quivering sea of flattened grass, took on a beauty for Gloria that was somehow reassuring in its symmetry and constancy. The next second she saw Charles waving his hands and shouting, "No... It's all right.... We're okay...."

She wondered what he was responding to when she noticed a thin line, a nylon rope and harness, being lowered by another man in the helicopter. Charles, cupping his hands and periodically making fantastically exaggerated signs as if he was addressing a classful of the hard of hearing, was doing his damnedest to indicate they weren't in trouble but were looking for a colleague. Still, the rescue harness kept descending until it was swinging forlornly over their heads, the man, forty-odd feet above them, encouraging them to put it on as one would frightened schoolchildren trapped on an ice floe.

"No... no... thank you..." shouted Charles, waving them away with a mixture of gratitude for their consideration and annoyance at their persistence, however well meant. The rope and harness were finally hauled up, disappearing into the rear hatch, which remained open. The helicopter came down lower, creating a minor whirlwind as it thundered and vibrated a mere fifteen feet above the boggy tussocks, each tussock with its long grass flattened on either side, eliciting the comment from one of the marines that from above the tussocks looked like a collection of neatly parted wigs.

The four marines dropped from the rear hatch like the expert gymnasts under whom they had trained, arms extended for balance, knees bent, ready to roll forward if necessary. But only one hit the ground awkwardly. Even so, he didn't fall but rather sprinted forward, running out the momentum of the jump.

Saburov came down in the harness. He wasn't at all embarrassed that he had to do so—they had their training, he had his—each served the party in his own way. He shook hands with the two Americans, explaining to them in very clear English that they had been worried on the mother ship that the survival shack might have been badly damaged by the storm and so had come to help if they could.

"No, thanks," said Charles. "The shack's fine. So are we—except for the mud." He pointed to his face and the marines laughed, one of them smiling at Gloria and pointing to his canvas leggings splattered in mud. Everyone laughed politely and could hear better now as the noise of the HIP had suddenly risen, hovering about a hundred yards away.

"But your friend," cut in Saburov. "We—"

Charles didn't let him finish. "Friend? Oh, yes, that's why we're out here. That's what I was trying to tell you. Just before the squa—"

The Russian clapped the American on the back. "Exactly. Exactly. Your friend. I know. You see, that is what

I have been trying to tell you through the—'' For a second, Saburov's English deserted him.

"Megaphone," put in Gloria happily. "You mean you've found him?"

"Yes, yes, exactly. He is back on the ship."

"Well," said Charles, nodding his head in relief. "That's good news."

"Is he all right?" asked Gloria anxiously. The marines were captivated by her. It was almost completely dark now, but they could see well enough.

"Ah, yes, but I am afraid his leg is cracked. He had rather a difficult fall."

"Cracked?" asked Charles. "You mean broken?"

"Yes. I am very sorry. Cracked is not correct. Yes, broken, I am afraid. But of course he is in our ship hospital. The doctor has put this cracked...I mean, broken leg in the plaster of paris. It will be all right. Three, maybe four months. Would you like to see him? We can take you there now, or in the morning if you wish. This is why we came, you see."

"Of course," answered Gloria unhesitatingly. "We could go now."

"Good. If you prefer we can bring you back tonight to your shack, or if you are very fed up with your cooking you may wish to eat with us. Stay during the night if you wish."

"Very kind of you. Thanks," replied Charles.

One of the marines took out a walkie-talkie from the side pocket of his jumpsuit and spoke briefly. Gloria couldn't tell whether it was Polish or Russian, but within seconds the helicopter was overhead. She saw what looked like a spotlight mounted on the belly and noted that the helicopter had no markings. There was a faint whine of the HIP's inboard winch and quickly the harness descended. One of the four marines slipped the canvas straps over his shoulders and was winched up into the black belly of the chopper. A second marine followed and then they teamed, standing by the rear hatch ready to assist Charles and Gloria, whose wet gear, backpacks and especially their down jackets ballooning with air gave them a comical appearance as they were winched up. The marines took a little extra time undoing Gloria's harness before they lowered it for Saburov. Inside the cabin Gloria could smell oil and the men, their faces barely discernible in the sickly yellow of the cabin's light.

The HIP rose to five hundred feet, then pivoted and headed north toward the survival shack. Saburov, reattaching his safety line to the overhead runner, made his way up forward, the instrument lights so dim as to be almost out, spoke to the lieutenant, then made his way back, smiling at the Americans. "We will be stopping at your shack," he shouted above the shattering noise of the rotors. "Your friend wanted us to bring some of his things."

For the first time Gloria was suspicious. Then a chill passed over her as she remembered noticing the helicopter was unmarked, was flying without any navigational lights, and that not once had the Pole or Russian, whatever he was, mentioned Julio by name. Of course, perhaps Julio had been unconscious when they had found him. Wait a minute—they'd said he had asked them to go to the shack.

"What did he want you to pick up?" she asked Saburov. "Perhaps Charles and I have brought—"

Saburov, smiling, cocked his ear, cupping it against the roar. "Again, please?"

Gloria leaned close to him. "His insulin?" she said.

"Yes."

"And I'll bet he wanted his cigarettes," she added. "He's a real addict. Lucky Strikes or nothing, right?"

"Yes," answered Saburov.

Gloria sat back, laughing with Saburov, shaking her head. "Julio, he's hopeless really. Tell Charles," she said to Saburov. "He'll enjoy it."

"What?" asked Charles, smiling at Gloria laughing. "What's up?" The deafening roar of the HIP was making everyone shout.

Gloria was still shaking her head, laughing. "Go on," she shouted to Saburov. "Tell Charles."

Saburov leaned over toward the professor. "Your friend wants us to get his cigarettes along with his medicine. He cannot go without them, yes?"

The four marines looked on, happy to see everyone else happy. Charles tried to look amused, too, but knowing, as Gloria did, that Julio didn't smoke let alone have diabetes, he didn't feel at all like laughing.

The helicopter was hovering again. "We are at the survival hut," shouted Saburov. "We will not be long." Gloria noticed that they were not bothering to use the spotlight, while Charles looked at the four marines and guessed they were half his age and no doubt twice as fit.

Charles was smiling, looking across at Saburov, and the three marines relaxed as the helicopter hovered, waiting for the marine who had jumped down near the shack to be winched up, after having ostensibly picked up Julio's insulin. Charles leaned over to Gloria, still smiling but talking so only she might hear him. "Ladies before gents," he said and before she could make any signs of protest, his smile broadened. "I insist," he told her, laughing as if sharing a joke. "On the count of three, okay?"

Gloria felt her heart thumping, faster, it seemed, than the rapid thudding sound of the rotors. "Yes," she said. "I love..."

He was counting. At "Three!" he suddenly charged across at the marines and Saburov in the confined space, taking them by surprise, his arms out like the embrace of a fullback, trying to stop the four men at once. Saburov fell back onto one marine, the other two already recovering, gripping Charles, pummeling him.

Gloria dived out of the helicopter, hitting the ground backpack first, sliding into the muddy darkness, then up and running away from the shack into the high, soaking-wet grass, even as Saburov, recovering, was screaming over the HIP's roar, telling the lieutenant to inform the marine in the shack. But by the time the radio crackled and the marine had run out into the darkness, there was nothing to see or hear but the chopper above him.

"I can use the spotlight!" the lieutenant shouted to Saburov.

"No, you fool! If that American ship sees a searchlight they'll know something is up. Radio the mother ship. Tell them I want the remaining eight marines fully kitted and ready to go. We'll pick them up and return to the island. They'll find the bitch!"

As the pilot radioed for the additional searchers, Saburov had already ordered two of the three marines on board to deplane. As the HIP rose they were already fanning out in the darkness, while the marine coming out of the shack was attaching the Mercury outboard engine by the hut to the harness rope. The remaining marine in the chopper had Charles pinned down, a paratrooper's knife to the American's throat. The chopper's winch vibrated loudly against its metallic runners while hauling up the Mercury, as the HIP swung hard to starboard over the eastern edge of the island, rising to twelve hundred feet. Saburov and the marine dragged Charles away from the open hatch, released the outboard, then threw him out.

"Now all we need," said Saburov, "are the other two."

"We'll have them by morning," said the marine.

"Yes, and when we get them," Saburov continued, "I don't want any of you doing an 'Afghan.' Understand?"

"Right," answered the marine, a tall, rough-spoken Georgian, amused by the political officer's puritanical streak. It was so typical of the party purist; the Georgian had seen a lot of action and wondered how on earth you could stop some of the Russian boys from having a bit of fun with the woman when they caught her, after they'd been away from pussy so long.

BEFORE THE SQUALL, Julio had thought all that was required was courage and cool determination. A hot head had got him into the mess, now a cool one would prevail. All he would have to do was go slowly and carefully. But the squall had changed everything. In the darkness the crazy pattern of fast waterfalls threatened to sweep him off the rock face if he dared go on. Tense with the realization of his position, and in spite of his mountainous pride in his self-sufficiency, in needing no one else in the world, Julio Suarez surrendered to the bare fact of the Pinnacle. The turbulent sea below and the darkness all around underscored the danger he was in, and he knew he would have to undo his pack and beg for help, by using the emergency flare to tell the professor and Gloria where he was, stranded humiliatingly by jealousy and bad temper seventy feet above the raging gap. He wasn't sure what they could do but he was afraid. He needed someone. But an even greater problem immediately followed his decision. The flare would have to be got out of the backpack and his foot and leg holds on the cliff were so tenuous that he dared not risk it, his body pressed precariously against the weeping rock face. He would have to find an indentation big enough to allow him room to take off the bag and fire the flare.

Then another fear assailed him—did these flares work after they had been soaked with rain? He had never bothered to ask, for like a young soldier until confronted by his first real battle, he had thought when he left the mainland that the possibility of such danger was remote.

Carefully he slid his left foot along the narrow ledge, feeling it tapering to solid rock face. Bringing his foot back, the tension in his back increasing until it was a throbbing knot of strained muscle, he rested for a few minutes before going on. The way down to the right was barred by a torrent at least ten or twelve feet across, the waterfall appearing as a series of thick white sinews against the impenetrably dark slab of towering rock. Whenever he

felt panic threatening, constricting his throat, he forced
himself to think of something else entirely: the order of
nesting among the birds he had left his beloved Mexico to
study; the gulls, whether they were Heermans, Califor-
nias, ring-billed or Bonapartes, would occupy the mid-
heights of cliffs, the higher reaches taken over by the cormorants, who could often be seen, their wings spread out
on the rocks, sunning the peculiarly nonwaterproof feathers in between dives so graceful that they reminded Julio
of the divers from the high rocks in Acapulco who risked
their lives to entertain the tourists. He tried to push this
thought out of his mind, for instead of taking his mind off
his predicament it only made him focus in on the roar of
the gap below, which was now so full, approaching high
tide, that the rush of water through the divide created a
phosphorescent caldron as legions of tiny, iridescent
planktonic forms were churned to the surface.

Pulling down his left arm in a wide arc against the dripping cold rock, careful not to put outward pressure on his
body away from the cliff face, Julio now extended his right
arm high above, stretching as if searching for a hidden
door key. He felt a crevice, and when it held, felt higher
with his left hand and found another hold. He gave them
his full weight. They held. Now all he needed was another
hold in order to move left, away from the waterfall and
toward the spot where he could see a dark hole within the
greater darkness as one sees a black hole in the night sky,
an indentation from which hopefully he could fire the
flare. He found two more handholds, tested them and
readied himself for a chin-up to raise his body to a ledge
closer to the recess in the rock. He breathed in, pulling
himself up; the right hand gave way. In a split second he
felt a damp softness in his hand, the sodden bird's nest
whose crust had fooled him. He tried to take all his weight
on the left handhold but the angle was all wrong, and he
fell backward into the night. Suddenly his head jolted forward, auras of light in front of his eyes that seemed to

come from the base of his spine, and he was sliding, feeling nothing, hearing only the screech of gulls as they exploded from the Pinnacle.

WHEN THE BIRDS' SCREECHING had stopped, although for how long Julio did not know, all he could hear was the mournful howling of the wind about the rock. Dimly at first, he gradually became aware that he was unable to move his neck or any other part of his body except his right arm, which he now used to feel for the pack strap. But all he could sense was a faint tingling, nothing more. Even when his hand slid over to his left thigh for his knife he couldn't be sure he actually had the handle in his grip but could only imagine it in the strange, detached way one sees oneself in a dream, knowing full well that it was a dream yet unable to wake. He knew he was paralyzed below the waist, there being no feeling down there at all. But how badly? The memory of Diego da Gama, an old fisherman he had known from childhood, came to him, of da Gama telling him, as he had so many times, that if a man could not live as a man then he should not live at all. The hand holding the knife lay limp by Julio's side, seeming detached, as if it belonged to someone else.

Unable to move his head even a fraction of an inch, Julio Suarez slid his finger down from what he could only guess must be the handle, trying desperately to feel for the blade.

Chapter Sixteen

A HUNDRED MILES to the east, near the mouth of the Columbia River, it was a different world in the cozy comfort of the Drift Net Café, down on Astoria's Marine Drive, where Johnny Hornby and his secretary, May, sat enjoying large crab cocktails and deep-fried razor clams washed down with ice-cold Olympia. Johnny had just returned from the phone booth when he saw a local fisherman, by the looks of him, sitting down and flirting with May. He probably thought the squaw was an easy mark.

"You selling something?" Hornby asked the fisherman.

May could tell by Johnny's cockiness that he had heard good news on the phone, or at least that he didn't have to go to sea just yet.

The fisherman was unfazed, looking up at Johnny. "Yeah," he said, grinning. "Good times."

"What?" Hornby scowled.

"I'm selling good times."

"In this town! Here, pull the other one!"

"Not such a bad place once you get to know it."

"Hey, fuck off! Got it?"

The fisherman got up, taking his beer with him, pointing it at Hornby. "Be seeing you, big shot."

"Fuck off!"

The fisherman smiled at May. "Nice company you keep." By then a waitress was hurrying from the bar, anxiously asking whether anyone needed refills.

"You should be careful," said May. "These fishermen stick together, Johnny."

"We could buy out the lot of 'em like that," he said, snapping his fingers.

May was interested in Hornby; he fitted a profile she'd been reading about in one of the night courses she was taking at Oregon U. The textbooks described the personality type as being "well-spoken, deferential," to those, like the Swiss boss, above them, but "tending to be domineering, aggressive and careless about verbal skills to those below them in the hierarchical structure." The textbook called them authoritarian personalities. On the reserve they called them shits. "What does Zurich say?" she asked.

"The *man* says that there must have been some rough stuff with that Beechcraft we hired. And—" he took a long pull at the glass of beer "—so it's time we played tit for tat." He smiled at the prospects. "We aren't going to put any more of our people in danger."

"Our people?" said May. "I didn't know the pilot was 'our people'—I thought we just hired her on a job-to-job basis."

"Hey, don't get fucking technical, sweetheart. What the *man* says is that we play it *cool*, right? We don't have to go anywhere." She knew this meant that Johnny wouldn't have to go to sea, which was why he was being even more bullying than usual. It was his way of celebrating a near miss at putting himself in danger, and the reason he was doing the silly nostalgia bit with "the man" and "cool" and all the rough tough business with the fisherman. It also meant she'd have to be with him while they waited for things to work themselves out in the storm that he was so afraid to go out in. It told her, too, that whoever was SRP's contact aboard *Petrel*, that is, whoever Johnny had bribed or blackmailed or both, was not only doing his job but must still have something up his sleeve if Zurich wasn't sending out Hornby. Altogether it confirmed what she had only lately suspected, that CANUS Ore had never been a legitimate mining business from the day it started shop but was merely a front, run by a local thug in a suit for a foreign thug in a better suit. She hated herself for being there, but the thing she hated worse was being poor and being lonely poor. If she wanted out of CANUS she knew she would need something, besides herself, that was worth selling.

"Hey, lost your tongue?" said Hornby, while signaling for another beer.

"No," answered May. "I was just wondering how our contact could stop *Petrel* and beat them ashore with the locations of sea gold. Didn't you say when SRP tried it one other time up in Canada there was trouble?"

Hornby looked down at her. "Yeah. And that's all I said. Besides that had nothing to do with the Portland office, with me. It was a Vancouver screwup. When Johnny Hornby says he'll get something done, it gets done."

"I know that, Johnny. I was just wondering...."

"Well, don't. Drink your suds and leave the thinking to me." He slid his hand under the tablecloth. "Christ, I feel horny. C'mon," he said. "Finish your beer and then I'll really give you something to think about."

She forced a smile.

"I'm gonna hurt you, honey," he said, his voice raspy, overcome with self-love. "I'm as big as a horse."

"Yes," she said. "A horse's ass."

He was feeling her again. She tried holding him off. "What's got you all excited, Johnny? Something about that *Petrel* boat, isn't it? Is the contact on the boat a woman?"

"I'm excited all the time, babe."

She'd make it slow, she decided, make him moan and groan a lot, pretend she was torturing him for information, get him babbling when he shot his load and was all glassy-eyed and stupid.

Chapter Seventeen

IT HAD TAKEN Julio a full ten minutes of extraordinary concentration to bring the knife across his stomach to his left side, and another fifteen minutes or so to begin sawing away at the padded nylon strap of the backpack on his left shoulder. Devoid of feeling in his hands, it was impossible for him to know how far, if at all, he had cut through the strap. As if by some strange compensation for his loss of tactile sensation, his hearing was much more acute than usual and he could hear the constant chittering of unseen birds, no doubt watching him from invisible perches high in the wind-filled darkness. As he stared helplessly up at the India-ink sky, an odd star visible now and then through the stratus, he recalled the fate of those lost in the deserts of his homeland, the birds waiting to eat out the entrails, and weakly, but with all the strength he had remaining, began to rub the blade against the strap once more.

GLORIA RAN for a half mile before she dared to stop, but then she was forced to halt before a jumble of grass-covered rocks that came at her out of the dark, echoing her rapid breathing so she was convinced that at least one of the three pursuing marines must hear her. The more she tried to stifle the noise, the louder it seemed. In her dash away from the helicopter, through increasing showers of rain, she had thought only of getting away, but now she realized that soon the chopper must return with reinforcements and that running would not be enough. Regaining her composure, breathing more slowly, she found it easier to think, and it occurred to her that the last place they would expect her to go would be back to the shack. If she could reach it safely she might be able to get some emergency supplies that she would desperately need to stay alive until the pickup ship arrived in four or five days.

She heard a swishing of high grass nearby and fell flat to the gravelly spill around the base of the rocks. Perhaps it had only been a high gust of wind? Or—Gloria suddenly felt a wave of hope—it might be Julio on his way back from the Pinnacle. She heard the rustling noise again. Suddenly she recoiled in fright, then went limp with relief. She had touched the cement foundations that had been part of the World War II radar station, and the noise she was hearing was the tall sword grass scraping against the cement. On her right more grass rustled against the walls of the long cement hut that had served as the radar station's barracks. Relieved that it wasn't the marines following but disappointed that it wasn't Julio, she was tempted momentarily to seek refuge in the abandoned building, then immediately rejected the idea as a move Saburov and his hounds, whatever they were doing on the island, would already have anticipated. Instead, she stuck to her original plan of doing the totally unexpected and headed back toward the shack. Besides, she would play safe, not go anywhere near it if there was the slightest sign of them around. Her one advantage, or so she believed, was that she knew the island much better than they did. The rain was easing now, and the moon, though eclipsed earlier by cloud, was waging its own battle to break through the storm line.

ONE SECOND Julio was cutting the strap, the next second the knife was in the air in front of him, the tension gone, the strap severed. He rested until he could drag the pack across his stomach and, fighting further exhaustion, he started to slowly undo the flap of the backpack. Then he lost consciousness.

When he came to a moment later he was aware of a metallic taste in his mouth and a faint warm sensation on his chin as blood trickled down onto his chest. He tried to raise his head to see the clasp on the pack he was trying to unfasten but fainted again from the effort.

When he next regained consciousness he discovered that his vision was blurring. It took him another agonizing five minutes that seemed to him like a half hour to undo the clasp and extract one of the two emergency flares. He began coughing, and the weaker he felt the more uncontrollable the coughing that racked him. Through sheer will he managed to hold the flare steady enough to pull the tape, praying that the rain had not ruined it.

The flare spurted to life with a crimson roar, streaking skyward, its glare illuminating the passing rock face in a spectacular splash of orange light and enormous flickering shadows of itself. Terrified bird colonies disbanded into a confusion of screeching and panicked flight as, climbing steadily, the flare reached an altitude of one thousand feet, seemed to hover for a moment, then began its slower parachuted descent. Finally, it burned itself out with such a brilliant incandescence that it could be seen through the curtain of rain for ten miles in all directions.

PETREL WAS TURNING even as Captain Tate, having spotted the flare, was asking for volunteers for a rescue party to embark for Eagle Island. When Frank entered the bridge he could hear the crackle of static and through it the broken English of the Polish captain, Novisk, telling *Petrel* that his ship had seen the flare and would dispatch a rescue team immediately.

"Your chopper won't see anything in this pea soup," replied Tate, only too willing to help even if it meant risking his own men. "Anyway, the barometer's falling. This lot will get worse before it gets better."

"Say again please, Captain?"

"I say the weather will get worse before there's another lull in the storm line. Your helicopter won't be able to see anything in the rain. We don't mind giving you a hand...helping. You understand?"

"Thanking you kindly, Captain, yes. But we are closer. We will send a party ashore. Thank you all the same. Yes." There was a pause. "Yes, my officer of watch saw the flare ashore arising from the northern part of the island. We will send our party immediately."

Petrel's third mate swung around. "Bullshit!"

Tate thanked the Polish captain for his kind offer, telling him *Petrel* would stand by in case it could be of assistance.

"Thank you, Captain…" The next bit was lost to static and Tate asked that it be repeated. The Polish captain was telling him that when the search party from the mother ship had found whoever was in distress, it would let *Petrel* know "in haste" as a matter of courtesy.

When he signed off, Tate swung angrily to the first mate. "What's eating you?"

"That flare came from the southern tip of the island, Captain. Not the north."

Frank had only spotted the flare descending as he climbed up the ladder from the stern deck to the bridge housing. "You positive of that, mate?" he asked.

"You bet. I did it by the book, Frank. Moment I saw that son of a bitch go up I took a sighting on it. Unless we're way the hell off course that line runs over the southern tip of Eagle Island. I'd say it came from that rock, the Pinnacle, but ten miles away I can't be that accurate. But it sure didn't come up from the northern part of the island."

"Funny," said Frank.

Tate was nonplussed. "What the hell's going on here?"

"That's exactly what I'd like to know," conceded Frank. "All I know is that Polish mother ship has been the closest to that trawler that went down, the closest to the plane that crashed and now this."

"Hey!" said the mate. "You're right. That's three out of three."

"Well, whatever it is," said Frank, "I think it's high time someone else got close enough to see what's going on." He turned to Tate. "Plus there's that little matter of the life raft from *Swiftsure*."

Tate was nodding his head worriedly. He walked into the chart room, steadying himself against the map table as *Petrel* rocked sharply then slammed hard aport through a double breaker. Beneath the blood-red glow of the chart lamp the worry lines on Tate's face seemed to soften, but Frank knew it was an illusion.

"Are you volunteering to go, Frank?"

"Yes."

"How many men will you need?"

"Oh—three'll do. One to stay with the Zodiac—two to lend me a hand if we have to get someone off that damn rock." He turned. "If you're right about that flare, mate?"

"I'm right."

Tate drew in a new course heading for Eagle Island's southern end. "Can't take you in closer than a mile offshore, Frank. Too many shoals."

"I'll manage," said Frank. "I'll take rations for forty-eight hours. All I need now is the other three volunteers."

"I'll go," said the first mate.

"Okay," said Tate. "That's two madmen."

"Ah," put in the mate, "I've always wanted to surf at night."

Frank grinned. "How many rubber suits do we have aboard, Captain?"

"We don't. We carry the oil rig survival suits now. Fifteen—one for each crew member. None for the scientific party, though. Supply screwup there."

"Ah, what the hell!" Frank returned, joining the banter that was going up against the danger. "I'll just put on a couple of T-shirts."

"Go on, you mad bastards," cut in Tate. "Get below and get ready. I'll ask for two more to join you and have Bosun ready the Zodiac."

"*CHORT!* DAMN!" snarled Saburov, his eyes fixed on the mother ship's radar. Amid the sea clutter he could see a recurring dot, the American ship *Petrel* coming out of the southwest toward Eagle Island. It was difficult, given the state of sea, to tell exactly what course the vessel was steering—whether it was heading for the northern tip or the southern end, which the mother ship had been using as a massive windbreak to aid the helicopter's takeoffs over the past few days. In any case, what was quite obvious was that the Americans were ignoring Novisk's assurance that the mother ship would go in and take care of whoever had fired the flare for help. "The bastards are coming after all," said Saburov, unusually agitated, turning to the electronics officer. "Keep me posted."

"Yes, Colonel."

Saburov was becoming more irritated by the minute. Making matters worse, Captain Novisk handed him a weather report indicating a lull of relatively fine weather sometime in the next thirty-six hours, meaning a loss of cover for the ship just at the point when it was in the last stages of its task, needing only another uninterrupted forty-eight hours to complete it.

"Well, at least," said Saburov, regaining his composure somewhat, "we don't have to operate in the dark anymore. We can use the HIP's searchlight now. After all it would seem strange not to in a rescue attempt. Correct?"

Even Novisk had to smile. He didn't like the Russian, but he was cunning as a Siberian fox.

AS TATE PEERED ANXIOUSLY through the spinning clearview window, its electric motor a comforting hum beneath the onslaught of the seas off Eagle Island, he heard the crackle of the radio console and Sparks asking an operator to repeat a message pecking its way through turbulent static. Following several repeats, the message, still incomplete but containing enough essential information, was handed to Tate.

"Contact the Polish ship! Then get Frank Hall. On the double!"

Sparks found Frank and the first mate in the forward wet lab, putting on the garish, tangerine survival suit of the type originally developed for off-shore Atlantic oil platforms, after rigs developed a bad habit of sinking before rescuers could get anyone off them.

"What's up?" Frank asked Sparks. "You coming with us?"

"You kidding? In a force nine? You know they tried to build a lighthouse on that rock once. Lost four guys just trying to get ashore. On a sunny day! In 1917. Read about it in the *Pilot*."

"You're a cheerful son of a bitch," said Frank. "Any other good news?"

"Yeah. This." He handed the yellow message sheet to Frank. Though it had obviously been a spotty transmission, name of the ship incomplete—something ending in *maru*, which meant it was probably Japanese—Frank could nevertheless tell from the coordinates, without looking at his 18007 chart, that the position, located between longitudes 127 and 128, meant that the latest Mayday in this storm was coming from at least 135 miles off the Oregon coast, putting it about seventy miles due west of Eagle Island, at the very outer range of the Polish fleet, all of whom would now be too far south to assist. At *Petrel*'s present seven knots in the heavy weather, it would take a minimum of twenty hours on dead reckoning to reach her, longer perhaps, given the resistance of the southward-bound Californian Current.

"What's wrong with her?" asked Frank.

"Engine trouble was the most I could get out of him. Japanese merchantman. English wasn't so hot and he sounded a bit panicky."

"How about the coast guard—air arm?"

"I've tried Air Station Astoria, Point Grenville, Lightship Columbia..."

"Cape Disappointment?" put in Frank.

"Everybody. Nothing but static. I'll keep trying but right now we're it."

"How about our helpful Polish friends?"

"Mother ship says she can't move too far from her trawlers. Apparently several of them are in trouble already—full holds."

"Did they say that? The mother ship?"

"Yes. Sent their regrets."

"First time that's happened," said the mate suspiciously. "Why are they suddenly all hell-bent to stay put?"

"That's what the old man wants to know," said Sparks.

"Because," said Frank, "they're not handling any more Mayday calls until they find whoever fired that flare. Now, why are they more interested in a few bird chasers than in a ship in distress—possibly sinking?"

"Search me," commented Sparks. "I just run the radio, guys." He hesitated. "Look, maybe we're blowin' this thing right out of proportion. They've got a much bigger ship over there."

"So?" asked the mate.

"Well, I mean their radar equipment might be better than ours... and they do have all their trawlers relaying messages and possible sightings as well. I mean they've got more eyes and ears than we have. Remember they were Johnny-on-the-spot with that Beechcraft and that trawler, *Lvov*, going down—and they're nearer the island. No denying they were closer to the flare when it went up."

"Maybe," cut in the third mate. "But that flare came from the south of the island. I don't care what they say."

"Well, anyway, the old man wants your opinion, Frank. Says you and he split the responsibility for deciding this one. Do we head west for this SOS and leave the Poles to find whoever sent up the flare?"

Frank, deep in thought, was looking down at the gear for the Zodiac, including a grappling iron for the landing, if they weren't smashed against the rocks before they got a chance to grapple with anything, and a telescopic pike to fend them off from the hidden rock ledges that, invisible beneath an incoming wave, could suddenly appear as rearing sawtooth projections striking out at the boat as it slid down into the suction hole created by a receding wave. Frank had seen two men lost like that in his time, trying to land on rocks, the memories still vivid in their bloody detail. He knew he didn't have to go to the island, not with the Japanese SOS and the Polish mother ship giving him the excuse to forget about the island and head west. It would be far less dangerous than going against the island. He pulled out a waterproof can of freeze-dried beans and lentils, solid camping fuel and, kneeling, slid them into one of the Zodiac's inboard elastic pockets along with coils of nylon rope. "We can have a go at both of them," he answered, realizing the moment he said it that the expression "have a go" had been unconsciously borrowed from Aussie.

"How the hell can we do that?" asked the mate.

"Our party of four goes in—to the island," answered Frank. "Then *Petrel* heads west." He pointed at the map of Eagle Island. "We can use this survival shack—to the north—if we have to. Anyway, one of us better cover the area around there, making absolutely sure the flare didn't come from that part of the island. No offense, Mate."

"None taken, Frank. I'll go to the hut if you like."

"All right, the other three of us'll head for that Pinnacle. We'll hide the Zodiac then search for whoever fired the flare."

"Hide the boat?" asked Sparks, perplexed. "Who from?"

"You know how it is," answered Frank enigmatically, buckling the waist belt of his first-aid pack. "Sometimes people don't want to invite you to a party, then hell, once you're there they can't bear to see you leave."

The mate grinned. Sparks was looking even more puzzled. "Don't like the sound of that...whatever it means."

"All you have to worry about is to watch that radar and help the old man. Drop us off as close as possible to this flat rock ledge below the shack."

"It's marked on the chart as table rock," the mate explained, "but it's about as flat as a porcupine."

"Agreed," said Frank. "Still, it's about the only place to land on the northern part of the island."

"Who's going with you?" asked Sparks.

"Byrne and Jamie," said the mate.

Sparks raised an eyebrow at Jamie's inclusion.

"He volunteered," Frank added noncommittally.

"Is he sober?" asked Sparks. "That's the question."

"He does his job when he has to," the mate answered tartly. "Why d'you think the old man keeps him on? He likes the sauce all right, but that's only when he's off duty. He cares about the ship when it counts."

Frank, pulling on his toque, said nothing about his surprise that Jamie was coming along, or about the fact that the mate was so protective of him. He'd have to take them, anyway; no one else was willing to take the risk. He couldn't place Byrne, the other volunteer, until the bird-faced man who had given mouth-to-mouth to Aussie turned up in his survival suit, as taciturn as ever but with a quiet competence about him in the way he helped load the Zodiac and lower it in a canvas sling suspended from the Austin-Western davit. The latter looked like a twenty-five-pound howitzer as it swung starboard, its steel telescopic arm suspending the eighteen-foot-long inflatable like some great stalk holding its young aloft.

Tate brought the ship bow-on into the seas, steadying her long enough for the four men to take up their positions, Frank in the Zodiac's middle, kneeling behind the steering wheel console, Jamie aft, the mate manning the starboard side, the tall, gangly Byrne in front of the console on the port side. The four tangerine suits were iridescent in the cone of rain-swept deck lights but became all but invisible the moment the Zodiac cast off and slid down, then up, a wall of water in a burst of noise, the twin fifty-horsepower Evinrude outboards driving the deep fiberglass V-shaped hull beyond the dancing aprons of light that undulated over the heaving surface of the sea.

As the tough rubber sides of the open craft first flexed then gave against the wind-streaked waves, taking on water that washed over the low freeboard, around the tightly lashed rescue equipment and the 300,000 candlepower spotlight mounted on the steering console amidships, Frank kept the boat well under its maximum of thirty-five knots, between six and ten depending on the swells. He didn't turn to run with the waves, but across them, until his eyes grew more accustomed to the darkness and he spotted a trough wide enough to allow him something other than a sharp turn on the downward slope. Gunning the engines, he stayed just ahead of the collapsing wall of water directly behind, and yet kept enough power to climb the wall buckling backward in front of him, threatening to reach its peak too soon and flip them backward into the air between the crests in an instant capsize. For a moment, speeding down the slope of the wave behind, approaching the jumping white line of surf that was smashing into the island less than a thousand yards ahead, Frank recalled that the last time he'd manned a Zodiac it had been in a fight against Klaus's hoods off the Canadian coast. He pushed the throttle forward to stay ahead of a cross wave curling grotesquely on the starboard quarter, its summit advancing with such malevolence that it seemed alive with an intent to destroy them before they ever reached the

island. He outran it in a burst of speed, then throttled
down as it exhausted itself and passed by. Frank caught a
glimpse of Jamie as the crewman dodged a spume of spray,
surprised by how fast Jamie had moved his head, not with
the tired or slow movements one would expect of someone in middle age but with the agility of someone much
younger. For Frank it was as if he was seeing another side
of Jamie, not the sluggish, easygoing guzzler from *Petrel*
but a man capable of suddenly galvanizing himself into
action, as his willingness to volunteer for such a risky rescue attempt had attested.

Now the Zodiac, its twin outboards unfaltering in their
throaty roar, was only three hundred yards from the rocky
shore, beyond any help from *Petrel*. As always Frank was
amazed once again at how, despite all a man's experience
at sea, the astonishing difference between seeing a surf-
pounded shoreline from the distance aboard a ship like
Petrel and from sea level is so awe-inspiring that in the final moments of his tiny craft approaching the shore, even
as he wills himself to go forward, every nerve in him is
taut, crying for retreat.

"Ready?" he called, and the mate, the boat's painter in
his hand, tensed, the Zodiac passing into the turmoil of
surf. Frank did not know what else he was heading into,
only that someone had fired a flare for help, and that even
if, like so many calls, it turned out to be a false alarm, he
had to go in.

"COLONEL! LOOK HERE!"

Saburov turned to the electronics officer and saw that
the plate-size radar screen with its dancing, orange static
was now expanding to the size of a big platter as the
E.W.—electronics warfare—officer switched up the mag-
nification, zeroing in on an area ten miles in diameter
covering the southern sector of Eagle Island. "Can't see
anything but clutter," Saburov responded, trying to keep
one eye on the radar as well as overseeing the loading of

the helicopter through the thick Plexiglas panel separating the bridge from the rear of the hangar.

The E.W. officer pointed to a blip that was shifting position in a more or less steady line amid the clutter of the heavy seas around the island. "That's *Petrel*," said the E.W. officer, "and that—" His finger traced a line slightly ahead of the blip to an even smaller dot.

"Is a smaller boat?" asked Saburov.

"Much smaller. I'd say a rubberized dinghy from the poor reflection we're getting, unless there's something wrong with our radar wave guide. But I don't—"

"You think it's from *Petrel*?"

"Yes, sir."

"They must be mad! In this weather? Are you sure?" he asked incredulously, while trying to block out background cross chatter between the bridge and the helicopter preparations.

"Yes, sir. It's definitely a boat. It has the configuration of—"

"Never mind that," Saburov cut in. "How can you be sure it's from *Petrel* and not from the island?"

The E.W. officer, his padded earphones giving him the appearance of a rabbit, looked up at the political officer, unfazed. "I've been watching the screen, Comrade. That's how I know. It's my job."

Swinging away from the rebuke to face Captain Novisk, Saburov threw up his hands accusingly. "Did you expect that?"

"No, Comrade." Novisk could see that once again Saburov was a true party man, immediately looking for someone else to blame. "Who knows what these Americans will do?" Novisk added.

"Then," said Saburov derisively, "if they are so anxious to play heroes why are they only coming to the island and not going to the Mayday?"

"The small boat," the E.W. officer broke in matter-of-factly. "It's heading inshore. Toward the area beneath the shack."

"To Table Rock," said Novisk. "Well, at least they fell for us telling them the flare came from the northern end of the island."

"Thank the stars for that," said Saburov, visibly relieved. "That will give us time to land our marines on the Pinnacle where the flare—"

"*Petrel* is turning," announced the E.W. officer as unemotionally as a surgeon describing an autopsy.

Saburov swung back to the screen, his mood now approaching exhilaration. "Heading?" he asked.

"263."

Saburov smacked the E.W. officer on the back. "West! They're heading due west. Well done, Comrade. Well done."

Chapter Eighteen

THE HOOD OF HIS SURVIVAL suit flapping furiously in crosswinds from sea and cliff, Frank, at the steering column in the center of the seventeen-foot boat, felt the gut-wrenching surge of a wave surge from the pitch-darkness behind him. The next second the Zodiac was planing at more than fifteen knots, racing toward the surf two hundred yards dead ahead, in the sharp beam of its spotlight. The inflatable was heeling hard aport, skimming over the huge mass of water. As the crest began to break, Frank continued the turn to port, completing a circle, avoiding the crashing wall of water and dropping down the back wall of the wave toward the beach in the calmer backwash, clear of the next wave's menace. It was a consummate piece of seamanship that Byrne, hunkering down in the bow, and the other two men fully appreciated as they saw the shoreline bursting white with the power of the collapsing wave Frank had so coolly outmaneuvered under pressure of timing and weather conditions that they knew would have panicked most men. It gave Byrne greater confidence, too, that he might ably fend off the rocks with the boat hook, as Frank told them he would swing the Zodiac on a sharp port tack, allowing the mate at the last minute to leap from the Zodiac's starboard side onto the exposed Table Rock and from there make his way up the winding cliff trail to the survival shack.

Knowing he would only have one approach in the surf where one wave was constantly rolling in on the heels of another, all melding into a hundred-foot-deep foam line, Frank kept the twin Evinrudes at low rev astern, in effect braking the boat against the forward momentum of the waves crashing in behind him, the men all the time feeling the rubberized gunwales flexing and giving under the battering as only a Zodiac could. The stratus cloud parted for a second or two, letting the moon peep through, but just as the four men, drenched in a hysteria of wind and water, thought the moon's glow would aid them by illuminating the sharp, fortresslike rocks of the shoreline, the clouds closed again, leaving Frank with only the spray-filled spotlight beam to judge distance.

For a split second he lost sight of the telltale forward line of surf, thinking he was closer to the rocks than he was. To compensate, lest he be overtaken by the waves coming in quickly behind, he reduced speed, alerting the mate to get ready. The mate rose to a half crouch, his orange survival suit vivid in the spotlight glare, his right hand on the gunwale strap, the other extended, ready to leap ashore.

APPROACHING THE SHACK from the high western cliffs, listening for the marines who she hoped were now heading south looking for her, Gloria saw a pencil-thin beam of light streaking out from the surf far below the shack like a long, ghostly finger feeling for the landing. Hurrying toward the top of the path that led down to the rocky shoreline, she ran as fast as the lumpy terrain would allow to meet them and warn them, whoever they were, about Saburov and his—

Suddenly she stopped, realizing she had no idea who they were.

"WAIT!" FRANK SHOUTED to the mate over the noise of the surf. "I'll get in clo—"

But the mate had already jumped for the landing and missed, a tangerine flash in the spotlight swallowed by whirlpools of foam. He reappeared moments later fifteen feet away, being sucked down again and swept away in the furious undertow. Frank gunned the outboards, swinging the Zodiac hard astarboard, the bow smashing up through the next wave down the incline, then rearing hard aport. The spotlight followed the tight turn, picking up the mate's arm as he struck out toward shore.

Without instruction, Byrne pulled back the pike and reversed it, thrusting the handle out to the mate, who didn't see it as he was caught in a cross wave and swept hard in to the shoreline. Next instant they saw him spread-eagled on the lip of Table Rock like some giant tangerine starfish precariously abandoned. He disappeared as the next wave engulfed him, but was still on the rock, slowly crawling up its slippery surface toward the bottom of the pathway leading up the cliff to the shack.

"Luck o' the Irish!" shouted Jamie. They held the beam on him until he turned and waved that he was all right, then Frank deftly turned the Zodiac around into the surf and beyond, before heeling full ninety degrees port, running south, parallel to the island's west coast beneath towering black cliffs thrusting a sheer thousand feet above the storm-whipped sea.

From what he remembered of the chart showing Eagle Island, the Pinnacle, off the island's southern tip, didn't offer any better landing places than Table Rock, but it struck him that if the flare did come from someone on the lone monolith, as the mate had claimed, then there had to be some way of climbing it. He switched off the spotlight, adjusting his eyes to the darkness, which enabled him to pick out luminescent shoals that spread out like tentacles from the base of the cliffs. Despite its shallow draft, the fiberglass hull would be sliced open like a can if it so much as grazed the razor-sharp reefs.

Byrne was pointing to something on the port side, at the base of the cliffs, Jamie nodding that he saw it, too, but Frank was so preoccupied, looking ahead for any signs of hidden rocks, that it wasn't for another minute that he could pay heed to whatever was obviously claiming the others' attention. Then he saw, running all along the jagged shoreline, splashes of white as fur seals and sea lions dropped into the sea, disturbed by something that Frank and his companions couldn't see. Gradually through the banshee wail of the storm they heard it, a faint chopping of the air, growing louder and more menacing by the second. But after all, he told himself, why shouldn't the Polish mother ship use its chopper for the search? Nevertheless, he couldn't shake the feeling of threat, that somehow he and the mother ship were engaged in some kind of competition, some kind of race.

"Frank?" Byrne was pointing up ahead, a couple of degrees to port in the slash of moonlight. "I think it's the Pinnacle—or maybe a headland."

Frank, detaching the spotlight from the quick-release gimbals mounting, passed it over to Byrne. "Check the chart," Frank told him. "Think we have a few miles to go yet."

Byrne switched on the light, crouching in the bow as they slid over roller-coaster swells. He compared the dim shape of the cliffs a quarter of a mile to their left with the contours of the chart. "No," he answered, passing the spotlight back to Frank. "Looks like we're still about a mile or so nor'nor'west of it."

Jamie shifted position, legs starting to stiffen. "A mile! I'm seizing up here."

"Hang in there, Jamie," Frank encouraged, and in that moment he sensed the camaraderie that only shared danger brings.

"YOU SEE THAT?" the HIP pilot asked Saburov. "A spotlight?"

"Yes. Must be the boat from *Petrel*."

"Want me to go down and take a look?"

"No. Let's find this Mexican first—this . . ."

"Julio," said the lieutenant.

"Yes. And the woman. They're the ones who've been on the island. That's our first priority."

"Then you think they know?" the lieutenant asked, marking the spotlight sighting on his chart and noting the time: 2214 hours.

"I don't know," admitted Saburov. "All I do know is there's only one way to be sure."

The lieutenant looked back over his shoulder at the eight marines the HIP had picked up from the ship and the tall Georgian remaining from the first contingent of four. All nine of them were fully armed and eager to have a bit of fun after the long voyage from Gdansk. "They'll make sure," said the lieutenant. "Their only worry is that their comrades we left on the island will have found her by the time we get there."

"They would have radioed us if they had," commented Saburov.

The lieutenant said nothing more. He wasn't going to tell Saburov what the marines had in mind if they found the woman first. One of them had told him that in Afghanistan, radio messages to base were often delayed when women in the villages were taken prisoner, so that the boys could have a little fun before receiving instructions from HQ. The lieutenant pressed the button for the red warning light to come on in the chopper's cabin, telling the Spetsnaz marines that they were about to be dropped off one by one to form the diamond search pattern specifically designed for capturing counterinsurgency elements. The lieutenant almost felt sorry for the Mexican and the woman. The lieutenant's English was not good but the situation reminded him of the American expression, "turkey shoot."

GLORIA DECIDED to take a chance, making her way as fast as the darkness would allow, down to the landing a quarter mile below the shack. If she kept a sharp ear she should be able to hear anyone coming up the track and hide among the rocks to the side of the pathway until she could determine who it was.

The rain had stopped now, high stratus finally giving way to the jet stream, allowing the moon to shine down on the tossing sea, giving it a deceptively calm appearance from the cliff tops. It was the beginning of the forecasted lull in the storm line, and Gloria took it as a good omen. The pathway down the cliff roughly followed the shape of an S and it was not until she reached the second curve in the S, after about ten minutes of walking, that she heard a trickle of loose stones behind her. She stopped, listening for footsteps, or had it been a small avalanche she had started, with the help of the rain-scoured soil, trickling down from the edges of the cliff?

The second fall of gravel was louder. She glanced around in the pale moonlight for a hiding place, could see none readily at hand, so kept on going down the trail. The sound of her breathing and the pounding of blood in her ears smothered any noise behind her, causing her to panic for a moment or two, sending her rushing down the steep path, speed overtaking common sense. Suddenly her feet were gone from under her. Coming down more lightly than she expected, she nevertheless slid in a mud patch for five or six yards until coming to an abrupt stop, her shoulder slamming into a honeycombed wall of rock on one side of the path. The impact sent pebbles running before her, splashing into potholes farther down the trail. She heard footsteps, not behind but in front of her, around a bend in the path. Seeing a large hole in the rock wall to her left, she made for it, fighting desperately to slow and silence her breathing, lying down, not knowing whether there *was* someone behind her as well as in front, and unsure whether the person in front of her was coming up the trail toward her or going back down.

"Hello! Anyone there?" The voice was labored. "First mate from M.V. *Petrel* here. Saw a flare."

There was silence. Then the man's voice was coming clearly through the moon-bathed night again. "Hello—anyone there?"

Gloria wanted to answer, but now she could hear another footfall a few yards behind her, coming down the trail, and a figure, looking monstrous in its full kit, a rifle unslung and held waist high, heading directly for her. He was so close she could smell his perspiration. Suddenly the man paused. It was one of the marines. She felt her throat go dry and gripped a loose rock, though she knew it would be a hopeless defense against an armed man. But then suddenly he walked on by. She knew he must not be far from the other man.

"Be careful!" she yelled as loudly as her lungs would allow. "He's got a gun!"

Her brain racing, she turned and immediately began running back up the path. She could do no more to help the man from *Petrel* other than get to the shack before Saburov's marine, who had probably been stationed at the shack waiting for Julio to return and who no doubt had come down to the landing rock the moment he'd seen the spotlight from *Petrel*'s rescue boat.

THE MATE HEARD the woman's warning about someone with a gun just as the Russian, traveling at speed, rounded the shoulder of rock. The mate put up his hands to stop the Russian, but it was futile. The marine had built up an enormous momentum in the downhill run, and the American's bright tangerine survival suit was clearly visible. The Russian smacked aside the raised arms with the Kalashnikov and kicked the American in the groin. The mate collapsed like a sack. He tried to get back up but the marine gave him a boot in the face, another in the back as the mate rolled over, his voice garbled in pain, spluttering through blood.

Saburov had been explicit about not shooting. As far as possible everything in the mop-up—like the American scientist they'd tossed out of the HIP and whose body would now be floating, if not eaten by sharks—was to look like an accident, a fall, if possible. You only shot them if they looked like getting away, but then you had to get rid of the body and not let it float around, on the remote chance of its being fished out of the water. And so the marine slung his rifle, then reached down, steadied the mate's head and, straightening up, kicked it again. This time there was no cracking of bones, only a soft crunch like a melon imploding. The Russian then lifted the American over his shoulder and made his way carefully down to Table Rock. Unzipping the American's survival suit he searched for cigarettes but found none, and rolled the body into the sea. He unclipped his walkie-talkie, wondering if it would raise the chopper at this distance below the cliff barrier. He was lucky. Though he had to repeat himself several times he managed to get through to Saburov, telling him that one of the would-be rescuers from *Petrel* was dead and that he was now heading back to the shack because he figured the woman would be up there ransacking the place for supplies.

"How do you know she's anywhere near?" asked Saburov.

"She tried to warn our visitor, Colonel. Anyway, it's like in Korea, and in Vietnam," the marine added matter-of-factly, though he hadn't fought in either war himself. "You can smell Americans a kilometer away. Body powder."

"Perfume," Saburov corrected him.

"Yes. Like some actress from the Bolshoi," said the marine, excited by the thought. "I'm going to get her now."

"Good work, Comrade."

"Thank you, sir."

"And, Comrade, make sure you destroy the shack. But no fire. Understand?"

"Yes, sir." The marine was pleased. If he kept this up he might even be rewarded with a Moscow residency permit, which would allow him and his wife to move out of the provinces. Shit, if he got the girl as well, a promotion could get him on the list for an apartment when he'd finished his ten-year stint. Just thinking about it all, he could smell the woman again, and as he headed cautiously up the path, taking nothing for granted, the image of her stripped naked gave him an erection that got harder and harder as he got closer to the shack.

Chapter Nineteen

IN MOSCOW, General Kornon pulled up the collar of his greatcoat as the chill preceding another snowfall rolled down from the Lenin Hills. Thick, leaden clouds blanketed the high tower of Moscow University, where he had spent his student days studying chemistry, the new math and the required intricacies of higher Marxism-Leninism and where he had excelled, not because he was the son of a highly decorated general of the Great Patriotic War of 1941-45 but because he was brilliant and studied hard.

He was considering the future, how he wanted young Svetlana, who had just turned twelve, to go to the Specialized Youth School for Gymnastics and in time become perhaps a gold medalist. Even if she did not excel, at least in the world of sport she would be as free from party intrigue as it was possible to get and still belong to a party family. Though proud of his own independence in faring well at the university and rising through the party's ranks on merit, Kornon was conscious that had his father not been a party member his children might never have been accepted into the university, and that no matter how good you were, no matter how good Svetlana might be, if a party member fell from grace, suddenly the doors would slam shut. He should know—he had slammed the door often enough himself. You could keep power in the Kremlin only by using it, and because he had used it unhesitatingly he knew there were those in the Central Committee who had not wanted to see him as an alternative Politburo member, let alone a full member where he would threaten their positions. They would not hesitate to oust him if his secret plan—his "Georgian plot" as Nikolai Borgach had called it—failed. An investigation would follow, and after that, exile in Gorky or a Siberian garrison, or as a supply officer on some squalid duty in the Afghan hills. He could not even take to Borgach his concern about the Polish ship's having encountered an unexpected delay—through the presence of the American ship, *Petrel*, and three ornithologists—without casting aspersions on his own competency. It meant only one thing—he would have to devise his own backup plan.

Walking northwest through Red Square in the first flurries of snow, past the yellowed plaster facade of the GUM department store, he was so deep in thought about the danger of his predicament that he didn't notice the long column of tourists waiting to get in to see Lenin's tomb.

The line stretched all the way back along the Kremlin wall
around the corner of Manege Square, south toward Gert-
sen Street and the Lenin Library. Some of the tourists recognized his rank from his collar tabs and board epaulets,
and a group of young schoolchildren from the Ukraine
began whispering, nudging and pointing that one of the
top men in all the Soviet republics was passing by. Normally Kornon would have acknowledged them with the
stiff formality expected of such exalted figures, but this
evening he walked by as troubled and preoccupied as any
Ukrainian official would be about a disastrous failure in
the grain harvest.

Then he recalled the report sent to him by his fisheries
and oceans experts in Geneva, that the American ship,
Petrel's search for strategically important minerals had
aroused considerable interest in Europe, especially from
Swiss Rhine Petrochemicals, with which his department
had several big contracts and of which *Petrel* was also an
old rival.

Suddenly Kornon stopped and looked up, as if noticing
the snow for the first time. The air no longer chilled him
but was instead refreshing. Turning back from Marx
Prospekt, past the Intourist Hotel, he was in a positive
mood, even bothering to acknowledge the smile of a child
in the lineup for the mausoleum and taking a childish de-
light in the simple purity and elegance of St. Basil's, its
snow-dusted cupolas stunningly beautiful in the steel-blue
light.

The moment he returned to his office inside the Kremlin walls he again read through the Swiss report, then
buzzed the reservations secretary on duty to ring Aeroflot
and book the earliest possible flight to Zurich, and to make
an appointment for him with Herr Klaus, head of Swiss
Rhine Petrochemicals.

Chapter Twenty

REACHING THE TOP of the pathway, Gloria saw the shack, a black square in veiled moonlight. She hesitated momentarily, began moving toward it—then stopped, looking around quickly for a pebble, anything, to toss at the door. If anyone was in there they would come out to— No, they wouldn't, they would stay still, silent inside the darkness, and when she entered...

She heard the approach of the helicopter but could not see it. The marine might soon return. The chopper was getting closer, its sound more frightening by the second. Where was Charles? Had they taken him back to the Polish ship or... The thudding sound of rotors was now so insistent it panicked her.

All she could think of was to run as fast as her failing energy could carry her to the Pinnacle, to where the rescue boat from the American ship must be heading to answer Julio's flare, and somehow warn them that they were heading into a trap.

As she started off she could hear the noise of the rotor blades neither increasing nor fading, remaining at the same nerve-racking pitch, meaning it was hovering somewhere nearby. She would keep close to the western cliffs on her way toward the Pinnacle, and if she was lucky she might be able to warn the Americans before they got there. But how to do it? She still had her pack, but what use was a flare? It wouldn't alert them but would pinpoint her position for her pursuers.

Far away to the south, she saw a bluish fork of lightning. It started to rain. It was crazy weather—it was a crazy island. What was the Polish ship doing there? There was more lightning, this time great sheets of it, followed by rolls of thunder. She kept running, the lightning, as if with malevolent intent, spitting angrily. It was then, in her fear, that she thought of a way she might buy time. Sodden with rain and mud, her fingers fumbling with cold, she reached into the pack, feeling among the bird rings, pliers, flashlight, some meager rations, past the smooth, tight package of a space blanket until she felt the hard, square slab of the first-aid kit. Although she thought the jacket would be sufficient cover, she nevertheless hooded the flashlight with the space blanket as she studied the standard international call signs, printed as usual inside the lid of the kit. Slipping the flashlight into her hip pocket, she headed toward the cliff, twenty yards or so to her right.

Halfway there she stopped and draped her jacket over a tussock of grass, pushing some of the blades back into the space inside the jacket's hood. Then she walked quickly northward parallel to the cliffs for another fifty yards, where she took off her thick sweater, her thin white cotton blouse plastered to her skin like plastic wrap, and arranged the sweater so it, too, was standing upright, stuffed with wild grass.

Counting off the paces she retraced her steps south in the gloomy darkness to where she had left her backpack and jacket, which was still upright though leaning in the wind. She rested as long as the cold and wet allowed her, which was hardly any time at all, gathering strength, knowing she needed all her stamina if her plan was to work. Taking out the two flares, she tore the protective strip from the base around the holding sticks and, using a fingernail, scraped the coarse, matchboxlike wick, stabbing the soft earth with the holding stock to anchor the flare. She began to run as she heard the first sputter of cordite.

Everything happened at once. Saburov and the pilot spotted the flare, coming from the north end of the island, at the same time as Frank Hall and the men in the Zodiac saw the helicopter's windshield glinting the color of pink grapefruit in the moving skirt of the flare's light. Frank saw the chopper banking out of the light, while Byrne caught the wink of a flashlight signaling a quarter mile away on the port side, high up on the cliffs that formed the faintest line against intermittent moonlight.

A split second later, the helicopter lost to darkness over the northern half of the island, Frank, also, picked up the pinpoint of light flashing on and off from the cliff tops. For a moment he thought it might be the mate in some kind of trouble, but the Morse was so poorly spaced and amateurish he dismissed the idea. He got A-N-G-E-R, all right, but then M-E-E-T-M-E-A-T-S-O-U-T-H-E-N-D were all run together "like a dog's breakfast," as Byrne commented. It wasn't until the message was repeated, without any stops in it, and he saw that the first letter was a *D* that Frank was able to sort out the words: DANGER. MEET ME AT SOUTH END. TWO MILLS— Then the yellow pinpoint ceased to exist.

"What's that all about?" yelled Jamie, as the Zodiac, now running parallel with the shore, was having a much smoother ride, heading at a good nine knots south toward the Pinnacle.

"Don't know," Frank replied. He confirmed his reading of the message with Byrne.

"That's what it says," Byrne answered, as perplexed as Frank. "Wants me to pick him up two miles down, I guess."

Jamie was shaking his head. "Don't make any sense. If the silly bastard, whoever he is, wants to head for the ass end of the island, why the hell fire a flare from the goddamn cliffs where no one can pick him up?"

ABOARD THE HIP, Saburov was already directing the pilot to descend quickly to where they thought the flare must have been fired, before the Mexican—or had it been the girl?—had any chance of disappearing in the darkness. "Don't worry about taking them alive," said Saburov, his face tallowed above the radar scope. "Shoot to kill! Remember, if they get away we'll all face—"

Saburov recoiled so fast his helmet struck the headrest with the force of a blow. A red streak shot past them to their left.

"What the—" began the pilot. "A second flare!" He threw the steering column hard aport and altered the incline of the blades, aiming the HIP's nose at a point about a mile away.

"We've got them!" he called into the intercom, startling Saburov, who, still recovering from the fright of the flare, whipped his headset off. The pilot, unable to hear him above the scream of the Isotov engine caught only a glimpse of the colonel's lips moving angrily, but otherwise ignored him, keeping his eyes glued to the altimeter—fifteen hundred meters—and to the spot his mind had fixed on as the position from which the second flare had been fired. Besides, it wasn't often that you saw a hardhead like Saburov get a fright.

Now the altimeter was reading nine hundred meters, and the lieutenant began leveling out and reducing speed, the roar above him shifting forward. He pushed the red Ready button, and the light went on in the cabin. The nine marines rose in unison, like some huge, multilegged insect, arms up, gripping the roll bar, the slings of their Kalashnikovs drawn tight for the impact.

Headset on again, Saburov pulled down the small mike. "Only four of you," he shouted even more loudly than the pilot had spoken in the excitement of getting the visual fix on the second flare. "The others," Saburov went on, "stay aboard!"

The pilot adjusted the trim, the HIP dipping its nose, the chopping noise more pronounced in its hovering position before the final descent above the sodden terrain. "Why do we need five marines to stay aboard, Colonel?"

"Because, Comrade, we don't know whether or not the Americans have landed on the island—or where."

"They won't come in now," said the pilot confidently. "Not when they've seen us directly over the flare position."

"Which flare?" Saburov asked.

The lieutenant didn't answer, his concentration focusing entirely on the slow but dangerous descent. He switched on the HIP's searchlight and from its belly a cone of brilliant white light illuminated a patch of frantically waving grass, twenty meters below, an ever-decreasing circle, as the chopper went lower, grass blowing over in the wash like silver wheat.

"It doesn't matter which flare," the lieutenant told Saburov. "Whoever it was fired two, just to be sure. That's my guess. Anyway, they couldn't avoid showing their position to us as well as to the Americans." He glanced at the rev counter, then back to the altimeter—ten meters. "Whoever it was, Colonel, we have them."

"Then why fire them fifty meters apart," countered Saburov, "instead of one right after the other?"

The lieutenant pressed the green Go button and compensated for the weight loss as the four marines dropped like falling shadows into the bright white cone. As the HIP swung about, starting to climb higher, the circle of light from its searchlight grew bigger but weaker, more than twenty meters wide, sweeping over the grass toward the cliff.

"WHAT ARE YOU GOING to do?" asked Jamie.

Instinctively, Frank reduced speed, moving in closer to the island, while considering the options. Jamie edged forward from the stern. "If you're right about that mother ship not being kosher, Frank, this signal could be a goddamn trap!"

"Maybe . . . I don't think so."

"So tell me why?"

"Don't think anyone on the Polish ship's after us. Not yet." He pulled the steering wheel hard. The raft lifted, then slid sideways over a massive swell. "Look," he continued. "That mother ship must have seen us shove off from *Petrel*, or picked us up on the way toward the island. They could have sent that chopper over and capsized us. Strong down draft from the rotors in this heavy chuck would do it easy. No, whoever's sending up the fireworks isn't from the mother ship. Whoever it is must trust us."

"What I'm trying to figure out is what the chopper's going to do."

"Meanwhile we're heading south," said Jamie, his tone one of implied criticism.

"You got any better ideas?" asked Frank.

"Yeah, get out from the coast a bit more. Uncharted reefs all around this island. We're in too close." He indicated the towering black cliffs before them, as if they were where the world ended.

"Don't sweat it, Jamie. I can smell a reef."

"Bullshit!"

"Serious," replied Frank. "You can smell the algae that're close to the surface."

"What if the wind's behind you?" Byrne put in shrewdly.

Frank gave a smile of admiration. "Well, I'll tell you, fellas, there's another reason." He pointed toward the rocky bastions curving gradually north to south, sloping down to the southern peninsula before the Pinnacle. "If I hadn't brought us in close we'd be back on the Polish ship's radar. The cliffs act as a shield between us and where she's anchored on the eastern side of the island. If we headed farther out from the coast she could pick us up on her radar. I don't want those jokers to know what Frank Hall and his mountain boys are up to."

"Smart cookie!" commented Jamie.

"But what about the chopper's radar?"

"So long as we're in close," said Frank, "same goes for the chopper. The angle from them to the sea is too acute. Their radar beams can't bend over cliff tops."

Suddenly, a cross wave flooded the Zodiac and they had to grab the gunwale straps for fear of being washed overboard. Byrne, his face chilled by the spray, found it difficult to speak, his question coming out as a mumble, which was just as well, thought Frank, who didn't want Jamie to start worrying again. Frank held the wheel firmly as they slid into an enormous valley of water. When they rode up on the next swell Jamie tapped Frank's arm. "What'd Byrne say?"

Frank caught a whiff of rye on Jamie's breath. "He wanted to know," Frank answered, "what happens if the chopper decides to come over the cliffs and makes a radar sweep."

"Good question," said Jamie.

"Very," said Frank.

Jamie waited for an answer. There was none. "You're a cool bastard, Frank."

"Calculated risk," Frank replied coolly. He jerked his head port aft toward the northern part of the island, at the finger-thick beam of light that hovered for a few minutes here and there, moving frenetically, eerily, like a visitor from another planet, disappearing altogether one minute only to reappear suddenly the next in its relentless probing. "Well, they're still busy," Frank assured Jamie. "It's when we don't see that beam darting all over the place that we'll have to worry."

"It's a gamble," said Jamie.

"So's life," replied Frank.

"I mean we still have a mile to rendezvous with whoever signaled."

Frank said nothing. Jamie had a point. Overcaution always does. It made Frank wonder why Jamie had volunteered if he was so damned scared. He wondered, too, what his, Frank's, opposite number aboard the chopper was like, the man in charge of rescue from the mother ship. Or *was* it rescue?

While the Zodiac's nose swung farther aport, heading toward the southern tip of the island, the three men in the Zodiac could see the Pinnacle sticking up from the sea like a swaying black pyramid. To the north, the beam continued its neurotic dance, and it wasn't until the Zodiac got closer in to the line of surf that Frank saw the beam fused to one spot.

"DOWN THERE!" called the lieutenant. Saburov leaned over, trying to see the beam but was unable to do so without unfastening the window on the right-hand side of the HIP's cockpit and manually readjusting the down-view mirror. The lieutenant, seeing his problem, touched the rudder bar, swiveling the chopper on its axis without significantly shifting the cone of light. It was a good piece of flying, and at the end of it Saburov was able to see clearly; the pilot was pointing to an area a hundred yards to the left. At the edge of the beam something was moving. The lieutenant palmed the searchlight's guide switch, and in another second they had their moving target dead center, bent over as if whoever it was thought that by hiding their face they could somehow avoid detection from the helicopter. It was, even Saburov thought, a pathetically hopeless gesture, as futile, he recalled, as the first Afghan tribesman he'd seen trying to fight a modern war with prayers and antiquated rifles.

Amid the controlled danger of the HIP hovering ten feet above the ground, unwilling to risk its twenty thousand pounds sinking into the spongy ground, the lieutenant kept his craft as steady as he could under the fierce vibration of the twin Isotov turboshafts. The shadows of two marines knifed the virgin-white circle of light as they dropped from the helicopter's rear cargo door. As they moved forward to the hunched figure, their Kalashnikovs unslung for action, the HIP rose suddenly to expand the marines' field of vision. Saburov knew it was against normal jump drop procedure to be exposing his troops to line of fire in the searchlight, but he was unwilling to kill the light and risk losing his target.

Then something happened that Saburov, with all his experience, had never seen before. He'd watched as targets actually disintegrated in high-velocity machine gun fire, but except for a small child in Kurdistan, the colonel had never seen a target literally blown away in the fierce wash of the helicopter rotors. But that was exactly what he saw happening now, as the first marine neared the figure. Of course, a second later he and the pilot and the two marines on the ground realized they had been *odurachen*, an old expression meaning "to be misled" or, more commonly, to be suckered, to be made a fool of. The parka, a woman's, already wind-bloated, given extra push by the blow from the screaming rotors, had quite literally been blown away into the darkness. The longer and better pair of grass-stuffed rain pants remained, however, shaking violently, comically, under joint assault from storm wind and chopper down-blast, the long blades of sword grass that had filled the parka now flattened against the ground.

"Shit!" It was the pilot, full of surprise.

Saburov said nothing for a few seconds, and when he did speak his voice was terse, ice-cold and unamused. "Bring them back up!" he said.

The rope ladder was lowered for the marines to rejoin their comrades. "The bitch is buying time," snapped Saburov. "To meet up with the Americans."

The lieutenant flicked off the searchlight, took the HIP higher, waiting for the colonel's next order. "She has to be on the western side of the island," he suggested.

Saburov looked, or rather stared, as if he had only just become aware of the other's presence. "Really, Comrade?" The sarcasm made the other blush. Saburov turned away, his mood of humiliating disappointment pervading the cockpit. He knew they could search the island all night and not find anyone, the waist-high grass making for perfect cover. Angry with himself for being tricked by an am-

ateur, yet at the same time not knowing how he might have
prevented it, he was most bitter because he'd been outwitted by a woman. He hated her type very deeply, the kind
whose independence both frightened and excited him.
More than that, he was angry with himself for becoming
angry, for not controlling his emotions as he had been
taught so often during training in the Leningrad academy.
Such behavior blinded you to logic. Even the time he'd
taken in venting his humiliation on the hapless lieutenant
meant valuable time lost from the job at hand, which was
to find the woman and the Mexican, to silence them, ex-
terminate them as enemies of the party—and of his own
advancement.

"The Mexican!" he said suddenly. "That was my mistake, Comrade. She won't leave without the Mexican."

"But," began the pilot and stopped. Why the hell
should he get himself into more... He hesitated.

"No, go on," Saburov said, his tone markedly conciliatory. "Go on. I apologize for my behavior."

"Well, Colonel, you said the two flares were fired a distance apart. Might not the Mexican be with her?"

"Perhaps..."

"At least," continued the pilot, encouraged by Saburov's apology, "if we search the Pinnacle and he is not
there, we'll be able to concentrate all the marines on the
island and..."

"Agreed," said Saburov impatiently, already figuring
out the logistics of using his twelve marines most effectively to capture the two in the twenty-six hours remaining
before the ship had to sail, before the lull in the storm line
that would mean the weather would clear enough for the
mother ship to be spotted on long distance radar or by
satellite. Yet how to flush them out? He thought hard, then
began nodding to himself. "Yes, that's it, Comrade." His
smile gave way to a chuckle of satisfaction. "The fools,"
he said, laughing. "They've unwittingly provided me with
the perfect strategy."

"Who?" asked the pilot, not sure he understood.

"The Americans," answered Saburov. "The fools from *Petrel* coming in so bravely to the rescue—or so they think."

"But sir," began the pilot, puzzled by Saburov's air of self-congratulation, "I still can't see—"

"Don't worry," Saburov cut in. "Just do as I tell you. First, pick up the four marines we put down earlier when we saw the flares."

The lieutenant shrugged as he put the HIP into a sharp turn. Saburov adjusted his co-pilot's seat to the reclining position, looking ahead into the wild night, barely able to contain his excitement. "Comrade," he said effusively. "Trust me. I am about to astound you."

Chapter Twenty-One

NOTHING HAD BEEN SEEN of another signal from the cliffs for half an hour. Frank was afraid that whoever had warned them of danger was either so exhausted that they couldn't make it two miles down the coast, or had, for some as yet unknown reason, run afoul of the chopper from the Polish ship.

"Can't wait here all night," said Jamie. "Coupla hours it'll be dawn. We'll be sitting ducks if there's something screwy with those Poles." He paused, then added, "I don't like it. Not one friggin' bit."

"None of us does," answered Frank, wondering again why the hell Jamie had volunteered if that was the way he felt. Probably, Frank thought, because he was paid, or rather wouldn't be if he didn't keep tabs on the competition. Or maybe he had been stoned when he volunteered.

If so, the storm's blow and the open boat were rapidly sobering him up.

"There's a break in that cliff," Byrne called out. "A point off the port quarter. We could shelter in there."

Frank saw the dark indentation a quarter mile off—a long fissure running all the way up a massive moon-polished rock face to about 150 feet above the sea. The wider base of the cliff boiled white every time several waves' backwash ganged up together to charge against the cliff, after which a cascade of foam could be seen spilling back into the sea, lasting at least ten seconds. This told him there must be a ledge of some kind, a rock skirting that might be used to beach the Zodiac—if he was fast enough between succeeding waves.

"Think we can do it?" asked Jamie, trying not to let his anxiety show.

"She'll be right," answered Frank, realizing once more he was using one of Aussie's expressions. Aussie had confessed that it used to traumatize visiting American executives because it usually meant everything wasn't all right, that in fact there might be nothing but trouble ahead.

Frank was aligning the Zodiac's bow with the long V-shaped cleft when Jamie turned so suddenly that Frank felt the boat's center of gravity abruptly shifting. "Watch it, Jamie. You almost—"

Frank couldn't hear Jamie above the head wind whistling in and around the cliffs, but he knew what his action meant when he, too, saw the weak yellow light winking from the cliff tops, about a quarter mile south of the cleft the Zodiac was heading for.

"Says L-A-N-D-H-E-R-E," called Byrne. "Must be a better landing spot down there we can't see."

"Tough tit," replied Frank. "We're going in here."

"Why the hell—" began Jamie.

"Because," Frank interjected, "we've no way of knowing who that is signaling us."

"We never knew that before," insisted Jamie.

"I know," agreed Frank, lowering the revs, allowing for the strength of the cross rips closer in. "So why walk into a trap?"

"What the hell you gettin' at?" Jamie called angrily.

"What I'm getting at, Jamie, is that we don't know if it's the same person signaling us now as before. Not since that helicopter's been flitting around."

"Jesus, you're a suspicious bastard!"

"I'm still alive, too," answered Frank, watching the cliff like a dark razor slash looming up five hundred yards dead ahead, its width increasing by the minute. He called out to Byrne. "I want you to take the painter. Okay?"

Without protest, Jamie crawled aft near the food and water pockets, relieved that someone else would have the unenviable job of jumping ashore with the painter, steadying the Zodiac until they disembarked.

"You go in after Byrne, okay?"

Jamie nodded. He didn't know whether to show gratitude or, as bosun's mate, to be insulted at not being entrusted with the task.

"Give Byrne a bit of experience," Frank told him, trying to be diplomatic. Jamie opted for insult, saying nothing.

"I'll go up the cleft," Frank called out to the other two, "and check things out. Give me half an hour maximum. If anything happens, if I'm not back by then, sit tight and wait it out till *Petrel* turns up. Okay?"

No one answered.

"What if you do walk into a trap?" asked Byrne.

"No sense in all of us getting caught. Right?"

Now the surf was all about them, rushing at them in a confusion of wave upon wave. Suddenly the wide sea had narrowed to a small, rock-strewn bay so wild with wind and raging water that Frank's answer was lost, carried swiftly away in a high wall of spray, the cliff rocking precariously toward them.

THE MOMENT the fourth marine was hoisted aboard in the blinding glare of the searchlight—making nine altogether aboard the HIP and three still searching the northern part of the island—the HIP banked sharply, heading south for the Pinnacle.

PAUSING FOR BREATH, Frank looked up through the chimney of the cleft at the moon-shredded night, hearing the steady throbbing of the helicopter overhead. The grappling hook was ice-cold against him as he waited to hear if the heavy pulsating sound would pass over him. Soon all he could hear was the pounding of surf below in the small, rocky bay where the Zodiac was beached, and thousands of seabirds protesting the invasion of their domain.

"REMEMBER," Saburov told the marines over the cockpit-cabin intercom. "Afghan hill drill. Three of you start working your way down from the top of the big rock, the other six moving up from the base. Divide each circle around the rock into equal segments—both your teams should meet about halfway."

"*Should* meet!" said one of the marines.

"Once you pick up the Mexican," Saburov continued, "find out what you can from him before you shoot him. But don't waste time if he won't talk. You'll only have twelve hours of daylight. Radio the ship as soon as you're done and we'll send back the HIP."

"Simple," said the same man. "Sounds like a picnic in Gorky Park."

"Yeah," called another. "This Mexican bastard could be anywhere on that pile of birdshit."

"If you ask me," said another marine, "I don't think the bastard is there."

"How would you know, Penkovsky? You're too busy tugging yourself off."

The others laughed but Penkovsky wouldn't be silenced. "Well, what would you do if you thought someone was after you?"

"Me?" asked the man next to him, a tall Georgian, famed in the Moscow Spetsnaz brigade as the most punished private in the Soviet version of boot camp but valued for his prowess as a sharpshooter and for his staying power over the grueling mountain obstacle camp in the Caucasus. "I'd get off that fucking rock as soon as I could."

"Exactly," said Penkovsky. "That's my point."

"Only trouble with your theory, Comrade, is that it's all bullshit. The Chinaman—"

"Mexican, you idiot!" someone interjected.

"Mexican...Chinaman...what's the fucking difference? We're going to shoot the prick, aren't we? Anyway, Penkovsky's still full of shit. The Chinaman doesn't know we're after him. Not like that bitch that got away from Saburov."

"Yeah," said a private with a leer. "She's the one I'd like to find."

"You wouldn't know what to do with her," said Penkovsky. "Probably put it in her ear." The others guffawed.

"Yes, I would," said the soldier.

"Don't worry about it, Dmitry," said the tall Georgian. "I'll show you where to stick it."

"Better not let Saburov hear you talking like that," advised the corporal.

"Yeah," said Penkovsky disdainfully. "He's a real *babushka*, all right." He used the Russian term for grandmother. "You know what political officers are like—purer than the dirty masses."

"Until they get a bit of cunt themselves," cut in the Georgian. "He's no better than the rest of us. You saw what he did to that woman in Kabul—a bayonet through

the guts. Six months big with a kid. Don't tell me about
Saburov.''

"You'd have done the same thing,'' said the corporal.

"We *know* that,'' said the Georgian despairingly. "Orders are fucking orders. That's what I'm saying. He's no
better than anyone else.''

"Not saying he is,'' replied the corporal. "But he
doesn't like any talk about sex. You'll end up on defaulters' parade if he hears you.''

The Georgian remained contemptuous. "Saburov's the
one who'll end up on defaulters', Comrade, if he doesn't
get this bit of American pussy and fix it like we did the
professor.''

"What d'you mean?'' asked the corporal, always aware
that his own career in the Soviets' special forces was as
inextricably linked to the success of his political officer as
it was by his own performance in the field.

"Well,'' the Georgian began, his tone not as cocky as he
saw the others looking away from him, sensing the danger
he was getting himself into, the kind that could get a man
posted to the Sino-Soviet border.

"Go on,'' pressed the corporal, sensing the Georgian's
sudden and uncharacteristic reluctance. "C'mon, let's hear
it or are you too—''

"All right, Comrade. If Moscow thinks a word of this
has leaked, friend Saburov is in for the high jump, isn't he?
Moscow'll cut off his balls and then some.''

The corporal affected innocence. "If a word of what
leaks out?''

"You know. Don't pretend you don't—''

"No, I don't,'' said the corporal. "If *what* gets out?''

The Georgian fell silent, the only sound that of the rotors slicing the cold air and the whine of the turbo fans.

The corporal, looking puzzled, leaned forward on his
Kalashnikov, his eyes moving up and down the two lines of
marines. "Anyone else know what he's talking about?''

No one answered. It was a political question.

"Come on, Comrade," pressed the corporal, sitting back and addressing the Georgian. "Let's have it."

"Well, fuck," said the Georgian, anger trying to roll over his fear. "I mean, it's no secret on the ship, is it?" He glanced around at the other eight for support. There was none forthcoming. He knew they would back him in a firefight, sticking with him to the very end, but not now. From childhood they had understood that the party was holy and that to know more than one should was dangerous, doubly so in the armed forces, more so still in the special forces. To be "political" was to walk the high wire above oblivion. It might well be common knowledge aboard the ship, as he claimed, but it was a state secret he was alluding to and everyone on the ship knew it was a secret and that Moscow would swat him, Saburov and anyone else who spoke of it. Perhaps, the Georgian thought, the corporal was KGB—or GRU or—

"Red light!" said Penkovsky.

"Stand up!" ordered the corporal. "Sling your weapons!" So saying, he slid open the rear cargo door. The icy slipstream whipped the marines' breath away as they shuffled unhurriedly toward the howling blackness above the great pinnacle of rock. For a moment young Penkovsky felt sorry for the Mexican whom they would start searching for in the dawn's early light. But then he remembered what he had been taught at the Moscow camp— it was either you or him. Besides, Colonel Saburov was right. So long as there was the slightest possibility that the foreigners had seen anything, they had to be eliminated as enemies of the state. Anyway, it was their own fault for being there in the first place.

The spotlight turned night into day as the Pinnacle's sharp summit appeared twenty feet below, so pointed, its craggy sides falling away precipitously into the darkness below to its quarter-mile-wide base. If a man didn't watch each step he'd be a goner. There'd be no jumping from the helicopter here—it would be a rope ladder all the way for the three marines landing on the summit.

The cockpit door opened and in its shaft of red light Saburov appeared, his hand sliding along the hold bar with the nonchalant confidence of a man who had overseen so many of what the Americans called search-and-destroy missions that they no longer held any surprises for him. Nevertheless, as political officer for the mother ship's whole operation, it was his duty to keep up morale, important to have the small contingent of marines feel part of the ship. Besides, if they didn't get the Mexican and the girl, Saburov knew *he* would take the heat. The knowledge that Novisk, as master of the mother ship, would suffer equally from his bosses in Gdansk or that Kornon would be just as ruthlessly punished by his enemies in the Politburo gave Saburov no comfort. It would mean the end of his dreams of retirement in Moscow and instead freezing in the perpetual permafrost of northern Siberia. Gripping the overhead bar, the HIP buffeted by high winds, he patted the corporal on the shoulder. "Don't take long. There's not much time."

"I understand, Colonel. We'll get him."

Saburov nodded. "Of course." The HIP steadier now, he relaxed his grip, moving back toward the cockpit as the green Go light came on.

Crouching in the clusters of outcrops around the Pinnacle, the two marine teams watched the HIP rising above them, the beam of its belly light rocking crazily over the rock like some huge Chinese lantern bobbing around. Then it was gone, the blips of its red and green navigational lights growing more visible to them as their eyes adjusted from the glare to the predawn darkness. The HIP headed out to where the mother ship lay at anchor a mile away, using the southern part of the island and the Pinnacle as windbreaks during the storm line. One of the three marines gagged and threw up. The stench of bird excrement was so overpowering that even his two comrades found it difficult to breathe.

"Shit!" said one marine in a hoarse whisper. "Don't know how they stand it."

"Who?"

"The silly bastards we're looking for."

"They like birds," said the other.

"Well, they're fucking lunatics. It's worse here than on the island."

"Keep it down," ordered the corporal.

"What for?" asked one of the two privates. "You think he didn't hear the chopper?"

It was the corporal's first assignment as a noncommissioned officer and the others resented his acting like a *babushka*, the weeks at sea having taken their usual toll on discipline. The corporal refused to be drawn in by his comrade's minor insubordination. Better, he thought, for the private to let off steam, then he'd settle down for the hour-long wait till first light when they could all start to move in on the Mexican.

The corporal received another blast of guano odor in his face as eddies of wind shifted about the summit, and he uttered an ancient Tartar oath and spit leeward, willing the dawn to hurry. The quicker they did away with the Mexican the sooner they'd be on their way off this shit pile. His only consolation was that bumping off the Mexican should be easy. Saburov had told them that because the flare had come from the Pinnacle, the most inaccessible part of the island, it meant there was a good chance that whoever fired it was injured, unable to make it to the island proper, and so would probably offer little resistance.

Chapter Twenty-Two

USING HIS FEET to push hard against one wall of the cleft, his back against the other, Frank inched his way toward the top of the chimney. Smaller fissures running off from the main shaft, weeping with moisture that soaked his toque, formed cobweb formations that he could not see but only feel. His legs and arms, aching from the effort, inched him up toward the moonlight that etched the jagged top of the chimney against a curdling sky of nimbostratus and low cumulus. By the time he reached the top and thrust the grappling hook over the edge, the sleeves of his survival suit were sodden with bird excrement, made softer by seepage from the rock. The stench of guano had been so overpowering in the narrow cleft that it was a great relief to find himself over the serrated edge of the top of the cleft, immediately blasted by a cold but invigorating south wind.

He lay there, catching his breath and listened for the sound of the helicopter. It was only when he got up that he saw its red and green pinpoints of light blinking several miles northeast of him, moving toward the island from what he assumed must be the huge mother ship hiding at anchor. The moon slid from behind torn veils of stratus, the island's long eastern coast showing up in a silhouette just as rugged as the western side, at once beautiful and frightening in its sudden and dramatic aspect. Treeless and windblown, the northern part of the island disappeared under a congestion of low brooding stratus, chased by the southern wind, while to the south the big Pinnacle thrust itself defiantly up from the sea, its stunning sharpness emphasized more than usual in an eerie wash of moonlight passing quickly over it like a silver cape.

Frank waited another ten minutes before he managed to see the tiny yellow light pricking the darkness again, not far to the south of him. The Morse code was still poor, but all the more entreating for that as it asked him to land on the coast where the light was blinking. For a moment he felt absolutely sure it wasn't a trap, but the very strength of his conviction made him uneasy as he started for the light, which he estimated was a half mile down the coast. After all, anyone could fake clumsy signaling.

HEARING THE HELICOPTER approaching, Gloria had crawled into the cover of sword grass growing right to the cliff's edge. Clothed only in her retrieved sodden sweater and jeans, she was shivering despite the frantic run she had made down the island during the time Saburov and his lot had been successfully distracted by the flare she had set off. Perspiration had now turned almost to ice, and she feared that if the party from the American ship did not land soon and get her into warm, dry clothing she would go into hypothermia, the shivering would stop, and the fatal sleep would overtake her.

When the roar of the helicopter rolled over her in a steady thunder her heart pounded so hard she could hear the blood rushing in her ears like a train, so loud in fact that for a terrifying second she was sure the chopper was coming down, that Saburov and his men were about to capture her. When she got up and looked out to sea every whitecap in the stygian blackness seemed to be the small boat she had signaled to from the cliff tops. But there had been no response to her last signal and she was afraid that it could have been picked up by the marines who, Gloria assumed, must still be coming down the island after having landed and searched the area near the survival shack. Then, seeing the helicopter a mile south, its lone evil white eye hovering over the Pinnacle, she was at the same time struck with cold fear and guiltily relieved they had passed over her. If nothing else, she told herself, it must mean that no one on the helicopter had seen her signaling. But why hadn't the American rescue boat seen her?

Scanning the sea once more she tried to put Julio's fate
out of her mind; perhaps they would only take him prisoner. Then to the east—or was it her imagination?—the
darkness seemed to be giving way to the first sliver of
dawn. She tried to remember exactly when first light came
on the island but couldn't recall, as she had never been up
this early. In fact, recalling the events of the past twenty-
four hours was all she could do with any clarity. The rage
of the squall, the terror of the Russian marine coming
down from the survival hut right behind her, the look on
Charles's face the instant before she escaped from the helicopter—all this had been etched in her mind from the
moment Saburov's smiling face had looked down at her
from the huge gray copter as it had winched her up into its
dark interior.

She kept stamping her legs and rubbing her arms to keep
her circulation going, longing for sleep, food and warmth,
for a glimpse of light piercing the sea to tell her that those
responding to the distress call would suddenly appear below on the small pebble beach accessible from the cliff top,
though barely wide enough for a boat to enter.

The moon slipped in and out of the stratus that was
moving moodily northwestward, and in the platinum sheen
it cast over the sea, Gloria could see and hear the pebbled
beach below, its rounded stones hissing in the bubbling
cream of the surf. But still there was no boat. She lifted the
flashlight and signaled again, her hands trembling so much
from cold and fear that she was sure the Morse must appear horribly disjointed. If they did not come soon, before dawn, it would be too late for her and, she knew, too
late to try to help Julio trapped on the Pinnacle. She knew
the quickest way across the funnel and . . .

She started to cry. How could she alone bring Julio off,
confronted as they would be by the soldiers she'd seen
lowered at the summit and base? Yet how could she leave
him, abandoning him to certain death?

There was a noise, off to her right, near the edge of the cliff, a hundred yards or so. It must be one of the marines dropped near the shack. She knew now she should have waited and not signaled out to sea again. She looked around for something to defend herself with, but there was nothing. Quietly yet quickly she opened the flap of her haversack, reaching in for the small pocket camping knife, but all she could feel were wet foil packages of dried food and a water flask. She heard the sound again and frantically searched for the knife, found it and opened the blade. She saw the silhouette of a man running toward her, about fifty yards away. Dropping to the ground she scurried into the tussocks of sword grass, stopping a short way from where she had last signaled. Lying perfectly still, biting her wrist to muffle the sound of her breathing, she could hear nothing but the faint murmuring of the shingled beach below, realizing she must be very close to the cliff's edge, or on an overhang above the beach itself.

She lay there for five minutes before she heard footsteps again, then she saw a flashlight bobbing above the sea of grass, moving away from her at first, then back toward the cliff, stopping, then moving away again. Her heart nearly jumping out of her chest, she fought the urge to scream, to have an end to it, to at least be freed from running until she could run no more. It might even be one of the Americans. Surely they must have seen her last signal and had landed somewhere farther up the coast? But then why hadn't they responded to her signal, unless—

Oh my God, she thought, unless they had thought it was some kind of trap, like the one she and Charles had so foolishly fallen into. She hardly dared breathe, think, do anything as the light began bobbing again not more than ten feet away.

It went off. She heard a rustle of grass snaking toward her but it wasn't the sound of footsteps. It was someone crawling through the undergrowth, coming after her. She broke cover and ran, stumbling, up and running again, the wind whistling about her ears, her body stiff and chilled but moving as fast as she was able. The moon sailed majestically out of the stratus and cast the grassy sea around the cliffs in a pool of light. She heard a yell, swung hard left, the air exploding about her. The moon disappeared again and all was suddenly blackness.

Gloria fell, got up, ran south in the direction of the Pinnacle, now a smudge in a light rain that was sweeping in from the sea. The footsteps were gaining, but now there were two of them chasing her, one on either side, one yelling in what sounded like Russian, the other grunting. The tussocks of grass were black lumps speeding by her, trying to entangle her, slow her down. She stumbled headlong into a muddy depression, was up and running again, hearing one of them closing in, his breath shunting like a locomotive, louder and louder. And then she crumpled, a huge weight crashed down on her, driving her into the ground. The second one's footsteps came in from her right. She lay there, unable to move, not wanting to face the larger terror of her capture.

She felt the man's hand roll her over. He was staring down at her, barely out of breath, it seemed, his chest heaving nevertheless, grinning over her triumphantly while calling out in Russian to the other man. The latter, too tired to answer, had stopped running and was now about twenty yards away, slumping to a walk and waving in a desultory manner while he paused for air, spit loudly, then resumed walking. Gloria saw the one bending over her slip some kind of catch on his telescopic rifle, take off his pack and bayonet, lay the rifle down on it, its muzzle on his pack, facing away from them. Without taking his eyes off her he began unbuckling his belt. She held her breath, her throat too tight to utter a sound as he watched her watching him, his face macabre under the helmet and camouflage. Grabbing her long hair he jerked her whole body forward to a sitting position and called out to the other man. Again there was an obscene grunt and a disgusting, animallike spitting noise.

Leaning over her, the marine tied her hands tightly with the belt. For a moment she thought he was tying her up to take her back to Saburov and it gave her a glimmer of hope, but then he lowered her again on the rough grass, flat on her back, her hands tied behind her. She tried to swallow but couldn't. He laughed as, her eyes shining with fear, she tried desperately to move back, away from him. He took off his helmet, unbuttoned his rain cape, then unzipped his fly. His hand went inside then came out.

"No," she pleaded. "No, please. I'll . . . no . . . no . . ."

He knelt down, slipping his hands beneath her sodden blouse, cupping and squeezing her breasts. She pushed herself back as hard as she could. He laughed, dragging her to him, then, clenching his teeth, tore off her jeans, throwing them aside, and drew his knife.

Gloria gave out a stifled scream. He slipped the knife up inside her panties and she froze, the steel blade razor-sharp, icy against her flesh. Laughing at her fear, he slit the panties' elastic, then gripping her thighs, pried them apart. His body arched over hers. She could smell his sour breath drowning hers and his hard body pressing unrelentingly down on hers. With all the strength she had remaining she rolled to one side, shoving her knee hard into his groin. He let out an oath, smacked her hard, back and forth across the face, calling out to his comrade a few yards off. Gloria saw the other man still hunched over but now silhouetted in moonlight. He had no helmet.

In an instant, the marine rolled off her, scrambling frantically for the gun, the other man running flat out straight at him. The marine flipped off the safety, the gun leaping to his side. Gloria saw the other man's foot come up fast, knocking the rifle as it fired, simultaneously bringing down some kind of club. The marine slumped forward into the grass and lay still, a grappling hook embedded in his head, blood gushing from a gaping hole in his forehead.

"You all right?" Frank asked her.

Still recovering from the speed and shock of Frank's attack, she couldn't find the words.

Frank leaned over and she felt one strong, warm hand effortlessly hoisting her to her feet while the other moved quickly behind her to untie the belt. Then he handed her the crumpled pile of her jeans and slashed underwear.

"Sorry I took so long, but for a while there I thought he was the one signaling to us, until I saw you running. I was out of gas, too," he added, turning his back, giving her time to dress as much as she could and recover some sort of composure. "I was a bit winded after coming up the cliff."

"You're . . . you're from . . . the American ship. . . ."

"*Petrel*," he said. "Yes. But we weren't sure if your signal—wait a minute, it *was* you signaling us?"

"Yes," she said, only now noticing he was wearing some kind of survival suit. "I—my name's Gloria. Gloria Bernardi."

"Frank Hall. I'm an oceanographer doing research work off *Petrel*. But never mind all that. We've got to get you off this place right now. There has to be more than one guy looking for you."

"There are. I—I don't know where to begin . . . I mean how to tell you what—"

"That can wait till later. Right now, we need to get you back to our Zodiac. We've got her beached at the base of a cleft about a half mile up the coast. We can hide out there until *Petrel* comes back—be about ten hours. Won't be very comfortable down by that surf, but it'll be better than being taken by this outfit." He glanced down at the dead marine.

There were so many things she wanted to tell him, explain, thank him for. She wanted to ask him where *Petrel* was, but all she could say, standing there shivering, was, "We can't."

"Can't what?" He pulled her down as the moonlight reappeared more brightly, making them visible to anyone who might be searching nearby. Frank began unzipping his survival suit. For a moment she was terrified. My God, now *he* was going to... She recoiled.

"No, no," said Frank, grabbing her, reading her thoughts. "No...look, you're freezing. Clothes are soaking wet. You put on the survival jacket or you'll be in real trouble." He glanced down at the marine. "I'll wear this creep's gear. Turn around." When she did so she could hear him rolling over the marine, the grappling hook clanking against the dead man's helmet. Ahead she could see the sharp peak of the Pinnacle touched by moonlight.

"What did you mean," he asked her, "when you said, 'We can't'? Can't what?"

"We can't go without Julio." She didn't want to say it but she knew just as certainly that she had to, that Julio wouldn't leave her, or anybody, for no matter how strong the temptation, you didn't leave your friends in the lurch.

"Who's Julio? Where is he?" asked Frank. "Look, Miss..."

"Bernardi. Gloria. He's a friend. He's on that rock."

Frank was zipping up the marine's trousers—right gut size, thirty-four, he thought, but too tight in the crotch. "On that rock," he said, touching her on the shoulder, handing her the survival suit, then walking away so that his back was to her as she stripped and slipped into the warmth of the suit.

"Yes," she explained. "The big rock at the tip of the island. It's called the Pinnacle."

"Yes, I know. Our mate thought that's where he saw the first flare come from."

"Yes," she cut in. "Julio must be hurt, otherwise he would've tried to get off."

She was standing beside him now, and in the pale wash of the moonlight he noticed for the first time just how beautiful she was. Gloria told him about seeing the marines disgorged onto the Pinnacle by the helicopter.

"How many?" he asked.

"Three at the top, I think—six below."

"Gloria," he began, as gently as he could, "I don't mind having a crack at it, but that's one hell of a big rock for even two of us to cover. First we'd have to get across the channel separating it from the main island. And if we did get across unnoticed, we don't know where he is. We're as likely to bump into more of these goons." He indicated the body of the marine, lying on his back, staring at the moon as it sailed into a gradually lightening sky.

"I know," she said, biting her lip, knowing she was hoping against all odds, knowing she had no right to ask any more of this stranger who had already risked his life and those of his friends, first in braving the storm line's dangerous seas, then in the climb up the rain-slicked cliff, and finally but not least, in saving her in the near-fatal, cat-and-mouse game he'd played with the heavily armed marine. "I'm sorry," she said, her words strangled by the overwhelming reality, the hopelessness of Julio's position; surrounded by the marines, he was bound to be discovered at first light. They would kill him as surely as they—

She gasped in fright, suddenly realizing that the man who had come ashore below the survival shack must have been aboard the Zodiac. "Did one of your..." she began, afraid to go on.

Frank swung around, wrenching her to the ground.

"What—" she began.

He put his hand across her mouth, his eyes searching for what he thought was another marine moving about. It was a tussock of grass bending in the night wind.

She gripped his arm tightly. "Did you..." she began hoarsely, "did one of your men land below the hut?"

"Yes," said Frank. "It was the mate's job to check out the hut. We'll go back and pick him up when—"

"Oh, my God." She told him of Saburov, of her escape from the helicopter, of seeing the Zodiac's spotlight offshore, of how she had gone down the path, a man calling out, asking if anyone was there, of how she'd heard the footsteps behind her, the huge marine passing her as she hid by the path, of how she'd shouted her warning to the American who had called out, and the bone-splitting sound when the marine hit him, of her running in panic up the path.

When she finished telling it she was in tears, leaning against him. He held her. For a moment the rage in him threatened to explode, but he held it in check, willing instead to *do* something more than merely voice outrage against the mate's murder. He could feel her body shaking against his.

"And . . . now," she began, "Julio. . ." She sat up, wiping her eyes. "I'm sorry. I didn't mean to. . ."

"How many did you say?" asked Frank. "On that rock? The Pinnacle?"

"Nine," she said, trying to compose herself, concerned that he might think she was trying to manipulate him into a suicidal attempt upon the Pinnacle instead of merely explaining to him what had happened.

"What the hell are they after?" Frank cut in. "This goon in the helicopter—what did you say his name is? Sak—?"

"Saburov."

"Saburov," Frank continued. "The bastard's out of control. If he's killed the mate, taken away the professor. . ." Frank was also remembering the Beechcraft exploding, *Lvov*'s Mayday, the name of U.S. *Swiftsure* on a life raft that should have had the name of the Polish trawler on it and Aussie murdered. "What the hell is this Saburov trying to do? Kill anyone who gets anywhere near his mother ship, the island, what?"

"It seems like it," she said. "If he killed the professor...the mate from your ship as well."

Frank suddenly saw a connection between Aussie, sea gold and Saburov. "Son of a bitch!"

Before she could say anything, Gloria saw Frank swing around her, sudden understanding replacing his look of perplexity of moments before. "Sea gold!" he said. "That's it!"

"I don't understand."

In a rush he remembered how the first station, only a few miles from Eagle Island, had yielded evidence of metalliferous muds. "Mineral deposits," he explained quickly. "The island must be a massive deposit of rich minerals." He raced on, caught up in the excitement of his discovery. "You see, some islands, in fact a lot of islands, used to be below the sea. Massive deposits of rock and minerals born under the sea were spewed out by volcanic upthrusting through vents that cooled off millions of years ago. When the level of the sea fell, the islands, like a lot of our coastal areas and some of our deserts, rose...or more accurately were left high and dry. Eagle Island must be stinking rich in deposits. That bastard Klaus *is* mixed up in this. I *knew* it. I could *smell* it!" He paused. "Ever since that night Aussie—"

Suddenly he stopped, realizing that his mention of Klaus, Aussie, all this, couldn't be making much sense to Gloria. "Look, what I'm saying is that a big Swiss multinational and Saburov's outfit—my guess is the Russians, maybe the Poles—are onto a big find, something so big they don't want anyone else to stake a claim or, worse still for them, to start mining operations on the island before they can take it out themselves."

"But how would anyone else know?" asked Gloria. "I mean how could *we* find out? Charles, Julio and me? We're biologists. None of us are trained in geology or anything. All we're here for is to study birds. And the mate from your ship—"

"I know," Frank interjected. "So that can only mean that somewhere on this godforsaken place—yes, by God, that explains the helicopter! They've been doing magnetometer runs back and forth over the island, registering changes in the magnetic field. Prospecting."

"But wouldn't there have to be something for us to actually see, for Saburov to be so—"

"That's just what I'm saying," said Frank. "Somewhere on the island they've set up some kind of drilling equipment or maybe recorder transmitters to keep sending out readings of the magnetics, soil conditions, that they can then pick up and monitor through their fishing fleets." He paused. "But *where*, dammit? That's the question. If you've been crawling all over the island and haven't seen any sort of equipment set up, then it must be—"

"On the Pinnacle!" said Gloria excitedly, anticipating him, a shiver of fear passing through her the moment she said it, realizing the terrible danger Julio had unwittingly brought down on himself.

"No," said Frank without hesitation. "No, you said they picked you up on the island, not the Pinnacle."

"Yes, but for all they know, the professor and I could have been on the Pinnacle days before."

"But the mate," said Frank. "He'd never been on the Pinnacle and there was no indication that he was going to be. Yet you said they killed him the moment he stepped ashore?"

"Yes. But they would have been afraid of what I might have told him. At the very least I would have told him about them trying to kill me. They wouldn't want that to get out, to draw attention to their ship."

"Makes sense. But look, they couldn't have set up any equipment on the island out in the open where anyone might stumble across it. It has to be somewhere not exposed, somewhere under good cover from wind and rain and—"

"It wasn't the survival shack," she said. "I can tell you that."

"Wait a minute. On the chart aboard *Petrel* I saw—"

Gloria beat him to it again, but he had opened the door for her. "There's an abandoned hut," she said, "from World War II, an old cement supply depot, I think. And some foundations."

"Have you been there?"

"No," she said. "Well, not inside. I mean there are thousands of birds nesting. It's a long hut, but we were only interested in the albatross that nest in the sword grass. Anyway, the place probably stinks to high heaven."

"Perfect!" he said.

She was realizing the full implications of what she had said as Frank bent down and picked up the marine's gun. "So you never went into the hut?"

"No reason to."

"Don't leave anything here," he ordered abruptly. "Pick up your wet clothes and bring them with you. Don't want the bastards to find anything." He snatched up the marine's helmet and cape, slinging the rifle, then kneeling, felt around the body for anything that might have fallen from it. Next he heaved the body over his shoulder, passing the grappling hook and the marine's pack to Gloria. "You manage?" he asked, already moving off.

She stood there, confused. Maybe he'd got mixed up after the fight with the marine. "You're going in the wrong direction," she told him. "You said your raft was back up the coast."

"It is," he said, but he was walking, or rather striding, south toward the old hut and the Pinnacle beyond. "C'mon," he enjoined her. "It'll soon be dawn."

"Frank . . ." she said. "Frank, it's impossible."

The body slung across his neck, its head lolling grotesquely in the moonlight, Frank kept walking south with no way of knowing that his theory was only half-right.

Chapter Twenty-Three

EVERY ONE of the twelve-man Spetsnaz teams had been trained in the use of close- and long-range hand weapons, but as each marine was a designated specialist for any one mission it had fallen to the tall Georgian to operate the infrared, a six-inch-diameter scope that transformed night into half-light. It squatted atop the rifle, short and stubby, out of all proportion to the sleek line of the 7.62 Dragunov. The Georgian sat uncomfortably in a niche of rocks, breathing close to the thick, hooded lens of the scope, fogging it up. Using his square of chamois he wiped off the salt spray that rose now and then from the gap between the Pinnacle and the island's southern tip like steam from a locomotive. Resting the sniper rifle's twenty-four-inch-long barrel on the edge of volcanic rock in front of him, he made another sweep of the rocks above him from left to right.

"Penkovsky!" he spit at the marine nearest him. "Pull your stupid head down!"

"See something?" asked one of the others in the six-man team staking out the monolith's base and waiting for the dawn.

"Yeah," answered the Georgian. "I just saw that American bitch. She's undressing," he went on. "You should see her tits. White as ivory! Swaying like a—"

"Yeah," young Penkovsky cut in, grinning like a schoolboy. "Tell us another one. After that trick she pulled on us with her clothes and the flare, she's not swaying. She must be frozen stiff."

"I'd fuck her anyway," said the Georgian.

Penkovsky, still capable of shock in sexual matters, shook his head and shifted the topic. "The Mexican must be frozen," he said.

"Well, I wouldn't fuck him," said the Georgian. "Besides, I don't think he's on this damned rock."

None of the others asked where he thought the Mexican might be, but the Georgian told them anyway. "I reckon the bastard's crossed over to the main part of the island." With that he turned around and, facing the island, did another sweep with the infrared from the island's rugged west coast cliffs on his left, across the sea of sword grass, to the equally jagged eastern coastline.

"If he left this rock," asked Penkovsky knowingly, "how come he fired the flare from here?"

"Because, you idiot," answered the Georgian, eye still glued to the scope, "the bastard panicked, fired the flare, then realized no boat could land on this stinking rock. That's why."

"Horseshit!" said one of the marines.

"Yeah, horseshit," echoed Penkovsky, though aware he might be pushing the Georgian's temper with such bravado.

But the Georgian said nothing. He thought he'd seen something move, about three hundred meters up from where the island's peninsula ended abruptly about thirty meters above him in the foaming caldron of the gap. The lens was spotting up again with crystals of salt from the high-flung spray, and the trouble was that every time you moved the scope, tiny deposits of salt moved, too, creating the optical illusion that you saw something moving. Pulling out the chamois again from his pocket, he cleaned the lens. He remained convinced that the Mexican kid, "Julio," Saburov had called him, was no longer on the Pinnacle. Once the kid had spotted all the other activity on the island he would have tried to get over the channel. And if he couldn't, if it had been full tide, then the kid was probably so badly smashed up that he'd die of exposure and couldn't possibly wander off and find out the mother ship's secret. Of course, thought the Georgian, Saburov was assuming the kid had found out something before he got to the Pinnacle to band more stupid birds. Political officers always played it safe. Whatever the reason, the fact that the Mexican kid was responsible for his being cramped up here in the bitter cold just before dawn only made the Georgian more determined to find him and finish the little bastard off as quickly as possible, so that they could get back to the warmth and hot tea and vodka aboard ship.

He lifted the rifle once more, this time beginning his sweep from the island's east coast.

Chapter Twenty-Four

ABOARD *PETREL*, now fifty miles westward, Redfern, the dour Scottish second mate, took the Gerber rule and, wedging himself in the corner of the chart room, slid the parallel rule across the Northeast Pacific chart, drawing a thin line from *Petrel*'s present position to the area of the Japanese SOS. "Aboot another eighty miles," he advised Captain Tate, who was busy glancing at the barometer and mumbling worriedly every now and then as he walked back and forth across the bridge, peering out into the rain-swept gloom, one eye on the overhead digital readout and Smith's chronometer, then checking the readout directly on the Arma compass in front of the helmsman, making sure that his ship's heading was kept as steady as the foul weather from an approaching low would allow. In the past fifteen minutes the barometer had fallen another point, and Tate was running his fingers through his thinning gray hair, knowing that the forecasted lull in the storm approaching Eagle Island from the south was about to be knocked for a loop once this blow from the west hit it broadside, whipping up the seas around Eagle Island into renewed frenzy.

"I think we should turn back!" It was Mary Crane, her face half in the darkness of the bridge, half illuminated by the red glow.

The Scottish mate looked up across the chart room at Tate. The captain had stopped his pacing, gripping the gimbals mounting as a wave punched *Petrel* hard amidships.

"It's—it's simply not worth it!" she added.

Immediately Tate tried to play down the danger of what would be a force-ten gale. "Frank and the boys have enough rations, Mrs. Crane, and if they manage to find cover of some kind and..."

She looked at him, puzzled. "You misunderstand me, Captain. I'm not talking about Frank or your 'boys.' I'm only concerned that this so-called SOS may be a fool's errand—a...a hoax even. I think we're wasting our time here when we could be back on our line of stations looking for sea gold and lowering some of the camera equip—"

Her greed made even the Scotsman more dour than usual, and Tate... Tate was so taken aback he had no reply but to resume stalking the bridge, only this time he was mumbling obscenities audible only to the helmsman, who just then was fighting a losing battle with the storm.

"Well?" pressed Mary Crane. "Do we go back now or not?"

Tate swung around from the starboard wing so fast, the helmsman was startled. "Mrs. Crane, we have no option but to go on. It could be us out there."

"Then why haven't they radioed their position again? If someone's really in trouble? Surely—"

"That's just the point, ma'am," Redfern cut in. "The fact that we've no' heard a whisper. Could mean they're in real trouble. Radio on the fritz or something, you see, and even if that's no' the case, static's so bad they could be transmitting at this very moment and we couldn't pick them up. You do see what I mean?''

"And it could be a trick, couldn't it?" Mary Crane shot back. "Just to lure us away from finding more sea gold. Do *you* see what *I* mean, Mr. Redfern?"

"We have no choice," repeated Tate, his temper barely under control. "It's the law of the sea."

"Of course we have a choice," she retorted. "Just turn the ship around. *I'll* take the responsibility."

"I'm sure you would," said Tate icily. "But I'm captain of this ship and we're not turning back. Not until we've checked it out. Understood, Mrs. Crane?"

"Perfectly," she replied, by which Tate knew she meant that she did not understand. To make matters worse, the next time he glanced at the barometric pressure he saw the needle had fallen another point.

The Scottish mate tried again to raise the stricken Japanese ship. There was still no answer.

At that moment the radio officer came onto the bridge, grabbing the compass mounting to steady himself and looking perplexed.

"What's up, Sparks?" asked Tate, eager to thwart further interference by Mrs. Crane.

"Got a message here, a transmit from Astoria station. They're on maximum power—much more than we have— but it doesn't make sense."

"Garbled or what?"

"No—oh, static's cut it up a bit but I got it all right."

"Well?"

A draft of wind fluttered the yellow message pad as Sparks, holding the roll bar with one hand, read the transmit. "Says 'To Tony Lee Many Happy Returns Signed Brenda.'"

"So?" said Tate. "Post it on the board. What's so funny about a birthday greeting? You've got plenty of those in the past."

"Yes, sir, but we don't have any crew by that name."

"Ach," said Redfern, "not to worry, Sparkie, it's the wrong ship they've got. Ask Astoria for a repeat."

"I did, Scotty," he answered. "Right after you tried to raise the SOS again."

"And?" Tate interjected, still irritable after his run-in with Mary Crane. "What did Astoria say?"

"Message was definitely asked to be sent to *Petrel*."

"All right," said Scotty. "Post the message on the board anyway—maybe a private joke."

"Huh," commented Tate gruffly. "Typical if you ask me. Whoever she is has forgotten what ship her boy's on."

"Typical of whom?" Mrs. Crane snapped. "I suppose you mean women in general?"

Ignoring her, Tate asked Sparks to try to raise the stricken Japanese ship again.

There was nothing but a fierce spitting noise like fat in a fire.

Chapter Twenty-Five

IT WAS A MOMENTARY BLUR amid the tall grass but this time the Georgian was sure. He had seen something move, but he wasn't about to be ragged by the other five marines until he was certain what it was.

It could be one of the three marines who had been left on the main island while he and the rest of Saburov's team were freezing their asses off waiting for daylight to begin searching the Pinnacle. Looking up from the rifle, blinded temporarily by the sudden shift from the eerie amber of the infrared to the relative darkness of predawn light, the Georgian stared ahead until he made out the line of the cliffs on the eastern side, and beyond them, a little more than a kilometer or so to the east, the long, dark shape that was the mother ship at anchor. Following the line of the rifle he focused hard again in the general area of the old cement supply hut. Maybe the marine, or whatever it was moving out there in the sword grass, was heading in out of the cold and the intermittent rain that was coming in from the sea.

He raised the Dragunov, his right hand firmly on the pistol grip, his thumb through the hollowed-out stock, and brought its line of sight to about a hundred meters or so west of the cement hut. High spray splattered across the scope. He swore and, reaching down quickly, pulled out the chamois.

Chapter Twenty-Six

IN ZURICH, halfway across the world, it was 2:45 in the afternoon, the late autumn sun soft gold on the shiny leaves of the evergreens, a thicket of them obscuring the big, square gray stone house set well in from the spear-patterned six-foot-high fence enclosing two acres. The mansion did not appear large, hidden behind the trees, and here and there red and russet-mottled maples caught the light in quick, vivid flashes of color made more brilliant by the more somber green of shrubbery. Outward show had never been Klaus's style. He made money not to show it off in what he considered vulgar displays of consumerism but merely to keep score in the game of power. There was, of course, since he *was* Klaus, also a prudential consideration, namely that if you were moved to flash your money about, then you were inviting someone to take it from you, creating all kinds of security problems and setting yourself up for all the horrible do-gooders and their pathetic causes to save humanity.

No, anonymity was by far the best policy. Very few of even his most active competitors, like Shell, Unilever and ATT knew much about him. Most, for example, thought he was married but were not sure. All this allowed him a low profile so that he could indulge himself in collecting art, women and his favorite wines. Lately though, he had given up wine, for the entry of the upstart American, this Hall person, had had a much more deleterious effect on his stomach than anything his private physician had antici- pated. He was now trying a new tablet, Gaviscon, pleas- ant, tasting of butterscotch. He chewed two more of the antacid tablets as he methodically examined a catalog of several paintings he wished to acquire for his private col- lection, all the time sipping a lukewarm cappuccino made, to his infinite disgust, from decaffeinated coffee so as not to further aggravate his distraught intestinal tract.

He paused to study the tension in several Cezannes and the vibrant angst of a Van Gogh but then passed on. Nor- mally he would have lingered here, for the madness he found in Van Gogh held a perverse attraction for him, in- sofar as he considered madness the worst fate, together with poverty, that could befall a man, and something that could be held at bay only by having control of one's life. Such control, he believed, was made infinitely easier the more power and money one had. Today the contempla- tion of the paintings caused him no discomfort, for today he knew he was in absolute control of his financial em- pire, that there were nothing but good omens.

The very fact that the Soviet general, an alternative member of the Politburo at that, was coming to talk was a signal that the general needed Klaus and Swiss Rhine Petrochemicals more than he needed the general. He looked at his watch and rang for the chauffeur. They would drive up and meet the Russian at Interlaken and, if time permitted, take the passenger train from Grindel-

wald, the picturesque little Alpine village below the towering ice of the Kleine Scheidegg. The cold mountain air
always cleared one's head for business, and besides, the
Russian would enjoy a day out in one of capitalism's cra-
dles—all expenses paid.

Feeling in an increasingly better mood, Klaus pondered
the desirability of owning Botticelli's *The Three Graces*,
the women clad only in their transparent amber garments.
Though it was in Florence, he saw no difficulty in acquir-
ing it. He often had masterpieces stolen from Italian mu-
seums; the only difficult part was getting the best forger on
the market, then arranging the swap beforehand so that
you had days, sometimes weeks, to get the real painting out
of the country. On such occasions he would sit for hours
watching the resulting outrage of the art world spilling
from the TV screens, deeply satisfied by the hypocrisy of
a business that he knew would buy the paintings back from
him, through his puppets, for far more than they were
worth prior to being stolen. He decided, right then and
there, that if his business with Moscow increased, he would
give himself the Botticelli.

Putting down his coffee, he pulled on his wine-colored,
lined gabardine coat. It would be chilly in the mountains
once they left the rental car. His chauffeur was always the
same but never the car. Often, after ordering a specific
make and color of car, he would refuse it at the depot, demanding a much more modest one instead. It was a little
security trick he had picked up from the Russian to throw
off would-be kidnappers and one of the reasons he was still
alive and head of the fourth-largest multinational in the
world.

He rang his contacts in Florence to get ready for the
Botticelli.

WHEN KORNON, in civilian clothes, arrived at Interlaken
he explained to Klaus, in German, how Moscow was hav-

ing a little difficulty and that the American, Hall, was involved.

Klaus nodded patiently for a while as Kornon talked, but gradually his impatience showed. "*Ja, ja,* General, but you did not come all the way from Moscow merely to tell me your troubles."

"No, to *request*," Kornon interjected. "To request assistance, Herr Klaus."

"But General, SRP has already supplied you with materials."

"Yes," Kornon agreed. "But this CANUS Ore 'office' of yours, as well as supplying lubricant and the like, using trawlers out of Astoria—could not your men, ah..." Kornon knew there was an English colloquialism that would better express what he was getting at.

"Check things out," said Klaus.

"Just so."

"Yes, I see how it would be difficult for you to show your faces there, other than when your ship has the cover of a storm—whereas SRP could conceivably find a way to—"

"Precisely," Kornon interjected, anticipating him. "To take appropriate action in our absence." They were nearing a small crowd of tourists at the train station at Grindelwald.

"Oh," said Klaus as they walked through the gate and gave in their tickets. "For this I would expect certain advantages, in other areas as well."

"You will be given preferential treatment and lucrative contracts, I assure you," said Kornon. "From Gdansk to Siberia. You will soon be the biggest multinational allowed to operate in the Eastern Bloc." Kornon was in effect also reminding Klaus of just how much SRP stood to lose if Klaus couldn't extend himself.

"Very well, General. Ah, let's sit at the end of the carriage. We can talk there."

As the train began its journey up the sharp incline toward the mountain of glacial-blue ice and snow, Klaus pulled up his collar and, despite the heating, could see his breath clouding the glass. "Is there anything else?" he asked Kornon.

Kornon ignored the scenery—he'd done a six-month posting as a young officer on the Kamchatka Peninsula and had seen enough ice and snow for a lifetime. "It may become necessary for CANUS Ore to do a little more—*now.*" He remained silent until the train had come to a stop several thousand feet up, across from the old hotel beneath Kleine Scheidegg that had hosted the great royal houses of Europe and now hosted the rich and bored.

"The train goes back in about a half hour," said Klaus. "Let's take a stroll."

Kornon grew more morose. In the foreign place, devoid of the usual surroundings and trappings of power to bolster his confidence, his fears took on the shape of a nightmare. He felt alone. Klaus was his only chance. He bent down and drew a map in the snow of where he wanted Klaus's boat to go and what it would have to do.

"But, General," Klaus protested, and then immediately sensed that Kornon thought he was getting cold feet. "No, no," Klaus quickly assured him, "I see the necessity. It is Hall or us."

The klaxon was sounding indicating that the train was about to return to Grindelwald, now a postcard village thousands of feet below, nestled in a sea of wildflowers of every conceivable color. "Then," said Kornon, "what is the problem, Herr Klaus? You've just said we have no option. We must stop Hall."

"Yes, I have no objection. I would like to kill him personally, but I've already activated Mr. Lee."

"*Your* man?"

"Yes," said Klaus, "but my concern, General, is that we simply do not have the kind of equipment one might need to stop Hall. Petrochemicals are one thing but ..."

Kornon, relieved, waved Klaus's concern aside. "That is already taken care of. It is on its way. By diplomatic pouch to our American West Coast consulates. The question is, will you do it if—how do the Americans say—push turns to the shoving?"

Klaus gave a passing thought to all the contracts he'd lose if he didn't, but most of all he pictured his nemesis, the American Hall, the man who had ruined SRP's chances of sea gold once before. Klaus was determined that this time he, and not Hall, would have the last say. He patted Kornon nonchalantly on the back as they took their seats for the trip down. "There will be no problem. I welcome the opportunity of cementing our good relations, General."

Kornon forced a smile, extending his hand in thanks. He'd never liked Klaus, but he knew that if anyone could help him stop Hall it would be the Swiss. The man's lust for power was as insatiable as his own.

Chapter Twenty-Seven

FOR JULIO ALL SENSE OF TIME had faded in a fever of confusion and recurring dizziness. As the moon had reopened its ongoing battle with the changing moods of the night sky, the dizziness had slipped precariously into a world of mad, unfinished dreams, where moons appeared and disappeared, interspersed with flares of sunlight intensity and other lights flooding the darkness high above the Pinnacle. Everything rolled about like a crazy ship on a crazy ocean, and amid the bright lights, surrounded by thunder and a black rain, thousands of cormorants and gulls shrieked, terrified by the light and noise. Dimly his brain had perceived another flare being fired after his—a signal of help on the way.

But then the lights disappeared as suddenly as they had appeared, and there was only a wild rush of air coming down on him from some unseen force, then it, too, was gone and in its place there was only the ceaseless moaning of wind around the rocky depression that encased him like a three-sided tomb. Ironically, it was the remnants of the heavy rain that had caused his fall that had also saved him, the rainwater allowing his body to do battle with the dangerous dehydration that otherwise would have finished him. Now the fever that had thrown him into confusion yet kept his body warm despite the external cold was gone, and in the occasional flashes of consciousness he sensed enough about his injury to know that if he was not found before another night he would die from exposure. Prostrate as he was it kept coming back to him that he must somehow manage another sign, to tell Gloria and the professor where he was, but then he lapsed into unconsciousness again, cradled in the warm, ephemeral embrace of a woman who was at once his mother and Gloria Bernardi, melding in and out of memory with a boundless and effortless grace.

APPROACHING THE ABANDONED HUT, and in that strange, shadowless semilight favored for attack, when the eye finds it well-nigh impossible to distinguish reality from myriad shapes, Frank, weighed down by the body of the dead marine, stumbled on a tussock of grass. The body slipped sideways, catching a sliver of the fading, washed-out moon being swallowed by day.

The Georgian spotted the movement, raised his rifle and saw a marine bending down in the grass. The next instant he saw the woman. "They've got her! They've got the bitch!"

"Where?" asked one of the soldiers.

"Who's got her?" asked another, realizing the Georgian had to mean the American girl, but wondering which of the three marines on the island had captured her.

"Can't tell," answered the Georgian. "It's a marine, that's all that matters, isn't it, so we can get off this crap pile."

"Doesn't help us," moaned another. "We've still got to get Pancho Villa."

"Well, it's one less," said the first soldier. "Be grateful for that much."

"Suppose so," said the complainer. "Wish it was the Mexican, though."

"Relax," counseled the tall Georgian, cockier now he'd proved to the other five that he *had* seen something on the scope the first time.

"Give us a look," asked another, to needle him. "Could be dawn delusion."

The others laughed.

"Here, smartass," said the Georgian, passing over the rifle. "See for yourself."

As the marine took the rifle from the Georgian, using the open sight beneath the infrared scope to line up with the long, abandoned shed more than a quarter mile away, across from the Pinnacle he did see two blips.

"Satisfied?" sneered the Georgian. "Dawn delusion?"

The marine now closed one eye on the scope, but there was enough light that a regular scope would be of more use. He switched to one of the two other regular rifles in the squad of six, his own weapon being a Kalashnikov. "Hey!"

"What?" said the Georgian. "She taking off her pants?" He turned, grinning at the other marines.

"You turkey! That isn't a marine."

The Georgian swung around. "What the hell are you talking about? I saw it with—"

"It's a marine uniform, but I don't think it's one of our men."

"Horseshit! Gimme that thing!" Snatching the rifle the Georgian, his face an angry twist of muscle, put his eye to the day scope. He saw the woman disappearing into the long, decrepit-looking shed. But now the man, who'd been in front of her, was nowhere to be seen, obviously having preceded her into the shed. "He probably had a goat rope on her," the Georgian explained. "Standard drill."

"Was she walking behind him or on his off side?" asked one of the marines.

The Georgian was thinking about it. So was the other marine who'd seen them. Both knew what the problem was; it came out of standard marine procedure. You might use a rope, especially when taking a prisoner at night. You might let a prisoner wander left or right, but never behind you. So the question of whether or not the woman was behind or offside the man was crucial in knowing whether or not the man was a marine. Saburov would reward the one with the right answer, but who was right?

The procedure for answering this problem wasn't learned at basic training but came from the intuitive sense of survival. You kicked the problem upstairs to the corporal, and with only eighteen hours before the ship had to set sail, you did it quickly. The marine who had the walkie-talkie passed it to the Georgian. "It's all yours, Mikhail."

It was no use; the static caused by the barrier of rock broke up the transmission so much that all the corporal on the summit could pick up was something about the "main island." And so the Georgian volunteered to climb up to the summit. If nothing else it would get him out of the painstaking job of searching every nook and cranny from the base up, in the boring spiral search pattern.

As daylight changed the color of the rock from a guano-smeared black to a white-splashed chocolate, the Georgian exchanged his long Dragunov for a more portable Kalashnikov and began his ascent, stopping every thirty feet or so to try the walkie-talkie. At times the curdling sky of gray invading patches of blue was darkened by thousands of seabirds rising, hovering and landing again on the Pinnacle, their noise and stench an overpowering assault on the senses.

Inside the concrete hut a quarter mile away on the island, Gloria Bernardi collapsed to the ground in a sleep of utter exhaustion.

IT WAS BECAUSE OF THE NOISE of the seabirds that Julio didn't hear the first few rushes of static, as the Georgian, pausing and craning his neck to see if he could spot the corporal, tried the walkie-talkie again. And it wasn't until the Georgian stopped about thirty feet above him in the honeycombed rock that Julio, barely conscious, saw the tall figure silhouetted against pale day. Within his body Julio could feel the frantic urgency to draw the searcher's attention to him, but now not even his hands would move. Vaguely, his mind fighting to keep conscious, he thought of trying to turn his left arm back and forth in an effort to throw a glint of sunlight off his watch that might get the tall figure's attention before he moved off again. The arm would not respond. He tried calling, but nothing more than a hoarse whisper emerged, his throat cracked and dry as the desert now that the rivulets of rainwater had ceased after the previous night's downpour. Julio swallowed, then with all the effort he could muster tried to move a leg, anything with which he might make some noise. His muscles refused the attempt, and in a tearing agony of frustration and surrender, the tension in his body collapsed like a pricked balloon, and a loud moan issued forth.

The Georgian looked down, flicking off the walkie-talkie in astonishment. "Well, I'll be . . ."

Julio thanked God and the Holy Mother as he saw the tall figure bending, tossing down the tiny canister as one would a crumb to a fish gaping hungrily from a deep dark tank. Julio willed his arms to catch the canister, but even in his flood of relief his arms lay stubbornly still, though he breathed easier for the first time in more than twenty-four hours. Thank God they had found him.

The grenade's explosion was a brilliant purple flash and a muffled *whump* in the crevice where Julio lay.

The Georgian continued his climb, cursing the steepness of the rock, but happy to be the one who would win Saburov's praise, the air over the Mexican's bloody remains thick with gulls squawking and descending, already fighting over the entrails.

INSIDE THE ABANDONED HUT, Gloria slumped by his side, still sleeping, Frank was sitting on the dusty concrete floor, ripping open a foil bag of freeze-dried food, when he heard the dull thump and the sound of cormorants outside still protesting at his and Gloria's arrival. Farther inside the darkness there was the scurry of something furry passing quickly out of a shaft of weak light that penetrated the opening of the sixty-foot-long hut, particles of dust dancing in the ray like particles of gold. Ten minutes later, he reluctantly woke Gloria. She sat up with a start, confused, staring blankly at him.

"Can't stay here," Frank explained. "Only long enough to look for stashed drill equipment, soil sampling equipment, stuff like that, then we have to move off again. If they've searched this place once for you, it doesn't mean they won't be back. At least we can leave the marine here—he'll be out of sight."

"What sort of drill equipment?" asked Gloria sleepily. "You mean pipes—that sort of thing?"

"Uh-huh, and chain lengths," Frank added. "Cans of lubricating oil...that sort of gear. It has to be pretty big—the drilling stuff, I mean. I'm not saying they're using the hut as a site, maybe just as a temporary storage shed from time to time."

Gloria ate a little of the dried food Frank offered her. She didn't like the Irish stew but it was better than starving.

"I don't understand," she said. "If they've already found minerals, I mean land deposits of sea gold, then why would they leave drilling equipment here?"

"Because they might want to come back and do more." He drew out the flashlight, its beam slicing the darkness, dust mixed with white flecks of guano. "Funny," he said, swinging the beam around two old wooden window shutters at the northern end of the hut, then moving it back toward them in a crisscross pattern.

Gloria gasped as the beam slid over the graying corpse of the marine. Frank was still staring into the black interior of the hut. Something seemed to be bothering him. "What is it?" she asked, only too happy to take her gaze from the marine.

Frank had got up and was now advancing farther into the hut past the cement foundations of old shower stalls. "What's wrong?" she repeated.

He was bending down, feeling something on the floor. "Don't know, but you're the bird expert, you tell me. Why isn't there any fresh bird dung here?"

She smiled and was conscious that it was the first time she had done so in days. "Guano," she said. "Not bird dung."

"All right." He smiled back. "Guano dung. All this stuff is dry as bone dust."

Gloria shrugged. "Sometimes birds prefer outdoor perches, open nests, especially seabirds."

"Yes, but they used to be here. This is old dung—or whatever you want to call it. Why would they suddenly move out?"

"All right," she conceded, "someone chased them out. So?"

"So someone must have been using this place."

"Then where's all the equipment gone?"

"Probably back on the ship. I told you it's probably temporary. Only used in bad weather when they can't be seen working."

Frank sat down, thoughtfully munching on the C rations, which took him back to his military service days. He was looking out from the hut's gaping mouth toward the Pinnacle and the vast, rumpled ocean beyond. Atop the huge lump of basalt rising more than two hundred feet into the air, two or three dots could be seen moving around. Frank walked over to his haversack, which was lying with the marine's rifle against the old two-foot-high foundations for shower stalls. When Gloria saw him lifting the binoculars toward the Pinnacle, she sat up excitedly, despite her fatigue. "You see someone?"

"Wouldn't get my hopes up," he cautioned, telling her as gently as he could about hearing the dull thump that had come from the Pinnacle. All he could see now was the cone of serrated rock, as cold and cruel as any natural thing he'd seen in all his years at sea.

"You think Julio's . . ." she began.

"Yes," he answered, lowering the binoculars, holding her, convulsed with fatigue and hopelessness and guilt. Drawing her to him he stroked her as gently as one would a stricken fawn and let her sob.

"What can we do?" she cried helplessly.

"It wasn't your fault," he tried to reassure her. "Don't take other people's decisions on yourself. From what you told me he got mad—stalked off. Common enough. Look—" he lifted her chin up "—that had nothing to do with them. I mean, those bastards were out to kill the three of you, no matter what happened between you. It's not your—"

"But now they'll be after you and just because you came to help."

She was right but he held her close again. "Look, honey. You can't worry about what-might-have-beens. Besides I have a hunch that we, that *Petrel*, was caught up in this long before we saw any flare go up."

"How do you mean?"

He told her about his previous battle with Klaus off the Canadian coast, and about how Klaus was the kind of well-dressed thug who never gave up, the kind of thug whose ego was as deeply invested in SRP as his money. "Mary and I never did believe he'd walk away from the hiding we gave him."

"Mary?" asked Gloria. She hadn't seen a wedding ring.

"Business partner. I used to work for her husband." He hesitated. "I stayed on after he passed away." The moment he said it he knew how it must seem to Gloria, and it bothered him. For the first time he realized that something was happening between them, and that she, in the tone of her question, was as aware of it as he.

"I'm sorry," she said, "for probing. It's none of my business. I..."

So close together, their body warmth merged in a cocoonlike embrace, they said nothing for what seemed like minutes but was in fact only seconds before they heard a terrifying noise, like splitting timber, several feet from them, a cloud of choking dust filling the air. An instant later they heard the sharp crack of the rifle being fired from the Pinnacle. He pushed her farther into the black interior of the hut, behind the cement foundations of the old shower stalls. "Quickly, put this on!" he shouted, handing her the dead marine's helmet as the shots kept slamming into the floor around them, fine cement particles mixing with the choking dry guano kicked up in the steady hail of bullets. Frank, his right arm over her as they lay behind the low shower stall, could feel Gloria's heart racing and held her closer as a new volley started up. Then he felt a warm trickle of blood from his forehead; a sliver of cement or bullet had cut the skin like a knife. "They're shooting wild," he said in a futile attempt to lessen her fear. "Gloria?"

There was no answer.

"CAN'T SEE THEM," complained one of the marines on the summit, pulling back the bolt on the rifle, clipping in another magazine with excited force. The other two, the corporal and the Georgian, were unable to contribute with their shorter-range Kalashnikovs.

"Maybe you've hit them," said the corporal hopefully.

"Hit them, my ass," cut in the Georgian. "If he'd hit 'em he'd've seen 'em go down in the scope."

"Not if they went farther into the hut," said the corporal. "Anyway, Colonel Saburov'll be happy enough if we pin 'em down. That's the main thing."

"The main thing is to kill the bastards," said the Georgian, unrelenting. "Saburov wants them dead, Comrade!"

"Well," said the corporal, as the rifleman, cheeks flushed as much by the excitement of his first kill as by the heat from the rifle's breech, began firing again. "There's no fear of that, is there?"

"No fear of what?" asked the Georgian.

"Of us not getting them." The corporal was pointing at the mother ship.

Chapter Twenty-Eight

AT THE BOTTOM OF THE CLEFT, waiting by the Zodiac, Jamie and Byrne were ignorant of what was happening. Frank was an hour overdue, and the Zodiac seemed alive, impatiently nudging into the mouth of the cleft.

"C'mon, Byrne," Jamie exhorted. "I'm damned sure those were rifle shots. We should go down the coast. See if we can help 'im out."

Byrne looked at him, surprised, having assumed Jamie's nerves would have counseled him to stay put rather than return to the heavy seas.

"Okay," said Jamie, his breath still smelling of overproof but more in control of himself now. "So I didn't like the ride in. Never do in the damn dark. Like to see what I'm up against, right?" Before Byrne could answer, Jamie belched and went on. "Look, Frank's a good head. He's helped us all out one time or another, that's all I'm sayin'. If we head farther south we'll be nearer to where that signaling came from."

"I don't mind," replied Byrne. "Only problem is if that mother ship sends the chopper over us, it'll be like them shooting fish in a barrel. I say we go up here on the rope and have a look see from there."

"No way, José," said Jamie, gazing up at the jagged cliff moving rapidly against a blue and gray sky. "I'll stay here and look after the Zodiac, or pick you up farther down the coast if you want, but I'm no mountain goat. I ain't climbing that thing."

"Better stay here then," said Byrne. "Pull the raft in—out of sight. I'll shimmy up here."

Soon Byrne began the slow and dangerous ascent. Now and then he could hear the popping of distant rifle fire.

"GLORIA!" Frank was shaking her now, ricochets zinging madly off the shower wall, wondering if the blood he'd felt on his forehead was really coming from . . .

Suddenly, she turned against him. "What?" She had been covering her ears so tightly she had had trouble hearing him over the noise of bullets striking and echoing throughout the hut.

"You okay?" he asked.

"No. I'm terrified."

"We've got to get out of here fast!" he called out above a fresh onslaught. There was a change in the noise, a metallic tearing, telling him the marines on the Pinnacle were no longer using normal bullets but dumdums instead, lead tips sliced so the bullets would spread on impact to the size of steel fists hitting the cement only a few feet away from the low protective shower wall. Soon the wall would start to disintegrate under the pounding.

"What do you propose?" she yelled.

"Next time he changes magazines, we'll go out one of the windows," shouted Frank. "Wait for me behind the end of the hut. Here!" He handed her the marine's pistol. "Can you feel the safety?"

"I don't know what you—"

He took her hand, wrapped it around the Makarov's grip, sliding her index finger back and forth on the warm metal that had been pressing into her as he held her down out of danger. "Push it forward," he told her. "Then hold the grip with both hands—take half a breath, then squeeze the trigger. Don't jerk it. Got it?"

"No."

He went over it again, then, rolling away from her, took up the grappling hook, throwing it in an arc at one of the rear shutters. It spun away from him, hit by a bullet in midair, clattering back to the ground. For a moment he couldn't see or breathe, eyes and nose filled with dust. Dragging the hook to his side, he threw it again and again until he heard glass breaking on the outside of the shutter and felt tension on the rope. He pulled hard on it during a lull in the firing. The whole shutter came apart, banging noisily into the hut, but the gunfire had resumed.

"Why don't you shoot back?" asked Gloria, looking at the rifle, waiting nervously for a break in the firing for him to help her through the window.

"Not a chance," he answered. "They'd zero right in on the flash."

A break came and Frank, lifting her off her feet, carried her quickly to the window. "Arms in front of your eyes!" he shouted, shoving her through. The shaft of light penetrating the hut was getting longer, making it easier by the minute for the rifleman on the Pinnacle to see into the hut's interior. The next second Frank heard glass whistling through the air. Hugging the cement floor, arms over his skull like a cowed prisoner, it occurred to him through all the mayhem and dust that it was strange how reckless they were about firing into the very place he had thought they might want to protect. It was then he understood that he might have been dead wrong, that there was nothing important about the hut at all. He waited, ears ringing with the noise, until he was sure the firing had stopped, but by the time he realized it the rifleman had reloaded and was pinning him down with a vengeance.

Outside, crouching against the rear wall of the hut, Gloria feared that the other two marines on the northern part of the island would already be moving down toward them and that those on the Pinnacle would soon be ferried across by helicopter. All around her the sea of grass came alive with menace.

ONE OF THE TWO MARINES halfway down the island had started heading south the moment he heard the firing starting from the big rock to the south. He spotted Byrne dragging himself over the cliff top, two hundred yards away on his right. Dropping to the ground, the marine waited to see whether any other Americans were coming up. Then he saw Byrne stand up after catching his breath and look cautiously about, shoulders rounded like an old man, orange survival suit ridiculously bright against the green grass. The marine couldn't see any weapon on him, but maybe the American was carrying a sidearm. Even if he was, the marine knew he could afford to get a lot closer and still have the advantage with his Kalashnikov.

Suddenly a submachine gun opened up a hundred yards farther on. The American turned to run, then the first marine fired. For a moment the American's body seemed to be shivering in the sunlight, heat waves rising all around him like a mirage, then, arching back, hands tearing at his stomach, he was knocked backward into the grass at the edge of the cliff.

The two marines emerged from cover, the first calling out to the other to be careful, that the American might be playing possum. It turned out he was correct in that the American was miraculously not yet dead, calling out some name again and again. The first marine was changing clips as he reached the man, but rather than waste another half clip, he used his knife on the American's throat and rolled him off the cliff.

Below, they could see a sky thick with thousands of screeching birds and the big breakers smashing in. After waiting, seeing no sign of anyone else, they continued south toward the old cement hut. Above the big blob that was the Pinnacle they could see the HIP hovering, ready to take their comrades off the rock.

Once across the treacherous channel, the marines would encircle the hut, go in with submachine guns and grenades and finish whoever they'd managed to pin down.

"Pity to blow away a nice piece of pussy."

"Well," said the other, "it's about time we got out of here. Be a clear day tomorrow if it keeps up like this."

"I'd still like to get a bit of that pussy."

"Maybe you will—if you're quick." The other laughed.

"Watch me, Comrade."

JAMIE HEARD THE CHATTER of the machine gun, the soft explosion of black and white birds scattering from the cliffs against the mottled sky, and a few minutes later saw Byrne's body tumbling down like a crumpled garbage bag through a hole in the canopy of birds, thudding on the rocks, splattering bright crimson against coal-black basalt. So badly shaken he couldn't think, Jamie retreated deeper into the cleft, staring out at the rolling sea as if its immensity might offer some consolation, some escape from what he had just seen, that somehow it would end the horror. But soon his eyes were drawn back to the cleft, where he sat trembling, and upward toward the rope that now dangled, swinging back and forth in the wind like a hangman's noose. He couldn't climb up and dislodge it even if his nerves hadn't deserted him, for then he'd be unable to come back down. But if he left it there and they, whoever *they* were, found it, it would lead directly to him. He thought of casting off with the Zodiac but was afraid he would be spotted at once by the helicopter he could now hear operating not far to the south. His hands shaking, Jamie took out his hip flask. It was empty as a virgin.

THE FIRING FROM THE PINNACLE ceased momentarily, the HIP's rotors a grayish blur, too close to the line of fire of the rifleman on the summit for the marines to take any unnecessary risk.

As Frank spotted the big chopper slowly descending beneath the Pinnacle's summit to pick up what he presumed must be the other marines Gloria had told him about, he dashed to the window of the hut, dropped the rifle through into grass and followed it.

Though he didn't see any marines approaching on land from the opposite direction, he thought he'd heard a stutter of submachine-gun fire earlier to the north. The moment he saw Gloria he indicated to her to follow him to the northeastern corner of the hut, the Pinnacle directly ahead of them a quarter mile away and the chopper's top half faintly visible above the man-high grass. All the birds that had been nesting and congregating earlier on the flat roof of the cement hut had fled during the firing from the Pinnacle; only one remained, staring fixedly, imperiously, at Frank and Gloria, completely unafraid, it seemed, staying put, turning its back toward them, then front and back again as if showing contempt for the whole human race. But at least, Frank thought, it showed courage, and kneeling down beside the corner of the hut, he thought of a man of courage, the mate, floating dead somewhere in the cold ocean, and of the young Mexican who had died.

Quickly, yet unrushed, he slid his left arm through the rifle's sling, made one turn on it, took aim at the greenish-brown dragonfly above the Pinnacle that jumped into the scope, bloated and bisected by the cross hairs. He began squeezing the trigger. The grass splayed before him in the barrel's hot breath and remained bent in obedience to the 7.62 mm bullets that kept streaming forth at a thousand yards a second.

The first bullet slammed into the port-side engine's cowling, with the sound of a puck smashing glass, taking out a piece of aluminum two feet in diameter, sending it spinning like a giant Frisbee into the Pinnacle, where it richocheted off, cartwheeling into the sea.

"What the—" Saburov began, but the pilot paid him no mind. Already the HIP was rising, struck twice more. A marine screamed. A sudden rush of icy air and the sound of torn fuselage flapping violently told the pilot his craft had been hit in the main cabin. The HIP veered away, Saburov feeling his gut wrenched by the unexpected acceleration and seeing one of the five marines they'd been about to take off the Pinnacle plummeting into the boiling channel like a rag doll. A second marine, this one hanging on for his life, was swinging wildly on the rope ladder, the lift winch still whining as the chopper swung hard to starboard once it had cleared the Pinnacle in a hasty retreat back to the mother ship. It almost skimmed the heavy seas, so low it threatened to drown the marine still in the process of being winched up.

The pilot was mistaken about the number of times the HIP had been hit. He thought it was twice, but on landing on the mother ship, using only the starboard engine as a precaution against possible electrical shorting and fire beneath the badly damaged port cowling, he discovered the helicopter had been hit four times in as many seconds. The second marine manning the winch had been killed. The first mechanic on the scene, hearing the groans of the marine who had hung on the ladder so grimly, found him

hanging by bloodied arms, the flesh scraped from the bone
by the quarter-inch wire that had kept winding him in,
though the winch operator was dead, his chest having im-
ploded with the second bullet.

"DAMN!" FRANK MUTED his swearing in front of Gloria,
but his expression of self-disgust was plain enough to her.
"I wanted to bring down that son of a— The scope must
have been knocked off center when I tackled that marine.
Either that or he was cross-eyed. Dammit! I had that
chopper dead in the cross hairs."

"But you've scared them off," countered Gloria triumphantly. "It'll give your ship time to—" She stopped.
"Frank!" Her voice was urgent but hushed.

He swung around, facing the sea of tall sword grass
stretching northward behind the hut.

"Over there," she said, pointing to a thick knot of grass
fifty yards away, her voice no more than a whisper.
"Something's moving."

But Frank could only see the ripples of wind running
through the grass and the thinning clouds of steam as the
grass dried out in the sunlight. Grabbing Gloria's hand,
leading her away from the hut, he headed quickly toward
the eastern cliff tops, where the wind was sending scurries
of dead grass and reddish volcanic dust racing along barren bulges of pockmarked cliff in which wind and rain had
carved out a honeycomb of caves in the rock face, giving
the lampblack- and, in places, reddish-colored cliffs an
acned appearance. Frank knew they would be momentarily visible going across the denuded margin that ran
crookedly in a long red scar between the cliff tops and the
edge of the grassy sea. He paused at the edge of the grass,
picking out the nearest hump of caves clustered in the
bulging formations of rock, which, closer up, looked like
pores on the skin of some giant, ugly nose. Glancing behind him, he could see the top of the hut like a cement table lying atop the dense grass, the haughty lone bird still

in the middle of it turning, then he saw a blur—someone or something, passing a corner of the hut and just as quickly disappearing.

"Let's go," he said softly, leading her in a crouched run across the margin.

On top of the Pinnacle a quarter mile south, no one saw them as, under a badly shaken corporal, Penkovsky and the Georgian moved cautiously down the summit, while the three remaining marines at the base made their way, too, around the rock away from the enemy's line of fire. The vital question was whether or not the chopper would be airworthy, and, just as important to the marines, whether Saburov would send the HIP in again to get them off the Pinnacle, if it was usable. To do so, the pilot would have to fly due east out to sea for several miles, then come in low, using the Pinnacle as a shield.

SURPRISED BY THEIR LUCK in not being fired upon from the Pinnacle, Frank and Gloria, like two players sliding for the same base, found themselves enveloped in a rust-colored cloud as they came to a stop at the cliff side of the dirt margin, then scrambled down a sharp incline and over the wind-chaffed lip of one of the caves on the bulbous projections that seemed stuck on the cliff three hundred feet above the sea. The projections, Frank could see once they were in the cave, were not so much volcanic outcrops pushed up like sea mounts from the metal-rich seabed but rather the sculptured remains of an ancient seabed itself.

Chapter Twenty-Nine

"YES?" SNAPPED SABUROV. "What is it?"

Captain Novisk handed him the latest weather forecast. "The predicted lull has begun, as you can see. Sea's down a bit already. Still, we'll have to start raising anchor by 2330 if we're to get under way by midnight, Colonel."

Novisk glanced at his watch, which only irritated Saburov further. He knew very well that he now had less than fifteen hours in which to kill the two Americans, without the Pole looking at his damned watch. He personally wanted to catch the girl and shoot her for all the trouble she had caused him.

"I know how long I have, Comrade," Saburov said tartly without looking at Novisk. He watched the HIP mechanics instead, asking the helicopter pilot anxiously, "Well? Is it all right or not?"

The lieutenant was wiping off the blood of the mangled marine after helping disentangle what had been the marine's arms. Saburov, he noticed, hardly seemed aware of the three marines the American had killed, totally preoccupied with preserving the secrecy of the mission from outsiders. In fact, it was quite obvious that the whole business had become much more than a mission to the colonel. It was now an obsession; Saburov would do anything to get the Americans. "We don't need the cowling, I suppose," replied the lieutenant. "We use it mainly as a maintenance platform when it's open. In the air it's really only a cover to prevent—"

"I don't want a lecture on helicopters, Comrade. Can it fly?"

"Have to check to see if oil pressure's up. Couldn't use it if you wanted to lift any crates again. The sling weight—" He stopped.

The colonel was furious. "You idiot! Shut your mouth!"

"I'm sorry, sir, I forgot that—"

"You forget again, Lieutenant, and you'll be a *private* on the Afghan front!"

"Yes, sir."

"Both engines'll be usable, Colonel. We can even operate on one if we don't have too big a— I mean if we don't have too many marines aboard."

"We haven't got that many left!" Saburov responded bitterly.

The PA speaker crackled to life on the afterdeck. Above, on the crowded pad, as mechanics and seamen swarmed around the helicopter, some of the mechanics taping over the punctured fuselage with fiberglass squares, there was so much talking that one of the junior officers, a Russian, had to bellow for silence.

"...Comrade Saburov is wanted on the bridge immediately...Comrade Saburov..."

As Saburov turned to go, he ordered the pilot to have the deck cleared and the HIP repaired in an hour to pick up the six marines still on the Pinnacle and ferry them across to Eagle Island, where they would close in on the hut.

"WHO SAW THEM?" asked Saburov after hearing Novisk's report on the bridge.

"I did, Comrade Colonel." It was a young Polish officer.

"How long ago?"

"Five minutes, Comrade Colonel. No more."

Saburov's eyes were sparkling with anticipation, but he couldn't afford any mistakes. If he had not left by midnight, Kornon, he knew, would probably put into effect his own emergency plan, which would include the end of Saburov's career. He could feel Siberia breathing down his neck.

"You are absolutely certain, Comrade?" asked Saburov.

The other officers on the bridge were also staring at the junior lieutenant. None of them liked Saburov, or any other KGB men, for that matter, but in their desire to leave this godforsaken island as soon as possible and get back to their loved ones, the Russians and Poles were as one. The young lieutenant was sweating; he saw Novisk calmly eyeing him behind Saburov, and the blur of assembled officers. The ship rose slightly, causing the young officer in his nervousness to tilt off balance. This made him even more nervous, but he stood his ground, reassured now by a slight nod of encouragement from Novisk.

"Yes, Comrade Colonel. I'm sure. Two of them, a man and a woman."

Novisk spoke next. "He's trustworthy. A good man on watch."

Saburov ignored Novisk's recommendation and picked up the huge East German binoculars. "Show me where."

The young officer pointed to a cluster of caves, high up on the cliffs more than two kilometers away on the mother ship's starboard side. Saburov could see nothing but flurries of red dust above the caves. "You're certain it wasn't two of my marines?"

"No, sir. I mean yes, I'm sure, sir. One was definitely a woman. I could see her long hair."

"Huh—" Saburov grunted. "That could be a Polish dissident!"

There was an attempt at laughter from the officers, but it died with one look from Novisk.

Saburov put down the binoculars, the peak of his KGB officer's cap pushed up. "A little joke, Comrades." He smiled. "Don't take it to heart."

"What are you going to do?" asked Novisk, who was glancing at the bridge's clock again. Now Saburov had even less time to get the Americans.

"What am I going to do?" Saburov echoed in feigned astonishment, still smiling at the Americans' fatal mistake of leaving the hut. "There's only one thing *to do*, Comrades." With that he strode over to the PA console, picked up the mike and pressed the button for the helicopter pad. "*Vooruzhite gelikoptery!* Arm the helicopter!" he instructed, putting down the mike, beaming at everyone on the bridge. "They are trapped, Comrades! Like rats in a cage!" Then, turning around, he asked the assembled officers, "Now, who can use a camera, Comrades? I mean a movie camera. Anyone?"

Chapter Thirty

MARY CRANE SAT in *Petrel*'s small wardroom, stoking a fire of resentment against Tate and his second mate, neither of whom could or would understand her arguments for turning back and resuming the search for more sea gold. She was angry with Frank, too, whose instinctive reaction in heading to Eagle Island she viewed as desertion of their joint venture to discover as much mineral wealth as they could off the West Coast before anyone else. Besides which, she thought, it was a blatant case of his putting someone else before her. She had seen something happening to Frank in the past few months, a drawing away from her, despite their fling, that she first put down to his preoccupation with the work of drawing up his secret list of probable sea gold sites. But now she wondered about her own part in his decision not to spend as much time with her as he once had.

In any event, sitting alone, hugging her coffee as *Petrel* continued to pitch and toss, the wardroom's breakfast dishes and plates held steady by the wetted tablecloth, the crockery clinking and rattling with nerve-grating irregularity, the more convinced she became that *Petrel* had been suckered away from the sea gold stations on a false alarm and the angrier, more moody she became—angry most of all with herself, when she recalled the argument she'd had with Frank weeks before they left on the voyage, when she was wound up, growing frantic that they might not find everything she hoped for, pressing Frank to press everyone else harder. "I thought," he'd said, turning to her with infuriating patience, "that we were going to enjoy this?"

"What do you mean?" she'd asked resentfully. "I want to be rich. Don't you?"

Frank had returned to coiling the fine wire for the grab's trip weight. "Not it if takes all the fun out of it, Mary."

"*Fun!* You think anyone is in this for *fun*? You think the competition, the multinationals, people like...like Klaus— you think someone like *him* is in it for *fun*?"

"No, he isn't. That's his trouble. He's power mad."

"Oh, and I suppose you're implying I'm power mad, too? Well, are you?"

Frank had taped the coil of three-eighths-inch wire to the grab with an unhurried competence that had only further infuriated her. "Well, are you suggesting I'm power mad, Frank? Answer me."

"No," he had replied evenly, "but I think we might be getting a little greedy."

"Really! *We!* I'm glad you included yourself!"

He shrugged. "It's something we all have to watch, I guess. No matter what we do."

"Oh!" she had countered sarcastically. "Spare me the philosophy. Or are you going to tell me *you* only do it for fun?"

"That's right—when you get right down to it. Look, Mary, I'm not saying I wouldn't like to make a buck or two...."

"Preferably *two*?" she interjected.

"Sure, but it's the searching that's half the fun, isn't it? The anticipation?"

"Not for me, Frank. I want to have it, to hold it, before I die. All of it."

With that she'd walked out on him, or, she wondered now, had he already walked out on her? Had they only needed each other for the job, a kind of peaceful coexistence? She had thought of trying to find someone else after one of their arguments, someone who would think as she did, but she knew Frank Hall was the best in the business when it came to oceanography and sea gold. More than that, it wasn't just the knowledge he had; he was by far the most able oceanographer on the deck of a ship, quick on his feet, especially so in emergency situations. And now he'd deserted her for some fool, or fools, who had probably twisted their ankle or run out of Perrier on some damn island that nobody cared about.

Reaching through the hatch between wardroom and galley, she threw the remainder of her coffee down the galley sink and, using both handrails, made her way against the roll. Once inside the pitch-blackness of the windowless cabin she closed her eyes, leaning back on the cold bulkhead, letting her loneliness possess her and tell her the truth, that she wanted him now more than ever, the only man who was completely his own and who hadn't yielded suppliantly to her will. If he'd come back to her, be with her, she would let him do anything....

There was a clacking noise, the latch of the toilet door probably. Sliding her arm against the bulkhead, she felt for the light switch.

"YOU OKAY?" ASKED FRANK, leaning the rifle up against the cave wall, which was dripping with moisture.

"A few scratches and bruises," said Gloria. "I'm all right. All I need is a month's sleep."

Frank nodded, smiling at her, catching his breath, too, from the dash across the margin and the slide down to the cave he had selected.

"Why this one?" asked Gloria. "It's farther down than a couple I saw."

By way of answer, Frank used the small scope adjuster he had unclipped from the rifle's stock as a pointer, moving it seaward. Gloria could see the long gray shape of the mother ship at anchor against the darker, white-flecked gray of the sea.

"Better view from here. Can keep an eye on them. See what they're up to."

"There's no mystery about that," replied Gloria, leaning against the damp basalt, the mouth of the cave before her a ragged, rusty oval shape against a skittish sky unable to make up its mind whether to give way to the high approaching from the south or maintain its unyielding mood. "They're trying to kill us," she said emphatically. "That's what they're up to."

Frank was adjusting the scope. "Doesn't mean we have to make it easy for them."

"No, but what can we do but wait till *Petrel*…" She fell silent, watching him stretch out on the floor of the cave, shift his pack so it provided a rest, place the tiny screwdriver beside it and aim the rifle out toward the mother ship.

"But," Gloria began, not knowing whether to be encouraged or terrified, "they must be almost a mile away from us, Frank."

"More than a mile," he answered without looking around, his left arm taking a turn in the sling. "Don't worry, honey. That's why they make telescopic sights. This isn't a squirrel gun, you know."

She watched as the long sniper's rifle snuggled comfortably into his shoulder, his navy-blue toque hiding the scope from her view.

"They're not going to like this at all," he said, pulling back the bolt then ramming it home. "Better cup your ears, honey."

Whack! into the HIP, high up. Oil sprayed down on the mechanics and then blind panic blew apart the crowd of seamen—running boots, oaths, one man down, the others fleeing, all the size of ants in Frank's scope.

Whack! The ants all but gone, one hobbling toward the dull silvery doors of the hangar, the helicopter pad deserted. Frank didn't know where the second shot went, lowered the sight a tad and saw pieces, like scraps of dark paper, flapping below the twin mounted turbojets. "The wind," he called out to Gloria, "it's pulling the shots too low." The long barrel lifted slightly and he finished firing the magazine of ten before the huge gray shape of the ship began slowly turning, using its thrust against the anchor to maneuver itself as much as possible bow on to the dozens of staring caves.

MARY CRANE TURNED the light switch on and, after flickering for several moments, the neon bulb cast its bluish-white glow over the eight-by-ten cabin. She was right, the latch on the toilet door was swinging like a tiny pendulum back and forth against the imitation-walnut plastic veneer, causing the annoying clacking sound. Torn between her impatience with the captain and with the Scottish mate's equally stubborn refusal to turn back, and the sheer boredom of waiting, she lay on the bunk, staring across at the bulkhead, watching a globule of moisture slowly sliding down the wall. She thought of going on deck, but no one was venturing outside unless absolutely necessary, the danger of being washed overboard growing as *Petrel* pushed on into the worsening weather.

The longer she lay there, the less aware she was of her surroundings and the more aware of herself, of her body, of her desire to have Frank make love to her. She knew they were drifting apart, that her vision of the financial empire she could build was no longer in concert with his and that sooner or later the distance between them would widen so far as to become unbridgeable, even in bed, *especially* in bed. But now, this instant, her need was simply biological, a need that gnawed at her like hunger, wanting to feel him in her, to revel again in the power she had over men, creating such expectancy in them, and to have the power to grant satisfaction. She switched off the light, began to feel herself, her head turning from side to side, murmuring, one hand clasping, her wrists taut then loose, taut again, her sighs, all but inaudible, becoming soft groans—when she heard the toilet door click.

Startled, she sat up, flushed, and her voice dry, cracked, called out. Just as suddenly she calmed down, her hand moving over her pounding heart as she remembered how, without the latch secure, the door often swung open partway during a roll, snapping itself shut as the ship rose on the next swell. It had been the momentary surge of guilt that had made her so quick to think someone was there. But why should she feel any guilt anyway? she wondered; everyone was entitled.... She walked over and pulled the door shut. It occurred to her to go up again to the bridge, or out on deck despite the strong seas for a breath of fresh air, but she still felt so aroused that she decided to stay a while longer in the cabin. Getting up to secure the toilet door's latch she flicked on the cabin light and, lifting the latch's hook, moved to put it in the metal eye.

The door burst open. She was hit in the stomach. Doubled over, unable to scream, trying desperately to get air, she heard the scuffle of sea boots and was hit again on the back of the neck. She glimpsed a face mostly hidden by the high yellow collar of oilskins. Feebly, like a stunned animal, she tried to stand, one arm on the cold metal floor, her other extended futilely above her in a plea for mercy. She was given none and was hit again; this time she saw a bosun's spike coming down to pierce her skull. She kicked out at the attacker's groin.

FROM TWENTY FEET inside the cave, the mother ship was no longer beam on to Frank and Gloria, but appeared as a sharp V facing them, above it a gray, rectangular slab that was the bridge. The helicopter no longer visible, Frank lowered the rifle. "That should keep them busy for a while. I think I hit the chopper's engine assembly twice. They'll have to try to fix it while the ship's beam on to the run of the sea. She'll be sloshing around like a great big whale. If we're lucky it'll keep them hopping until *Petrel*...Gloria?"

Now that all was silent save the sound of sea below and the monotonous moaning of the wind, her exhaustion, aided and abetted by their temporary safety, by the hope of finally getting off the island alive, had made her sleepy again. Her dark hair, dried by wind and the intermittent sunshine, had taken on a chestnut-brown sheen, made more sensuous by the wisps of air sucked in from outside the cave where huge, moving shadows of cloud played teasingly with the light so that one moment she was in shade, the next in sun, its rays penetrating the cave in clusters of golden spears. She was turned to the sun, hands pressed between her knees, Frank's dirtied survival suit several sizes too big for her, making her appear even smaller, more in need of protection, the front of the suit torn by shards of glass as she'd gone through the window of the long hut. The zipper was open to her waist. Watching her lying there, her body instinctively seeking the sun's warmth, Frank felt stirring in him a combination of longing and affection that, in the short time they had known each other, could only be explained, he thought, by the intensity of their present danger. He wondered whether his feelings for her would last only for as long as they were trapped on the island or whether, if they ever managed to get off alive, he would still feel the same.

He watched her draw up into the fetal position for more warmth and, putting down the rifle, went over and, as gently as he could, pulled the zipper all the way up. A strand of hair blowing across her face brought her hand up, and her eyes opened. Slowly, but as if it was the most natural thing in the world, her arms enfolded him, drawing his body to hers, her silken hair falling across his face, her lips softer than her hair, yielding, meeting his as he slid his arms about her, bringing her up to him, her back arching unprotestingly, the spicy smell of her and the feel of her arousing him so suddenly, so unexpectedly, that it excited him more than he could remember. Her embrace tightened, his hardness insistent, pressing, feeling wonderful against her, then harder as he pulled her in to him, his arms taut, fingers digging into her, so strong it took all her strength to breathe, her lips parting in an ecstasy of anticipation, eyes lost in his, so intense in their blueness she momentarily sought respite, looking away, out beyond the cave toward the sea. "My God! Frank—"

The rough circle of turquoise-and-gray-mottled sky that filled the cave's mouth was bisected by the blur of the HIP's rotors, its twin turbojets the bulging eyes of some monstrous fly heading directly for the area of the caves, its short wings, suspended from the fuselage, weapon outriggers, a proboscis protruding from its front like a short, sharp stick beginning to swivel from side to side. A 12.7 mm machine gun. Then it was gone, above their line of sight.

"My God, Frank! Where did it come from?"

"From the ship," said Frank. "Didn't do as much damage as I thought."

They could hear the rotors chopping the air, probably two hundred yards or so away, to the right of the cave, then it was coming nearer, directly over the cliff tops in a muted roar somewhere above them. There was a string of popping sounds as the 'copter passed overhead.

"Machine gun," Frank explained as they both stared up at the dark roof of the rock, Gloria wondering aloud whether it was thick enough to...

There was a muffled explosion, another louder *crump!* followed by multiple whistling noises as fragmentation bombs exploded against the cliff face, sending rust-red dirt streaming down over the cave's entrance.

"They don't know what cave we're in. They're trying to flush us out—make us panic."

"They're succeeding," said Gloria. "What are we going to—"

"Sit tight."

"For how long? It'll be hours before *Petrel* is . . ."

"Until the bastards move off," he said. "Then *we* move."

"Where?"

"Back to the hut. I've been thinking . . . why didn't they come at us with this heavy stuff while we were in there?"

"I don't know. . . . I—we—only got there before, just before dawn. Maybe it was too dark for them to use any—"

"No," said Frank. "I was right. There's something about that damn place they don't want us to—" Another explosion farther off, but they instinctively ducked as the cave shook from the vibration, layers of slate coming down from the roof. Then they heard the chopper moving off. For several minutes there was silence. She clung tightly to him. Then they heard it returning. More bombs started to fall. Frank got up, moving toward the cave's entrance.

"Frank!"

He turned to see her pale face. Her voice had trembled with fright. She was screaming above the din of the explosions above them and the crash of falling rock. "What are you doing?"

Frank clipped a magazine into the rifle, passing her the hand gun. "I'm going up front. We can't sit here and wait for Saburov to get lucky with one of those bombs. Anything happens to me, take the pack and head back, as far as you can, into the cave."

"I'm coming up with you."

Frank shook his head. "No point in you—"

"Frank—"

He paused. "Stay here," he said softly.

There was another explosion to the south, along the cliffs toward the Pinnacle. "What'll I do?" she shouted frantically. "If you don't come back? Frank!" She took his arm, clinging to him.

There was more debris falling over the cave's entrance. Then a bomb exploded nearby. Soon it was several minutes since the last bomb had detonated. Then the dirt stopped falling. Silence. Had they given up? Minutes were ticking away.

Think, he told himself. Think like that bastard, Saburov.

Chapter Thirty-One

AT FIRST CAPTAIN TATE was not worried about Mary Crane's not being in her cabin; after all, she could be anywhere on *Petrel*, sticking her nose in wherever she thought she stood a chance of dissuading officers and crew from going on to the rescue position, still several hours away to the west.

"Have a look aft," he advised Scotty, his attention on the Simrad depth sounder and compass as *Petrel* battled increasingly truculent seas. "She's probably sulking somewhere up by the winch. It's a favorite cubbyhole."

"Aye," said the Scottish mate, who saw it as his job to smooth things over before everyone's anger ballooned into a major problem on board. He and Tate were old hands and understood how what on shore might be simply an argument or tiff soon forgotten could, in the close and often claustrophobic quarters of a ship at sea, quickly become an irreconcilable rift between people. "Like married couples," the mate had once explained, both partners knowing that if either of them doesn't soon move to mend the damage, things swiftly enter the no-talking phase, pride swelling ego until reconciliation is well-nigh impossible.

Tate blamed himself for not having kept his temper in check; he should have simply refused politely to yield to the woman. But her pushy, aggressive manner had a way of piercing his normally calm demeanor so that when he did get his blood up, all his annoyance with her over past incidents had poured out. What was making him feel worse, however, was that he was beginning to think she was correct, that the SOS was a decoy, *Petrel* being suckered away from Eagle Island, now more than eight hours to the east, because of some damn scheme aboard the mother ship. Through the whirring clear-view window, Tate watched a wandering albatross, admiring the bird's effortless grace as it skimmed low up and over the chaos of foam-streaked sea, belying its notorious awkwardness on land. The sweeping ease of its youthful flight contrasting so much with *Petrel*'s ploughing progress transported him back to the confident days of his own youth, when all the world seemed to be waiting for him to discover it and make it his own. Now he was a few years away from retirement, his career all but over, yet the thought of sitting around his wife's manicured house and garden filled him with a cold horror that turned him back to the sounder.

The depth was over eighteen hundred fathoms, which meant *Petrel* was now well beyond the Juan de Fuca Ridge where the ocean plate and continental plate meet and enormous buckling takes place in a never-ending war of tremendous pressures. Sometimes a battle lasted centuries, at other times occurred with such lightning ferocity that whole coastlines and cities were realigned overnight, resulting in hot upwellings of sea gold and a profusion of life in the otherwise cold ocean.

They could not find Mrs. Crane, and a growing mood of unease was settling over the lonely ship. Next to experiencing fire at sea, one of the seaman's greatest fears, that of being swept overboard by a freak wave, was being discussed. Most of the crew had at least one memory of being on a ship when this had happened, usually at night. A monstrous wave, a scream drowned out in the roar of sea across the deck, and a seaman was washed away with the suddenness of a gull plummeting in a wind shear.

"Have you searched the engine room?" Tate asked Redfern.

"What would she be doing doon there, Captain?"

"How would I know, Scotty? But have a look, will you?"

As Redfern left the bridge Tate had a sinking feeling in the pit of his stomach—a board of inquiry, lawyers, newspapers, the verdict of people who hadn't the slightest idea of what a different world it was in the maelstrom of a Pacific storm. Why the hell had they called it Pacific?

"Captain!" It was the lookout on the bridge's starboard wing.

"What is it?"

"Wreckage, sir. Three points starboard!"

BY THE TIME THE GARBAGE SACK was dragged by *Petrel*'s seaman along the corridor from the freezer room, then shouldered, taken the short distance out on deck and, as was done every day at this time, tossed overboard, some of the crew were coming out onto the for'ard deck to see the wreckage. Astern, the weighted garbage sack disappeared in the ship's wake, and the seaman, careful to use the lifelines rigged especially for the storm, moved down the starboard side, joining his fellow crewmen on the for'ard deck, shaking his head, too, as they saw more and more debris floating lifelessly on the uncaring waves.

"Poor bastards," he said, lighting a cigarette, hands cupped against the wind, then offering one to an oiler next to him. "No thanks," said the man. "Don't use 'em.

The crewman drew in heavily on the cigarette and as he blew the smoke out, the wind took it away. "A Chink boat, wasn't it?" he asked.

"Japanese, I think," said the oiler. "No lifeboats yet."

"Ah," said the crewman, smoking, his tone encouraging. "Never say die. Could still be someone out there. Visibility's the shits but we could pick 'em up yet."

"You're hopeful."

"Better'n being down!!"

"I guess. One of the new stewards, aren't you?"

"Yes and no. Signed on just before this cruise but I've been with old man Tate before. Years ago."

"Oh, yeah?"

The steward nodded. "Yeah—he's a good head."

"Not like of some of 'em."

"No," said the steward, knowingly, taking another drag on the cigarette and moving smartly out of the way as several other crewmen, deckhands, passed by, readying boathooks as *Petrel*'s bow thrusters defied the run of the sea, pushing the ship toward what little debris could be seen.

Chapter Thirty-Two

GENERAL KORNON DELAYED taking the call from the Commander of VTA-East, the Eastern command of the Soviet Military Transport Wing. To have snatched the phone up would have signaled to his aide that the general was more concerned than he should be, or, more dangerous, that he had been anticipating the call. He let the aide answer it instead. "Commander of Transport Aviation, General," said the aide.

Kornon glanced up at his aide, a young, efficient lieutenant in immaculate uniform, then immediately returned his attention to the sheaf of reports on an unexpected drop in the catch of the Soviet North Sea fishing fleet. "I'm too busy," he said. "You take it, Kolya."

Kornon kept studying the reports but not focusing on the words, even as he turned the pages, frowning with mock interest, marker pen in hand. He was listening intently to Kolya's responses. When the aide finished with the call and began to speak, Kornon motioned him to stop until he had turned another page. The report in his hand, he swiveled his chair toward the bluish light from the snow. Finally he asked in a disinterested voice, without looking up from the fishing reports, "Yes... what is it?"

"General, Commander Korol reports that the auxiliary generators you ordered for our Eastern fleet have been delivered."

Kornon grunted, indicating he had received the message, and kept on reading. Kolya got on with his other work, and after a few minutes rose and asked if the general would like some tea.

"No, thank you, but go and make some yourself."

Alone in the tearoom, Kolya wrote a short note to Nikolai Borgach, Minister for the Committee on State Security to inform him of the message General Kornan had just received about the successful flight of one of VTA's planes, an 11-76 CANDID long-range transport flying out of Vladivostok with in-air refueling. Kolya was careful not to sign the note. He simply put it in a Defense Ministry envelope for Borgach's attention only.

Kolya had nothing against General Kornon, his boss for the past two years. In fact Kolya quite liked him, but when the minister responsible for the KGB asks you to "keep him informed" of Kornon's "Tartar" scheme so that he might take credit for it if it succeeded, then there was only one answer to give.

"SHE'S GONE, CAPTAIN. We've searched every inch of the ship."

Tate said nothing. Down below, through the misted glass of the bridge's starboard side, he watched crewmen dragging aboard what were clearly the remains of yet another victim of the ferocious Pacific storms. Now his guilt about Mary Crane assailed him with the same intensity as his anger had vented itself against her. Scotty was right—they had lost her.

After what wreckage they could find was brought aboard, *Petrel* turned back toward Eagle Island, ten hours away, the wind behind the ship, increasing her speed. Tate entered the wardroom, carrying with him the oppressive silence he had felt on the bridge. Despite the wailing of the wind, the silence was all-encompassing, for it was the silence of death. The fact that he had found wreckage, vindicating his decision to go on to the SOS position, offered him no consolation. Even if he had felt triumphant, the looks of his officers, and especially his steward, only made the silence heavier to bear. He had lost men before—it was the nature of the sea to take its yearly toll—but never, in all his years at sea, had a woman been lost under his command. That alone was enough to churn his insides. But something else weighed him down, too, haunting him in a vague, undefined way.

It was not until he was on his way to the bridge that the dark possibility came welling up inside him with the burning sensation of bile, declaring itself with the vividness of a nightmare. It was the growing conviction that Mary Crane's death, like Aussie's, might not have been accidental, but that both could have been murdered, and that if he was right, the murderer was still on board.

When Tate reached the bridge, Redfern was taking a loran bearing. Tate, fingers trembling despite his efforts to control them, drew the Scottish mate aside. The two of them had been together on *Petrel* for more than ten years, and Tate trusted him absolutely.

"Scotty?"

"Captain?"

"I want you to go down and get the keys to the cabin Mrs. Crane was using. Search it for anything, anything suspicious, a sign of a struggle, anything. Say nothing about this to anyone."

Redfern nodded. "Aye, but Jesus, man, you don't think—"

"I don't know...."

Tate took over the wheel. The necessity of paying attention to the course heading forced his mind back to the job at hand, to his immediate responsibility to steer the fastest route back to Eagle Island.

Below, Redfern entered the darkness of Mary Crane's cabin—what had been her cabin.

Chapter Thirty-Three

THE FRAGMENTATION BOMBS had all been used. The pilot instinctively tightened his seat belt as he swung the HIP hard up over the red margin between the concrete slab of the hut and the cliff tops, preparing for what would be a gut-wrenching drop to port and another tight turn. He clicked on his helmet mike, informing the other two men aboard, the machine gunner in the nose directly below him and the electronics officer behind, that all bombs were gone. The machine gunner flicked off the safety on his 12.7, picked out a colony of sea lions at the fringe of surf and tested the belt feed with a burst. A spill of red appeared as two or three sea lions flopped about, thrashing helplessly into the lacy white surf. The electronics officer began activating the six suspended packs, each containing thirty-two air-to-surface rockets, and the four "Swatter" homing antitank missiles mounted in slots above.

The HIP banked against the mottled sky, then leveled out, its nose inclined below the Azimuth bar and its tail rotor above so the gunner could see all the caves and not only those dead ahead. The electronics officer deactivated the heat-seeker circuits so that if the rockets were needed they would explode at point-of-aim rather than on the warmer parts of the cliff, which would not be the cooler cave entrances but rather sheer slabs of rock warmed by the sun.

Frank and Gloria heard the chopper approaching. The roaring echo of the turbo engines rebounded off the chocolate-red cliffs in a crescendo of noise that assailed their ears and stomachs. The staccato pounding panicked the thousands of seabirds dotting the sky like confetti. Frank and Gloria could not actually see the chopper, their arc of vision cut by the oval shape of the four-foot-wide, five-foot-high opening of the cave. They quickly moved farther back into the cave. Frank took up position so that the scope's circle covered the cave mouth. Using his haversack as support, spreading his legs out behind him, he brought the carbine up to his right shoulder, laying his cheek against the stock. He took in a long, deep breath, then exhaled a little, holding it, waiting. In the scope, the specks of white and black confetti were farther apart, and as the gray background lightened to a patch of blue, he could see that the dots in it were snowy-white gulls.

From the HIP all the machine gunner could see through the birds were the black mouths of caves all over the cliff face and not a sign of life or opposition in any of them.

FRANK SAW A LONG SHADOW knifing through the birds, the helicopter passing overhead, high above them to the left.

He put down the rifle and began to breathe normally again. "Thank God for those birds. They're keeping the bastards from coming in too low to machine-gun the caves. Russkies don't want the rotors to hit—"

They heard the chopper turning high above, pivoting over the cliff tops, its roar steadying.

"It's hovering," said Gloria. She no sooner had the words out when they heard the long rattling of a heavy machine gun and saw a gap in the sky that moments before had been the curtain of seabirds. Even before the machine-gunning stopped, tiny scarlet explosions and puffs of feathers could be seen midair a few hundred feet from the cave's mouth.

"Dammit!" said Frank. "Now they have a clear run at the caves. They'll come in lower—and closer. We've got to get them at a disadvantage."

"How?"

"I'm working on it."

"You'd better hurry."

The chopper, still out of sight, was moving out over the sea, then got louder as it wheeled in, nose down like some airborne tracker dog, racing at the cliffs.

THE LIEUTENANT PULLED DOWN his visor, scanning the cliff face. "See anything?" he asked.

"Lots of rock!" came the gunner's reply. The birds dispersed even more now that the HIP was coming in at just over fifty knots, around a mile a minute, too fast, the pilot knew, for any detailed look at the cliff face but fast enough that he could wheel away quickly if necessary.

"They're hiding in there somewhere," said the gunner. "Shitting themselves."

"I would be," said the E.W. officer. "We've got enough firepower on here to sink a battleship!"

"Or two!" said the gunner.

"Or three!" said the E.W. officer.

"Shut up! Watch the cliff, gunner!"

"Yes, sir."

The lieutenant pulled back the control column just as the RV-3 altimeter's dangerous-height light started blinking. He kicked the left rudder bar, the HIP responding beautifully as it rose without hesitation. The jagged line of the cliff top ran downhill from the HIP toward the sea as the chopper wheeled around for another run.

The lieutenant turned up the R-860 VHF transceiver to 125 megahertz, reporting to Saburov on the mother ship. Someone had said the political officer was gutless for not going on the HIP's mission. But as much as he disliked the man, the lieutenant knew Saburov had only given up direct command from aboard the HIP because he didn't know airborne drill and so that more rockets and ammunition could be carried in his place. Saburov heard the pilot's report of "no sighting." The pilot knew that the American, wherever he was, was no coward, either; he'd proved that much already merely by landing on the island, never mind taking on Saburov's marines.

Saburov's crackly voice told the lieutenant they couldn't afford time to play hide-and-seek all day, with the American obviously trying to draw fire from him. It was now noon, and in another six hours it would be dark again, and they must clear the area by midnight.

"Do another straight run," ordered Saburov. "If you still don't draw fire go in and take them out by grid. It's slower, I know, than if he'd show himself but it'll be sure. An hour should do it...." Saburov said something else but was momentarily drowned by static, then came on again. "...I said there are fifty-three caves that we can make out from the ship."

The pilot flicked on his close-in radar and watched the amber circles pulsating into wider iridescent greens that started bleeding at the extremities. He made a mental note to report the bleeding to the ground crew—too hard on the eyes in combat flight. The radar registered the cave openings as "hollow" blips, giving a density readout of more

than seventy on the cliff face. The computerized echo de-
tector was unable, despite its fine calibration, to distinguish between cave entrances and fissures in the rock.
"How many caves did you say, Colonel?"

"Fifty-three that a man and woman could crawl into.
But you don't have to count them." The HIP hit a down
draft, dropping beneath the lip of the approaching cliff.
The pilot was ready to go in on grid at a much lower speed,
in some cases hovering momentarily to fire a high-
explosive rocket into each cave by the radar's line of sight.
Saburov was correct; it was much slower but surer. All you
had to remember was to start off with the highest target,
the highest cave in each grid. That way the only way the
American could get any kind of shot up at the chopper—
if he had the balls to try—was to show himself momentarily at the cave mouth below the HIP and get a shot away
at the acute angle. Then you either machine-gunned the
bastard or simply "air-hopped" it over the cliff's rim and
returned at an oblique angle, hovering about two hundred
meters to avoid shrapnel throw-back. Then you computed
him in, firing whatever you damn well pleased into the
cave, blowing it apart like a rat hole.

"THIS IS GETTING ON my nerves," said Frank. "Here." He
handed Gloria the rifle.

"Lord!" she said. "It's heavy."

"Not really," said Frank, unclipping the haversack.
"But I'm not lying around here all day trying to hold it
steady. Sooner or later the scope'd start shaking just from
fatigue."

"What are you doing?" she asked.

"Oh, they think we're too scared to do anything." He
handed her a grenade, its dull khaki paint chipped here and
there from the marine belt's metal clasps. "You press down
on the lever—hard. Got it?"

She nodded.

"All right," he said. "Then when you're ready, pull the pin. Don't pamper it. Pull it—hard but don't yank—otherwise you might drop it...."

She looked harried.

"Hey..." He patted her arm and moved a strand of her hair back gently. "Don't worry." He paused. "Okay then, worry. Who wouldn't? But pull it clean when I tell you, then drop it like this—"

"Frank, I'm terrified. I've never done anything like this. I don't know how. I'll make a mess of—"

"Look," he said, "you ever play baseball?"

"No."

He was incredulous. "What kind of crazy school did you go to, anyway?" Before she could answer he went through the motion of a slow underarm throw. "Got it?" They heard the helicopter, its steady drone taking on a sharper edge by the second. Then a long, terrifying roll of machine-gun fire tattooed into the cliffs above them, to the left or right of the cave, they couldn't tell because of the echo on echo, a hail of splintered rock falling down the rock face. "Come on," he said. "Now we've got no choice." Her hand gripped by his, his right hand holding the rifle, they moved toward the cave's mouth. The HIP zipped sideways like a dragonfly, moving in short, frenetic zigzags, seemingly going backward for a second or two. The Mondev rockets streaked out in pairs, leaving smoky trails that curled and wafted away.

The explosions inside the caves hit were as varied as each cave's depth, some of the detonations shaking the cliff, spewing out fierce orange tongues of flame and rock fragments that came arcing out like masses of tiny meteorites, like a hot rain sizzling into the sea far below.

The machine gunner kept raking the cliff's wall randomly as added insurance, knowing as well as his two comrades that while they were coming in in straight lines in order to lock onto the cave targets, they were vulnerable to a quick shot. The American wasn't about to show his face, but the gunner was taking no chances. Whenever he had to change ammo belts for the 12.7, the lieutenant would take the HIP high over the cliff until the gunner had laid a new belt, ready to start raking the cliff again. He enjoyed the freedom to select whatever target he wanted while the E.W. officer fired off his rockets.

"Russian roulette!" the gunner joked as he selected a cave midway down the cliff and gave it a long burst. A few shots entered the cave but most chopped off guano-covered encrustations, sending up white dust that he thought looked quite pretty against the rusty red of the rock. The HIP shuddered again; another two rockets screamed toward another cave. It was a process of elimination, one by one, and they had more than enough rockets.

"TO THE LEFT OF ME!" instructed Frank. "That's the girl . . . stand flat against the wall." They could hear the chopper firing, away to their left but high. Cunning bastard, thought Frank. No set pattern. He's not working the cliff to any pattern, he's blasting a small grid here, then another somewhere else, so we can't anticipate where he might be.

Out through the cave's mouth he could see the sky was becoming grayer, not as good a background as a nice open blue, but it would have to do. He checked to make sure the safety was off and smiled across at Gloria. "Ready?"

"Yes." She nodded nervously. The wind was blowing into the cave and lifting her hair across her eyes, giving her such an air of vulnerability that she looked even younger than she was.

The machine gun's thudding suddenly exploded all around them. Both of them fell to the floor, arms locked protectively over their heads as part of the burst raked the lip of the cave, splinters of rock singing around them. Frank heard Gloria gasp, then the thudding abruptly stopped, starting up seconds later farther away.

"You okay?" Frank asked, reaching over to her.

She was holding her leg. A rock sliver the size of a pen nib had cut open the survival suit, clean as a scalpel. Frank opened the slit wider and saw blood. He turned to the first-aid kit.

"No," she said. "After."

"We'll take care of this first," he said, taping gauze over the wound and applying pressure.

She was still holding the grenade tightly in her left hand. "No, Frank, let's do it now. My leg won't matter if I'm dead."

"Okay. But will you be able to move to the back of the cave fast enough? I want you back of me, honey," he insisted. "Not in front."

"Sure. Looks worse than it is."

He lifted the rifle and dropped on one knee like a runner readying himself to start from the blocks. "Go!" he said.

Gloria pulled the pin as Frank braced himself, using his thigh as support for the left arm that cradled the rifle. Gloria went a few feet in front of him and simply tossed the grenade in an underarm throw. Immediately she turned, moving fast, crabbing it along the cave wall opposite Frank. The grenade exploded thirty feet below them against the cliff.

The machine gunner saw the flash at the same moment as the pilot. Their teamwork was exemplary, the lieutenant yawing the gunship hard to port, dropping its nose in the direction of the flash of light, while simultaneously adjusting his pitch and roll for a steady point-of-aim rocket attack, the HIP's computer taking over the final millisecond adjustments.

In the few split seconds it took for this maneuver, Frank, hearing the chopper off to his right, moved three feet closer to the cave's edge. He saw the HIP, lifted the rifle, the chopper completely filling his scope, and fired one-two-three-four shots at the blob of Plexiglas in less than two and a half seconds, then ran deep into the cave.

The HIP went wild, its computer firing rockets in all directions. Its pilot, his face like a smashed cantaloupe, miraculously was still breathing, but his torso was shaking loosely in the seat harness like a bloodied carcass, an asthmatic sound coming from some part of him, changing into the soft bubbling of a fountain as the HIP spun around and blood poured from him. The electronics officer tried to control the madly spinning craft that first rose high, belly to the cliff, like some enormously dignified flying lizard, rockets still firing skyward. The machine gunner struggled to get up into the main cabin, while the electronics officer fought furiously to stop circuits shorting near the oxygen feed line. Suddenly the HIP stopped its climb, dropping like a stone, flung from the cliff face the moment its rotors touched the rock. Its rotors' lack of synchronization now sent the HIP down in a grotesque parody of its normal flight, in a spastic shuddering that ended only when it hit the rocks, its tail rotor still intact, snapping off, churning the water in a circle of foam that moments later was gone. The bodies, or rather parts, of the three men scattered over rock and sea, a lone orange foam seat floating between incoming waves.

UNZIPPING HER SURVIVAL SUIT, Frank lifted Gloria's leg gingerly onto the Russian groundsheet and checked the wound. It wasn't deep but was bleeding again so he applied a pressure bandage. She put out her hand and rubbed his arm as it flexed to tie the knot. "You're a sweet man."

He grunted something. Gloria propped herself up against the wall. "You'll have to leave without me, Frank. I'm just too tired."

"No way I'm—"

"You know you'll have to leave me here," she said matter-of-factly. "If you're to go and get help when *Petrel* comes back."

"We don't have to wait for *Petrel*," he answered. "There's still Jamie and the Zodiac."

"No matter who you go to you'll have to leave me here. I'll only slow you down. Your Jamie doesn't know where we are, and it'll take me a lot longer than you to walk back across the island. You'll have to go up to the cement hut— it's the highest point—light a signal fire!"

Unable to deny the logic of her argument, Frank pushed the haversack toward her. "You're a stubborn lady, know that?"

Despite her exhaustion she forced a smile. "Guess so. What's in the bag?"

"Thought I could at least leave you some food," he replied, but she could see his mind was on something else.

"What's wrong?"

He picked up the rifle. "The old hut. You're right. It is the highest part of the island."

"So?"

"There's something that keeps bugging me about it."

"You mean no drilling equipment, no crates? Didn't you say they could have stashed it anywhere on the island?"

"No, I mean something about the hut itself. Keeps coming back to me like a dream...something doesn't fit...but I can't quite—"

Frank saw a trickle of dirt falling over the cave's entrance. Someone was descending the slope above the caves, maybe the two remaining marines Gloria had told him about.

"But they can't know what cave we're in," whispered Gloria.

"No," answered Frank, "but what would you do in their shoes? I'd check out every cave," he answered himself. Taking her by the arm he moved her to the rear of the cave twenty feet away. "Shhh..." he said. "Keep moving. When you get there lie flat on your face and—" He stopped.

They heard another spill of dirt and then small rocks toppling over the cliff.

"Frank! What are you doing?"

"Thinking like Saburov. That Russian bastard must have been watching the cliffs through the chopper attack. They're still watching it. We've got to go to the front of the cave."

A foot from the cave's mouth Frank fixed the bayonet to the Dragunov, making it longer than the four-foot diameter of the cave's opening. Reaching high so that the rifle with bayonet was wedged across the cave like a beam a few feet in from the entrance, he hurriedly undressed and draped the Russian tunic, undershirt, trousers and rain cape from the rifle in a crude curtain. Shivering, clad only in the drab Russian-issue underpants, he pulled out the Makarov 9 mm pistol, the paratrooper's knife in the other hand, and placed them by his side as if kneeling in prayer. He then weighed down the roughly made curtain of wet clothing with fist-size rocks from the cave's floor so that the curtain was taut. And then he waited, looking up through the narrow slit between the rifle beam and the curtain out at a sliver of blue sky, imagining for a second or two that the clear patch was a sign of change to fair weather—a good omen for him and Gloria—and hoping no one would appear at the cave's entrance but sure that Saburov was as ruthless as he was cunning.

Then quite suddenly, as if the gods were against him, gray clouds invaded the blue, at first staining it but then, while another shower of pebbles and dirt sounded somewhere above, obliterating it. He heard an explosion, smaller than the bombs and rockets had been but fiercer, sharper in intensity, then more dirt and veils of guano dust followed. More explosions, some farther away—he guessed a hundred yards or so to his left. The ones on his right, however, were coming closer and, he thought, more frequently. They were bombarding the cliff face in a systematic pattern, and in the sun-deserted gloom of the cave he knew that he and Gloria would only have a split second to act.

"Gloria—quickly. Take off your Mae West!" He reached down for his, jerking the red cord attached to the carbon dioxide cartridge. There was a hiss of air as the canary-yellow life preserver inflated into an enormous bosom. "Do the same!" he told her, grabbing for the haversack as he spoke, pulling out his roll of sodden clothes he'd worn from *Petrel*. "Now, take off your survival suit," he said. There was another explosion, this time only twenty feet or so from their cave.

"I'll freeze," said Gloria, hastily doing what he told her.

"Better than being dead," he replied. "Hand me those rocks by the wall." As she hurriedly passed over the baseball-size rocks to him, Frank added, "Anyway, I'll keep you warm." Finished with his clothes and in a sweat from the fast, furious effort demanded by his plan, he next turned to help Gloria do the same with the vivid tangerine survival suit she'd been wearing. Though only in her bra and panties she, too, was perspiring as he explained exactly what she must do. There was another trickle of dirt, growing bigger by the second as it cascaded over the cave's upper lip like red water. "Now," he whispered hoarsely, urgently. "Go to the back of the cave and remember—"

The cave shook, this explosion no more than six feet outside, near another smaller cave, then a brief silence before he and Gloria heard the clamber of boots. A marine AKM submachine gun blazed at close range like tearing linoleum, another detonation followed by a 600 rpm burst that Frank knew would disintegrate anything in its path, the echo of the long burst rolling from the nearby caves like muted thunder.

There was a hand. Frank tried to grab it, missed, saw a dark green concussion grenade. Throwing himself against the rock wall, Frank fired the pistol as the grenade hit the taut curtain, bouncing off below the cave. He fired twice more, one bullet hitting the thrower's shoulder. This time a grenade exploded on the rebound just below the cave's lip, blowing the marine, screaming, off the overhang into space, its concussion lifting Frank off his feet, throwing him back. The curtain, now holed and ripped, flapped like a torn sail. Frank's nose was bleeding, his ears ringing loudly as he threw out the two dummies, a man and a woman, each torso filled by a Mae West. The trousers' legs and the arms were pinch-tied at the bottom and filled with rocks. Frank's toque pulled down hard on one. The survival suit Gloria had been wearing was particularly lifelike, filling with air as it fell from the cave. Gloria's primeval scream rang out against the cliffs.

Momentarily stunned, her pink underwear lacerated and clinging to her, Gloria nevertheless saw that Frank was much worse off. Gloria started to feel faint but busied herself quickly with the first-aid kit as she attended the multiple lacerations on his chest and face, the worst a cut across his left eye that at once made him want to close it but that stung unbearably when he tried to do so.

Even as his hearing returned, the ringing in his ears remained shrill like a train whistle, altering its pitch now and then but refusing to go away. "Well," he said, "we've had—" he paused, regaining his breath "—what Aussie would have called 'a bloody nice time, mate.'" He winced despite himself as Gloria dabbed iodine on his cut.

In turn, he cleaned a cut on her face made by a piece of shale thrown up by the grenade's blast.

"Well," she said, forcing a grin, "I think you were brilliant."

He grinned, too, sitting up, looking at the cave's entrance then back at Gloria, an expression of cautious hope spreading over his face.

"What is it?" she asked.

"Listen," Frank said, getting to his feet, surprised at how much better he felt after Gloria had come to him, her gentle touch, her closeness, her smell, arousing him despite the danger all around them. He felt certain now about something he had only suspected earlier, that he loved her.

There was silence above. "They've gone," she said jubilantly. "We can get out of here." Her breasts rose and fell quickly in her excitement.

"No," he said. "Not until it's dark. *Then* we get the hell out of here. We—"

She began to laugh. He looked at her quizzically, smiling in return but not seeing any joke. She pointed at the ripped curtain of wet clothes. "You're going to look awfully funny in those." She kept giggling as he got dressed. The khaki Russian tunic was an "absolute write-off," he said, and she fell into a hopeless torrent of laughter. She tried to contain herself, but try as she might she couldn't stop laughing, her sides aching with the sheer joy of being alive. To her amusement, Frank turned away as she took her wet jeans and sweater from the bottom of the Russian's backpack and got dressed.

When she'd finished, Frank sat down beside her, his arms holding her to him. He kissed her and thought that now it might all be okay. If Saburov and the marines, seeing the two "bodies" fall, believed they were dead, the Polish ship would sail away from Eagle Island and unknowingly let them be. Then *Petrel* would return. Soon, when the pent-up tension had ebbed from her, they kissed long and hard, again and again.

WAITING FOR DARKNESS to fall and envelop the island, they clung together in the cave. The cold wind howled around the caves like some giant's breath blowing forlornly over a deserted hive. In the distance they could see the faint bobbing of the motor launch that had come to take the marines back to the mother ship. Gloria snuggled closer to Frank, not only that they might share their body heat but to feel safe at last, to finally unwind after the terrible ordeal of the day. For Frank, relaxation was impossible until they finally left the cave behind them and he could find out what had happened to the two men who had landed with him in the Zodiac. Then, once Gloria was safe on the deck of *Petrel*, he could relax. But where *was* the *Petrel*?

"Frank, what's wrong?" The cool touch of her hand on his forehead was reassuring.

"Don't know exactly," he replied. He felt a deep throbbing headache beginning behind his left eye, spreading along the side of his left temple and down into the muscles of his neck, sending them into a spasm that locked in place so he found it impossible to turn his head without inviting a sharp, needlelike pain in his shoulders. "Something doesn't fit about that hut," he said, his right hand trying to massage away the stiffness in his neck. Outside they could see the dot of the motor launch in the swells, nearing the mother ship's side.

"Well," said Gloria, "it doesn't matter now they've left the island."

Frank's fingers dug deeper into his muscle, as much to clear his head as to relieve the pain so he could think clearly. Gloria handed him several aspirins from the first-aid pack. He took them but they made no difference to the pain. It was almost, he thought, as if he was punishing himself for something with the pain. Maybe he was feeling guilty about falling head over heels for Gloria even though Mary must have known months ago that any romantic involvement he had had with her was over. No, it wasn't Mary Crane that was bothering him.

Gloria made him lie facedown. After all he'd been through, she said, was it any wonder he still felt tense? She kissed him, then sat up and, despite the cold seeping into her very bones now that nightfall was almost there, she massaged him until she could hear him sigh and groan with relief.

"I love you," he murmured. "Know that?"

"Yes."

Outside in the failing light she could see a dot crawling up the side of the mother ship. The motor launch was being winched up. She told Frank. Her fingers caressed his neck. "Pain gone?"

"Yes," he lied.

Chapter Thirty-Four

"WHY WASTE MORE TIME?" asked Captain Novisk, anxious to start weighing anchor. "You've been insisting we leave no later than midnight. So why wait any longer if we can get a head start on our way back to Gdansk?"

Saburov was only half listening to the Pole. "Because," he said, "I'm waiting for the film to be developed. It'll be ready in fifteen minutes."

"But Comrade Colonel, you said you saw it with your own eyes."

Saburov loosened his collar and took off his cap. "I saw it through binoculars," he said.

"So?" asked Novisk. "All the better. More effective than the naked eye."

The colonel took out a khaki handkerchief and wiped the back of his neck. "We'll wait for the film, Comrade!"

Novisk shrugged and rang the engine room. "Not yet, Chief."

The chief engineer's profanity was so violent that even Saburov was moved to explain further. "A film will show us more," he told the captain. "The eye sees it for a second—then it's gone. The camera records."

Novisk glanced at the clock above the bridge's console and sent one of his senior officers down to the darkroom to hurry things up.

ABOARD *PETREL*, Scotty reported back to the bridge and saw that the barometer had fallen to the line below 7 that separates Storm from Very Stormy. By the time they reached Eagle Island there would be no lull left in the southern storm line flowing over the island. Instead the area would most likely be engulfed again in a storm, this time struck from the west instead of the south. Tate and Scotty withdrew into the relative privacy of the chart room, the ship's motion smoother now that she was running with the sea, the wind behind her.

"Find anything?" asked Tate without preamble. "Any sign of a struggle?"

"No-o, sir. Cabin's tidy as can be. And I think that's the trouble."

"What do you mean?" asked Tate.

"Ach, sir. Perhaps there's nothing to it."

"Scotty!"

"The bed was made."

"So she made her bed?"

"Or the stewards made it, sir. I mean it was fresh linen."

Tate was biting his lower lip. "And today isn't change day. Is that it?"

"Exactly, sir. A complete change—pillowcases and all—is kept in the drawers beneath the bunk. 'Course she could have done it herself. Trouble is, there's no sign of the stripped linen."

Could be nothing. Maybe, as Scotty said, she had made the change herself. But if she hadn't, then the bed had been made afresh for a reason. To hide a sign of a struggle? Or—he didn't want to think about it, but if any blood had splattered . . .

The port side door to the bridge opened and a cold draft of sea air flooded the bridge and chart room. One of the ship's three stewards, the oldest of them, a man who Tate recognized had sailed on and off with him over the past ten years, stood at the door of the chart room. "Excuse me, Captain. . . ."

"Yes. What is it?"

"There's something a bit queer in Mrs. Crane's cabin, sir, and I thought I—"

"What's queer?" asked Tate hastily.

"Well, sir," said the steward, looking from the Scottish mate to Tate, "I'm responsible for the linen count and the wash. And when I counted up this afternoon, 'bout half an hour ago, I didn't get the right number. I thought I counted wrong so I went over it again, sir, but I was right. There's a set missing. The whole lot. Sheets, top and bottom, pillowcases, too. So I checked crews' quarters. No one knew anything about 'em so I checked officers' and scientists' cabins. All had the spare change set in 'em except Mrs. Crane's."

Tate nodded, then looked at his third mate. "What do you make of it, Scotty?"

Scotty shrugged noncommittally. "Don't know." He looked over at the steward. "You have any ideas, Steward?"

The steward's lips tightened.

"Go on," said Tate. "Spit it out."

"Well, I'm no detective, Captain, but well... Mrs. Crane's missing and we've searched the ship top to bottom. If she'd been..."

His eyebrows knotted in deep suspicion and Tate finished for him. "You mean if she'd been... killed?"

"Yes, sir. If she has... if she was killed in her cabin and there was blood or anything to mop up— Oh, I almost forgot, all her towels are gone, too."

Tate thought for a moment, then pushing himself away from the chart table he patted the steward on the shoulder. "All right. Thanks for telling us— Martin, isn't it?"

"Yes, sir."

"Keep it to yourself."

"No sweat, sir."

"Good man... and Martin?"

"Sir?"

"Keep your eyes open."

Martin nodded accommodatingly.

"If you see anything funny, tell Mr. Redfern or me."

"Yes, sir."

As Martin left the bridge Tate called over to the man at the wheel. "Helmsman, you hear any of that?"

"Most of it, sir."

"Not a word. Got it?"

"Yes, sir."

Tate and the second mate went below for coffee. "So, Scotty. What do you think? Is it Martin? Being so help-ful? Or is he on the level?"

"Or did the laddie see me go into her cabin and just happen to come up noo—to cover his backside?"

"Well," said Tate, perplexed, "he does do the linen check and you have to take your time. I mean, you have to be pretty damn sure of something missing before you go crying theft on a ship, Scotty. Most serious charge a man can make."

"Except murder!" said Scotty. "Besides, who's inter-ested in stealing bloody sheets?"

"Whoever killed her," said Tate pointedly. "If she *was* murdered."

"Christ," said Scotty. "What do we do?"

"Damned if I know."

"Keep an eye on him."

"Who, Martin?" Tate grunted. "If it's him he'll be the first one to know he's being watched."

"Aye. It's a right bastard."

For a fleeting moment Tate had the horrible thought that it could as easily have been Scotty as anyone else aboard. Besides, the last people seen with her, arguing fiercely with her, were Scotty and himself. It was as if fate was on the murderer's side.

SABUROV LIT another cigarette, taking a long pull on the rich, coarse Turkish tobacco, holding the smoke captive as it coursed through his lungs while he waited impatiently, trying not to show it, for the junior officer to start the 16 mm projector. The first frames flickered fitfully on the screen. Nervous in front of the political officer, knowing so much was riding on the films, the junior officer—the same man who had seen the two Americans running down from the hut to seek refuge in the cluster of caves—had threaded the film too quickly so that it was now off the sprockets. The film shuddered violently on the screen as the latter rose and fell with the mother ship. There were some good-natured booing and some sarcastic remarks in the darkness of the wardroom as the junior officer worked quickly to rethread the film in the dim glow of the projector's pilot light. But after another futile attempt, he had to call for the main wardroom lamps to be switched on in a humiliating admission of defeat. Whistles and catcalls ensued, some of the Polish officers taking the opportunity to blame the delay on Saburov, who studiously ignored them, staring impassively ahead and smoking.

Captain Novisk leaned over, telling the junior officer to take his time, sending the youngster into greater panic so that it was another five minutes before the film was again on track.

"Sound!" someone shouted as the overhead lights went off.

"There is no sound, you fool!" It was Saburov, swinging around, his wide Soviet officer's cap prominent in the curling haze of thick smoke. There was silence as he turned back to the screen. A slightly flickering black-and-white film showed the high cliffs, a quick shot of the cement hut appeared briefly at the top of the screen, then a sweep over the tall grass bending beneath the southern wind, and then, jerkily, back to the cliffs again. A zoom shot toward the cliffs showed what looked like insects crawling around over the cluster of cave openings, which in the film were no more than dark blobs, though some, caught in the shifting sunlight, were clearer than others. About every thirty seconds or so, one of the caves suddenly became a smudge of black on black, as some of the marines, slightly bigger than insect size now in the zoom, stopped moving. They continued moving carefully over the bulbous projection of rock, each marine responsible for clearing a cave with a grenade followed by submachine-gun fire. Occasionally Saburov could see a wisp of smoke from the small-arms fire, but none of this interested him.

Novisk hunched over his wristwatch in the darkness, but if Saburov saw him the Russian gave no sign as he lit another cigarette. The only satisfaction Novisk got, the only indication that Saburov was as aware as he of how little time they had left, was beads of perspiration on Saburov's brow beneath the peak of his cap. Novisk thought, however, they might simply be caused by the heat in the overcrowded wardroom.

Suddenly the glow of Saburov's cigarette darted forward. "Stop! There it is! Run it back. Stop!" Saburov leaned forward, pointing at the screen. The whirring sound of the projector on hold seemed to fill the room as all chatter from the audience of officers halted. Now all of them, including those who hated Saburov and what he stood for, were attentive, knowing that what they saw in the next few minutes would decide whether or not they would be weighing anchor and heading for home. On top of that, despite official party policy against gambling, wagers had been made throughout the ship. One of the motor launch petty officers who had gone in to pick up the marines was running a book on the outcome, the bets involving thousands of rubles, vodka allowances and even prized digital watches smuggled from West Berlin. It was about an even split: most of the crew said that Saburov was *wariat*, nuts, that he was so worried about what Moscow might do to him if he *zawalil*, cocked it up, that he was cracking, seeing Americans under every damn rock on the island.

The officers who had had an opportunity to observe Saburov at closer quarters pointed out that up until things had started to go awry a couple of days before, when the American woman had escaped, Saburov had been on top of things. They grudgingly admitted that he had done a pretty good job—for a Russian! Yes, they admitted Saburov was no one's fool, least of all Moscow's, and he wanted it kept that way, which was why, they said, he was playing it so safe. "Wouldn't you?" some of them asked their comrades.

The motor launch bosun didn't like their assessment at all. "Too close to call," he said, which was his way of noting that whoever was correct—those who thought Saburov was just seeing things or those who suspected he was right—a bookmaker could only hope to come out even. To add to the bookie's anxiety, somebody who had been up to the wardroom for coffee reported to the lower decks that the damned film had broken, so now there'd be another delay until they got it spliced.

"Marvelous, isn't it?" complained the bosun, talking to some of the twenty or so bosun's mates who were gathered around the soccer-field-size engineering and repair shop deep in the bowels of the ship. "Marvelous. The Russians've got satellites as sophisticated as the Yanks but their stupid projector is a museum piece. Typical!"

"Well," said another defensively, ticking off repairs that had had to be done on the launch that had picked up the marines, "hate to tell you this, bosun, but the projector's probably one of ours."

The bookmaker grunted. That wasn't the point. What he was afraid of was that Saburov might be right. If so, he saw another postponement in getting under way, and if that happened he'd have to entirely revamp the odds for his estimated time of arrival based on leaving the island at midnight. Like so many others aboard he was starting to get very tired of the two Americans; they were fouling up his timetable, the ship's, Moscow's and everyone else's who wanted to get home after the wearing two months at sea.

THE TWILIGHT LASTED less than a quarter hour. The moment darkness fell, Frank and Gloria got up and, with Frank leading, cautiously made their way out of the cave. Frank drew the sling of the rifle tight so his hands would be free to steady Gloria as she sought firm toeholds in the shale-covered rock, which was proving more treacherous on the way up in the pitch-dark than when they had come down in their haste from the old cement hut.

After several minutes they stopped to take their bearings, trying in the faint and intermittent wash of moonlight to follow the shortest, yet at the same time safest, route back. But rocky outcrops, so distinctive on the way down, now all looked the same, preventing a clear view of the cliff top so that they were forced to go much more slowly than they'd intended.

Frank sensed Gloria's fear and tried to reassure her. "Don't push it, sweetie. Now they think we're kaput we've got all the time in the world to reach the Zodiac."

"How do you know your friends'll still be there? Didn't you say you told them to move farther down the coast if you weren't back in time?"

"That was before all the firing started and the chopper attack. My guess is they'll still be there, not wanting to show themselves. Anyway, even if they're not exactly where we landed, as soon as *Petrel* comes in sight, they'll pop up somewhere. And by then the mother ship will be long gone."

"Hope you're right."

"Know what Aussie would have said? 'Not to worry!'" Unable in the darkness to see the expression on his face, only hearing his voice, full of confidence, she had no way of knowing that his headache was so bad the steel band he felt around his head was now tighter than ever and his optimism nothing more than an attempt to comfort her. He was in fact as worried as she was about the Zodiac's having moved since he'd landed, and he wondered how long Gloria could last in sodden clothes and shoes and with all their food now gone. They could rest up in the cement hut, start a small fire with the wind-dried grass, at least until first light. But they could only do this after the mother ship had left the island and not before she disappeared out of view beyond the northern headland.

ABOARD THE MOTHER SHIP the mended though scratchy film started up again, and when it got to the part where the zoom lens showed one of the marines suddenly and silently blown from the face of a cave, followed seconds later by two other bodies, Saburov was on his feet. "There!" The film stopped, not as bright now, the two falling figures suspended in midair. Saburov walked up to the screen, holding in one hand both his cigarette and a navigator's two-piece magnifying bridge, usually used to slide over charts to enlarge finely drawn depth markings. He held the magnifying glass closer to the screen, swiveling his officer's cap back to front. The cap and his shoulder boards blocked most of the screen, casting a huge shadow of himself across the tall cliffs and the white streak of stilled surf along the bottom of the screen. The female figure was lower, falling ahead of the other American whom he had never seen but felt that he knew now as well as any man can know his enemy face-to-face.

Saburov moved the navigator's glass directly over the woman. "No hair that I can see," he said to no one in particular.

"Tucked in the parka's hood," suggested Novisk.

"Not a parka," Saburov corrected pedantically. "A survival suit. Same one as the marines saw from the Pinnacle when they were being fired upon."

"Well, survival suit then," conceded Novisk in a spirit of conciliation.

An officer came up and whispered to Novisk. The chief engineer was grumpy as a bear, demanding to know how much longer before he could get steam up.

Novisk waved the officer aside, giving his full attention to the screen. "The point, Colonel," he continued, "is that her hair would be most likely wrapped up in the parka's—survival suit's—hood, correct? You know how women are about their hair. They won't—"

"Another frame!" ordered Saburov, and the projector ground forward then stopped. The woman's arms were hanging down limply, "As if she was already dead," commented Novisk, "before she hit the rocks."

"But what are they doing so close to the edge?" asked Saburov. "Wouldn't they have been farther in the cave?"

"Not if they wanted to try and stop the grenade, Colonel," said Novisk. "What would you do—retreat to where there's no way out? You'd get chopped to pieces by shrapnel in a confined space like that."

"Yes," agreed Saburov, "I, too, would try to meet the attacker up front—kill him before he could throw in a grenade."

"Then they got it half-right," said Novisk. "Only trouble is the blast sucked them out as they killed your man. Now we can go home?"

"Hmm," murmured Saburov, feeling better about what had happened, but still trying to match up what the camera had seen with what he thought he might, or might not, have seen with the naked eye in what had been less than a few seconds through the binoculars.

The next frames he peered at closely showed the woman hitting the rocks at the bottom of the cliff, bouncing a little as bodies will from such a height, he knew. Then it lay still, crumpled on the rock, looking like a sky diver whose parachute had failed to open. The second figure, a toque barely visible, could be seen hitting the water, the splash on the stopped film a white blur frozen in time. The next jerk of the film took the American farther into the water until frame by frame the splash finally disappeared.

Saburov lit another cigarette as more frames were shown. Nothing but water. The figure did not reappear. Saburov had the film rewound and again ran the man hitting the water and disappearing.

"My God!" It was one of Novisk's senior officers who saw it, too, who confirmed Saburov's initial skepticism when he'd watched the figures tumbling down, first the marine hitting the water, his dead body bobbing up, washed to and fro near the cliff like an errant cork, then the American, going under and failing to reappear.

"Exactly," said Saburov, taking absolutely no pride in discovering that his suspicion about a human body that plunged into the sea and didn't float had been proved right, that he *had* seen what he thought he'd seen. Instead he was merely acknowledging the fact, knowing how little time they had, five hours at most, before they must leave. Knowing that he now had only one option.

He turned to the assembled officers. "The Americans have made fools of us all, Comrades. If we fail this last part of our mission, this ship will be in great danger, never mind disrepute."

Even Novisk felt something cold turn over in his belly. He might dislike the Russian but the colonel was right, and in one stroke he had made the most telling of appeals to seamen. Not to their love of country—he knew better than that, with Moscow running every country in the Eastern Bloc. No. Comrade Saburov had hit their most vital nerve, the seamen's tie to their ship. They might hate her at times, love her at others, but whatever she was, the great thing was theirs. Above all, even on the least sentimental level, on the most practical level, they knew if the ship fell into danger, if she died, so would they. They had no choice. In this, Saburov's enemies were their enemies. Some of them were already more than merely "put out" with the Americans, they were mad at them. The Americans shouldn't have been on the damn island in the first place.

FRANK AND GLORIA reached the top of the cliff, pausing for breath and trying in vain to talk above the screeching of the gulls and cormorants, which filled the night with their raw and primitive cries. By the time the two of them reached the hut, gulls were rising in a black hail across the moon, having grown afraid over the past few days of the approach of any humans.

The roof of the long cement hut was devoid of all birds but one as Frank climbed up to see whether or not the mother ship had left. She still lay at anchor, though he could see her building up steam, threads of wind-whipped smoke disappearing in the translucent seas of nimbostratus. He estimated that the ship would have a full head of steam in a few hours and that by midnight she would be gone. He wasn't particularly religious but said a prayer of thanks anyway for their deliverance. As he was making his way along the roof of the hut, he was able to smile again, seeing the same determined bird calmly perched in the middle of the roof, turning abruptly every now and then as if oblivious to any of the concerns of men.

Before dropping down from the roof Frank took another look at the bird, full of renewed admiration for its courage, or was it really stupidity? It moved around again, then quickly back the other way. Now that he had time to look more closely at it, there was something odd about its turning, fluid yet so abrupt at times it seemed to be swiveling or pivoting on one spot. Another gust of wind played around the hut and the bird quickly turned back and forth.

He crawled through a slime of bird droppings to within a foot of the gull, holding out his hand. It looked directly at him, swung away, then turned back again. He touched it, took gentle hold of it, and there was no protest. The bird's body was ice-cold as if stone dead. But there were no feathers, though the shape and proportions were so exact

that Frank had to admit it would fool anyone under normal circumstances. The plastic was the same kind, he
guessed, as was used to make duck decoys and the like for
hunters. The bird was mounted with a small cotter pin on
an inch-long tube sticking out from the roof, the tiny well
or moat around the tube—it felt like copper tubing—
greased so that the bird could rotate easily.

Frank tried to lift it off the mount but the cotter pin
held. He had better luck smacking it from the side. A few
good clouts and the bird came off, the body still attached,
however, to some kind of fine wire, about three-sixteenths
of an inch in diameter, leading down into the hut. He
couldn't recall any piping or wiring visible inside the hut.
Perhaps it ran along through the ceiling or inside the wall
panels. Or maybe it was part of the wiring left over from
the old radar complex in World War II. But the plastic bird
was in too good condition, too recently made for that. It
was obviously some kind of wind vane, an anemometer,
but what for? Unless you were drilling at sea, what was the
use of a wind indicator?

When Frank entered the hut he heard a low, rumbling
noise. He stopped, listening intently, holding the bird, then
realized it was Gloria snoring. He had wanted to see how
her leg was but judged it better for her to get the rest.
Though tired himself, he wanted to check out the wire, but
until the mother ship left he couldn't risk using the flashlight or lighting a fire. He looked at his watch. Nine-thirty.
The ship would be gone in a few more hours. His headache had abated now that he'd finally had time to rest. He
started to doze off, increasingly mesmerized by the moaning of the wind, but then got up, determined not to drift
off until he saw the Polish ship steam away. He walked
outside to stretch his legs and get a few blasts of the cold
wind to keep him awake.

Emerging from the hut, still thinking about the bird, of
what possible use an anemometer would be for drilling on
the island, he saw the sea sliced here and there by moon-

beams, and then watched the moon disappearing behind cloud so that the sea once more was in darkness. He noticed the patch of flattened grass where the dead Russian had been; no doubt the other marines had taken him back to the ship, not even burying their dead on the island for fear of giving their presence away. He was struck again by how far men would go to protect their claim to gold, whether it be in some hidden mine in High Sierras or in the form of untold riches under the sea. He thought of what he had told Mary Crane, of how it was the search that motivated him—whether, as part of his oceanographic business, it was to help the Navy find and refloat sunken ships, or the Air Force a downed fighter. Whatever form they took, it was the discovery of the ocean's secrets that excited him. He had seen that Mary didn't believe him, or rather that she didn't want to. Gloria, on the other hand, would.

The moon reappeared, and while he had the opportunity he took in the wild beauty of the place. He looked northward across the grasses, then south to the Pinnacle, no more than a massive hump a quarter mile southeast of the hut. He couldn't hear the birds as clearly as before because of the strong westerly howling behind him and because his ears were still ringing from the explosion of the grenade. He saw the dark slab of the mother ship, though now there didn't seem to be any smoke trail, either that or the smoke was invisible against the dark patches of sky beyond the moon's corona. Though exhausted, he felt elated that he and Gloria had returned safely from the cave, and for a moment pride won out against his usual reserve and he chuckled at having beaten the opposition.

The clouds broke temporarily, bathing the entire island in moonlight. The seas of grass bent all around him and the ocean was transformed to crinkled silver. Closing his eyes he took in a deep breath of the cold, bracing sea air, spiced with the tangy smell of the grass and seaweed that momentarily overcame the stink of guano from the cliffs.

When he opened his eyes, half expecting the moon to be swallowed up again by cloud, the moonlight was even brighter, the silvery race of sea between the cliffs and the mother ship flecked with what he assumed must be white-caps starting up as a result of the westerlies in spite of the island's protective bulk.

His stomach tightened. "Son of—" He went into the hut, took up the rifle and, using the side of the hut as a stand, put the scope to the silvery sea. There were so many that at first he thought it must be spotting on the scope's lens, but on his second look there was no doubt. It was an armada—motor launches towing lifeboats towing smaller craft, all jam-packed with men. Here and there he could make out the black stick of a rifle among them as they pitched up and down the swells, heading for the island. There were so many, more than twenty boats in all, that he knew there must be at least two hundred men coming for them. Almost the entire mother ship's complement—no doubt led by Saburov and the marines.

THEY WERE RUNNING, the wind-dried grass swishing past noisily, the end of the hut a blur in the moonlight, the wind howling around their ears. Gloria tried to speak, tried to make sense of what was happening. Was she in a night-mare? Frank had shaken her awake, dragged her to her feet, snatched the haversack, and now she was trembling, cold. She had seen what looked like a dead bird near where the haversack had been, heard Frank yell something about boats and men. She assumed for a moment that *Petrel* had returned, but then Frank kept shouting that Saburov hadn't finished with them after all, that the wily Russian hadn't fallen for the decoys, and was now coming to kill them once and for all.

"There's something in that damn hut," Frank called out as they ran.

"I didn't see anything in the hut."

"Too dark," he answered. "Yesterday we didn't have time...."

Only then did Gloria's head clear enough for her to realize where she was, not heading for the western side of the island but for a promontory jutting out high on the eastern cliffs, overlooking the approaching invasion force from the mother ship. "Frank, shouldn't we be heading for—"

"And do what?" said Frank, dropping down by the haversack and taking another look at the armada through the scope. "Go where? To our Zodiac? They'd be swarming all over the place by the time we got there. *If* it's still there. Besides, they'd simply sail around the other side and trap us there. More than twenty boats against us. We wouldn't stand a chance. Anyway, they're armed as well. We've only got the rifle and the grenades from that dead Russian." He lowered the scope. "See the line of boats? Four abreast. Coming in waves." Shorter than Frank, Gloria couldn't see the boats closest inshore, but could plainly see the remaining fifteen or so a half mile from the cliffs, bunching closer together, forming a wedge.

"It's because there's only one landing place," Frank explained. "Where the launch picked up the marines. They can only get one, maybe two, boats in at a time, otherwise they'd pile up."

"What can we do?"

He was leading her out to the very tip of the promontory. "C'mon," he said. "I'll show you."

Chapter Thirty-Five

AS OFFICER OF THE WATCH, Redfern took an obligatory look at *Petrel*'s radar. It showed nothing but interference. He turned his attention to the compass, reading out, "Zero-eight-five degrees," making sure the helmsman was on as steady a course as the worsening weather would allow. Despite the urgency to reach Eagle Island before the heart of the westerly storm overtook the ship, Redfern knew from long experience that there was always the danger of nodding off. The constant whine of the clear-view window spinning, the constant buffeting of wind and sea, the steady, rhythmic thumping of the four G.M. engines all combined to take the edge off the men's concentration on watch, especially when they knew that it would be at least another four hours before the ship was in sight of Eagle Island.

Now and then a blast of wind would catch the ship on the port side and rattle the heavy oak door that separated the bridge proper from its wing. Redfern would turn around sharply to see the door thud back on its hinge as if taunting him with the constant suspicion that someone was trying to come in. He half expected to see Mary Crane's face suddenly appear to give the lie to the mystery of her disappearance; or was it, he wondered, that he had begun to suspect everybody and anybody of being the murderer, of prowling the ship amid the wild gale? Had she simply been washed overboard, in which case the steward's report about the missing linen was either mistaken or made no sense?

The door groaned again and he swung around. Damn! He'd be glad to reach Eagle Island, pick up Hall and head for home. The compass needle had swung to 089 and he told the helmsman to stay sharp.

IN MOSCOW the snow was deep and still falling on the spires of St. Basil's as General Kornon took off his coat, accepted steaming tea from his aide and without a word sat down to read the most urgent dispatch—a decision in a court martial of a junior officer, drunk on duty, charged with running a patrol boat aground in the Black Sea.

"No one farther down wants to deal with it, General," commented Kolya.

The general glanced at his aide. "Why?"

"Related to the Minister of the Interior, isn't he, sir?" said Kolya in as neutral a tone as he could manage.

"I believe so," replied Kornon, "and General Borgach has passed it on to me. Kind of him." The general used the delicate question of special privilege for the drunk officer as a convenient excuse to steer away from the subject to the matter of the fishing fleet quotas. "Any information on the catch in the Northeast Pacific?" he asked.

"Nothing this morning, sir. Should I try to contact them?"

Kornon shook his head. "No, it's just routine for the books. Anyway, Gdansk will let us know in time, I suppose."

"I can phone Gdansk if you wish."

"Don't bother." The general took another sip of the piping-hot tea. "No pastries this morning?" he asked lightheartedly.

"Hadn't arrived when I got here," answered Kolya. "I'll go check."

"Good. Bring me two."

"Yes, sir."

"Kolya?"

"Sir?"

"Better make that one."

Kolya smiled. "Only one. Yes, sir."

When his aide left, Kornon telephoned Gdansk. "No, Comrade," reported the commissioner for fisheries, there was no report that the Northeast Pacific's fleet was on its way home.

"Then the mother ship?" asked Kornon irritably. "Has *she* left for Gdansk?"

"No, sir. Not that we've heard. Mind you, there's a lot of bad weather and the static is—"

Kornon heard Kolya's footsteps coming down the hall and hung up softly. When his aide entered the room the general was studying the court martial file closely. It seemed appropriate, he thought, that he should be studying how quickly an officer's career could fizzle out. It made him more determined that it wouldn't happen to him, that if he didn't hear by midnight northeast Pacific time that the Polish mother ship had left, he would have to play his ace card.

His aide noticed that the general ate, or rather devoured, his pastry so quickly that he could hardly have tasted it. The general, he was sure, was extremely worried, but Kolya would not yet report this to Borgach. Kornon had survived crises before, and Kolya had a hunch the general would survive this one as well.

Chapter Thirty-Six

BY THE TIME FRANK and Gloria had reached the spear-shaped point of the promontory that stuck out more than two hundred feet above the sea, their hands and faces were lacerated and stinging from the now dry, sharp sword grass. To make matters worse, the moon had disappeared again so the sea had lost its sheen, and instead they found themselves looking down on a dull metallic ocean against which the boats were difficult to distinguish, except for the first line. These were backlighted against the effervescent surf. The waves, after pounding themselves to exhaustion against the rock face, could be seen constantly dissipating in an increasing backwash of foam and spray that washed up against the slabs of shalelike rock, four or five feet above sea level, that had been used earlier as a landing platform for the mother ship's launch.

The first boat, a motor launch crewed by a bosun and two seamen, carried fifteen men, one of them the corporal of the marines. The other fourteen consisted of one Russian, who, most suspected, was KGB, and thirteen seamen ranging from deckhands to oilers not on Saburov's essential list. All were armed with standard-issue Polish PMK rifles and one hundred rounds of ammunition. The corporal was touting his AKM, a gas-operated version of the Kalashnikov 7.62 mm, capable of emptying a thirty-round magazine in four seconds. In addition, the corporal had distributed two grenades apiece to each man in the boat, keeping six for himself, attached to the canvas webbing belt around his middle. Every man in the armada knew that the man who stood between them and home was called Hall and that Colonel Saburov had authorized special rewards for the man who killed him.

As the launch neared the rock slab that was level with the top of its superstructure, the bosun swung the wheel hard aport, bringing the boat hard astarboard, its gunwales racing toward the slab. Another wave pushed the launch high into the line of foam, then, just as suddenly, it was sucked away, the gunwales one moment level with the slab, the next in the deep trough of the retreating wave. The bosun shouted something. Though Frank couldn't hear what he said, he saw two seamen's arms suddenly grow long, two pikes thrusting out, steadying, keeping the launch away from the slab until all fifteen men were ranged along the starboard side ready to leap ashore on the next swell. The launch rose again, its mast arcing quickly at the apogee of the swell. Frank fired four shots.

Three bodies slumped in the crowded boat. There was a rush by the remaining men from the launch's starboard side, which was nearest to the cliff, to the port side. Frank saw the launch's mast swing wildly from the bottom of the scope to the top. He then shifted the scope to the four life-boats pitching and tossing behind the launch, knowing as well as the bosun in command of the launch that the sudden shift of the human cargo from one side to the other meant the vessel had rolled beyond the point of no return. And as he fired into the lifeboat immediately behind, he could hear screams thrown up against the boiling surf as the launch turned belly up, some men trapped beneath, others—about six dark blobs—struggling frantically to stay afloat in crashing waves. The second boat didn't roll over, but its helmsman, Frank's prime target, slumped over the tiller, his weight keeping the wildly rocking boat on line, heading straight for the overturned launch.

At the last second someone managed to swing the tiller so that the boat began to come about. But instead of smashing its bow on into the capsized launch, which might have acted on it as a brake, it sheared alongside the launch and, lifted by an incoming wave, was dumped hard astarboard as the wave collapsed, capsizing the boat. In the process it scraped off several seamen who had been hanging on to the ribbed bottom of the upturned launch.

The men in the third boat had quickly cut themselves free of the common towline connecting it to the capsized crafts ahead, but its seamen, like so many in the age of diesel, had no tradition of dealing with longboats of any kind. The lack of discipline and training caused most of their deaths. Without firing a shot, Frank watched while men who had little or no experience handling anything smaller than a five-thousand-ton freighter scrambled hopelessly and ineptly to steady the third boat as she, too, came about to face the merciless battalions of storm-driven waves. The boat rode over the first two waves all right but was already taking on too much water. As quickly as her conscripted crew bailed, under futile shouts of a bosun, more water slopped into her. There was a belated effort to man oars either side of her but it was like a tragicomedy. The boat sank ever more certainly, the oars out of sync, whipping up the sea around her in what was meant to be a lifesaving effort of sculling but was nothing more than the frenzied panic of men who had never rowed anything together, who jerked the long oars against the oarlocks instead of pulling rhythmically and in unison. It was the chaos of each man acting alone, rowing himself farther under.

As the third lifeboat disappeared from sight, four or five men struck out for the landing. Only two made it to the slab, washed ashore more by the wave's high peak than by their own efforts. Frank didn't have to think of Julio's death, of the professor's, or of any of the cold-bloodedness of Saburov's intent to murder him and Gloria; all he reminded himself of at that moment was the simple fact that out of about two hundred men who were coming to the island to kill him and Gloria, some of them were bound to make it ashore despite the chaos he had helped inflict on the first wave.

Three lines of boats were still approaching the island. He shifted the scope to cover the spray-polished slab of the landing rock. Three men, all armed, were making their way toward the steep rocky trail that wound and snaked its way to the cliff tops. He fired three times. One of them fell, another was flung backward off the cliff, lost to the darkness of rock.

Already the last two boats in the initial wave of five were nearing the slab now that the pileup of the first three boats had been swept aside by the swirling current at the base of the cliffs. Frank could see the flashes of semiautomatics from the boats behind them and heard bullets passing overhead, some thudding into the cliff face directly below. "Time to move!" he called out to Gloria.

With that he took up another box magazine of the 7.62 mm, clipped it into the Dragunov, grabbed the Russian haversack and withdrew twenty yards from the tip of the promontory. He then swung in a wide semicircle, out of sight of those in the boats below, to a position a hundred yards or so away farther around the cliffs, almost exactly opposite where he had last fired.

In the few minutes it had taken him to confuse those shooting up at the cliffs there had been time for more men to land. Their rifles and packs intact, they started up the cliff by the trail, much of it hidden from Frank's sight by protective arches of rock. This made it impossible for him to know how many were already on their way up and from which of three exits that spread out at the cliff's top the men would emerge. He might take out a few if they broke cover in moonlight, but more likely they'd wait until the moon passed into cloud. In either case, he knew he and Gloria would quickly be outnumbered, surrounded and outgunned.

Crouched beside him, Gloria knew, with a wave of certainty as inexplicable as it was fast, that Frank would be killed.

The moon vanished and the sea went dark.

"Damn it!" said Frank.

"RIGHT!" the tall Georgian ordered the bosun leading the second wave of boats. "Let's get in close!"

"What about the men in the water? We'll have to pick them—"

"Are you crazy?" snarled the Georgian. "That moon comes out again and we'll be sitting ducks!"

"But—" protested the seaman, seeing so many of his comrades floundering in the angry sea only yards away.

"But, nothing!" the Georgian cut in. "You mess around picking them up and you'll be joining 'em. We've got to get that damn Hall before he gets us and now's our chance. Go!"

Swinging the tiller hard to his chest, the bosun steered a course a few points to the right of the slab so that when he pushed the tiller from him the launch slid up and over a swell, coming about smartly and parallel to the slab. The Georgian bellowed that anyone who tried to disembark before he gave the order would be shot, so that even when the launch began rocking precariously in the trough that opened in the darkness as a swell sucked it back, not a man moved. The bosun's mate leaped ashore on the next wave's upswing, securing the painter, while two seamen at the stern used poles to fend off the rock. Only then did the men take their turn, most jumping out, the lucky ones stepping ashore as the launch rose high, pushed against the rock in the sea's constant attack.

Nevertheless, the wind, the noise of the surf and the darkness took its toll, another seven men lost as the second wave of boats unloaded as fast as the hidden moon would allow. Still, despite the wild conditions at the cliff's base, more than one hundred armed men landed on the slab, making their way up the winding path that led to the three exits. The seamen, most of them Polish, were divided hastily into three contingents of about thirty men each, under the command of three marines: the corporal, young Penkovsky and the Georgian. Even if the moon suddenly came out and Hall was able to pick off a few more of them, the marines knew the critical point against the two Americans would come at the moment of exit from the cliff top. That was where Hall would try to stop them, knowing that if he didn't they would quickly break out, spread out, then close in and overwhelm him.

THE MOON CAME OUT from hiding and Frank looked down at the sea-slicked rock hundreds of feet below. It was deserted. The boats that had unloaded the men, about two-thirds of the total, were heading back to the mother ship. He used the scope to look over toward the west for any sight of *Petrel*'s lights, but all he could see in the moon glow was a circle filled with tall grass. In fact, from where he and Gloria were, the western sea couldn't be seen at all. For all he knew, *Petrel* might be just off the western shore, or thirty miles off, another two or three hours away.

"Could we make it to the other coast?" asked Gloria.

"No point. Where could we go? They'd swarm all over the island and pick us off easily from the cliffs. No, we have to make our stand here." He clipped another magazine—ten rounds. His last.

Barely audible above the sound of the west wind, a noise came up from the cliff, difficult to discern at first. Frank, his ears still ringing, had to listen intently. It was a subdued grunting noise, like some huge animal—the sound of more than a hundred men coming to kill them.

THE SHUDDERING VIBRATION of *Petrel*'s engine could be felt up on the bridge as Captain Tate opened the port side door, letting in a draft and causing Scotty to start.

"How far off?" asked Tate.

"Thirty-seven miles," replied Redfern. "ETA a wee bit more than three hours."

Tate's eyebrows rose in a frown. "Should be sooner than that with this tail wind, Scotty."

"Aye, but we're running into a bit o' bother now with that storm belting up from the south, Captain."

"Thought there was supposed to be a break in that one?"

"True enough, but it's not as much as we expected."

Tate grunted. "Well, I don't imagine another hour or two will make a hell of a lot of difference to Frank."

"Hard to say."

Tate detected something unsaid in Scotty's voice. "Go on."

"I'm thinking, sir, of whoever fired that flare. Our ETA might make a bit o' difference to them."

Tate scanned the instrument panels to see if they could squeeze any more out of *Petrel* but the engines were on maximum revs and the course was as steady as conditions allowed, the compass needle hovering east northeast on 088. "Nothing more we can do," he said, looking at the Smith's chronometer, estimating they would arrive at Eagle Island about an hour past midnight. Tate switched on the intercom to the radio room. "Any traffic yet, Sparks?"

"Nothing but buzz, Captain."

"Keep me posted."

"Will do."

Tate went into the redded light of the chart room and double-checked the course. 088 it was and there was nothing he or God could do about it.

SABUROV WAS BUOYED when the mother ship's weather officer informed him that the break in the southern storm wouldn't be as long-lived as they had thought. It meant they might be able to stay a few hours more on station, hopefully until a few hours before dawn, giving the colonel additional time to finish off the two Americans then get his men off the island. He watched the sharp-peaked line of cliffs through his binoculars but even with the aid of the moon could not see if his men had started to deploy.

ASHORE, THE TALL GEORGIAN, the corporal of marines and Penkovsky, the marine who had helped Saburov throw the professor out of the HIP, conferred. They were about fifty feet from the top of the trail, where it split into three exits about thirty feet apart through honeycombed rock. In the moonlight the area took on the look of a lunar landscape.

"Wait until the moon goes behind cloud cover again," instructed the corporal, looking skyward at the scattered islands of cumulonimbus. "Should be in about ten, fifteen minutes. I'll fire the first one, then." He turned to Penkovsky and the Georgian. "Your two groups follow. Penkovsky, take the far right, I'll take the center opening." He pointed over at the Georgian's group. "You rush the far left and try to pick out where they are as you're spreading out."

"They might have taken off," Penkovsky suggested, wanting to show he could figure out strategy as well as anyone else.

"No, they won't." The Georgian sneered. "This is the bastard's only chance to try and stop us. Not that he's got a chance. He'll be there, don't worry, sonny."

Wanting to shut them up but figuring the noise of the hundred or so men clustered behind him would prove as unnerving to the American as it was objectionable to his professional training, the corporal contented himself with acting as impromptu traffic controller, his submachine gun clasped in his left hand, moving down the line, directing odd bodies into one of the three assault groups.

WHILE THE CORPORAL was counting off his men in the deep-cut rock, Frank and Gloria, bent low to avoid making a silhouette, ran toward the first exit. Gloria branched off toward the far right-hand one. An attack, Frank told her, was the last thing the Russians would expect, with odds against the Americans of more than fifty to one.

Crouching low above the southernmost exit, Gloria did as Frank had told her, laying the four high-explosive grenades by her side and waiting for his signal. Above her, the moon was sliding in and out of cloud. Tense from fear and determination, she no longer felt cold. She was flushed from the run to the cliff's edge, and adrenaline pumped through her veins. Her senses were more acute than they had ever been, than she could ever have imagined, her skin more alive than ever before, her nipples engorged tightly against her bra. The wind-dried grass rattled against her thigh like spears on a shield, her vision was so clear that the mother ship lay silhouetted more dramatically than ever before. Above all else her sense of smell was so sharp she could detect the sour odor of sweating male bodies barely forty feet below and the overwhelming and invigorating saltiness of the sea.

The next moment she heard a loud bang. Mistaking it for the sound of Frank's first grenade, she pulled the ring out cleanly as he had shown her, felt the urgent push of the release spring against her palm and tossed her first grenade down the rocky chute of the exit just as the Russian's first flare blossomed in a beautiful salmon-pink, five hundred feet above the exit. Frank threw four grenades, at one-second intervals, and Gloria her remaining three. Both she and Frank then ran from their positions in toward the center exit as the eight grenades went off in a series of vivid purplish flashes, exploding in the confined space of the rocky trails like gigantic flashbulbs. The crescendo of the explosions came amid screaming so horrific that its echoes overcame the wailing howl of the gale-force westerlies.

THE CORPORAL WAS KILLED outright; Penkovsky, stunned, his face wet with hot blood, stared at the stump of what had been a man's left hand. A seaman next to him and others farther down the line seemed untouched, but the twenty-five or so of his group were either dead or so badly wounded in the confined space, that it looked like a depth charge had gone off inside a sub. Out of thirty men in his group, Penkovsky realized that all but a handful were out of action.

Penkovsky felt his face carefully, fingers shaking, expecting to find a gaping wound, but realized the blood was from the seaman who had lost his hand and who now lay unconscious before him. The man's face showed a grotesque agony visible in the flickering light of the descending flares, whose eerie glow died as they hit the dirt and pebble-strewn margin between cliff and grass. Penkovsky wished he had never heard of Eagle Island, the professor, Julio or the American called Hall.

"C'mon!" It was the Georgian shouting, abusing, exhorting every one of them who was able—still more than fifty of the original hundred or so in the three groups—to get off their asses, to attack, telling them there was no other way out. The Georgian joined by Penkovsky made his way to the front of the column. They sent up another two spotter flares, then leading, firing from the hip, they charged the southern exit, ignoring the middle one. Expecting another grenade attack, they burst quickly through to the cliff top. Everyone peeled off, left and right, spraying the AK-47 machine-gun fire in wide, protective arcs.

The fusillade of automatic and rifle fire as they rapidly advanced across the twenty-yard margin to the edge of the grass lasted a full two minutes before the tall Georgian yelled for them to cease fire. Sporadic shooting continued, as many of the younger sailors were so charged up with thoughts of vengeance against the two Americans that they were unable to take their fingers off the triggers until the Georgian repeated his order, accompanied by oaths that finally got the sailors' attention.

When the firing stopped, the banshee sound of the wind and grass was all they heard. Once in the tall grass, the Georgian knew, many of the sailors would be their own worst enemies, prone, in their inexperience of man-hunting, to let fly at anything that moved, particularly anything near them. For a moment, cold and dry as it was, he wished the heavy rain of twenty-four hours ago had kept up. If nothing else it would have taken much of the spookiness out of the unnerving rustling sound of the dried grass. He gave orders in Russian, repeated by one of the ship's officers in Polish, and the sailors spread out four yards apart either side of him, forming a sweep line of well over two hundred yards, ready to advance. The Georgian called out again, this time the order being only to shoot in front and not to the side. The line would stop and reform every thirty paces. He gave one more order before the line moved off.

LYING DEAD STILL in the tall grass seventy yards from the line, Frank and Gloria heard the Georgian shout one more order, which was immediately followed by a clanking noise, like the sound of a tank, as the line fixed bayonets and advanced, preceded by the crashing sound of sword grass being trampled by boots. From their right—Frank guessed about a hundred yards away, near the hut—there came the sound of a smaller group of two or three who, with the Georgian leading them, had detached themselves from the main line of searchers and were now scrambling atop the hut. The next moment the windy darkness was pierced by a high-intensity spotlight, its beam, sharply delineated in the salty air, beginning to sweep methodically south to north across the wild expanse of grass.

"We can't stay here," Gloria whispered, though realizing they were trapped between the advancing search line and the men on top of the hut behind them. "Can we use grenades?"

"No," Frank whispered. "Might take a few out but that's all. Give me the first-aid box. Hurry! Cotton bandages, rubbing alcohol. Quickly!" As he urinated into the empty water bottle they could hear the search line halt, someone yelling, then another voice, a moment or two of silence, then the line starting up again, crashing forward. The spotlight crisscrossed the tall grass in advance of the searchers but never so close to the line as to present any of the seamen or marines as targets. As the line advanced, the distance between the spotlight's moving pool of light and the hut it was being directed from steadily decreased. Frank and Gloria were now about equidistant from the line and the hut's roof from which the tall Georgian now commanded.

The Georgian turned to the man working the beam. "They've got to be hiding around here somewhere. Wouldn't have had time to get farther." For a moment the beam stopped, then raced to an unusually low clump of grass almost flattened by the force ten coming out of the west. "Anything?" asked the Georgian, his tone betraying anxiety for the first time during the mission, now that the corporal of marines was dead and he alone in charge. It would be his head that Saburov would mount if the Americans weren't killed quickly, before morning. His finger tapping the AK-47's trigger guard impatiently, he sincerely hoped he would be the one to get the opportunity to finish off this Hall and the bitch. The Georgian was not moved by revenge—or mourning his comrades who'd gone down in the American's grenade attack; it was simply that he had been on more than a dozen covert operations, from Korea to Afghanistan, and not one had been a failure. He wasn't about to become what the Americans called a loser now.

The line halted again to straighten itself, get its bearings. Its southern end, like the tail of a long, dark snake, was no more than a hundred yards from the hut, while the remainder of the line stretched northward. "Want me to start a different sweep pattern?" asked the man behind the spotlight. "Might confuse 'em?"

"Good idea," agreed the Georgian. "Flush 'em out."

Gloria, her fingers aching with the cold, unrolled the seemingly endless cotton bandages as fast as she could, letting the four-inch-wide cloth unravel loosely like a ball of heavy-gauge twine. She then emptied the small bottle of sterilizing alcohol, dripping it on both sides of the bandage. By the time she had finished and Frank had tied one end of the bandage securely around the now-heavier water canteen and the other end around the base of sword grass, Gloria's hands, wet with alcohol, had almost seized up on her.

"All right," he whispered. "You ready?"

"You sure it'll work?" she asked.

"No."

"But will it be fast enough? I mean—"

"That's a force-ten wind," he said in hushed tones. "I've played out enough cable in my time...." He took one more turn of the bandage around the canteen for good luck. "Force ten's about sixty miles an hour," he continued. "Almost a hundred feet a minute."

He felt in the first-aid box for the Bic lighter and handed it to Gloria. He then raised the Dragunov, the spotlight a dazzling sun in the scope, and fired. There was a tinkle of glass, and shouting above the high wind. The filament faded to a dull orange, then died.

Frank dropped the rifle, snatched up the canteen, and Gloria flicked the lighter, igniting the canteen end of the bandage. "Down!" came Frank's hoarse command. As she dropped flat he rose like a javelin thrower in the darkness at the end of his run, throwing the canteen far to his left, the flame racing back along the alchohol-soaked tail trailing fifty yards behind.

ALL SABUROV SAW through his binoculars on the mother ship's bridge was a tiny speck of light arcing like a firefly atop the cliffs. He guessed it must be between cliff top and grass, for he'd given explicit instructions that no flares be fired once they had reached the grass, for then instead of the flares coming down on the barren margin between cliff and grass, they would topple into the tall, wind-dried sword grass and cause a fire. He was wrong, though; it wasn't a fire he was seeing, it was a disaster.

A WALL OF FLAME RACED back from where the canteen fell into the grass, along the entire length of the bandage taper, leaping ten to fifteen feet high above the grassy sea. The tangerine-streaked inferno fanned by the sixty-mile-an-hour wind blowing from the west, raced pitilessly toward the line of men to the east, which one second was advancing, the next fleeing, the pursuers becoming the pursued.

The feral roar of the flames and exploding grass was so fierce, so swift in its terror, that Gloria momentarily felt sorry for the hopelessly doomed line, many falling, others dropping rifles and whatever else impeded their retreat, and through it all, the sickly-sweet smell of melting flesh. Her own flesh seemed on fire as the intense heat from the blaze radiated to where she and Frank watched.

"It was their party, not ours," said Frank as they heard the screams of the dying men, who tried futilely to cover the more than two hundred yards through the thick grass to the margin before the wind-driven fire swept over them.

The three men atop the hut were brightly outlined, and Frank fired again. Now there were only two, and they quickly vanished. "C'mon!" he shouted above the roaring flames. "Let's go before they snap out of it!" The next instant they were running west, the hut now a little more than fifty yards to their left, its northern wall dancing madly with shadows.

ON THE ROOF, the tall Georgian shook the man next to him who was lying down, hands over his head. The Georgian couldn't stand the damned sobbing. "C'mon!" he shouted at the man. "You stupid Polack! Get a grip on yourself." The sobbing kept on, so the Georgian kicked the man's leg. "Damn you—" One of the man's arms slipped off his head, and in the glow of the fire the Georgian saw he was quite dead, whatever he had once looked like no longer of consequence in that his face had disappeared, in its place a mashed pulp of bone splinters, greasy with blood.

"Could—could've been me," said the sobbing seaman on the other side of the dead man. "Could've been m-me."

"Well, it wasn't!" said the Georgian, adding a few curses. "So get off your arse and do as I say. C'mon, move, you bastard or I'll shoot you." The man got up, still shaking. "Now, you listening?"

"Y-yes."

"Look, Comrade. One or two stragglers in the rear might have gotten out. Get off the roof and start down where this damned fire has already burned its way to the margin, while I stay here and see if I can spot—"

The Georgian stopped talking. He thought he'd seen a glint, possibly metal—from the American's gun perhaps—a hundred yards north of the hut. Or was he imagining things? Problem was, you couldn't bet on the American bastard hightailing it, he'd already backtracked on them once. For the moment, the Georgian knew, the American wouldn't attack, because the fire he'd created was so intense it had cast a moat of light around the hut, so bright that no one could get close enough for an attack. But would the American stalk back later after the fierce but short-lived fire had burned itself out? Probably not, the Georgian decided. In the confusion, he'd try to make his getaway. Besides, he was protecting the woman come hell or high water, so he wouldn't leave her alone. So what could—

Then it hit the Georgian like a bolt of lightning—how the American had unwittingly trapped himself.

Chapter Thirty-Seven

"THREE POINTS TO STARBOARD, sir."

It was *Petrel*'s lookout indicating the scratch of pink no more than an inch long reflected from the cloud cover on the horizon east northeast. Even through the big 8-by-24 Minolta binoculars, Scotty Redfern could make out only a larger blurring of color through the spumes of spray splattering the *Petrel*'s bridge. He checked their heading. Still 088 against the line of sight.

"Mother o' God, it's coming from Eagle Island!" He reached for the intercom to awaken the captain but stayed his hand, realizing that there was no reason for waking up the old man. Nothing on God's earth could make *Petrel* go any faster than the fifteen knots the wind and the four G.M.s were giving her so that it would be another two hours before *Petrel* reached the island and they could find out what exactly the fire meant. Had it been lit as a signal beacon? Was Frank in some kind of trouble?

Redfern had been so preoccupied with the task of keeping the ship on steady course he'd all but forgotten Frank Hall and the three men who had gone with him. Redfern thought for a minute how unpopular he was about to make himself but decided to get the radio operator up anyway, to see if he could pick up anything at all that might explain the fire.

Five minutes later, Sparks delivered his verdict. "There's nothing," he answered irritably, having gone all around the dial.

"Can you transmit?" Redfern pressed. "Find out whether any other ships are near the island?"

"No," said Sparks over the intercom, sitting in his Chinese silk robe, as grumpy as the two dragons glaring at each other on his back. It wasn't his job to man the radio twenty-four hours a day. "Anyway, I'm still getting static." He then took off the earphones and made his way complainingly to the wardroom, where he poured a mug of coffee from the pot on the gimbals-mounted hot plate. It tasted good, always did on *Petrel*.

As he became wider awake at the wardroom table, he started drawing, more like doodling, with a teaspoon on the linen cloth, which had been moistened so as to cling to the table in the heavy weather. He found himself dwelling on the static. It was odd that there was so much of it. There'd been no lightning in the past hour or so, at least as far as he knew. But then he'd been in the sack. Through the serving hatch he could see a steward sitting at one of the red-and-white square-patterned Formica tables of the crew's mess, sipping coffee and flipping through a girlie magazine, pausing now and then as he turned the magazine upside down and cocked his head like some kind of bird.

"Steward, you hear any lightning? Thunder?"

"Only Cook farting."

"Huh," said Sparks, getting up with a groan for a refill. The disturbance was, he recalled, what you'd call a steady interference, not rising and falling in the kind of surging static you got, for instance, on some long distance calls. It was more constant, at the same level, as if someone might be deliberately jamming all radio transmission in the area.

"Thanks, Sparks," Redfern acknowledged when the radio officer rang through with his hunch. The Scottish mate, a dour look clouding his face, made a careful entry of Sparks's report in the log, putting the log in the waterproof safe when he was finished. He was a cautious man, and if for any reason—God protect them—*Petrel* went down, then at least, like in an airplane's black box, there'd be a record of what the radio officer had said. The only trouble was that someone would first have to find the ship in the vast deep of the Cascadia Basin more than twelve thousand feet below. And the best man for that was Frank Hall, who right now depended on *Petrel* staying afloat.

In view of what Sparks had said about the possibility of jamming, Redfern decided to wake the captain. The pinkish glow on the horizon, about twenty-five miles northeast, was getting bigger. The question was, was the fire spreading or was it that the ship was getting closer?

FROM ATOP THE HUT, facing directly westward, the Georgian had fired three flares in a fan pattern—one to the southwest; the next one due west, straight in front of him; the last to the northwest. They started three separate fires in a giant semicircle three hundred yards west of the hut. If he was lucky, the fires would have started well ahead of the fleeing Americans, cutting off their escape. The fire set by the Americans was now burning itself out behind the hut, along the edge of the margin, leaving a plain of black, burned-out tussocks of grass, which looked like giant, abandoned anthills. Ash scattered on the wind, some smaller lumps grotesquely curled, where flesh had melded to bone. The horror of the swift yet tormented death was captured forever in the charred corpses, gazing, eyeless, at the moon.

The Georgian could see the Pole he'd sent to gather up whoever had managed to reach the margin, but only a handful of men, seven in all, were left. Two of them, like cardboard cutouts in the dying firelight, were doubled over, staggering around, coughing and moaning. The Georgian decided he'd have to leave them to be picked up later and press ahead with the remainder to find the bodies of the Americans, who would now be suffering the same fate as most of the search line. The Georgian had badly wanted to shoot the American himself, and the thought of having the woman before they finished her still appealed to him so that in a way he thought it a shame that she would shrivel to charcoal before he could stick her. But at least he would have stopped them, thwarting Saburov's wrath and earning a few points for himself in the bargain.

He watched, listening to the growing roar of the three fires, now each more than a hundred yards wide, whipped to frenzy by the west wind. They raced to meet one another, with only two channels of grass, each no more than fifty yards wide, separating them until they coalesced into one massive wall of flame. Lying on the roof of the hut, he could already feel the intense heat building and knew that soon he'd have to move down behind the protection of the hut, and if necessary move back into the burned-out area behind him as the inferno burned itself out around the hut. But for now he remained stretched out on the roof, setting his binoculars to zero in on the rapidly narrowing gaps between the three fires, which were now cracking and exploding like volleys of small arms. The Americans would have no choice but to try for the gaps if they were to make a run for it at all. With one hand holding the binoculars, he pulled the Kalashnikov closer to his side.

THE MOMENT HE HAD SEEN the flares streaking high overhead, smoky blue trails snaking behind, Frank knew his own strategy was being turned on them. They headed for the nearest gap, between where the middle and far left flares had come down. They saw the first sparks of fires that would spread quickly, cutting off their escape across the island.

"Sign of an inferior ball team," said Frank. "Copying tactics—can't think of their own." It was an attempt to keep Gloria going, but he realized his error as soon as he'd said it. *He* was falling into the trap, doing exactly what would be expected. All he could remember was an old childhood trick, one you played in hide-and-seek, but would it work? He had less than three minutes to find out.

"Come on, sport!" he coaxed Gloria, reverting to one of Aussie's devil-may-care expressions.

Meanwhile the Georgian shifted the binoculars right to the northern gap. It had narrowed from a seventy-yard-wide corridor to forty yards in less than a minute, the fire's roaring, crackling noise in competition with the wailing of wind as it rose in intensity—bad news for the Americans. The flames raced in faster to close the gap, leaping twenty, thirty feet into the air like mad spirits in a Georgian tale. When he saw nothing in the northern gap he shifted his binoculars to the southern one. It was closing a little more slowly, and so he lay watching it more intently and longer than the other. That was *his* mistake; so occupied with peering through the glasses, he ignored the foreground. Out of the wild, swaying grass a figure burst forward so fast the Georgian only caught a glimpse of the Russian helmet, a jagged flash of light, the fire from the Dragunov directly in front of him. He dropped the binoculars, grabbing the Kalashnikov. It jumped to his shoulder, then clattered to the ground, his body crashing down a second later. He was dead.

"C'mon!" shouted Frank, snatching up the Kalashnikov, the flare pistol and its ammo pouch. "Into the hut!" As the two of them rounded the southern side to the entrance and slipped inside they saw a line of seven men walking up from the margin toward them. For a second the men, faces black in the fire's reflection, stopped, looking up toward them, then there was shouting as they spread out, weapons hugging their sides.

The fire behind the hut was now only forty yards away. Its heat washed over the cement building in waves, backlighting it like a long adobe in the middle of a blazing desert. Tussocks of grass exploded into flame with such force that the line of men advancing from the direction of the cliff momentarily went down and several minutes passed before they started to move forward again.

"That's good," whispered Frank, gasping for air in the oxygen-starved hut as the fire roared toward them. "They're nervous."

"Unlike us," Gloria responded weakly. "Frank...I...I can't run any more.... I'm...I just..."

"I know," he replied as he gazed upward, all but mesmerized in his own exhaustion by the fantastic shapes on the walls as the fire, burning itself out in a final surge of rage, met the already burned-out area stretching from the hut to the margin. As he flipped out the 7.62 mm bullets from the Dragunov's magazine, he topped up the Kalashnikov's magazine until the spring felt tight. Then, checking that the last two grenades were in the right pocket of his torn Russian tunic, he took out the 9 mm Makarov pistol and handed it to her, butt first. "Tuck it inside your pants," he said, showing her again how to disengage the safety catch.

She took the gun but shook her head as if she either hadn't heard him correctly or, if she had, didn't understand. "Why can't I just hold it?"

"Because they'd see it."

She looked blankly up at him. He kissed her and lifted her to her feet. "You've got to walk a little farther, honey. Okay?" He said it gently, softly, so full of consideration in the circumstances that she felt more afraid than ever. "It's our only chance," he said. She tried to answer, to tell him she understood, that she'd try to be brave, but no sound came. "That's my girl," he said. She felt so weak she put her hands out against the hut wall, afraid she'd faint.

"You all right?" he said again, tenderly.

"No," she answered quietly, gripping his arm so hard he could feel her nails digging into him through the tunic. They waited. Outside, the fire was in its final throes, the last of the grass before the blackened-out area going up like straw before it turned crimson and fell.

CAPTAIN NOVISK WATCHED Saburov. The colonel was so beside himself that for a moment Novisk half expected the Russian to throw the binoculars across the bridge. Instead, Saburov raised them again as if to verify the horrendous vision before him. "The fools—the incompetent, idiotic fools! They've set half the island on fire!" His hands were now clasped to his temples as if that was the only way he could contain the explosion of rage inside him. His voice lowered, its tone, however, more disturbing for his forced restraint. "Why did the idiots think I ordered them *not* to use any flares beyond the margin? My God," said the Russian in disbelief. "Don't they realize what they're doing? Lighting a beacon for twenty miles!"

"Can't blame our people, Colonel," interjected Novisk. "If the American started it, our people couldn't very well put it out."

"Each body..." said Saburov, with all the determination of a man solely responsible to Moscow. "Because of that damned fire every single corpse will have to be taken off the island before we leave. The high tides would have taken care of the helicopter debris, but on top of the island there mustn't be any trace of us being here, of being anywhere near that hut.''

Novisk had seen the face of fanatical dedication of KGB officers to duty before, but he also knew what was impossible in the time remaining. "By the time we landed a cleanup party,'' said Novisk evenly, matter-of-factly, "and buried our comrades . . .'' He said *comrades* without irony but with a genuine, heartfelt compassion for all those who had died trying to keep Moscow's plan secret. "The fact is, Colonel, we don't have enough time left, even if we were to get more cover later on from this westerly storm. It's as simple as that. We must leave now while we still have cover of night and cloud.''

"The fire, of course, could be attributed to anything,'' Saburov said, thinking aloud. "Any number of things could have caused a brushfire in the wind-dried grass. . . . But the bodies—'' He turned to face Novisk. "No, they must disappear into the sea.''

"Colonel, if the American is not caught in two hours, we *must* leave.''

"Yes, yes,'' replied Saburov, speaking rapidly. "I understand. I'll take a party ashore. We'll stay behind if necessary. First we will finish off the Americans once and for all, then clean up. Besides, I must check up on our depot after the fire. No point having protected it if we can't use it, eh?'' Saburov's smile and rapid delivery struck Novisk as maniacal, unhinged, the actions of a man nearing the end of his tether.

"I agree that would be the best plan, but we can't spare any more than a handful of men—six at the most. My ship needs at least a crew of—''

"That'll be all we need,'' said Saburov. "Six.''

Novisk nodded uneasily, noticing as he did so that the bridge had quietly emptied of almost all the remaining officers and men. The few members of the skeleton crew who did stay on the bridge were merely intrigued as to what

Saburov could do, except for the serious young officer of the watch who had so impressed Saburov and wanted to stay, and the two lookouts who had to be on watch. "All right," said Novisk, seeing his chance to escape finally the mad carnage of Moscow's plan. "I'll draw up a list of six 'volunteers' to stay with you. What trawler do you want to pick you up?"

"I don't care," said Saburov. "As long as it's fast enough to reach here in the next few hours and has enough cabin space for an extra dozen men."

"Dozen? I thought you are only going to take six."

"I'll get another six volunteers on the island. Six men who are fresh—six who already know the terrain."

"Sounds reasonable," replied Novisk. The truth was, however, that after seeing how the American had been operating over the past thirty-six hours—which had seemed more like thirty-six days—Novisk had assumed there would be nobody left to help Saburov once he reached the island. *If* he reached it.

But Saburov guessed what the Polish captain was thinking. Grinning, eyes alive with promise, he responded, "Don't fret, Comrade. Oh, the American is good, I grant you. He's very good, but I have a few tricks of my own."

He then turned to the young Polish officer. "Have we any antitank rockets left over from the HIP?"

"Yes, sir. Two pods—sixty-two rockets."

"A shoulder launcher?"

"Yes, sir."

Saburov turned to Novisk. "We know the Americans aren't on the cliff top because they had to be farther inland to start the fire and to try to make good their escape. They'll be—what is it the Americans say?—hightailing it back to the western side to wherever their boat is hidden."

"So?"

"So this is what I want you to do...."

As Saburov began his explanation, he was pleased to see that one of the six men who had been assigned to him was the young Polish officer who had been correct about the decoy bodies falling from the cliff, and who was clearly interested in party career possibilities. He showed great promise and, above all, initiative.

THE FIRE IN ITS FINAL STAGES was still crackling all around the hut, and Frank and Gloria could hear shouts growing in volume as the remainder of the search line neared them.

"Know any Russian?" Frank asked Gloria, who was standing by him at the hut's entrance. She shook her head. Though he wasn't surprised, it further pressed home the terrible risk they were taking. But to stay holed up in the hut was an invitation to annihilation.

Frank pulled down the strap of the marine's helmet, and yelled out, *"Da!"* as he poked Gloria from behind with the Kalashnikov. She emerged from the hut, hands held high, her body, if not her features, clearly visible against the dying flames behind them. The thin line of seven searchers raised their weapons nervously, but Frank pushed her arrogantly forward with the muzzle of the Kalashnikov, using only one hand, prodding her so hard she stumbled, swearing loudly at him. In his other hand, unseen on his off side, he clasped a grenade. When they were thirty yards from the search line, amid a torrent of Russian and Polish, firing erupted halfway down the line. Gloria had already fallen as Frank opened up, taking out two men as he hit the ground. He threw the grenade. The wind quickly scattered the ash from where they had all gone down so that now no one could see anybody else. The grenade split open with the sound of a tree hit by lightning, its white-hot fragments whistling, killing a third Russian outright, wounding another so badly he, too, was out of action.

Now it was three against two, but Frank knew it would be their turn for a grenade attack even as he tossed their last one in the general direction of the line. It was a dud but caused one of the men to roll away from it. Frank saw the plume of ash rising against the moon and fired two long bursts. There was a scream. Now it was two on two, or so he thought, but the Kalashnikov's magazine was empty. He took out the Russian's flare gun, opening the pouch only to find that all the flares had been used. He reached down to the leg sheath and slipped out the paratrooper's knife. All the firepower they had now was in Gloria's 9 mm Makarov pistol. But she hadn't yet fired.

Was she so frightened, or was it jammed with ash? Christ, he thought, if she fires it like that it'll blow up in her face. Slowly, inch by inch so as not to raise too much ash, he dragged himself in the general direction of the line, knowing that the two remaining men had the advantage with the wind blowing in their direction, for the slightest sound he made would be immediately carried to them while their movements remained muffled. What he had no way of knowing was that one of the screams was a put-up job, that there were in fact three men lying in wait for him, not two.

There was a loud squeaking sound, like metal on metal. Frank lay absolutely still, trying to figure out what it was. If he didn't know better, he thought to himself, he'd say it was the sound of a tracked vehicle of some kind, but this he knew must be impossible, unless Saburov had somehow managed to land an armored vehicle or troop carrier on the island. No, that wasn't possible. But the sound came again in the distance, now more like that of a tractor pulling chains.

Suddenly, submachine-gun fire ripped high overhead like angry hornets, a few of the shots hitting the hut, sending cement chips flying above the cherry-red embers of the exhausted fire. Then more shooting. This time bullets struck the ground, but the bursts, well apart, landed nowhere near him and Gloria. Obviously it was random firing. A cement fragment struck the rim of his helmet, spinning it off him. But despite the unfocused firing, he dared not move a muscle to retrieve it. He became aware of the faint sound of loose gravel somewhere ahead of him—probably on the margin—and behind it—it was difficult to tell just how far—the metallic sound again, no longer constant but an unoiled, creaking noise.

"Drilling pipes!" he told himself in a whisper. Then there was a high, shrill sound like a train whistle. He heard another sound, shuffling, close to him, a few feet away. He spun around and lunged. There was an explosion of air, a cloud of ash choking him and his attacker, and a high-pitched scream from the shape.

"Frank! Frank!"

He released his grip. "Gloria! Jesus—I nearly..."

She'd flung herself back on the ground, now half-lying, half-propped up on her elbows, her face white with ash and fright. "You nearly killed me. Anyway, they've gone."

"What?"

She pointed out to sea. The big gray slab of the mother ship was slowly moving on her own axis, her anchor being laboriously hauled up. Again the ship sounded its whistle. "Afraid they'd miss the boat," she said, laughing, her voice verging on hysterical relief.

Frank said nothing, watching the ship as it swung slowly with the tide. The massive clanking winches wound slowly, the slack of the huge chains slipping occasionally, then tightening in a vice-like grip as the links were slowly but surely coiled around the house-size drums. After a while they could hear a launch, coming in to pick up the remaining seamen.

"After all that," said Gloria. "Frank, they're going— why?"

"Don't know—maybe it's the weather," Frank proffered, looking up at the sky. "Running out of cloud cover, temporarily at least. Might mean they've run out of time. Have to move before they're spotted?"

"But they're giving up. Frank, darling, they've given— Frank? Don't you think they have?"

"No. But let's get out of here while we can. Over to the other coast. *Petrel* should be due soon."

They made their way through the moonlit devastation of the grass fires, up past the hut, heading westward. Gloria remarked on the absence of birds following the fire, reminding Frank of the plastic one he had found atop the hut.

"Probably a wind indicator," said Gloria. "Left over from the war."

"That's what I thought at first." He began to slow down, looking back at the sea, part of which was now blocked from view by the cliff tops. He could still make out the mother ship, though, building up steam.

"What's bothering you?" asked Gloria.

Frank had now stopped walking and was looking back at the long rectangle of the deserted hut. "The rod," he said, turning to her. "The copper rod the bird was perched on was new, well lubricated against the weather. That's why the bird kept moving around with every little shift of wind. I mean, it was well oiled, perfectly balanced."

She shrugged. "It was probably put there for—I don't know—maybe something to do with all this drilling business. What did you call it—metalliferous...?"

"Sea gold," he answered, "metalliferous muds." His attention was drawn more and more to the hut. "Wind direction doesn't tell you anything about drilling. Holy—"

Before she could say any more he had dropped the haversack and was running over to the hut. Striking the lighter, shielding it with his other hand, he held the flame high overhead, looking up at the roof. He tried to recall everything he could about the hut in the daylight: the absence of birds' nests for one thing, and the pipe the bird had been perched on and the wire that went through the roof, probably connected to some kind of wind gauge.

"Where the hell is the pipe?" he asked aloud without turning around, hearing Gloria's footsteps behind him on the cement floor. "Where the hell does it go?"

"Does it have to go anywhere?" she asked.

"Sweetie, people don't come over eight thousand miles from Poland, or wherever the hell they came from, to stick little plastic birds on the top of huts." He walked to the center point of the long roof and looked up again. It was eerie in the hut, the wind groaning outside, the old shower stalls catching an eddy as the westerly changed direction momentarily, blowing over still-warm embers of the grass fires. All the time Gloria, at Frank's instruction, kept an anxious watch at the hut's entrance so as to reassure themselves that the mother ship was still making steam and that no one else was about to appear suddenly on the cliff tops.

Frank moved the wavering flame back and forth over what he was sure must be the point immediately below the short projection of pipe on the roof. He saw a faint hairline fracture in the cement, the fissure all but invisible to the naked eye, being the same color as the old gray cement, thus arguing against the recent installation of the pipe. He scraped the cement with the knife. When flecks of cement-colored paint appeared on his hand instead of cement he knew he was onto something. "Where's the ship?" he asked Gloria.

"Still drawing up the anchor. Getting harder to see her. Moon's hiding under cloud."

"Well, keep watching. I don't trust that bastard Saburov."

"Can't think why."

"You see a launch heading back to the ship?"

"Can't see anything now but a lot of waves."

"Well, I guess a launch could have already been and taken them off." He scraped excitedly at the cement, the latter giving way much faster than cement should have; instead it was some kind of industrial putty that looked like

cement but was breaking up as he worked the knife harder
and harder.

"Hello!"

She saw he was pulling down on a length of wire that
was now exposed, leading along the ceiling from the pipe
on the roof. The more he pulled, the more wire became
exposed, like ripping up a hidden tendril of morning glory
from a garden, only here the dirt was putty raining down
on them as Frank kept pulling hand over hand until he'd
reached the far end of the hut. Then, after a bit more digging with the knife, the wire began to peel away from the
wall. Now and then it would resist more strongly where the
Polyfilla-like substance had hardened more than else-
where, but soon he had pulled out wire all the way to the
base of the far northern wall—more than a hundred feet
from the hut's entrance. In a sweat but too curious to take
a rest, he started to dig away at the cement floor. "Remember," he began, "how I said it was funny that they
didn't use the chopper's heavy stuff on the hut? Wasn't
until—" The knife's point broke.

"Damn!"

"Wasn't until what?" asked Gloria.

"Wasn't until we'd reached the caves that they stopped
the small arms and started using the heavy stuff." He
stopped digging with the blunted knife. "This isn't going
to work. It's solid cement here."

"Frank!"

"What the hell—"

"No, no, I'm sorry. I mean, it's all right. Everything's
all right. The mother ship. It's leaving. Frank, Frank." She
was throwing her arms around him. "I love you. . . . I love
you. . . .

Chapter Thirty-Eight

WESTWARD, AT A POINT that Jamie estimated must be about fifteen miles from the island, a green light could be seen winking now and then as a ship dipped and climbed the swells. It was about the right time for the return of *Petrel*, but given the heavy weather she must have encountered on the way out to the Mayday, and the time it would have taken her to search, he was surprised that she would be back by now. Perhaps she'd been lucky and reached the site of the SOS without having wasted any time searching for the stricken boat; or, and the thought made him feel selfish, the boat in trouble had sunk by the time *Petrel* had reached her.

Jamie didn't know what to think now, but stuck alone in the cleft, his rescue was all he had been thinking about. Not to hold the hope would have been to let the horror of seeing Byrne so brutally murdered overtake him. He had unclipped the Evinrude outboards from the stern slats, lifted up the rubber raft and placed it as a lean-to against the base of the cliff, which spilled out a few yards like a large, rough-hewn fireplace. It was a good hiding place, almost impossible to see when looking down from the top of the chimney, because of the kink in it that had given Frank a few anxious moments on the way up. Still, Jamie looked up for the hundredth time to check that the rope was still dangling, and wondered, after all the distant firing he'd heard and the pinkish glow he'd seen reflected in the sky, when Frank was coming back.

Reaching into the Zodiac's rations pocket he pulled out what seemed to be a piece of dried apple from the feel of it, or was it a banana? Whatever, it reminded him of a holy wafer, of his boyhood as a server at Mass and of his one-time beliefs. He wished he could believe again, to give him some hope in this stormy, lonely, barren place, and he struggled to remember the ancient prayer for times of peril, for men who go down to the sea in ships. He looked westward again and waited. The green light had vanished.

HOLDING EACH OTHER tightly in their excitement, Frank and Gloria kissed. As Frank came up for breath, his resolve to find out where the wire led to, what it meant, weakened, for right there and then he wanted to make love to her.

But still, he was thinking about the wire. What was it that had so obsessed the mother ship that Saburov had been prepared to kill so wantonly? He held Gloria against him, feeling her lean closer to him, wanting what he wanted, yet so desperately tired that all her strength was drained. Lowering her to the ground, Frank pulled the groundsheet around her. "We'll rest here awhile," he said softly, propping her against the hut wall. "I'm going to find out where that thing leads to. You catch forty winks, then we—"

"How?" she began weakly, holding his hand and barely able to keep her eyes open. "How are you going to find out?" She indicated the broken knife. "That's useless now."

"I'll get a bayonet from one of our late friends," he said, nodding toward the killing ground of the burned-out grass.

She shook her head.

"Look, I know how badly you want to get away from this damn place but we have to find out."

Her hand reached up and her delicate fingers touched his lips. "Grenades," she said.

He, too, was so tired, it took him a second to realize she wasn't suggesting the hut was a storage depot for grenades, ammunition and the like, but that as well as getting a bayonet he could get grenades from the bodies and use them—now that the mother ship had gone.

He looked down at her admiringly. "Very good, Miss Bernardi! Top of the class."

"I've just thought of something else," she added. "Won't the fire have blown them up?"

"No. That kind of heat won't do it. You have to pull the pin to start the detonation. Besides, we would have heard them going off in the fire."

"Well then, it's not such a dumb suggestion of mine, after all."

"Wait here," said Frank. "It'll only take me ten minutes or so. When I get back, though, you'd better do your resting outside the hut."

Whether it was from weariness or from the waves of relief washing over her in the wake of the mother ship's departure, Frank's seriously delivered advice that Gloria vacate the hut while he packed a grenade charge at the base of its far wall struck her as incredibly funny. She was still giggling as he kissed her, called her a nut and went outside into the howling night to get the grenades.

THE FIRST BUNDLE OF GRENADES made a bowl-shaped depression but failed to penetrate the cement floor, despite the fact that Frank had packed them hard into the pot-size hole he had excavated with the paratroop knife. He took another four grenades, ramming them hard into the larger cavity, and warned Gloria to take cover again as he piled on what debris there was, ready to pull the trigger pin.

The explosion filled the hut with thick dust and a hard, piercing light. Heat rushed out into the night, hitting the cold west wind, creating a steamy mist that shrouded Frank and Gloria outside the entrance before it vanished. Lifting her to her feet, he put his arm about her. "C'mon," he said. "Let's see what's under that floor."

"A cellar," she joked. "Full of champagne."

"Or vodka!" he answered just as casually, walking back into the hut. He flicked on the lighter, its flame resembling a tiny candle in a cave full of choking, chalklike powder. "That cable from the wind indicator wasn't put—" he began coughing "—wasn't put there for..." The tickle in his throat made his eyes water and sting so badly both of them retreated into the clean night air.

"What's that smell?" Gloria asked. "Like something burning."

For a moment Frank thought that she was smelling the grenade, but then he detected it, too—an acrid odor like that of a burned-out electrical connection yet more astringent, like spilled vinegar. But though they could see the jagged black outline of a man-size hole, blown out by the second charge, and knew the smell must be coming from it, the dusty halo around the flickering flame of the lighter still obscured their vision. Suddenly Frank snapped off the lighter. "Could be gasoline fumes, something volatile," he explained, reaching out for her in the pitch-darkness. "Don't want to torch ourselves."

Gloria said nothing but rested against him to feel his strength in her exhaustion, dreaming of home, of the end of this island nightmare, of being with him in a warm and peaceful place, afraid that here inside the hut there was an evil that would somehow destroy the dream.

"Damn!" he said impatiently, the fresh cold air failing to drive, or rather suck, the acrid fumes out of the hut. Gently he pushed her toward the entrance. "Wait outside while I have a look."

"No! Stay with me, Frank. Frank—where are you? Frank...?"

"Go on, honey—wait outside."

"Bully," she said in mock petulance.

"I love you," he said. "Go on...."

As THE LAUNCH TURNED slowly in the chop for its approach to the landing slab, Saburov heard what sounded like the dull *crump* of an artillery shell high up on the island. He was at a loss to explain what it might be. Perhaps, unlike the small group of seamen whom he could see anxiously awaiting him to take them off the slab and back to the mother ship, one or two of his men might still be on the island, fighting it out with Hall and the woman.

"Get below," Saburov curtly ordered the men as they leaped and scrambled aboard the launch. His tone showed his contempt for their being outwitted by the American. "And get warm. I want you ready for action in twenty minutes."

Below, in the cramped space, there was a heavy stench of gasoline fumes, acrid coffee, and vomit. One of the men had been violently ill, the result of shock from what had happened on the island, the rolling sea and the plain fear of going up against the Americans again. On the other hand, several of the men, fresh from the ship, a marine among them, were so full of hatred for the Americans they were willing to go ashore and help Saburov finish the job he had started, especially when Saburov informed them that whoever got Hall or the woman would be given more than a medal on his chest. There would also be hardship allowances, the kind you got for volunteering for construction projects in Siberia, in the form of vouchers for the party's "specialty" shops that officially didn't exist but were stocked with luxuries from the decadent West and from East Germany. He even hinted at a Moskvich subcompact. They all knew that this must be a lie—such a thing, a brand-new car—well, one might as well wish for a private apartment on the Black Sea. "Maybe a used Moskvich?" suggested one of the seamen, to at least bring the offer down to earth. The sick man wasn't interested in a car, new or used, or anything else, but for the remainder, "used" carried with it a faint air of possibility, an ex-government vehicle, perhaps. The mere possibility was enough to firm up what had been a flabby resolve when they'd come aboard and had had their hopes of immediately rejoining the mother ship dashed by Saburov's determination, whatever the cost, to get the Americans.

As the launch rounded the Pinnacle on the first leg of Saburov's plan, they began talking about their own plan to share whatever any one of them won. It was, the marine told them, only proper for socialists. His real reason was that alone, none of them could afford to run the car on their pay, even with "full catch" fish bonuses—the cost of the gasoline would be prohibitive.

Overhearing them, Saburov poked his head beneath the deck canopy. "I assure you, Comrades, I will keep my word!"

"By God!" said one of the seamen excitedly when Saburov withdrew again to the deck. "He means it. A car!"

Leaning forward on the hatch cover, hands free to use the binoculars as the launch heaved and slopped against unpredictable side rips, Saburov scanned the base of the cliffs, the moon's occasional and ghostly light startling as it illuminated the splashes of seals and sea lions dropping from the bumpy shoreline.

IN THE SENIOR OFFICERS' CLUB in Moscow General Borgach glanced down at his cards with a bored expression, having mastered the art of deception in bridge and everything else during his long years of survival in the Politburo. Either side of him two junior officers sat stiffly, honored by the invitation to join Borgach but too intimidated by Borgach's exalted rank. Sitting across from him, half-lost in shadow beyond a smoke-filled cone of yellowish light, his protégé, General Kornon, tried to look as equally unconcerned as Borgach with the hand he'd been dealt. But if Kornon's facial features showed no sign of strain, Borgach could detect a faint movement of the green baize tablecloth as Kornon's knee went into an involuntary spasm that the young general cursed lightheartedly as an old wound from his days as "adviser" to the Vietcong. Borgach knew that Kornon knew he was putting on the bored expression, but there was no way the younger general could know whether his superior's inscrutable gaze concealed a good hand or not, a trap, a pretense behind the pretense.

Kornon's aide entered the officers' club, his dull khaki uniform relieved only by the stiff red epaulets reflected in the dim lighting of the card room. Kolya begged pardon and whispered his message to Kornon. Kornon nodded as if the information conveyed was of no more than passing bureaucratic interest, but soon after he played his hand, losing but with such good grace that Borgach suspected it had to be good news. Kornon threw up his hands. "Ah, outranked again!"

"Outranked?" Borgach said, grinning, signaling the waiter for refills. "'Thrashed again!' is what you mean, Comrade."

"Exactly!" responded Kornon enthusiastically. "Exactly. Outmaneuvered." Kornon downed his vodka so vigorously Borgach was certain it could only be the best possible news, that Kornon's scheme on Eagle Island was going according to plan—despite some earlier hitches young Kolya had reported—that the mother ship must be under way, having sailed, as ordered, at midnight. The question, however, was whether he, Borgach, should now announce his unqualified support—and more than that, his partial initiation of Kornon's Eagle Island plan—before the younger general could take all the credit himself, making Borgach seem no more than a bandwagoner if he waited. Or should he wait a little longer? From experience Borgach knew how subordinates were tempted to pretend everything was in order till the last possible moment. What if, for example, the earlier difficulties that Kornon's aide had secretly reported to him had not been resolved? Borgach knew what he would do in the same circumstances—cover his backside, buy time to correct any "errors."

After Kornon excused himself, Borgach walked slowly to the vestibule, stopping to chat briefly with other members of the club, particularly those who were also mem-

bers of the Politburo and those, like Kornon, who were
slated for full membership, providing they kept their noses
clean. Reaching the vestibule, he paused a moment by the
granite bust of Lenin, buttoning his greatcoat and looking out to see if it was still snowing. The distance to his
chauffeur-driven Zil was only a matter of a few yards, but
still the swirling gusts chilled his vodka-flushed cheeks.

As the jet-black limousine drove off silently, Borgach
took off his gloves and pulled out a note that had been
neatly slipped into the right thumb space by Kornon's aide.
It confirmed that the mother ship had indeed sailed, the
message having been sent by the ship's captain to the Polish minister of fisheries in Gdansk. Borgach lit an American cigarette, then burned the message. He would play
safe, wait until the Polish minister heard from the political officer, Saburov, as well as from the ship's captain.
Lifting the Zil's phone he asked for the officers' club, then
for Kornon's aide.

WHEN THE PHONE RANG in Gdansk, the apartment's
shades were drawn but the commissioner for fisheries was
wide-awake, humping like a beached whale, in the final
approaches to climax, his secretary moving faster and
faster beneath him, her cries of pleasure belying the practiced, almost mechanical, rhythm of her movements. The
phone was insistent. The commissioner increased the pace
even more before the ringing could turn her off; he was
gasping and telling her not to worry and damning the
party—but it kept ringing and ringing. Then she slowed
but he kept on trying to keep everything alive, grunting
and cursing as the phone kept ringing. Finally he stopped,
fell off, and they lay panting together, lathered in perspiration, which dripped from him as his hand stretched out
in defeat. He wanted to scream into the receiver, swear at
everything and everyone, but she motioned for him to be
calm. It had to be party business; no one else would have

let the phone ring at her place for that long without hanging up.

"Yes, Comrade," she heard him say breathlessly. "Of course, Comrade. Right away." Putting down the receiver softly he turned to her. "Moscow."

She was frightened. "They've never called here before."

"I know," he said, sitting up, reaching over for a cigarette. "It means they know about us." He lit the cigarette, inhaling deeply, trapping the smoke. "Kornon's aide. It's a message I have to send—off the record. I cooperate or else." He flopped back onto the bed.

"Who to?" she asked.

"A political officer on board one of our mother ships."

"So?" she said. "There are political officers on most ships."

"This one's different."

"Why?"

"I don't know. It must be important, though, for the bastards in Moscow to be covering their asses, channeling everything through us. We'll get the shit if anyone else finds out."

"What do you have to do?"

"Request an ETA in Gdansk. Right now!"

"Poof!" she said irreverently. "Call later."

"What—"

"Comrade Commissioner," she said, slipping her hand beneath the sheets, "your secretary will book the call in earlier. My record book will show you called the minute you received instructions from Moscow."

The commissioner frowned. "What if they check with the ship later?"

"The captain's Polish, isn't he?" She squeezed harder. "Let them wait!"

The commissioner extinguished the cigarette, crushing it so hard that the rice paper burst, the tobacco oozing out. "My God, I want you."

''No,'' she said. ''Leave the light on. I want you to watch me.''

''On. Yes.''

Neither of them could know it, but as they fondled and kissed, rekindling the passion made sweeter in their defiance of Moscow's instruction to send the message, they were unwittingly giving Saburov that much more time to stop his enemies from escaping, to stop them from telling the world the secret of Eagle Island.

Chapter Thirty-Nine

HOLDING THE LIGHTER over the jagged hole blown out by the grenades, Frank saw that he was looking down fifty feet at the secret of Eagle Island. They were not as sleek as photographs he had seen, but then, he thought, what was? There was a glint from the grease-creased hydraulic legs folded, drawn in close to the body like some monstrous grasshopper, the legs ready to extend upward, lifting a mechanical steel cradle to any desired angle. It was the smell of the grease on the hydraulic legs that Frank now found so overpowering in the huge, underground chamber, the size of a ship's engine room. For the first time he realized that the cement floor he'd so unceremoniously blown a hole in was massively hinged, only a hairline separating the two steel halves that would open by virtue of the hydraulic legs.

Descending into the chamber, holding the flickering lighter high, he saw four more pairs of hydraulic lifts, smaller, arranged in series. Each pair was the shape of five-foot-high fence posts or columns placed six feet apart, the top of each column a flat, six-inch-square steel plate. All in all they looked like the legs of a front-end loader, only turned upside down, the flat tops to be used to push upward into matching female receptors, thus raising the two halves of the steel trapdoors, cracking through the relatively thin veneer of cement.

"Drilling pipes!" he said aloud, mocking his earlier certainty. "Pipes, my foot!" He had to admit that what the Soviet designers had done was truly impressive. They had taken an ordinary thirty-foot-long cradle and fitted it on six pairs of squat, soccer-ball-size runners, so that each of the six remote-controlled missiles would pop up horizontally into the cradle. The hydraulic elbows would push the cradle upward and forward at the same time, so the cradle would, in effect, become a trolley as well, carrying each missile in turn beyond the hut's entrance where it could then be swiveled and elevated in any direction.

Frank stood for a moment, holding the light high, transfixed by the brilliance of the Russians' bunker. He wasn't sure exactly how much time Moscow would save, but you didn't have to be an expert to know that for the six ICBMs, capable of being triggered from anywhere in the world, the distance from Eagle Island to the United States mainland was a mere spit, taking much less than half the time it would to launch them from the Soviet Union. He was looking at a massive Russian preemptive strike, "in place," only seventy miles off the continental United States!

Lowering the lighter but keeping it away from a small pool of leaking hydraulic fuel, he noticed the rollers were stamped with the letters SRP, Swiss Rhine Petrochemicals, and that the missiles weren't black as he'd first thought, but had been painted instead with an ugly wavy dark green and brown, as if camouflage paint would make any difference. They would come in so fast....

Suddenly he was in darkness. A gust of wind had blown out the light.

Chapter Forty

UPON LEARNING that the mother ship was headed for home, General Kornon had been in a celebratory, expansive mood. His hand swept over the huge wall map of the Pacific, eastward from Eagle Island to the enemy's heartland. The attack plan called for fourteen targets—the Bangor Trident sub base in Washington State, a little to the north of a very short Oregon trajectory; the NORAD center in Colorado Springs, a few minutes from Eagle Island; the four major ICBM silo complexes in the Midwest; assorted SAC bases; the vital sub transmission antennae in Maine; and, of course, as he had explained to General Borgach, a cluster of four of the eighteen SS-20, 150-kiloton warheads for the Washington, D.C./Andrews Air Base/Pentagon area, one of the prime purposes being to annihilate the seat of the enemy's government and command. Destroying Andrews into the bargain would have the added advantage of preventing the American President from reaching his much touted Ever-Ready Airborne Command Post.

"It will give us such an edge," Kornon explained to Kolya. "Even if anyone in authority is left in the United States to order a retaliation, their command systems will be in a shambles." His hand was slashing the air now like a Cossack's. "And never mind the effect of the EMP."

Kolya knew Kornon meant the enormous electromagnetic pulse that would wipe out all United States communications, from every TV and radio set to the big defense computers, but he asked the general exactly what he meant, anyway. When it looked to Kolya as if you had backed a winner, it was best to curry favor immediately, for it was at such moments that a winner's generosity was at full flood. Kolya took care, however, to say nothing about the message being sent through Gdansk asking for

Saburov, specifically, to reply. If Saburov did reply, then everything would be all right. If he didn't reply, then Kolya would simply tell Kornon, explaining it as a double check to safeguard Kornon; Kornon would appreciate Kolya's loyalty and initiative. On one hand, if Kornon's present gleeful mood of self-congratulation turned out to be premature, then Borgach would be grateful for the warning. Either way, as Kolya saw it, he couldn't lose.

Kolya's phone was ringing in his outer office. At first he ignored it as he poured Kornon's tea, but it was so persistent that the general told him to go answer it. As Kolya closed the door to the general's office and lifted the receiver in his beautifully furnished, but much smaller office he noticed that ice was building up on the windowpanes. "Yes?" he said with exactly the right bureaucratic tone, midway between subservience to high officials and brusqueness for the *narods*, or lower orders. As he listened, he affected an air of official unconcern should anyone suddenly appear and overhear the conversation.

When he told Kornon that it was Gdansk reporting that Saburov could not be reached, the general stopped sipping his tea, uttering an obscenity he hadn't used since the Afghan war.

"Are you certain?" Kornon pressed.

"He doesn't answer, General."

Kornon was facing the windows; snow swirled madly outside. "But the mother ship is on the way?"

"Yes, sir."

"Try him again," ordered Kornon grimly.

"Yes, General."

The tone of celebration had completely vanished. "Kolya!"

"Sir?"

Kornon was still facing away from him, staring out at the icicles building on the Kremlin's walls. "There are more ways than one to skin a cat."

"Yes, sir." Kolya didn't know what the general meant, only that they were all in deep trouble if Saburov didn't "finish the job." The one promising thing, Kolya reminded himself, was that Saburov had been handpicked, he was the best they had. The odds were on Saburov's side, and Kornon, in his rapid rise to the inner sanctums of power, hadn't picked a loser yet.

Chapter Forty-One

COLD SOBER AND NOT KNOWING what had taken place on the island, Jamie was filled with such unrelieved tension that when he spotted a bobbing mast light about twelve miles southwest of the cleft he suspected it might be the Polish mother ship they had sighted when they'd first entered the area two days before. He decided not to signal until the ship came closer and he could make her out, if not in the occasional wash of moonlight, then at dawn. At least that was his plan. But isolation and fear made him so anxious for rescue from the endless smashing of the sea against the granite fortress of the island that his resolve was already weakening.

He heard a low growl that at first he thought was from one of the nearby colonies of sea lions. Then he recognized it as a motor, an inboard by the stroke, possibly a hundred yards or so out to sea.

DESPITE THE COXSWAIN'S SKILL, the launch was rolling so badly in the chop that it took Saburov all his time to prevent the sniper's rifle from sliding back and forth on the gunwale. Never mind his keeping the night scope scanning the rocky shore as the launch determinedly, though slowly, made its way up the western coast of the island. Below in the cramped cabin the sick seaman, unused to anything less than a ten-thousand tonner, continued to retch, his head lolling from side to side, his eyes glazed as if possessed by some primeval spirit. Some of the other ten men told him to shut up but his agony was beyond admonishment, and he kept on so that three of the sailors retreated to the deck even though it meant confronting icy wind and spray. To their collective amazement, Saburov seemed to be actually enjoying himself, his lean body pressed hard against the port side hatch cover, telling the coxswain he was convinced they would find a way of cutting off the Americans' escape.

Having given his eyes a rest from the constant and disorienting corkscrew motion of the launch, Saburov now seized the opportunity to look through the scope again in the relative calm of a trough. He saw a white splash at the bottom of the cliffs. It was a huge bull sea lion this time, disturbed by the proximity of the launch. Then Saburov saw more splashing as surf pounded a small, shingled inlet, and above it what appeared to be a long crack in the towering granite. For a second he saw a shape move on the edge of the shingle then disappear into the face of the rock. He assumed it to be another sea lion, except that this one was much smaller, more the height of a fully grown seal.

The moonlight was poor at this angle to the cliffs, and Saburov had to wait another five minutes until the fissure was almost out of sight behind a craggy outcrop before a sheet of moonlight revealed, without benefit of night scopes, that there was an indentation several yards across at the base of the fissure. In the scope, Saburov saw something move again then disappear beneath a startlingly geometrically-shaped rock, very pointed at its top, almost a perfect triangle, its base lost in a crumble of shingle. He looked again. No movement now, but the apex of the triangle was so fixed, so geometric as to be unnatural.

"Of course!" he shouted, eye glued to the scope, his right hand excitedly adjusting the focus. "A rubber raft—stood upright. All right, Comrade," he said to the coxswain, indicating the cleft. "Take her in!" Next he assembled nine seamen, readying them to disembark but warning them not to fire for fear of alerting Hall and the woman.

WHEN JAMIE SAW the launch's dark prow looming out of the sea, he searched, panic-stricken, for something with which to defend himself. There was nothing but the paddles from the Zodiac, and it was with one of these that he attempted to do battle as nine blackened figures leaped from the launch onto the shingle before the boat turned around to wait offshore. Beneath the din of the shingle being rolled, sucked to and fro in the crashing of the surf, the sound of Jamie's lone and desperate battle was lost to all but the seamen as, already out of wind, he swung the Zodiac's paddle. None of them bothered to get too close, content instead simply to let the American wear himself out.

It was only when he started yelling loudly, his voice carrying up the chimney to the top of the cliffs, that Saburov gave the word to stop messing around. They went in, rifles extended to ward off the American's wild blows, until they managed to drive him back into the cleft, knocking him down and using the rifle butts to crush his head against the rock wall. It was then that Saburov saw the rope hanging in the chimney like a rope in a belfry. Would Hall and the woman return to look for the Zodiac? he wondered. Or would they decide to stay clear of it, suspecting their raft might have already been discovered by earlier marine patrols? Saburov tried to put himself in Hall's place.

The waves seemed to be pounding the shore with greater frequency now, but whether it was because of the westerly or his imagination pressured by his urgency to stop the

American, Saburov couldn't be sure. He knew only that he had to act swiftly, with the same kind of initiative his enemy had shown, and for which General Kornon had chosen him. "Quickly!" he said, turning to the nine-man team. "Two stay here by the raft—and don't make a sound. If the Americans return, let them get well down the rope before you fire. Understood?"

"Yes, sir."

"You others follow me."

Saburov holstered his .9 mm Makarov, clipped the holster shut and showed why, whatever else he might be, he was grudgingly respected as he led the way up the dangerous 150-foot chimney, not having asked anyone under his command to do anything he wasn't prepared to do himself. In the shaft of weeping granite he had a hard time of it, his age and lack of conditioning working against him, his muscles as unused to this as his dead marines had been used to it. The pain, however, made him even more determined to kill Hall himself.

"FRANK?" GLORIA'S VOICE was weak. He didn't hear her, intent as he was on examining, admiring, the elaborate and compact bank of lithium-battery-run computer consoles that, among other things, were constantly monitoring the vital variables of wind strength, resistance and direction, adjusting launch mode and the missiles' inboard computers accordingly.

"Frank?" she repeated, her voice quavering. Turning around and looking up in the halo of dust he saw her, a blistered arm around her throat and something resembling a human face, bloodied and soot-covered, breathing openmouthed against her clotted hair. The sound of the breathing was animallike in its wheezing. The high foresight of a Kalashnikov rested, or rather pushed back, against her bosom, its tip pressing up hard under her chin.

Frank didn't move, but watched the marine's singed epaulet dangling loosely from the scorched uniform, his eyes bloodshot, exhausted. He was staring at Frank with such hatred that Frank knew intuitively that any sign of fear on his part would be the same as pulling the AK's trigger himself. His senses straining for any sign of advantage over the Russian, Frank became very aware of everything around him, the howl of the westerly, the salty air, the Russian's labored breathing and the broken paratroop knife that still lay at the edge of the man-size hole, about a foot to the right of the Russian's right boot. But Frank had spotted the knife with his peripheral vision, not once taking his eyes from the Russian. "Gee," he began in an intentionally casual tone, "I guess we missed you at the barbecue?"

The Russian pulled the AKM tighter against Gloria by way of telling the American to shut up and making it clear to Frank that he didn't speak English. As if the sound of Frank's voice had suddenly reminded him where he was and what he had originally intended when he had crept up on the girl outside, the Russian began gesturing fiercely for Frank to come out of the missile bay—now. Frank knew that this would make it easier for the Russian to shoot them both together and that the badly scared Russian realized that to fire the automatic rifle into the missile bay could start any number of small fires either around the hydraulic fuel lines or in the electronics. The nuclear warheads wouldn't go off, but the missiles' solid propellant would go up like the *Challenger* in '86.

Frank motioned toward the manhole opening by way of confirming that that was what the Russian wanted him to do. The Russian nodded. *"Da!"*

"Fine." Frank's left hand pointed up at the lighter held high in his right, and at his knees, indicating half in pantomime that he couldn't very well climb out of the hole while holding the lighter. He made to turn it off. The Russian suddenly moved back, gripping Gloria so tightly she winced in pain. *"Nyet! Nyet!"*

"Okay, okay," said Frank. "Take it easy. I won't flick it off and jump you. Here..." So slowly there could be absolutely no mistake about his intentions Frank held the lighter aloft and pointed to the Russian. "I'll let *you* hold it...okay...or her." He nodded toward Gloria. "Okay, whatever you like." He stood still, his head just below the manhole's opening. He could hear the faint click-click-clicking sound of the anemometer cable running from the hut's roof down into the missile bay, but all his attention was centered on the Russian, who indicated that the lighter be placed on the ground.

"But it'll go out!" he said to the Russian, going into more pantomime. "It's an open-flint lighter—you have to keep your finger on it or it goes out. A Bic—you understand?"

The Russian nodded. "Bic!" He understood.

"Yes," said Frank, adding, "Thank God for advertising. I have to hold it...the *Bic*...okay?"

The Russian nodded again but gestured with his rifle, keeping its tip hard under Gloria's chin.

"All right, all right," answered Frank. "Watch me then. No funny stuff, right?" The tone conveyed his meaning to the Russian, who thrust his head up and sideways for Frank to get out.

"Watch the light then..." said Frank, placing his left hand on the edge of the manhole, then lowering his right hand, with the lighter still flickering, on the right side of the hole, to lift himself up. The flame wobbled for a minute, their three enormous shadows thrown against the wall as the Russian shifted Gloria around toward Frank, shielding himself.

Frank was coming up very deliberately from the crouch position at the edge of the manhole when his right hand almost dropped the flickering light. "Oops," he said, grabbing for it. In that moment the Russian, like Gloria, had glanced at the flame. Frank slipped, his right hand bringing the lighter close to Gloria's face. She recoiled as

Frank's right hand did two things in one movement: his
thumb hooked the AKM's barrel, shoving it violently up
and away to the side and his left hand slammed the jagged
paratroop knife into the Russian's side.

A hot jet of blood shot out, and the AKM fired a short
burst, sending down more dust. Gloria staggered away
from the Russian in horror, both hands clasped against her
mouth. He had dropped his AKM, and was swallowing
frantically as he stumbled backward, one hand clawing
frantically at his throat, the other reaching vainly for the
wound in his side, trying to stop the flow but only creating a hand-over-hose effect, spraying plum-colored blood
all over.

Frank walked over, picked up the Kalashnikov and
emptied the magazine into the Russian. "I'm getting
damned tired of these jokers."

Gloria was hysterical, backing away, whimpering like a
child.

"C'mon," said Frank. "C'mon, honey." He shook her
hard until she finally began to sob uncontrollably, throwing herself against him, her hair wet with tears and blood.

"Listen . . ." Frank said, as softly as he could. "I've got
a little business to do here, then we'll go home. What do
you say, kiddo?"

Her only answer was to hold him so tightly that he found
it difficult, without hurting her, to break free.

Chapter Forty-Two

ON BOARD THE MOTHER SHIP off the northernmost tip of
the island, Captain Novisk was handed the second transmission from Gdansk in as many hours, requesting Sabu-

rov to give the ETA of the mother ship in Gdansk. Novisk turned to the radio officer. "We can't answer in Saburov's name, and that's all there is to it. What happens when we get to Gdansk and he isn't even aboard? Then we get it in the neck."

The radio officer was visibly agitated. "But sir, I have to tell Gdansk something."

"Then tell them the truth! What the hell did Saburov ever do for us? Tell them he's not aboard. And radio all trawlers to be clear of the island by dawn. No use us leaving if they're going to get caught in a satellite photo and screw up the whole business."

"Yes, sir."

BY NOW *PETREL* WAS five miles from the southern tip of Eagle Island. The mother ship, blocked from her view by the island's mass, made full steam ahead for Gdansk. In the predawn darkness, *Petrel* was assembling men on the forward deck, preparing to launch the aft-stowed Zodiac to go and try to find out what had happened to Frank and the three crew members. Running with the sea, *Petrel* was making good time. Captain Tate and Scotty felt sure they'd have the answer to the fire on the island within a few hours.

Sparks tried again to contact the United States Coast Guard air arm, from Cape Deception to Astoria, in case anyone had been badly injured on the island, but there was still nothing but static. Sparks was more and more convinced that something quite apart from abnormal sunspot activity was effectively jamming the system. From his cabin, Sparks could see the cluster of men on the forward deck all pitching in to help get the Zodiac in position so that the Austin-Western hydraulic arm could lift and swing it over once they were close enough to the island. One of the busiest members of the crew, he noted with admiration, was not a deckhand but one of the stewards, head

· bent against the force-nine's wind and spray, trying to be of assistance wherever possible.

Petrel's radar was also acting up under the electrical interference so it was not until they were four miles from the island that visual contact was made with what appeared to be another ship about *Petrel*'s length in the binoculars' sighting. Scotty said it was six miles off and closing due east of *Petrel* and southeast of the Pinnacle off the southernmost tip of the island.

"Where's it heading, Mate?" asked Tate. "Toward the island?"

"Ach, I think so, Captain, but I'd no' bet on it. Have to wait and see."

"Probably a trawler," commented the lookout.

"Aye, I think you're right there, laddie. Aboot that size."

"Well," said Tate, "it's got nothing to do with us. Let's look lively on that deck, Mate. I see there are only one or two wearing hard hats again. Thought I'd made myself clear on that."

"I told 'em," said Scotty, "but whoever makes the rules ashore, Captain, has never worked in a force nine."

"Maybe," said Tate grudgingly. "But someone could get hurt."

SABUROV STARTED his men in a run as soon as they reached the cliff top and heard the stutter of gunfire eastward from the direction of the hut. After a few hundred yards, four of his men had to stop, unfit, unable to go on, but the young Polish officer and five comrades kept pace with Saburov. Even if they slowed down or rested later on for a moment or two, the colonel estimated they'd still reach the hut, a half mile off now, in less than fifteen minutes. Glancing back, he spotted the four who had rested starting off again about three hundred yards behind him and his front runners.

FRANK AND GLORIA WORKED feverishly, tearing up the uniforms of the dead Russian and three others around the hut, then began knotting together the strips of what had once been Russian khaki shirts, trousers and singlets. In the distance they could see the bobbing mast lights of two ships, like two erratic stars, five miles apart. They knew that the one southwest must be *Petrel*. The other ship to the southeast was unknown. Both were heading for the island.

"No, not that one," commanded Frank, as Gloria, all but dropping from lack of sleep and food, was about to tie a piece of bloodstained cloth above the missile bay. She looked up at Frank, bewildered for a moment, and it wasn't until he took it from her and threw it away that she realized, looking down at her hands, that it was damp with blood. "Oh," she said tiredly. "I'm sorry, Frank... I'm..."

"Never mind," he said, trying to keep the urgency from his voice as he watched the ship from the southeast closing in on the island. "You're doing fine," he assured her.

"How long?" she asked him.

"What? Oh, fifty feet should do it. Just keep those knots coming!" He'd spoken lightheartedly, but she was too cold, too undone by the constant, awful danger of the past forty-eight hours, to even give him a smile. Hopefully that would come after—if there was an after.

Chapter Forty-Three

THE BRIGHT, UNDULATING LIGHT that was *Petrel*'s forward deck went out.

"What the hell—?" began Captain Tate. Instrument panels on the bridge's console flickered in multicolored frenzy before the alternate generator kicked in. Someone entering the bridge bumped into the captain and Tate felt hot liquid running over his hand. "Christ!"

"Sorry, sir, I—"

The ship rolled to starboard and Tate could smell as well as feel the gush of coffee. "For Christ's sake . . ."

By then Scotty had the emergency lamp clamped over the bridge's window and he switched it on, flooding the bridge with twice as much light as was usual when they were running or on oceanographic station. One of the stewards, the younger one, was down on his hands and knees, trying to recover a cup that, having rolled across the raised cedar slats of the bridge's floor, had wedged itself between the Marconi radar and the wall of the chart room.

"Sorry, sir," said the steward as he reached in behind the Marconi set. "Martin told me to bring up some coffee."

"Don't go blaming Martin, son, and don't worry about any refills for the time being . . . not until we get that Zodiac launched and our boys back here. All right?"

"Yes . . . yes, sir. Sorry, sir."

"Steward?" It was Redfern, putting down the bridge phone.

"Yes, sir?"

"I thought it was Martin's shift?"

"Yes, sir, but, well, seeing everyone's keen to get our boys off that island, well, Mr. Martin and me decided to stand by . . . make a few pots of brew."

"Where's Martin now? Thought I saw him on deck?"

"He was, sir, but he's been down in the galley the last little while making sandwiches for the boys."

"Ach, well, then thank him for us. Nice of you. Above and beyond the call, eh?"

The young steward didn't get the Scotsman's reference to "above and beyond," only that the mate seemed to be thanking him and Martin. "Thanks, sir." He left the bridge as all the deck lights came back on, and Tate, in a bravura performance, mopped himself with paper towels, using only his legs to counter the ship's heavy rolls.

Scotty lifted the bridge phone again, looking through the overhanging angle of bridge glass, moving his gaze from the seamen who had been keeping lines taut on the Zodiac. Her sides were ripped end to end, flapping helplessly and uselessly in the wind. When Tate saw the damage he stopped worrying about the coffee, his whole body immobilized. "What in the name of Judas—?"

"Bosun said it must have happened when the lights blew a fuse. Somebody probably wasn't holding a line tight enough, let the raft have her head for a moment, probably gashed herself open on the shackle pin or against the edge of the Austin-Western's arm."

"Damn it!" said Tate, looking incredulously around the bridge. "Goddamn it!"

Scotty was looking directly at Tate but was indicating the helmsman, who was busy keeping *Petrel*'s head into the wind while they'd come around momentarily to steady her for the Zodiac launching. "I'll take over," Tate told the helmsman. "Go below and get me a towel from the steward, will you? My arm feels like a sponge." Then he turned to the lookout. "And I want you to go aloft while we're with the wind and get a fix on that other ship east of us. We might need her help."

"Yes, sir."

"Use a safety line all the way up."

"I will, sir, don't worry," and he was gone.

"'Don't worry!' he says," commented Tate. "Well, I am. So, Scotty, what the hell's going on down there? You don't think a gash like that could happen so quickly?"

"Ach, it could, sir."

"But you don't like the coincidence. Mary Crane, Aussie and now this."

"That's right, Captain. If the ship's jinxed, some-body's doing the jinxing."

Tate suddenly looked much older as he tried to keep balance in a heavy roll that pushed, then dropped, *Petrel* hard aport. "You think it's that fella, Martin?"

"Could be anyone."

"He came and told us about Mrs. Crane's cabin, re-member?"

"Aye...the business aboot the sheet missing an' all. All palsy-walsy!"

"But he was in the galley—making sandwiches when the deck light went out."

"But have ye no' seen the stewards' bread knives, Cap-tain? Great bloody cleavers they are. Take the leg off a bloody great bull they would! Never mind a rubber raft."

Tate braced himself defiantly against the next roll, but his stance was more bluff than power and at the last mo-ment he grabbed the roll bar. "Can we fix the Zodiac? I won't launch a longboat in this weather."

"We could inflate the rubber sides and try patching her with aluminum tape. Might hold it for a wee while."

"It'll have to be longer than that, Scotty."

"I think it'd last to the island and back."

"There's no time to test her, Scotty," said the old man worriedly.

"Noo, any testing I'm afraid will hae to be done on the job."

"We've no option, then," said Tate. He stood back from the wheel as the helmsman returned to the bridge, handed him a towel and took back the wheel. "All right, we'll patch her. But I won't order anyone to go, it'll have to be—"

"I'll take her," said Scotty. "All I need is two more."

For the second time in two days Tate found himself asking for volunteers to do battle with the heaviest of seas, and had five volunteers within two minutes. By the time he'd refused two of them as being needed on the ship—in fact they were both married men with children—Tate had tears in his eyes, never having failed to be moved by the goodness in some men as much as by the evil in others. Then, toweling himself down, something occurred to him that he'd never had the slightest inkling of before and he called Scotty aside. "The young steward. Look, if it *was* sabotage, it could have been him—not Martin. I mean he timed it nicely to be up here, with coffee, just as the lights went out, didn't he?"

"Glory!" said Scotty. "And he'd know about the sheet drill in Mrs. Crane's cabin and—you're right, the young bugger could be settin' up Martin."

The bosun was ringing the bridge. He told them they were taping the Zodiac now and should be able to launch in half an hour, which at *Petrel*'s present speed would mean they'd only have a short run in to the cliffs to pick up Frank Hall and the crew—if they were still alive.

As FRANK WATCHED the pinpoint of light of the unknown ship emerging from the darkness of the southeast there was no doubt in his mind that it had something to do with Saburov. But where was Saburov? There had been no more gunfire, no flashlights weaving their way ominously across the island's sea of grass. In fact, it was the very absence of his enemy that made him anxious. Gloria, handing him a length of torn khaki trouser, asked him about the number of grenades. "Aren't there enough?"

"Plenty. These jokers have left us ten at least," he said, slapping the haversack on his shoulder. "And enough ammo if we want to scrounge around, but the trouble is, the longest fuse on the grenades is about seven seconds."

"Are you sure?" she asked, not meaning to doubt him so much as to keep her mind occupied with the present danger rather than let it drift back to the horrors of the fires.

"I know it's seven seconds," said Frank, grunting as he made sure of the final knots and tested their strength. The segments now formed a cloth rope almost sixty feet long. "Because of the ones we used against them when they landed below the cliff. Longest is seven seconds. Believe me."

"I do," she answered, her tone so precise, so definite despite her fatigue she sounded like a drunk trying too hard to be sober, at the same time finding it difficult to get to her feet because she felt so weak.

Frank reached out his arm, steadying her as he hurriedly took out the margarine-size tub of solid camping fuel in his rations and the three cheap cigarette lighters he had found on the dead Russians around the hut. While breaking open the seals of the lighters and prying off the lid of the camper fuel with the broken knife, he kept looking out into the darkness beyond the hut for any sign of trouble, ears straining for any other sound than the dirge of the wind.

"But why don't you just use the grenades?" Gloria pressed obsessively, determined to get an answer. Maybe, Frank thought, he was as done in as she was; he was sure he'd already told her.

"Grenades blow in seven seconds. With all the missiles' solid propellant in there, seven seconds isn't going to do the trick, honey. What I'm saying is, it'd work all right but we'd go up with the damn missiles."

"What about the nuclear warheads?"

He said nothing, thought he heard something metallic. Listened again. It was the cable from the anemometer he'd ripped out from the ceiling, now clanking loudly, unnervingly, at about six places between the rooftop and the missile bay.

"Don't worry about the warheads," he said. "They can't be set off by an explosion like this—they'll be programmed to go off over preselected targets in the U.S. There's a city or a base's name on each one of those little wonders. What we've got to worry about is getting the hell away from here before the solid propellant goes. Okay, we're all set," he said, lifting up the ball of cloth rope and handing her the AKM, loaded with a full magazine. "And remember..." She was looking at him but he wasn't sure she was listening. "Honey?"

"Y-yes."

"If anything moves out there, shoot. Got it?"

"Yes."

He ran back to the manhole and descended into the bowels of the missile bay, unable to use the lighter to see by for fear of igniting the cloth rope. Once he felt the stickiness of the big, cold hydraulic elbow he took a turn around it with the cloth ball, then, edging several paces to his left, did the same where the six-foot-long, four-foot-wide liquid gas cartridges were stored. Each of the cartridges, atop one another like bullets in a magazine, were ready to be pushed up against the base of each missile as it came into position, so as to effect a "cold launch." Frank wound the end of the cloth wick around the nozzle of each of the six-foot-long cartridges. Each cartridge was not much more than a gasometer under enormous pressure, ready to literally blow out the missile when the mobile erector launcher cradle rolled out beyond the hut. Quickly taking another turn of the cloth around the top cylinder's neck, Frank retraced his steps back along the dark bay, past the cold hydraulic elbow, out through the manhole to the hut's cement floor, all the while taking care, despite his haste to be rid of the place, to unravel the cloth so as to allow for slack. Any tautness along the way could result in a knot giving way, causing the flame to fizzle out before it reached the missile bay.

NOW SABUROV AND HIS MEN could see the hut five hundred yards away.

Frank took the AKM from Gloria and lit the cloth wick. He waited a few seconds until he could see the flame blossoming from a small orange tongue, slowly eating its way into the cloth, to a run of flame that he figured would put them ten minutes, at least five hundred yards, away.

As they ran into the windy darkness, Frank glanced back and saw the warm, golden glow in the hut, as if coming from a lone candle dancing in a phantom draft.

Saburov saw the two figures running south from the hut two hundred yards to his right. But the colonel was out of breath and not even pride or determination could force any more oxygen into his lungs. He had to stop, bending over, a stitch in his side so painful he knew he couldn't take another step until he got his second wind. "Stop them!" he wheezed, urging on the young Pole and his front runners, pointing excitedly as the two figures disappeared into the darkness. "Kill them!"

Immediately the Pole unleashed a burst from the hip in the general direction of the fleeing Americans.

Frank and Gloria, now three hundred yards from the hut, heard the burst. Frank crashed to the ground, Gloria falling behind him, hitting his haversack so hard she was momentarily knocked out. When she came to she heard Frank yelling, "Gloria! Back to the hut—quickly!"

She tried to get up but something was pressing down so hard on her she was unable to move. "Back to the hut!" she heard Frank repeating urgently, shouting above the wild chatter of machine-gun bursts coming from somewhere off to her right. She tried desperately to get up again, to run back to the hut in time for them to stamp out the burning taper and take refuge in the cement building as they had done not so many hours before. But she couldn't move and, still dizzy from the impact of the fall, couldn't make out anything more than a foot away. Then she heard a Russian's voice, Saburov's, shouting. Abruptly the wild shooting ended, to be followed by other shouts. As the dizziness passed she realized it was Frank's arm pressing down hard on her neck.

"Don't move!" he whispered.

"But—" she began.

"Be quiet," he whispered again. "Didn't you tell me he speaks English—Saburov?"

"Yes." Her breasts were hurting, pressing so hard on the coarse blades of grass she found it difficult to breathe. "Why are you—"

"Shh." And then Gloria realized why Frank had been shouting so loudly for her to return to the hut.

Very soon the voices faded as the Russians closed in on the hut, and Frank and Gloria headed off quickly southward again, wheeling to the southwest. Frank's hand shot out as Gloria stumbled but not in time. She twisted her left ankle, groaning in despair.

Shifting the weight of the haversack, Frank knelt, hoisted her across his back and kept running, the blood pounding in his temples, the wound across his eye bleeding profusely, stinging like nettles as the west wind struck him full blast. He figured they had only about two minutes left.

By now Saburov, getting his second wind, had resumed running toward the hut, still at right angles to him. He could see his team of nine men just entering the glow, their shadows so long they looked like giants entering the mouth of some great cave. Then they were gone, in an orange flash so enormous it could be seen forty miles out to sea, the hut exploding with a roar that shook the whole island, the saffron fireball racing at subsonic speed, cascading over the nearby cliffs in a molten lava, curdling the surf and lighting the sea farther out to a black mirror. The sky turned a marble-white and the sea below could be seen boiling for a hundred yards out.

The shock wave knocked Saburov off his feet, sending him tumbling backward like a sagebrush, the sword grass flailing his body until, bleeding and bruised, he lay gasping, infinitely grateful for the icy rush of air from the west, a blustery stream of oxygen without which he knew he would have died from asphyxiation. Had it not been for the intense light cast over the island, Saburov knew he would not have glimpsed the two Americans, who had almost reached the safety of the western cliffs.

BUBBLING IN A PLASTIC and metallic porridge, the crater where the long hut had once stood was a hundred yards across, belching forth a toxic stew of melted materials whose pungent odor carried eastward on the west wind, engulfing thousands of seabirds, sending them reeling out of the sky, splattering the sea in a hail of scorched bodies. The intensity of the flames immediately around the crater decreased rapidly, but the center of it was still burning fiercely, its edges crumbling and suppurating with a yellowish discharge looking for all the world like some giant carbuncle oozing pus. Sufficient light was emitted to create an unmistakable beacon for *Petrel* and the other ship, which Tate, though still in shock at the awesome size of the explosion, had identified in the fire glow as a trawler of several hundred tons, flying, as he had expected, the Stars and Stripes.

With his Zodiac hastily repaired yet unproved as they closed in on the island, it was a small relief for Tate to see there was another American ship he could call on. But as Sparks tried to raise the ship, realizing that it was probably trying to raise *Petrel*, the crackle of static was still so powerful that he knew it was futile for both of them.

THE TWO MEN WAITING for Saburov at the base of the cleft gazed up the chimney of rock for any sign of his approach. For several minutes after the explosion had lit up the stormy sky, the two men, in sheer fright, had frantically signaled the launch standing offshore to come in and get them. Calmer once the terrifying crash of the explosion had rumbled away to the east and the glow had clearly outlined the trawler coming to rescue them, they waved the launch back to wait a while longer for Colonel Saburov and their comrades to show up, even though they were already half convinced that some, if not all of the team that had gone to kill the Americans must have been killed themselves. They heard dirt and rocks falling down from the cliff top but didn't have time to do anything as the crash of thunder blew them to pieces on the shingle, their disintegrating bodies briefly visible to the launch's coxswain as cherry slashes in the electric blue of the grenades' explosion.

The coxswain, so terrified he yelped like a puppy, spun the wheel, and the launch, bashing the waves at full power, headed out toward the trawler. For a moment he heard an incongruous buzzing sound, like that of a bumblebee in a flower bed. It disappeared as big waves struck the launch but then resumed, and he recognized it as one, possibly two, outboards—a Zodiac coming in from the American ship.

WHEN HE AND HIS seasick comrade boarded the trawler the coxswain was taken straight to the captain and accused of cowardice for leaving the island. Stunned, the coxswain began to defend himself; after all, Hall and the woman must have been the ones who dropped the grenades into the cleft of rock. There was little point in waiting around; besides, if Colonel Saburov was still alive he—

"He would not have scampered away from the island as you did, Comrade," the captain cut in. "He would have at least waited a while to see whether or not any of his comrades had survived and were signaling for help."

Only then did the berated coxswain notice the Pinnacle looming up a mile to starboard and realize the trawler was still heading in for the island.

"Yes," said the captain, his angry tone unabated. "Colonel Saburov has been signaling us ever since you so *bravely* scampered. He's waiting to be picked up, *Comrade*!"

"But . . . but . . . how do you know it's the colonel?"

"Have you been drinking?"

"No, Comrade Captain, but I don't understand."

"His call sign, you fool. He's been signaling us in the emergency code for the past fifteen minutes, from the eastern side where the American ship can't see."

The coxswain tried to redeem himself by reporting that he had heard what must have been a rescue craft coming from the American ship now about eight miles due west, but this information only further incurred the captain's wrath. "If you'd stayed on you might have been able to stop it picking up the Americans."

"How?" the coxswain blurted out. "I only had one rifle."

"You could have rammed them!"

The coxswain made no reply; even the trawler's officers, dim figures on an even dimmer bridge, knew as well as the captain did, that a launch was a ponderous whale to maneuver next to a small, zigzagging Zodiac.

"All right," said the captain, more to end the conversation than excuse the coxswain. "You'd better get back aboard the launch. Two of my men will go with you to the eastern landing to pick up Saburov. No lights. And be quick about it. We've got a transfer to make, and now this thing's blown sky-high no Soviet or Eastern Bloc ship can be seen in the area. We've orders from Gdansk to be completely out of the area by dawn. That means we only have two or three hours till first light. Understand?"

"Yes, sir. Ah, Captain, this transfer. Will it be taking Colonel Saburov to the mother ship?"

"That will be up to the colonel," the captain answered brusquely.

"Oh," said the coxswain, crestfallen. "Then I suppose none of us will get the car now?"

"Car! What the hell are you talking about?"

It was depressingly obvious to the coxswain that the idea of the Moskvich auto as an incentive in hunting the Americans must have been Saburov's alone.

"What d'you mean, a car?" repeated the captain hotly. "Are you ill?"

"No, sir I . . . Doesn't matter, sir," and he was gone to pick up Saburov, leaving the trawler captain completely nonplussed, asking all his officers whether any of them had heard anything about cars. None had.

HEADING BACK to *Petrel*, spray totally enveloping the Zodiac, Gloria clung to Frank. Both of them huddled under blankets and oilskins that were flapping noisily in the wind. The fire's glow on the island was dying, the missiles were destroyed. The full realization of Mary Crane's disappearance had yet to sink in. Frank wished that the whole nightmare would recede in his own and Gloria's memories as quickly as the island was being left behind on the moonlit horizon tilting sharply behind them.

In their own shock at what had happened both on and off the island, no one else on the raft, except Scotty, commanding, said anything. The tragedies of their fellow seamen were so oppressive that they attended carefully, almost gratefully, to the mate's instructions in the mounting seas, wanting, like Frank, to leave Eagle Island behind and to get Frank and the woman safely aboard *Petrel* and then head for home.

"Frank?" It was Gloria, her head tucked in close against him, the sting of the sea wind reviving her enough to ask, "You don't think Saburov survived, do you?"

Despite the pain of Mary's disappearance and his bone-aching fatigue, Frank nevertheless managed to shake his head. "No, he didn't survive. Not if he was one of those in the hut."

"What if he wasn't . . . ?"

"No, honey. Whatever else the bastard did he would've been in front, leading them."

"I suppose," she said and watched, all but detached in her own exhaustion, as *Petrel*, ablaze in lights, rocked against her sea anchor, bow into the wind, beckoning to them to take them away from the island forever.

Chapter Forty-Four

KOLYA'S EXPRESSION TOLD Kornon all. The mother ship had finally caved in, conceding that Colonel Saburov was not aboard but was now about to be taken off the island by one of the fleet trawlers. And worst of all, the innocuous-sounding message in "plain" language but couched in prearranged fishing terms ended with "main catch aborted due to equipment failure." This told Kornon his whole scheme had ended in disaster.

Kornon, slowly pulling the heavy scarlet drapes shut against the blizzard, looked like a man closing the massive doors of a redoubt, readying himself for the final battle.

"It's too late to do anything, General," said Kolya.

Kornon's face was hidden in the shadow of the lamp, his voice slow but as threatening as Kolya had ever heard. "If our plan gets to the President of the United States—" he turned full on to Kolya, his eyes bright with menace "—we're *all* in trouble, aren't we, Comrade?"

Kolya was visibly troubled by the General's deliberate use of *we*—and by his tone as much as by the word itself.

"By which," Kornon continued, "I mean everyone in the Kremlin. Surely you don't think, Kolya, that only my head will fall?"

Kolya was very pale.

The general sent his aide out again for more strong tea, and when Kolya had gone, made a long-distance call to Zurich. As the number was ringing, he entered in his log that the call was "a discussion concerning Soviet contracts with Swiss Rhine Petrochemicals." The Swiss secretary answered him fluently in Russian, typical, he thought, of the capitalist nation's ability to adapt, to be able to do business with any regime and to do it discreetly. It was an ability much admired in Moscow by the men who had learned the art of survival, no matter what the official communiqués proclaimed to the masses. It was also an ability that he would need to practice now but one made easier, he congratulated himself, because he had already prepared for it.

Kornon lamented the fact he could not signal the trawler armed with the Exocet to simply blast the American ship *Petrel* out of the water. But with Klaus's informant aboard the ship to gather vital information about possible sea gold sites, that was not possible. In any event, it would soon be dawn and none of his fleet could be seen in the area.

When Klaus came on the line Kornon was brief, his pleasantries heartier than usual, despite his urgency. "I thought you should know, Herr Klaus, that our metals production may be under quota this month. We were wondering if you could assist us by drawing on your reserves for the time being?" He paused. "Naturally we would reimburse you at current prices or add the amount, in tonnage, to our final shipment—as per contract."

"That will be no problem, General. These inconveniences happen. We will be glad to absorb the shortfall. For the time being."

Kornon thanked him and hung up, relieved that his request for the Swiss Rhine backup, which he had hoped he would never need, was being met with such swift equanimity. Of course it had always been a quid pro quo arrangement, an ongoing case of I'll-help-you-if-you'll-help-me. Even so, Klaus had seemed particularly agreeable. But then Kornon remembered it was Klaus himself who had once said that he would have liked to kill the American,

Hall, with his own hands. It was obviously much more than just plain business for Klaus—it was personal.

Kornon next sent a message to Colonel Saburov's trawler to try fishing another area and gave coordinates.

IN ZURICH, SITTING at his usual table overlooking the olive slate of the Limmat and beyond to the lake, Klaus popped another antacid tablet. The burning sensation in his stomach came not so much from anxiety this time as from excitement, that now, finally, he would get to settle his old score with the American commoner who had beaten him in the race for sea gold deposits a few years before. Only this time SRP's subsidiary would have the help of a Russian diplomatic bag en route to the Soviet consulate in San Francisco. Diplomatic bags could not be searched.

Klaus asked that a phone be brought to the table and, while waiting, calculated that it would be 5:00 a.m. on the American West Coast.

Chapter Forty-Five

WHILE GLORIA SLEPT and *Petrel* steamed through the darkness of the gathering storm, heading toward the coast of Oregon more than seventy miles away, Frank sat in the wardroom, his injured eye patched, three days' stubble and salt-encrusted hair doing nothing to improve his battered appearance. He tried to command every ounce of energy he had, bolstered by the strong black coffee the senior steward kept pouring, forcing himself awake until he wrote out a succinct yet informative message describing what the Russians had tried on Eagle Island. But when he sent it up to Sparks for immediate transmission, the radio officer returned promptly, message in hand with Scotty in tow, painfully embarrassed by his inability to send the message to the Astoria station and thence to Washington as Frank requested.

"But dammit," said Frank, "you told me there'd been a break in the static."

"I was wrong. Oh, there were a couple of minutes after we got you aboard when I thought we had a clear channel, but it was crowded out by a lot of chatter from the Polish fleet. Then the moment they were done, back came the static like a football crowd. No way I could—"

"Okay," Frank cut in, holding up his hand and turning to Scotty. "Could I have a word, Mr. Redfern?" The steward was fast to comply and vacated the wardroom. Sparks took offense as if they were going to be talking about him and departed moodily, but Frank had no time to stroke bruised egos after what he and Gloria had been through in the past thirty-six hours.

Frank turned to the second mate. "Scotty, I know we haven't had a chance to go into all the details yet, but you said you're sure now we've got a plant aboard?"

"Noo doubt aboot it, Frank, if you ask me. After Mrs. Crane's disappearance I was convinced and, I might add, so was the captain that Aussie's death was no accident." He went on to tell Frank about the tear in the Zodiac.

"Then," Frank went on, "the moment the plant leaves us, we're done for!" He looked up at Scotty, who was staring at him uncomprehendingly. "I'm sorry, laddie, I've noo idea—"

"The static?" Frank raced on. "They don't want us to get any messages out, right? And you said our radar's blanketed, too?"

"Yes, but—"

"Don't you see, Scotty, this is what all the static's about. The bastards aren't finished with us yet. They tried everything to stop anyone finding out what was happening on that island. They're sure as hell not going to give up now that we're off. We've just moved into a different area as far as they're concerned. Fact is, that trawler east—''

"You mean," Scotty cut in, "all this static is being pumped out by that trawler to stop us from sending.... But it's an American trawler, laddie. I saw the Stars and—" He stopped. "Oh, you stupid Scot," he told himself. "It's a bloody ruse."

"Right. They've probably got a flag for any country you can name."

"But still and all, laddie, they can't keep pumping static around us forever. I mean once we reach Astoria all the bloody static in the world won't—oh, Jesus!" said Scotty.

"Right again," said Frank. "They mean to get us *before* we get to Astoria. The moment their plant, whoever he is, is off this ship with that list of sea gold stations stolen from my safe we're a sitting target." All the anger and sorrow about what had happened to the Australian and to Mary and what they might yet do to him and Gloria and everyone else on *Petrel* churned inside him, but rather than oppressing him, physically and mentally exhausted as he was, the memory of what his enemies had done and the realization that they were not yet finished made him fighting mad.

"Come with me!" he said to the mate. "Bring a flashlight."

As they stepped astern over the dry lab's sill into the heaving blackness, a wave broke high above the prop and water gushed through the A-frame with such force that both men were pinned to the bulkhead. With the flood subsiding, pouring out through the scuppers, they began checking each lifeboat, especially its block and tackle, for any sign that someone was preparing for what Aussie would have called a "moonlit flit." If Frank was right, he knew the trawler they had seen standing off the island must be somewhere nearby in the darkness, waiting, ready to pick up Klaus's spy.

Chapter Forty-Six

JOHNNY HORNBY WAS amazed, exhilarated as he stood in the cockpit of the CANUS Ore vessel, *Sea Dart*—a stripped and converted PT boat. It headed fast westward toward the storm, its running lights out, only a faint orange bulb for the skipper, Joe Mawley, to see the chart by. Hornby reveled in the boat's bashing against the sea and the rush of sea air in his face. Keeping May close to him, he held her hand in his pocket, rubbing it against him.

The action was so blatant that she knew Joe Mawley must know what Johnny was doing. But she couldn't bring herself to object in front of the skipper; besides, she knew Johnny would only make another squaw joke about her— he always did whenever she complained about his forwardness or vulgarity. He was in one of those big moods of his, the kind he always got into when he'd made some fast, smart deal in North America on behalf of Swiss Rhine Petrochemicals, full of telling everyone forced to listen just how goddamned shrewd he'd been. Only this time it wasn't any deal he'd pulled off; all he'd done was take delivery of a big canvas bag in some back street from some European who'd flown up from San Francisco.

As usual, he'd celebrated his deal in bed, swearing at her a lot, telling her to stop moaning all the goddamned time about how it was too big, how she might choke, acting like she didn't like the taste of it, and all that "crappola!"—telling her she should start acting like the "whore squaw" she was, admit she enjoyed it and quit trying to play the part of Lady Muck!—telling her to shut up and just keep on gobbling.

Then he got the call from Switzerland informing him he would have to go to sea for CANUS, after all.

It had made May very happy, remembering his gloomy expression a couple of days ago in the Drift Net Café when he'd confessed to her that he couldn't stand boats, how they made him "sicker'n a dog."

Getting sullenly out of bed after the call, he'd told her to "move ass," that she was coming with him. May didn't mind. She liked boats and she was looking forward to seeing him "sicker'n a dog," part payment for all the humiliation he'd heaped on her.

Yet here he was now, an hour out of Astoria, the wind screaming and cold as fish, and the son of a bitch standing up in the cockpit, high on his discovery that he loved the sensation of the fast boat, going on about how all the times before when he'd been seasick it had been aboard some big closed-in ferry, or a ship with all the "fucking windows closed."

"Portholes," she said.

"What?"

"They're called portholes, Johnny. Not windows."

"Portholes, assholes, what do you know, eh? What I'm telling you is that I feel great! Just fucking great! It wasn't the up-and-down upset my guts, it was being locked in, right? All that stinkin' fuel smell an' crap. That's what must've made me puke." He looked past May at Mawley, who was lighting one cigarette with the butt of another, holding the wheel firmly with a boxer's hand as the *Sea Dart* kept shuddering against the oncoming waves in a bone-jarring staccato that had May thinking her eyeballs would soon shoot out of their sockets. "Isn't that right, Mawley?" Johnny shouted.

"Whatever you say," said Mawley, taking a long drag on the cigarette, then starting to cough so badly that even in the weak light of the cockpit May could see his rough face turning a dark red, like an overripe plum.

"Well," Hornby continued, "that's what I say. When we gonna reach that trawler? Been over an hour since we left Astoria. Don't you miss the friggin' thing!" He said it like you might miss a train, as if all you had to do was turn up at the station on time.

"More to it than that," shouted Mawley, between hacking coughs. "We haven't hit the storm area yet. Forecast says two systems, one from the south, one from the west, are gonna meet out here." He pointed to a spot on the map clipped to a pullout board under the cockpit's windshield. "About ten miles farther west. And that's where your trawler is, buddy."

"Well, we've got to make the swap before dawn. I dunno how the goddamn things work," he said, nodding back at the aluminum storage trunk aft of the cockpit, where May had seen them put in the big canvas bag, packing it carefully with Styrofoam chips.

"Don't worry," said Mawley. "Didn't you say the trawler'd be lit up like a Christmas tree?"

"That's what I was told."

"Well then. We'll see her all right. Don't worry."

"*Hey!* I'm worryin'. I'm responsible, right? No one else knows you're here. For you it's strictly free lance, one job here, one job there. You don't give a shit. It's my career, Bozo. I have to do it right every time, right?"

"Don't worry," said Mawley. "They know we're coming, right? When they see us on their radar they'll light up."

He'd no sooner spoken than May spotted pinpricks of light arcing in the great, black, wind-filled expanse of ocean, then gradually she could make out a blacker black, within the overall darkness, advancing on them and dimming the lights of the trawler. "What is it?" she asked Mawley.

"Squall," he said. "Running ahead of the storm."

"Well," Hornby urged. "Let's move ass!"

"You scared?" asked Mawley, laughing. May didn't like the laughter, it had a crazy edge to it, as if Mawley didn't care about danger one way or the other. The other thing she had trouble with was how come smart Johnny Hornby had hired Mawley in the first place—a man who'd sell his mother for a bonus? Surely the big boss in Switzerland wouldn't approve?

When she and Johnny went below to the galley for a coffee from the big thermos, which, like everything else, was braced firmly for rough weather, she asked Johnny about his choice. He smiled.

"Come here." He slid his hand under her skirt, grabbing her roughly, making her gasp with pain. "Ever had it on a speedboat before?"

She shook her head and was filled with shame, because despite the pain she did want it, and God forgive her but she wanted it from him. God love her but she loved the danger. It had nothing to do with money and security or supporting her mother or her kid or anything else; she loved the danger of being around him and when he told her not to worry about "old morbid Mawley," how the storm would make it wetter'n hell all over Oregon that weekend and how Mawley couldn't drive for nuts, and told her to pull him off right then and there as hard as she could, May knew that after the job, Johnny was going to kill Mawley.

The sea was becoming rougher so she sat on his lap and lost herself in the savage beat of the enormous, pulsating engine, feeling its every vibration and shudder as the *Sea Dart* neared its rendezvous.

Chapter Forty-Seven

"YOU NEED REST, Comrade," the trawler captain told Saburov. "Let Major Gorbak join the CANUS boat and we'll proceed with you back to—"

"Captain," began Saburov, "I've had an hour to rest. And besides, I don't need any more rest than Hall." Saburov was having difficulty breathing in the thick atmosphere of fish smell and tobacco smoke that filled the Russian trawler's wheelhouse like a fog. He took another sip of vodka-laced coffee.

"Comrade," interjected the captain. "I am in command of this ship and Major Gorbak is assigned to this ship. It's therefore my duty to insist—"

"Major Gorbak?" said Saburov, hunched in coarse woolen khaki blankets and wedged into the starboard corner of the trawler as she rode in relative ease, running with the sea toward the new "fishing" coordinates Kornon had given them. "Major Gorbak? Are you not junior to me?"

Gorbak, a small, thickset man leaning against the depth sounder, saw what was coming but felt obliged to put up some kind of token resistance. "Yes, I am, Colonel, but if I might say so respectfully I think—"

"Major, I will be joining the CANUS boat. That is an order, Comrade. Understood?"

"Yes, sir," replied Gorbak, feigning disappointment for the record. "I understand."

"Good," said Saburov with such authority that not even the ship's captain felt disposed to object further. "How far are we from the CANUS boat?" asked Saburov.

"Only five miles."

"Have they signaled?" asked Saburov, sipping the vodka-laced coffee.

"Not yet," replied the captain. "But we have them on radar." He paused. "It would have been much easier if their cargo had been sent with us, Comrade."

"New models, Captain," explained Saburov. "Moscow hasn't even had time to test them—certainly not in battle conditions. In any case it would have made no sense for you to have them. The CANUS plant has yet to get off *Petrel* and you can not afford to wait—it will soon be dawn. You must be out of the area by daybreak. On the other hand, the CANUS boat is American. It can stay in the area as long as it likes. That's why I will go and join it."

"Could not the Americans on the CANUS boat activate the new models?" asked the captain. "Work it out themselves?"

Gorbak smiled knowingly across at Saburov and now that the trawler was running with all lights blazing they could see one another quite clearly. "Oh," Gorbak began, "they might work it out eventually but that would take too long. *Petrel* would be in port by then."

Saburov closed his eyes and lay back against the bulkhead, relishing the warmth of the vodka's fire. "What Comrade Gorbak is saying, Captain, is that we don't want our CANUS friends to 'work it out.' They are our friends only up to a point. I will activate the new models, then after *Petrel* is sunk and I have rested at our consulate in San Francisco I will fly home to a long vacation."

"And where will you go, Comrade?" asked Gorbak good-naturedly. The two men had taken a liking to each other.

"Oh, I think if I can get a special permit I will go to the Black Sea."

"Permit?" The captain chuckled. "I think somehow, Comrade, you will get permission, after all you have done." It was meant as a compliment but suddenly the bridge went quiet. Gorbak wasn't joining in the hilarity, and it quickly dawned on the others that any vacation or reward Saburov might have coming would not be forthcoming until *Petrel* was sunk and with it the secret of Eagle Island.

Gorbak, bracing himself against the turbulence, walked across and offered Saburov a drop more vodka.

"Thank you, Comrade," said Saburov. "But not too much."

"Colonel?"

"Yes?"

Gorbak's voice was low as he tipped the bottle of vodka. "What happens if the CANUS contact does not manage to get off *Petrel* and back to Astoria? Will you still sink the ship?"

Saburov drained the cup of hot liquid. "What would you suggest, Comrade?"

BY NOW, FRANK and the Scottish mate had been battling the fierce wash of waves over the stern and rushing down the walkways of the ship for a half hour. Explosions of foam more than forty feet high leaped up from the bow, sweeping back, drenching them and *Petrel*'s bridge and reducing visibility to near zero. The two men continued their search down both sides of the ship, looking for any sign of disembarkation ladders, coiled and stashed ready for another ship, her lights out, coming in unseen by *Petrel*'s jammed radar to pick up the plant. But they found nothing and now sought temporary refuge beneath the fo'c'sle's overhang, water streaming down before them, the wind screaming around the forward winches and well deck with such fury that, though only a foot apart, they had to shout in order to be heard.

"Bloody mad for anyone to go over in this lot, laddie!"

"Bloody mad to stay," Frank retorted at the top of his lungs. "What would you do, Scotty, if you were a spy? Stay on *Petrel* and risk being sunk or take a chance on them picking you up?"

"Well, laddie, if I was a rat I'd leave the ship."

"Precisely."

"Then why bother searching?" shouted the mate. "Let 'em stay aboard whoever they are. Insurance against us being attacked on our way in!"

"Because, Scotty, if we don't find out who it is, they could sabotage *Petrel*—stop us dead in the water. Make us a sitting target before they leave the ship. Besides—"

Suddenly he was flung hard against the starboard bulkhead six feet away, the wave lifting him up, knocking him over. He grabbed the web lashing holding the long, twenty-foot core barrels in place, and stood his ground.

"You still sure that the trawler's mixed up in this?" asked Scotty, looking at it five miles off *Petrel*'s port quarter.

"Yes, but I can't make out why she's all lit up. Our lookouts would see her coming up behind us."

Scotty took heart. "Ah, maybe we're worryin' aboot nothing, Frankie boy. She seems a wee bit slower than bonny *Petrel* anyhow."

"Let's keep an eye on her anyway. Scotty?"

"Aye?"

"I've got another idea about the plant."

"Hope it's a bloody warmer one than this."

"It is. Whoever's going over *has* to be ready now. If they wait much longer we'll be in too close to the mainland and in daylight."

"Aye, makes sense. So what's your plan?"

"Let's go inside," said Frank, starting down the well deck's port side, using the raised cargo hatch as a handhold. The whole business was reminding him of a hard lesson he'd learned on *Petrel* years ago—whenever you were in a fight with the likes of Swiss Rhine and their hired hands, you were better to suspect everybody, even those, particularly those, who appeared to be helping you most. He was going over what Sparks had said about trying to send the message but being unable to because of the continuing static. How could anyone be sure the radio and radar jamming wasn't caused by Sparks himself? Who else would really know? Who else had the expertise? He could easily fake it. Or maybe, as Scotty believed, it was the steward, Martin. Or maybe it was the man right behind him—the dour Scot much more helpful on this cruise than he'd ever been before.

Staggering under the heavy, glistening oilskins and the roll of the ship, Frank and Scotty opened the for'ard door, shutting it quickly behind them as water slopped about the sill. Immediately they were assaulted by the smells of the ship, a thick, headachy stench of dieseline exhaust being forced back down the funnel by the swirling vortices of wind, the pungent aroma of coffee grounds mixing with the sickly-sweet smell of hot chocolate, and now and then the bracing tang of the sea in a blast of chilly air rushing through whenever someone stepped out on deck. The sudden change in temperature, from cold to stuffy warmth, gave Frank a dull ache across his forehead and he took an aspirin from the wardroom bottle. The mate, deciding to pour himself a coffee, was lifting the pot from its cradle when he saw Frank go through the wardroom's open doorway, walking along the passageway, chewing on the tablet. "My God," he shouted, "an' tha's a good way to burn your gut oot—without a drap o' water."

"We make 'em tough in Oregon," said Frank, taking the small red hammer from its wall mount and smashing the fire alarm glass.

"Jesus Christ, mon!" began Scotty, the ship resonating with the din of the alarm. Frank went into the galley and poured himself a glass of water as deckhands, some in working gear, others in civvies, some half-dressed, half-asleep, dragged themselves up and down the steel gangways, shuffling, shouting and moaning, all combined in general confusion. Tate's voice could be heard shouting over the intercom from his cabin. Someone else was swearing at an oiler who turned up smoking two cigarettes at the same time, walking somnolently, vaguely trying to remember his proper fire station.

Frank raised his glass to Scotty.

"You've flipped, laddie. What in the name of living..." He hesitated, his coffee cup swaying in unison with the ship. "Ach, you crafty bugger."

"Aye," said Frank, adopting the Scotsman's mood. "Noo then, Scotty, we'll see who's here and who's busy packing for a wee trip. I'll take the boat station roll call. You see what the others are up to."

"Yes, you wicked man! I will!"

"Fire report!" bellowed a bleary-eyed Tate. "Goddamn it—where's the fire?"

Despite the urgency of the search for anyone who might even look as if they were ready to hop ship, Frank's fatigue found relief in watching the age-old disorder he'd seen on every oceanographic salvage ship, submersible and, of course, ferry. There were always a few who didn't know or couldn't remember where the hell they should be, running, turning, bumping into each other. The Marx Brothers on parade.

But his mood abruptly changed. After the roll call, allowing for the engineer and oiler who had to remain below and those on the bridge, the only ones missing were the junior steward, nicknamed "Sonny," the senior steward, Martin and Gloria Bernardi.

Tate and Scotty saw the stunned look on Frank's face, had a quiet word with each other and took over. "All right," said Scotty. "It's only a drill, fellas. Back to byebye, or to your watch. C'mon, be smart aboot it!"

"That man there," Tate called. "Jardin, is it?" It was the spaced-out oiler, grinning at the bulkhead. "Come here!"

"Yes, sir?"

"Stop looking at me like that, you fool."

"Peace, man."

"Bosun's mate?" Only then did he remember Jamie had died on Eagle Island, that they might all die. He called over to cook.

"Yes sir?"

"Keep Jardin in the galley and fill 'im with coffee. Don't want him falling into the prop."

The oiler was smiling. "Off duty, man...not working below till dawn, Captain."

Tate looked him straight in the eye, trying to get through the haze of whatever the oiler was on. "We're all on duty now, sailor. If we aren't, we may not see the dawn."

The passageway was soon cleared, the dispersing crew's murmuring filled with speculation and growing apprehension that so soon after rescuing the oceanographer from the island they were now all in grave danger of being attacked in the very last hours of the long, nerve-exhausting cruise. And all because in the first place their ship had responded to a call for help. Soon only Tate, Frank and the mate were left in the passage.

There was a long, agonizing silence. "Frank," Scotty said. "What do you want us to do?"

Frank's voice was quiet, barely audible beneath the onslaught of the storm as *Petrel* battled her way toward the dawn—and hopefully Astoria, another fifty miles on. "Find them," he said.

As the mate and deckhands organized a search party, Frank was reeling inside from the shock. It didn't make sense. It didn't fit that Gloria, after all that had happened...unless she'd been in on the search for sea gold from the start. But how was that possible? His brain was racing so fast, tripping over the possibilities, the myriad contradictions....

Damn it, she couldn't possibly have had anything to do with the Russians. But if Klaus had managed to plant her on—

"Bridge to captain!" It was the voice of the third mate. Tate took the call on the wardroom phone.

"Captain to bridge. Go ahead."

"That trawler, sir, has heaved to—riding her sea anchor. 'Bout seven miles to starboard."

It meant the trawler had fallen back, bow into the wind, to keep herself as steady as possible. But what for?

"Don't know, sir," came the junior officer's reply. "Couldn't be putting down nets in this weather, could she?"

"No, mate, she could not. She's either decided to ride out the storm or—"

"She's waiting for someone," Frank cut in, his tone matter-of-fact with an overlay of bitterness he found difficult to contain. "Keep the glasses on her," he continued and called out to Scotty, who had quickly rounded up a dozen men to do a sweep of the ship.

"Where to first?" asked Scotty, deferring to Frank in anything that involved the woman, a woman who had changed Frank Hall's mood quicker than anything else the mate had witnessed in all the years he'd known the oceanographer.

"Well," Frank began, "we've tried topside, the lifeboats. And they sure as hell can't hide in the Beauforts," by which he meant the tightly rolled inflatable life rafts contained in forty-four-gallon-size drums attached to long rip cords that, once the drums hit the water, would unfold and inflate by means of small carbon dioxide cartridges.

"How about looking up for'ard?" hollered the Scotsman against the crosswinds on the stern deck, which made the search party look as if they were all in violent tremor, the wind vibrating their oilskins and puffing them to twice their normal size.

Frank disagreed. "No one'd try slipping off up for'ard. Even in this weather someone might spot them through the bridge glass." As he spoke, the mate was nevertheless glancing forward through the partially opened forward hatch leading from the main passageway out onto the well deck.

"Bridge to afterdeck . . . Bridge to—"

"Yes?" answered Scotty.

"Trawler's disappeared." It was Tate's voice. "All her lights have gone out. Lookouts can't pick her up."

Scotty turned to Frank, but before he'd put the question, the oceanographer said, "Kill ours. If they try to creep up on us we'll see 'em better without our own glare."

"Agreed," said Tate, and gave the order, "Douse all lights—deck and running! Close all porthole shutters. Secure hatches, interior lights on dim."

"Captain," Frank interjected on the stern phone. "Can we have a man or two on every main switch?"

"Done!" said Tate. After giving the order, he turned back to the intercom, addressing Frank and Scotty. "Gentlemen, you tread carefully out there!"

"Aye, aye, sir," answered Scotty.

Frank split the search crew into two teams, one for 'tween decks, one for the upper deck, leaving himself and Scotty to check out the main deck again from stern to bow, one of them moving up each side of the ship to the windlass then back.

THE PT BOAT HAD COME IN on the off side of the trawler so that her much smaller silhouette could not be seen from *Petrel*. Mawley made three passes until he was close but not too close for any of the massive swells to suddenly drive him into the trawler's side, or vice versa. The trickiest part was to judge the pitch so that the Russian need only jump a few feet down onto *Sea Dart*'s foredeck instead of finding himself tumbling through three times the distance and being crushed between the two vessels at the lowest point of a trough when everything opened up like the mouth of a whale.

Mawley gunned the Rolls-Royce Merlins to get their measure, then throttled them back, all the time watching the trawler's roll. From the corner of his eye he saw the Russian, clad in black oilskins, an automatic rifle wrapped in plastic tightly slung across his shoulders, clamber over the trawler's side, perched on the strake, waiting to jump. The *Sea Dart* lifted, the figure jumped, or more accurately, dropped. There was a thud on the foredeck and

Colonel Saburov made his way cautiously along the starboard rail.

From the first moment, Saburov didn't like Hornby or Mawley, and he could see they didn't like each other. The woman, Saburov decided, was merely another bourgeois whore along for the ride. It wasn't the kind of team they'd pick in Moscow—all he could smell on the PT boat was greed. Their being here had nothing to do with ideological commitment, nothing to do with the will to defeat capitalist America, but Saburov didn't let it worry him. Their reasons might all be different, but at least he knew they were all agreed on the one thing: to stop Hall. They drank to it quickly in rough camaraderie as Mawley passed a bottle. It was a kind of whiskey Saburov had never tasted before. He refused a second swig, turning immediately to work as the trawler moved off northward, home to the Baltic, and the *Sea Dart* turned east.

"What do you call it?" Saburov asked them about the whiskey, as Johnny and May, bracing themselves hard against a violent yawing, passed him the round, gray, eight-inch-diameter, sunflower-shaped objects from the Styrofoam packing. "The booze?" answered Hornby. "It's Southern Comfort! Why—don't you like it?"

"It's delicious, Comrade."

"*Hey, hey, hey.* Easy with the fucking 'Comrade,' eh?"

Saburov, sitting at the small galley table, was working on the "sunflowers" with a jeweler's small screwdriver, adjusting them by means of a tap screw that was at the heart of the beeswaxlike surface of the sunflower pattern. The *Sea Dart* crashed through the top of a cresting wave, throwing May into Saburov, sending the screwdriver flying from his hand, skittering across the table. "Christ!" bellowed Hornby at May, dragging her off Saburov. "You'll set 'em off!"

"I'm sorry..." May began. "I didn't mean to..."

"Don't worry," said Saburov. "This is only a crude adjustment. There can be no explosion yet."

He retrieved the screwdriver from where it had been stopped by the antiroll edging of dowel that ran around the garishly red-patterned Formica tabletop, and resumed working in the pale cabin light shaded in part by a compact disk player that had been securely lashed to the bulkhead. "How long to *Petrel*?" Saburov asked matter-of-factly. His businesslike tone conveyed neither liking nor dislike of his companions on *Sea Dart*, his only interest getting the job done as quickly as possible.

Hornby called up the voice tube to Mawley, who told him the sons of bitches on *Petrel* had doused their lights too, so now he had to get them on the Decca-II.

"Don't go all friggin' technical on me, Mawley," growled Hornby. "What the hell's that?"

"Radar," Mawley replied, "but the signals are hoppin' all over the place."

Saburov looked up from unwrapping a small, six-inch-square package from the Styrofoam and said something in Russian that the others instinctively understood from its tone to be a curse, and a violent one at that.

"What's up with you?" said Hornby.

"The jamming," said Saburov. "Our trawler must keep jamming all radio and radar signals in the area so *Petrel* cannot broadcast or see us. But if now *Petrel* has doused its lights then . . ."

"We can't see *them* either, right?" said Johnny. "Fucking lovely, Ivan. That's just hunky fucking dory that is."

"We had no choice," Saburov snapped back, unused to such insubordination. "Did you want *Petrel* to transmit—to let the world know that your Mr. Klaus was going to provide maintenance for our installation? That CANUS is merely a—"

"All right, all right, keep your shirt on," said Hornby, turning back to the voice tube and hanging on to the side of the doorframe leading up the few stairs to the cockpit.

"So, Mawley, what's the drill? How we going to find *Petrel*?"

Mawley didn't answer, letting them stew, saving his reply for maximum effect.

"Well?" bellowed Hornby. "How you gonna find 'em? How we gonna pick up our contacts if you can't—"

"Use your head, Hornby. What the hell would you do if you were hidin' out on board there ready to ditch near us and they suddenly switched out all the lights on you?"

"All right, big shot," Hornby called back. "What would you do? If they switched out all the lights on you?"

"Switch 'em back on," said Mawley, guffawing into the tube, making a sound like a clogged sink.

"Jesus Christ!" said Hornby, shaking his head, first with disgust, then, surprisingly to May, with wholehearted and unreserved admiration. "Mawley...you're right, you horse's ass!"

Saburov looked up, appalled by the use of such foul language in front of a woman, common as she was. He was equally appalled by Mawley's answer, in that it was clear to him that while *Sea Dart*'s captain was undoubtedly very able at handling a speedboat and would get them close enough to do the job, he obviously had no idea how formidable a foe Hall was and would be until he was as dead as the czar. Did they really believe, Saburov wondered, that Hall, knowing there was a plant on board *Petrel*, would have all *Petrel*'s lights put out so no one could see them and yet leave the switches unguarded?

"Your friends on *Petrel*," said Saburov, "will have to think of another way to show us where the ship is."

"So, now you're the expert?" Hornby said, grinning crookedly.

"Yes," said Saburov, looking at him evenly. "Because I have fought with him already, and one thing I know, Comr—one thing I know, Hornley—"

"Hornby, Comrade!"

"One thing I know, Hornby, is that we cannot under-estimate him."

"We'll handle him," said Hornby easily.

"*I* will handle him," said the colonel. "You will do what I say."

"Listen, fella—"

"No, you listen." Saburov lifted up a shining, five-inch compact disk he'd taken from its cardboard sheath and glanced down at the dozen or so metal sunflowers he'd been working on. "Do you know how this system works?"

May looked from Hornby to Saburov and back again. For a Russian, she thought, he was very attractive.

"No," said Saburov, "you don't because this is the lat-est...what you Americans call, I think, state of the art. No, Hornby, you will do what I tell you if you want to get your contacts and the sea gold information off that boat—and if we are to get Hall. Understood?" Saburov noticed May was staring at him, and for the first time since coming aboard *Sea Dart* he allowed himself to take in more of her than KGB discipline normally advised. He knew he was impressing her with his authority. Her admiration would be even greater after he had finished with Hall.

"Well, you better know what you're doing, Ivan," said Hornby. "Because if you don't—"

"I do," said Saburov, and turned back to the table, picking up the screwdriver as the PT boat pitched so high that six of the sunflowers slid crashing into one corner. Saburov put his arms out over them to prevent them slid-ing back.

"Did you bring the floats?" he asked Hornby, who gave a surly nod in the direction of two large gunnysacks con-taining clusters of basketball-size, blue plastic floats, clearly visible through the burlap sacks, which were lashed to one of the bunks.

Mawley, oblivious of the preparations going on below, was busy maintaining *Sea Dart* at quarter speed, heading toward his last sighting of *Petrel*, seconds before she had shut off her lights.

Saburov put the compact disk into the player and, placing each of the sunflower receptors in front of the two speakers, he pushed the start button, turning the volume halfway. Then, after telling Mawley to head *Sea Dart* into the wind and cut his engines, he slid each of the sunflowers from one side to the other as the speakers rumbled, soon shaking with the deep throbbing sound of a ship's prop under water.

"What's *that*?" asked May, looking to Hornby for an explanation.

Hornby mumbled something about "state of the art," then told her it'd probably be better if "Ivan" told her.

Saburov was brief—only so far as need-to-know might help them to help him on the job and no more. "Every ship, like every automobile, has a different sound print."

"Like fingerprints?" said May.

Saburov glanced up at her. "Yes, yes, that's correct. But it is more like the human voice in this case. Every voice has its own particular print or pattern of speech, you see. Ships are the same. You tape their sound underwater with hydrophones—"

"Ah, that's microphones," cut in Hornby self-importantly, crossing his arms. "I know about that."

"Yes," said Saburov, looking back at the disk console, adjusting the sound so that the volume fell away, all but inaudible, at least to the human ear. "You collect a library of such sounds," continued Saburov, "of all shipping in fact, friendly and...otherwise." He gave May a smile.

Hornby glowered. "Hey!"

Saburov went on, undeterred. "You make the best recordings possible of these sounds." He turned the volume up, pointing to the disk that, although unmoving as the laser needle took from it the gut-wrenching throb, looked as if it was a small platter of silver. "And when you have the sound—or, if you like, the 'voice print' of every ship's engines and prop—you simply adjust the mine to detonate—'' he indicated the honeycombed centers of the ten sunflower-shaped mines ''—when its receptors hear the identical sound for which you've programmed them. Many of you Americans use the same idea to open garage doors, switch on television. A certain frequency switches it on. Here a ship's frequency sets off the mine.''

''Is . . . is that what you're doing now?'' asked May. ''Programming them?''

''Yes, with the recording that's been sent out.'' He smiled. ''But I seriously doubt we will need all ten of them.''

Suddenly May realized what the Russian was saying, that it wasn't just Hall they were going to kill but everyone aboard the ship. It also struck her, from the way he looked at her, that she was someone he might possibly desire but could not afford the time to find out, that he was a man possessed by his job, a man who would rather die than live, so long as it meant achieving his ultimate goal—in this case his enemy's certain destruction.

''Why don't we just run ahead of them and lay the mines on the sea bottom?'' asked Hornby. ''Why all these floats?''

''Two reasons,'' replied Saburov. ''First, *Petrel*'s destruction must look like an accident. A mine, you see, will make it look like an internal explosion at sea. That would hardly appear to be the case, however, if other mines were found or detected on the sea bottom, would it?''

''Huh, suppose not,'' conceded Hornby.

''That is one reason for attaching them to the floats, but there is another equally valid scientific reason, Comrade.''

Hornby was so absorbed by the explanation he didn't mind the ''Comrade.'' ''What's that?'' Hornby asked.

''Because—''

Suddenly there was a loud burst of laughter followed by a hacking smoker's cough. Mawley's beefy red face appeared like that of a malevolent Santa Claus in the hatchway. "Got 'em!" he shouted. "They signaled. Marked 'em heading due east. Smack on zero-eight-six degrees. You finished, Professor?"

"In a few minutes," answered Saburov. "Did they use Morse?"

"Nah, not enough time for that. Molotov cocktail, looked like. Just one flash. Yep, I'd say a bottle of gasoline over the stern. Whoosh! Went up like the Fourth of July."

"All right!" bellowed Hornby, officiously snatching back command from Saburov. "Let's go!" he shouted, grabbing May and squeezing her, throwing back his head in the tiny galley, making a loud Indian "Whoopee!"

Chapter Forty-Eight

THE SCOTTISH MATE on the starboard well deck was the first to spot the flash of light, or rather the reflection of the Molotov cocktail tossed off *Petrel*'s stern, and ran aft to intercept whoever had thrown it. Moving as fast down the starboard side as dripping oilskins, gale-force winds and sharply inclined deck would allow, he could hear the muffled sound of sea boots coming toward him and moving parallel to him on the port side, as Frank, feet out and hands on the rails, slid down like a gymnast from the upper deck where he'd been searching before seeing the same flash. As Frank hit the afterdeck he saw a figure, black on black, taking the diagonal course from the A-frame at the stern, heading over toward the mate's side.

"Scotty!" Frank called out. "Coming at you!"

"Got 'im!" came the Scotsman's reply. The next moment Frank was clinging to the port side of the winch, its bulk rising above him, hissing with the sound of the water jets shooting out of every nook and cranny. The ship then heeled in a counter roll, its starboard side smacking the wave dead amidships, creating a huge wall of water. Scotty, too, was clinging to the winch on the other side from Frank, but in the fury of the wave's onslaught the two shipmates might as well have been a mile apart for it was impossible to hear anything over the roar of the sea's attack until the helmsman managed to bring the ship back on even course. As *Petrel* regained her heading, Frank made his way over the slick deck to the intercom box by the A-frame and called the bridge.

"Bridge here...go ahead," came the ready response. It was Tate's voice.

Frank, turning his back on another high wave he saw looming just yards off the stern, tried to get his message off as soon as possible. "Change course at least ten points now our position's known to whoever's—" The wave thundered beneath the A-frame, lifting the props above water, sending *Petrel* planing, adding a good three knots to her present speed.

"Roger," came Tate's reply. "Altering course..."

Frank didn't hear the rest of the confirmation. He was knocked off balance by the Scottish mate who had started toward him and had slipped on the deck, driving Frank head first toward the A-frame, knocking the deck phone from his hand, splitting it open. Frank, like a man out of control after falling on ice, felt himself sliding toward the stern, his hands clownlike in their frantic grabbing for anything that would slow him down before he smashed against the A-frame's pylons. Instead, he felt the whack of a cable against his neck and suddenly he was still, stunned by the blow, but only for a second as the wave dumped hundreds of gallons of foaming, ice-cold water over him.

"Jesus, Scotty!" he shouted back to the mate who, losing his footing again, was now flat on his back by the winch. "Could've told me you were coming. I'd have baked a cake!"

Frank immediately got up and offered the downed mate his hand. "See who it was, Scotty?" In the next instant he knelt, clutching a bollard for support where some of the kerosene used in the Molotov must have spilled on the deck, making it treacherous. Then he felt the water sloshing around him warm as soup. The seaman's spike was embedded deep in Scotty's gut; his eyes were still open but difficult to see in the India-ink night. Frank felt for a pulse, but his own hands were so cold and stiff he couldn't be sure whether it was his own pulse he was feeling in the tips of his fingers. He got behind the mate, dragging him back along the few feet to the entrance of the lab, opening the watertight door and lifting the body high enough to clear the sill. When he slammed the hatch shut he heard a shuffle of feet behind him. It was the search party from below decks still looking for Martin, the young steward, Sonny and Gloria Bernardi.

"Christ!" said one of the crewmen when he saw the blood on the mate's hands, now clasped tightly around the spike. "He alive?"

"Not sure," answered Frank. "Get Larson down here!"

While the seaman went to get the assistant cook, who also doubled as the ship's medic, Frank told two of the others to stay in the lab, the rest to follow him. Running down the passageway of the ship, he told them to check every starboard and port side door. "Nothing here!" came the repeated reply as each man checked the hatch entrances. It was at the last hatch, on the starboard side of the forward lab, that Frank saw the telltale puddle of water spreading into long fingers across the dull green floor. But there was no one hiding in the lab, only piles of aluminum trunks holding oceanographic gear and stacks of clear plastic liner for the core barrels, all stacked and lashed vertically in the lab's corners.

"Here!" said one of the three crewmen. He had been using a flashlight, sweeping it closely over the floor. One of the long fingers of water was streaked with blood, and then, closer by the opposite door leading from the lab into the main passage, more blood. As they moved into the passageway, *Petrel* climbed high over the summit of a wave, hesitated, swung hard right, landing heavily on her belly, completing the corkscrew motion with such violence that Frank and his helpers were flung along the passageway. The flashlight clattered to the floor, rolling around like a live thing before they could retrieve it, its glass broken but its spiderwebbed beam still intact as they followed the blood up the stairs where it abruptly stopped. Suddenly they knew. The officers' cabins!

"Which one?" asked a seaman, whispering despite the rage of the storm, which was growing by the minute.

"Whichever one it is, they aren't going to give up easily," said Frank.

"We'll need the keys," someone else chimed in. "In the wardroom."

"We're going to need more than the keys," said Frank. "Wait here," he told them, hurrying as fast as the sodden wet gear would allow to his cabin on the far starboard side to get the Kalashnikov, and, in case they proved necessary, the six grenades he had brought from the island.

When he opened his door he saw the Kalashnikov pointing straight at him from the darkness behind the chief scientist's desk lamp. "Sit down!" Martin said. "On the floor. Now!" The steward's voice was strained, hoarse—stretched, Frank could tell, to the breaking point. On the floor he could see chocolate-colored stains where blood had congealed, changing color under the soft peach glow of the lamp.

"You're going to get us off here," said Martin.

"So you can blow us sky-high?" said Frank. "No way."

"You haven't any choice, asshole."

"No?"

"No," said Martin, his body still nothing more than a dark shape in darker shadow, sitting in the scientist's chair, resting the gun on the desk, its high foresight pointing directly at Frank's head. "Keep your goddamn hands out in front of you. Against the wall." Frank did as he was told.

"All right, Sonny." Suddenly the room was suffused with the eerie green light of the cabin's washroom and, outlined in it, Gloria's pale white skin was visible through the long nightie that had belonged to Mary. A hairy arm was around her neck in a headlock; Sonny's other hand held a flick knife against her throat. Frank moved.

"Get down!" Martin screamed, and Gloria's head was jerked back so her strangled cry to Frank came out as an unintelligible whimper, Sonny's knife arm high against her throat. Frank stopped halfway, as Martin kept screaming.

In the ghoulish light Gloria's face looked wan as well as terrified, the dark circles of exhaustion more pronounced, her despair in stark contrast to the sheer physical beauty of the naked body showing through the sheer nylon, which was now atremble with fear and cold.

"You bastards," said Frank. "Cover her up. She's freezing."

"Shut up!" screamed Martin. "Shut up! Shut up! Now." He couldn't speak for a few seconds, his rage, his nerves, more in command than reason. "You...you...go out and tell them to put on all the lights. Got it?" Suddenly he screamed, "All the fucking lights, you got it, asshole?"

Sonny was so startled by Martin's outburst he retreated into the washroom, bracing himself, almost falling with Gloria on top of him as *Petrel* heeled to starboard then slipped hard astarboard. "You get all the lights on, then you get a fucking inflatable overboard. Sonny goes over— then me and your sweetie. Any screwups and I'll personally cut her tits off. Like I did Mary Mary. That right,

Sonny? Mary, Mary, quite contrary." He laughed maniacally.

"That's right," said Sonny.

"And you don't cut that raft loose till Klaus's boat picks us up. Got it? And tell Tommy Tate to drop the fucking sea anchor. Nose into the wind. Keep this fucker still. Understand?"

Frank's whole attention was on Martin, the friendly, helpful steward who'd murdered Aussie, then Mary Crane and done God knows what else. Your classic psychotic, as much interested in sea gold as dirt. He took jobs to kill. Mad.

"And then you'll let her go?" said Frank.

"When we get aboard the pickup boat . . . sure."

Sure, thought Frank, and leave a shipload of witnesses afloat. Now, more than ever, he knew that once Klaus's men were off *Petrel*, she was a doomed ship. Yet if he let them take Gloria, he knew he'd never see her again.

"C'mon, move!" said Martin. "All the lights on right now, and a life raft over the stern on a line."

By way of support, Sonny, whom Frank now saw as much skinnier and shorter than he'd remembered—maybe it had been the cook's hat—hurt Gloria some more just to make the point. As she gasped from the pain, her body arched, Sonny jerking her back, her nipples thrust out hard against the nylon as Frank started toward the door.

"For God's sake, have some decency," he said. "Cover her up. At least keep her warm. She'll—"

"You shut your yap, Romeo, and get those lights on. Now, you hear?"

"Yeah," added Sonny. "Now."

"And I don't want to see anybody on the way down. Understand?"

Chapter Forty-Nine

"WHERE IS IT NOW?" asked Saburov, still sitting at the galley table, calibrating another of the five-kilogram mines and activating them by feeding in the sound print of *Petrel*'s engines and prop from the master compact disk.

"Same heading," Hornby reported.

"Zero-eight-six?" said Saburov.

"Yeah," replied Hornby. "Mawley said it wasn't a Molotov cocktail, though. This time it looked like light coming from the ship itself. A hatch opening and shutting probably. You gonna be ready soon?"

Saburov said nothing, leaning forward, concentrating on adjusting one of the sunflower's screws, pushing his side holster farther back on his belt so he could better steady himself against the table.

"We haven't got all night, you know," Hornby pressed, miffed at the Russian's dismissive silence. "That trawler of yours is heading north. She'll soon be outa jamming range. That happens before we pick our people up, and *Petrel*'ll be able to send out messages. Blow the whistle on your boss, well as mine."

"I am aware of that, Mr. Hornby."

"Then you'd better get a move on. I figure your trawler is almost out of range now and—"

"Don't bug him, Johnny," said May. "He's workin' as fast as—"

Johnny swung around, arm outstretched, fingers almost in her face. "Hey! In the teepee! Got it?"

"You were asking me before about the floats," Saburov went on calmly. "The reason we're using them is that the different salinity layers in the sea have different densities, different thicknesses. These interfere with the transmission of the target ship's sound waves so that by the time the sound reaches a mine on the sea bottom it can be very distorted. Using floats we bring the mines to just below the surface.''

May smiled at the Russian. "Hey, that's pretty smart.''

"Never mind all that scientific crappola!'' Hornby cut in. "When you going to have those things ready? Thought you said—''

"Ready now,'' said Saburov, returning May's smile, his voice raised over the steady thunder of *Sea Dart*'s engine.

"About time, too,'' said Hornby, pulling May to him tightly, his left hand sliding down her thigh.

"Cut it out!'' she said. It was meant for Saburov's benefit, yet despite her obvious dislike of Hornby there was, Saburov thought, a sluttish reluctance about her response, her tone suggesting not so much genuine repugnance as much as a desire to appear more virtuous than she was, or really wished to be. Underneath it all she seemed to like his behavior, and Hornby knew it. It also struck Saburov that Hornby, for all his offensiveness, was right, that the trawler would soon be too far north to keep up the jamming of *Petrel*. And yet it would take at least half an hour before *Sea Dart* could hope to pick up Klaus's plants, for the PT boat would have to get close to *Petrel* without her spotting them. By that time the trawler's jamming would be too weak. He couldn't take the chance.

Deciding three floats per mine would be sufficient, he asked May and Hornby to undo the burlap bags and pass the floats to him. Hornby had to shout to Saburov, asking the Russian to repeat himself, the noise of the storm and engines together making it almost impossible to hear anything else.

Hornby tore open the loosely stitched bags with his bare hands, enjoying the display of strength in front of May, passing her two of the blue plastic floats. When she turned to the Russian her mouth flew open. Hornby dropped the floats, his hands going up in front of his face, his slide to the deck cushioned by the floats, his head bumping, sending the floats bouncing crazily around the galley. Still in the sitting position, Saburov lowered the Makarov for May, shooting her twice between the breasts and once more, aiming the last time for the forehead but thrown off balance in the next roll, so that the .9 mm went instead through her left eye, exploding out through the top of her head. Topping up the magazine, Saburov holstered the pistol and quickly began tying the floats, three to each of the ten mines. When this was done, he took the mines two at a time into the cockpit where he reached over and placed them in the Styrofoam trunk again, ready to toss them overboard when the time came.

"What's Hornby doing down there?" asked Mawley. "Wanking himself off?"

"Wanking?" asked Saburov.

"Y'know," said Mawley, letting go of the wheel with his right hand and going through the motion.

"Ah, no," said Saburov. "The woman is very seasick. He is, how do you say, comforting her."

"I'll bet." Mawley guffawed. "Eh, listen, we're getting pretty close now. If that *Petrel* is still on the same heading we should be right up to them in about ten minutes. Should get a signal then from whoever we gotta pick up. Then we go in. Right?"

"No," said Saburov. "First we run ahead of them and put these over. Then we pick them up." He explained to Mawley about the trawler soon being too far north to jam *Petrel* any longer. "Much easier anyway," Saburov went on, "to pick up two CANUS people when everybody's abandoning the ship. Don't you agree?"

"Dunno," said Mawley. "Hornby's paying the shot. He says to pick his people up first then—"

"May I ask—" Saburov cut in, but he had to begin again as *Sea Dart* took three twenty-footers head on in succession in a din that Mawley said sounded like Niagara Falls. "May I ask," shouted Saburov, "how much you're being paid?"

"None of your goddamm business. Why?"

"I will double it if you do what I say. Run ahead of *Petrel* first."

"What's Hornby say about this?"

"He's dead."

"What?" Mawley spun the wheel to avoid a cross rip. "Jesus Christ! And May?"

Saburov didn't answer. It was ten seconds that seemed much longer to Mawley before he considered his option, which was that Saburov would shoot him as well if he didn't agree.

"Yes or no, Mawley. Which will it be?"

"You can't do it yourself," said Mawley in an effort to save face. "If I say no, you can't do it yourself."

"Of course I can, Mr. Mawley. This is nothing more than a very fast speedboat. But your help will make it faster, and we have to sink *Petrel* within the next half hour. You help me lay the mines first, and I'll double what you are being paid."

"What guarantee do I have, eh?"

"None, but I promise you, Mr. Mawley. You will be paid."

"All right, seeing I got no choice." He paused. "Double'll cost you ten thousand."

Saburov smiled, sure that Mawley was lying, more than doubling his price, like any good capitalist. "Agreed," said Saburov. "Ten thousand. Now go ahead of them."

"In U.S.," said Mawley.

"What?" asked Saburov, taking out the first cluster of floats.

"Dollars," Mawley explained. "I don't want it in friggin' marbles."

"Rubles," corrected Saburov.

"Whatever," said Mawley, watching Saburov insert a small cranking rod about the size of a roller skate key into the underside of the sunflowers. "How'll we do this?" he asked Saburov. "I mean, drop 'em all in a straight line in front of *Petrel*?"

"Run ahead of her in a fan shape, a big semicircle."

"Gotcha," said Mawley, entering wholeheartedly into the spirit of the proceedings now he had time to think what he could do with ten grand. Nontaxable. "One of 'em's bound to get her, right? Take the wheel for a mo?" he asked Saburov. "Heading is—"

"I know what the heading is. I've been watching you."

"You are a suspicious bastard, aren't ya?" Mawley joked. "All right, I just want to go to the head."

Saburov nodded reluctantly. "Hurry."

As Mawley opened the hatchway and disappeared down into the galley, Saburov shifted to the starboard side of the cockpit, holding the wheel with his right hand, unclipping his holster and taking out the Makarov with his left. When Mawley came up he'd expect to see him on the port side. Saburov held the gun level with the open hatch, one eye searching the darkness east of *Sea Dart*, watching *Petrel*, the other on the hatch.

Chapter Fifty

WITH MARTIN and his Kalashnikov behind him, followed by Sonny with Gloria, Frank began the slow, step-by-step descent from the officers' and scientists' deck, down the deathly quiet and emptied passageway to the stern. There a Beaufort container was already going over the stern roller, hitting the water, splitting open and unfolding its tentlike shape like some monstrous, misshapen mushroom undulating with every rise and fall of a wave. *Petrel*'s port lookout reported a wake of foam visible a quarter mile off the stern quarter and closing fast. The craft, whatever it was, the third mate reported, was now starting to show up as a slight blip on the radar screen, indicating that the jamming of radar and radio signals appeared to be weakening.

"Too fast for the trawler we expected," said Tate anxiously, his attention torn between the stern deck and radar screen.

"Lot smaller, too!" said the third mate.

"Well, the sooner they come and take these bastards off, the better."

"Yes, sir."

Tate could see Frank leading the way to the A-frame as the ship continued to drop her sea anchor, steadying herself into the wind.

Below the bridge, in the second mate's cabin, the medic did what he could for Scotty, giving him another shot of morphine, leaving the spike where it was, afraid that if he tried to remove it, the hemorrhaging would kill the mate for sure. The least anyone could do, he thought, if the man was to die, was to ease the pain.

As MAWLEY REAPPEARED from below he looked over, surprised, at Saburov holding the pistol.

"You took a long time down there," said Saburov.

"Don't worry, Comrade. Just a few souvenirs." Mawley grinned, tossing two wallets, one a man's, Saburov noticed, the other a woman's, over the side, minus a bundle of cash from each that he stuffed in his hip pocket.

It was then, as Saburov was about to reprove Mawley for his greed, that they suddenly saw their quarry almost stopped, fully lit, turning into the wind.

"Beautiful!" said Mawley, and then he began to laugh.

"What's the matter?" asked Saburov, unnerved by Mawley's exuberance.

"Look." Mawley was pointing at his Decca-II radar. "Just as they sit still and light up for us our radar starts to pick up."

"What?" snapped Saburov. It meant that the trawler's jamming would end within ten, fifteen minutes at the most, good news for the trawler, now out of the danger zone when dawn would break, but meaning *Petrel* would be very soon able to transmit her news about Eagle Island to the world.

"Hey," said Mawley, pointing along a line about 080 degrees, almost due east, dead ahead of *Sea Dart*. "There's a raft astern of her. Looks like Klaus's people made it off, after all, Comrade."

"Too late," said Saburov. "We can't waste time picking them up now. By then *Petrel* will be transmitting." Then in the binoculars Saburov saw *Petrel* was lowering her sea anchor. This would mean more time before she got under way again and, without her full noise imprint, the mines would not detonate. She had to get under way as quickly as possible. He would have to help her.

"Jesus!" said Mawley. "You're not going to run them down?"

"What?"

"The CANUS people. You're not going to run 'em down, are you?"

"And run the risk of fouling our props?" snapped Saburov. "Of course not."

SEA DART WAS now bearing down on *Petrel* in the heavy seas at a bone-jarring twelve knots. Martin, increasingly agitated, standing braced against the A-frame's port pylon, forced Frank to kneel on the deck, arms outstretched, holding the rail cable, his head down facing the dying wake of the stopped *Petrel*. Excitedly Martin saw the *Sea Dart*'s sharp prow ripping open the crest of a wave, disappearing then rising again, its spray cast high like a white net in the *Petrel*'s undulating sheet of light. The tent-shaped raft rose and fell only feet astern. Several crew members were in the process of rigging a bosun's chair to the Austin-Western arm to lower Martin, Sonny and Gloria to the raft.

Tate stood helplessly on the bridge, knowing, as did Frank and everyone else aboard the ship, that once Martin and Sonny were free of *Petrel*, the ship was a sitting target for the fast boat. Without turning to the junior officer at the steering console or the two lookouts, Tate was watching every move on deck. "Well, dammit," he said, "we're not going to take it sitting still like some damned rubber duck. Tell the chief—"

"Yes, sir."

Tate watched *Sea Dart*, now only seventy yards off.

"You think they'll release the woman?" asked one of the lookouts anxiously.

"What do you think?" asked Tate. "You think they want to keep any of us alive?"

"The bastards!"

"That," said Tate, "is an understatement." He turned to the junior officer. "Did the chief acknowledge?"

"Yes, sir. Ready to go whenever you are."

"Very well. Stand by!"

HIS BACK AGAINST the starboard winch, his knife still precariously close to Gloria's throat, Sonny watched apprehensively as three crew members held guy lines taut on the bosun's chair that, once picked up by the Austin-Western arm, would first lower him and the woman over the side into the inflated raft now riding impatiently on the swells that were passing under *Petrel* in great hills of water, one moment visible in the apron of light, the next moment lost in the darkness.

Looking up from his kneeling position, facing the stern roller, Frank glanced back over his shoulder at Martin, resplendent and mad in the vivid orange survival suit. "Take me as hostage instead of her," said Frank.

Martin looked down, his twisted grin conveying a mock civility that belied the crackling tension on the stern deck.

"Oh, no, Frankie. We'll have a lot more fun with her."
The grin disappeared. "Turn your face to the sea, asshole, or I'll blow it off!"

Frank saw the Austin-Western davit lowering ten feet to
his left, its hook about to engage the eye of the swivel atop
the bosun's chair. The Austin-Western's control panel,
situated right next to the two main switches for the deck,
which were housed in a flip-up-sided metal box, was being
worked nervously by a seaman on the starboard side near
one of the A-frame's stanchions, a distance of six feet from
the arm itself. Trouble was, Frank knew he'd be dead before he got halfway to the main switch box. Six feet was
point-blank range for the Kalashnikov pointed at his back.
"You be careful," he told the operator. "If you—"

There was a crack of bone. Martin's kick drove hard
into his ribs, knocking him sideways, sending him sprawling in agony by the port side stanchion. "I told you to shut
your goddamn face!" roared Martin, close now to losing
all control. Sonny was so alarmed by the outburst that his
knife nicked Gloria beneath her chin, and the white nylon
negligee became spattered with blood.

"I'm...just telling him..." Frank gasped, "that...if
he doesn't watch it that hydraulic arm'll jerk the chair out
of control and..."

Martin was about to whip him with the stock of the
Kalashnikov but, sensing that Hall's concern for the
woman could pay off for him when it was his turn to go
over in the bosun's chair, he hesitated, then shouted,
"What d'you mean?" Out of the corner of his eye he saw
the speedboat turning, vanishing into the darkness, obviously waiting for him, Sonny and the girl to get aboard
the raft. Its skipper, to Martin's chagrin, was obviously too
cowardly to come any closer to the oceanographic ship
than was necessary; to Martin's further disgust, he obviously preferred to let Martin and Sonny take all the risks
of disembarking from *Petrel*. "What the hell you mean?"
he shouted again at Frank, who had been explaining it to

him but whom he had trouble hearing in the racket of the hydraulic arm's high whine, the thumping of *Petrel*'s engines on standby and the never-ending howling and wailing of the storm front.

"I said," Frank repeated as loudly as he could, "that the arm doesn't glide down, it goes in a series of jerks. If you're too slow lowering the chair you'll have it crashing in against the side of the ship. If you're too fast, you'll dunk it." He nodded at the seaman operating the arm, which was, as he had just explained, jerking spastically toward the shackle on top of the three-sided canvas chair. "He hasn't operated it much," Frank continued, his frame contorted from the pain of the kick. "That was Jamie's job—and mine—when we were on station. I don't want to see Gloria—"

"All right, smartass," said Martin. "You're so goddamn clever, you work it, and if there's one slipup, you're dead. Got it?"

"I don't want to work it. I'm just telling you—"

"Work it! Move!"

Favoring one leg, his left arm bracing his rib cage, every breath seeming an effort for him, Frank looked like a much older man as, holding the starboard rail, he made his way over to the control panel. "No offence," he told the seaman who had been operating the control lever and variable speed buttons.

"No sweat," said the seaman gratefully. "Better you than me. He's crazy."

"Hey! Yeah, you!" Martin called, waving the Kalashnikov at the seaman. "Piss off from there. Get on with it, Hall!"

Ten feet away to Frank's left, Gloria tried to turn toward him, but Sonny jerked her head back, telling her not to move. The sheer terror of what was happening to her made her feel like throwing up, and she could feel Sonny pressing hard against her buttocks, his left hand fondling her front under the pretense of steadying her against the heavy swells. The oilskin jacket they'd thrown around her was open at the top, whether through accident or by design, revealing the sodden negligee.

"All set to go," one of the seamen working on the chair told Martin as he walked back toward the after lab after shackling the chair's swivel joint to the arm's hook. "Can't use the safety chain across the front of the chair, though," he cautioned, "not with two instead of one squeezing into the chair."

"Yes," Frank added, his hand on the control lever ready to take up the cable's slack. "Should only put one person in at a time. It'd be—"

"Yeah," Martin interrupted, the bright, mad look in his eyes again. "One at a time…you'd like that, wouldn't you, assholes? Take more time for me to make a mistake, eh…eh?"

"No, listen," began the seaman. "I'm just telling you for your own—"

"Shut up. Sonny, you and Sweetie Pie get in the fucking chair."

"Right, Marty."

"Wait a minute!" said Marty, going over to the chair, testing the shackle to make sure the flanged edge of its through-pin was flush, that it hadn't been sabotaged in any way.

Using the palm of his hand to better control the jerkiness of the hydraulic arm, Frank showed his long experience despite the heavy rolls of the ship. He took up the slack in one smooth pull, the loose five-eighths-inch cable becoming taut, creaking, salt dust flying from it like talc as it took the strain. Sonny sat in the canvas chair with Gloria on his lap, a scarlet patch of blood spread over her bosom, so vivid in the harsh white glare of the stern deck's spotlights it took on a dirty brownish tinge. The chair began to ease off the deck and move higher into the glow of the A-frame's powerful arc light. From the chair, Gloria glimpsed long shadows spearing the deck below as three seamen struggled to maintain their balance while keeping the guy ropes on the chair tightly reined.

The arm swung outboard over the starboard side, twenty feet above the water. "Tell your friend he can put away his knife now he's out of reach," Frank told Martin. "He'll need his hands free to help fend the chair off the ship's side."

Martin thought about it, suspicious as ever, but saw it made sense and told Sonny to do it. Frank looked down into the ship's shadow, his eyes straining, particularly his injured one, to judge how far the oil-sheened telescopic arm needed to be extended in order to bring the chair slightly in front of the raft, where Sonny and Gloria could be lowered to its entrance and not onto the inflated roof. He began lowering the chair until it was deep in the ship's shadow and, he guessed, only about ten feet from the crests of the swells. It began swaying precariously close to the ship's side, its guy ropes slack, trailing down into the sea like spaghetti. The three crewmen who had been holding the ropes were now busy manning long boat poles, pushing hard against the cable, trying to help keep the chair from smashing into the ship.

There was a thud as the arm stopped its steady descent. "Need to swing the A-frame's light outboard to see what the hell I'm doing," Frank advised Martin.

"All right, all right, hurry it up. But no funny stuff," Martin replied, poking the Kalashnikov's barrel forward.

"For Christ's sake," said Frank, grimacing with each breath. "I'm not going anywhere. The main switches are right here next to the arm's controls. Besides, I'm hardly going to try anything with Gloria—"

"Just hurry up!" shouted Martin, taking a split second to check out the speedboat. He couldn't see it but could hear the steady throbbing of its engines.

Frank, still favoring one leg, his left hand firmly on the ball of the arm's lever, moved a pace or two right to the stern deck's control box, flipped up the cover, threw the two main switches and shoved the arm lever up. The stern was in darkness, the bosun's chair smacking the water in free-fall. The blackness was ripped open by the Kalashnikov's burst, but Frank had already hit Martin in a battering knee tackle as shots streamed overhead, slamming and sparking into the bulkhead above the winch and ricocheting across the blacked-out deck.

Frank punched Martin in the groin. There was an explosion of air, the machine gun clattering by the A-frame. "Turn on the lights!" Frank yelled. The ship's bow was dipping sharply as the deck was floodlit again. Frank saw Martin doubled over in the A-frame, pulling a switchblade, his arm and one foot going back for the thrust. The stern suddenly dropped, the ship yawed, and Martin was gone.

Now there were three of them in the water, Gloria swimming for the ship's side, reaching frantically for one of the dangling guy ropes, Martin and Sonny striking out for the raft.

IN THE PENUMBRA OF LIGHT visible in his binoculars, Saburov could see one of the men in the water aft of *Petrel* slashing wildly at the painter tethering the raft to the ship. Then he saw the two of them clambering aboard the raft, and at the same time the distance increasing between the raft and the oceanographic ship. His glasses moved to *Petrel*'s stern, and he saw for the first time the man who he guessed must be Hall, obviously in charge, overseeing the raising of the hydraulic davit, and the woman, who fell from one of the ropes only a few feet from a phalanx of hands stretching out for her.

Saburov handed the glasses to Mawley. "You should see this, Mr. Mawley. It's quite entertaining."

It took Mawley a second or two to focus as Saburov kept *Sea Dart* riding high into the wind, and by the time he could pick out *Petrel*'s stern, heaving up and down in the circle of the binoculars, he could report to the Russian that someone was taking off his oilskins, jumping over the side to help the woman.

Saburov shook his head. "These Americans!"

"I'm an American," Mawley said proudly.

"Yes," said Saburov, putting out his hands for the binoculars. "And to think all this heroism—" he spoke the word *heroism* distastefully as if it was some kind of terminal disease "—will be wasted."

"What do you mean?" said Mawley, lighting another cigarette from the one he already had going.

"I mean that in another half hour our hero and his Ninotchka will be dead."

"We gonna dump those gadgets of yours now?" said Mawley.

"Not until *Petrel* heads off under full power—to detonate the mines. I'd say take or give fifteen minutes."

"Give or take," corrected Mawley. "It's give or take."

"Yes," said Saburov. "Of course."

FRANK WAITED until he saw Gloria safely aboard and until Larson, the medic, told him her knife cut wasn't as bad as it looked, before he would hear anything about changing into warm, dry clothes. As he saw her carried by two seamen off the deck, shivering, almost delirious with hypothermia and the horror of what she'd been through, he walked toward the stern, looking at the raft now about seventy yards away. He took up the Kalashnikov and, holding on to the rail, made his way over to the intercom, telling Captain Tate that he could douse all lights and head for home, and adding that all they had to worry about now was an attack from the PT boat.

"What about those bastards?" said one of the crewmen, astonished that Frank hadn't fired at the raft.

"They're not worth a murder charge," said Frank simply, adding with a shrewdness that bypassed most of them, "Anyway, the more time it takes their friends to pick them up, the more time we have to leave that PT boat behind."

"But that boat could catch up to us, Frank. It's a hell of a lot faster."

"Yes," admitted Frank. "It could. But in another hour it'll be dawn and by then all that radio static we've been getting should be gone. We'll be in the clear." He said this to calm the crew's fears, but knowing Saburov, he spoke with more confidence than he felt. *Petrel* was picking up speed, her pistons thundering in renewed effort. In a matter of minutes she would be on maximum revs.

Then, as if in perverse denial of what he had just told the crewman, the moon lit up the sea to reveal the streak of the *Sea Dart*'s wake, as the PT boat could be seen racing a hundred yards out on the port side, parallel to *Petrel* as her chief engineer brought the four G.M.s to full power on a direct heading for Astoria. At the same moment *Petrel*'s third officer observed the patrol boat showing up more frequently on the radar between the clutter of the westerly-driven swells. Through his binoculars the race of moonlight became a wide, silver band flexing bright and dark, and at one point he reported to Tate that it looked as if the PT boat had thrown something over the side.

"What the hell are they up to?" inquired Tate.

"No good," answered the young mate.

"I know that," Tate retorted caustically, worriedly watching the radar sweep and the rev counter simultaneously. "What I mean is," he continued, "why are they going ahead of us and what are they tossing overboard? Thought they'd be tracking behind us until they could pick up those two bastards in the—"

The deck-to-bridge intercom button blinked urgently. It was Frank, wind and sea trying to drown his voice. "Captain, that PT boat's running ahead of us."

"I know, Frank," Tate responded, telling him what the mate had seen. "I'm just trying to work out—"

"Can't be any kind of mortar or depth charge," said Frank quickly. "Otherwise they'd stay windward of us. Going ahead of us like this would mean they'd have to be firing against the wind. Plays hell with any kind of trajectory. Remember how we throw our seismic charges downwind—"

"Yes," Tate cut in, "but we haven't any dynamite charges aboard to defend ourselves."

"Then it has to be some kind of magnetic mine," Frank said.

"Jesus! How can we stop them?"

"We can't. But I think we should stop engines. Drift awhile."

"Westerlies'll still blow us east into the mines or whatever it is they're laying down."

"Yes, but not as fast as if we keep going full ahead. Once they lay mines they won't be able to keep track of them any more than we can. They'll have no idea when we're supposed to run into one. That gives us a little time."

"For what?" Tate demanded. "So we drift awhile longer before we're blown out of the water. What's the difference?"

"How far ahead are they?" asked Frank.

Tate glanced at the radar. "Only a thousand yards, cutting out a semicircle. Hemming us in nicely."

As Tate spoke, Frank could hear the ship's telegraph clanging over the intercom, her engines slowing. But he knew that somewhere, no more than a thousand yards ahead, there was probably a line of explosive charges, magnetically activated, whatever, any one of which could either stop *Petrel* dead, for the PT boat to come in and finish her off at their leisure, or, if it hit *Petrel* amidships, could tear her apart, sinking her in minutes. His index finger was tapping the Kalashnikov's trigger guard as he thought.

Tate came back on. "They're heading down our port side."

Frank couldn't see them, for the moon was gone again and all he had to go by was the pulsating roar of the PT boat's engine. Only then did he see a faint flickering of light, not the PT boat but a light several hundred yards astern, which he knew could only be the tentlike inflatable with Martin and Sonny aboard, having a fit, no doubt, that if their buddies on the PT boat didn't see them, they wouldn't be picked up. But that didn't concern him; for all he cared, Martin and Sonny could drown, the sooner the better. What he *was* concerned about was what would happen after they were picked up.

Frank switched on the intercom again and asked for four seamen not on watch to come immediately to the stern deck.

Chapter Fifty-One

SABUROV CHANGED POSITIONS with Mawley so he could man the .50 mm Browning machine gun on the starboard side of *Sea Dart*'s cockpit, but when he saw what a fat target the lit-up inflatable made, like a big incandescent jellyfish sliding up and down, he decided instead to use the Makarov and save the more punishing .50s for when *Petrel* started to go down and he had to go in close to finish off any would-be survivors. He fired four shots before one hit part of the inflatable's skirting tubes. The raft collapsed in on itself with a sigh of air that contrasted markedly with the hysteria of the two men inside, who for a moment looked like two mad ballet dancers, leaping around until the canopy collapsed around them and the raft flooded, disappearing slowly beneath the waves.

The raft and the PT boat being no more than a few hundred yards upwind, Frank and the crewman could hear Martin and Sonny screaming along with the short, sharp cracks of the pistol shots.

"What the hell—" began one seaman. "They're killing their own people!"

It was no surprise to Frank, who knew by now that Saburov wasn't going to leave any witnesses.

WITH ALL HER LIGHTS OUT, *Petrel*, at dead slow ahead, was coming about into the wind as crewmen, in response to Frank's request, emerged stumbling and cursing from the after lab. They bumped into bulkhead and doorsills, dragging out all the bedding they could find, dumping it into the loading net Frank had quickly spread out on the stern deck, while Tate used all the considerable seamanship he had to keep the ship's bow pointing westward. The swells kept pounding her, but her direction was such that the wash on the decks was kept to a minimum as the crew kept dumping mattresses into the sling. Frank then slashed them, looking out now and then to starboard where he could hear the PT boat's engine throbbing, waiting like a hidden vulture for *Petrel* to run into one of the mines.

SABUROV SCANNED eastward with his binoculars, but *Petrel* was all but invisible due to the darkness and the awkward angle *Sea Dart* was in after maneuvering to sink the raft. But the colonel was taking no chances, telling Mawley to run a north, then a south arc, during which he tossed over more of the floating sonic mines at fifty-yard intervals so that *Petrel* was in effect between two semicircular arrays of mines. "In the event they decide to come about and run astern!" Saburov explained to Mawley, unable to keep the tone of satisfaction out of his voice. "They are trapped."

"Smart thinking," said Mawley, offering Saburov another filter tip, which the colonel gratefully accepted, tucking it in his tunic pocket for a relaxing smoke later when his job was finally done.

"Not long now then, you reckon?" said Mawley happily.

"No, Comrade ... very soon."

Mawley was trying to decide whether he'd take the ten grand in thousand dollar bills or hundreds.

WHEN THE HALF DOZEN or so mattresses were in the loading net and Frank had slashed all of them, he told the two off-duty oilers they could now pour on the gasoline, and some, "but not too much," bunker oil. Then he took three of the six grenades from the haversack he had brought from the island, handed them to a seaman and, stuffing the other three in his pocket, switched on the control for the Austin-Western, lowering the arm. The second it "clunked" to a stop a few feet above the deck he attached its big hook to the sling of the patched-up Zodiac, and climbed in with the Kalashnikov. One of the seamen moved to the rear to man the Zodiac's twin outboards and steer by the tiller handle.

"Frank?" It was one of the seamen crouched low around the loading net. Frank tried to see who it was but couldn't recognize him in the dark, despite a faint suggestion of dawn in the overcast sky. "What is it?" Frank asked quickly.

"That aluminum patch on the bottom of the Zodiac. I dunno how long that's gonna hold, buddy. It was starting to rip by the time we got back from the island."

"I'll take a chance," said Frank, then turned to the seaman at the twin Evinrudes. "How 'bout you, sailor? You're free to—"

"No," said the sailor. "I'll take a chance, too."

"Right!" said Frank. "Let's go!" As the Austin-Western arm began to take up the Zodiac's slack, ready to swing them out over the port side, the PT boat's engines still sounded a good way off to starboard. Frank shouted his last-minute instructions. "Remember, he's not going to leave anybody alive if he can help it. Jimmy, where are those bottles?"

A seaman handed him the haversack. "One of 'em's Torio—one of Aussie's bottles."

"Okay," acknowledged Frank. "Appreciate it. You ready with the flare pistol?"

The seaman held it up.

"How many flares?"

"Dozen at least. Ship's stores has got lots of these babies."

"Christ!" said another seaman. "You won't need that many, Jimmy."

"All right," said Frank. "Who's got the other three grenades?"

"Me," said Jimmy. "Three for me, three for you. Right?"

"We're all set then," said Frank. "Don't forget you've got seven seconds with those. So get 'em over fast, boys."

"She'll be right," said Jimmy. There was subdued laughter on the deck at Jimmy's deliberate use of the phrase, a bittersweet memory of one of Aussie's celebrated sayings, designed to reassure but ironically signaling alarm.

The arm lifted, extended slightly, swung to port then down. The moment the Zodiac slapped water Frank and the seaman were drenched, the Evinrudes already sputtering low. Frank hunched like a protective mother over the haversack to keep the bottles as dry as possible, and despite the strong wind, the stench of the black boot polish he and the seaman were using for camouflage and the overwhelming smell of gasoline fumes enveloped him, starting another headache that he knew would take hours to abate.

It happened much more quickly than either Frank or Tate or any of the crew had anticipated, but all of them had underestimated not only Saburov's obsession with finishing off *Petrel* but how much closer in the PT boat was. They had thought she might be half a mile out, but in the few minutes it took Frank and the seaman in the Zodiac to go up *Petrel*'s port side and swing starboard around her bow, heading out in the general direction of the sound of the PT's engine, Saburov had decided to come in to less than a thousand yards from *Petrel*, trying to pick something up on the binoculars in the coming dawn.

AS INSTRUCTED BY FRANK, the seamen on the stern deck brought back the Austin-Western arm as soon as the Zodiac had cast off, hooking the arm to the loading net that was bulging with the gasoline-soaked mattresses and other assorted items individual seamen had deemed expendable, including pails and empty kerosene tins. Jimmy and another man pulled out the grenade pins, holding down the spring levers until the net was lowered below the rail, then in unison, under Jimmy's command, they dropped the three grenades into a V formed by the mattresses. The operator, remembering Frank's warning that he would only have seven seconds, was already extending the telescopic arm even as he was inclining it seaward at full speed to a few feet above the water.

The *thump* of the muffled explosion, its enormous fire and sound of metal shrapnel erupting ten feet out from *Petrel*'s port side, looked, from even a few yards out on her starboard side, to be the result of an internal explosion that had ripped her belly open. Immediately the crew on the stern began shouting and swearing, making whatever noise they could. Fire hoses were unraveled from the interior of the ship, as well as from two hand-held extinguishers quickly unclipped from the stern deck's bulkhead. In seconds a crisscross of water jets poured forth from all of them, aimed at the flames but, unable to be seen from the starboard side, going through the flames, avoiding the gasoline cargo burning fiercely below the extended arm.

THROUGH THE CIRCLE of his binoculars, Saburov saw an enormous fire leaping up from *Petrel*'s off side. The American sailors were desperately trying to fight it in the storm, as the wind played havoc with the hoses' jets. The black figures of the sailors were rushing in all directions in the panic that nearly always accompanies a fire at sea. No matter how well trained the crew, a fire onboard ship was the sailor's worst nightmare.

"Holy Toledo!" said Mawley. "Didn't think your gadgets'd cause that much damage."

"They're very powerful," replied Saburov, so smugly that even Mawley knew the Russian was really as excited as a schoolboy with the deadly results of the sonic mines.

"What now?" Mawley asked.

"Wait a few seconds, I think," said the ever-cautious Saburov. "That kind of explosion will sink her, all right, but let us wait until—" He hadn't finished speaking when they heard a loud pop like a firecracker going off.

Saburov's long experience told him it was a flare even before he saw the phosphorous streak arcing well forward of the stricken ship, leaving its bridge and after section in flickering shadow as men astern, a little more clearly now at least for a few seconds, continued to fight the fire. The forward section of the ship was bathed in the flare's bluish-white light, its reflection running out to sea like a huge circle of white fish trying to escape.

"SOS," said Mawley, flicking the stub of his cigarette overboard. "You were right. They're going down, all right." Then, turning to the Russian, he asked, "Should we help 'em out, ya think?" They could see several Beaufort inflatable canisters being frantically thrown overboard from the forward well deck and men donning life vests in the continuing confusion on *Petrel*'s deck. Through it all could be heard the nasal sound of a PA system announcing Abandon Ship.

Feeling victorious, Saburov couldn't help a smile and, adopting Mawley's tone, answered, "Oh, I think we

should—how do you say it, Mr. Mawley—lend a hand."
With that he manned the .50 mm Browning and fired a
burst to test the feed belt as Mawley pushed the throttle
forward.

Skirting the edge of the flare's light, knowing their Zodiac was too small for the PT boat's radar to pick up in the
increased wave clutter, Frank and the seaman saw the machine-gun's tongue spitting in the dark. They waited until
the flare reached its zenith and began its descent, seeing the
knife-edged bow of the PT boat clearly then about seven
hundred yards to the southwest, with *Petrel* a thousand
yards due north. When the flare hit the water and fizzled,
they headed out on a starboard tack, aiming at an intercept point midway between the two vessels.

Added to the cacophony coming from *Petrel*, the persistent noise of the storm's wind and the ear-pounding
throb of the PT boat's own engine as it raced toward *Petrel*, there was now the fierce stutter of the Browning machine gun. Saburov was already raking the inflatable rafts,
intent on gunning down anyone who might not go down
with the ship. So occupied were he and Mawley that neither of them saw the Zodiac coming in, up and over the
mountainous waves, until the very last moment. Mawley
shouted, pointing off their starboard side. Saburov swung
the machine gun around, and Frank fired at the khaki figure whose head he had glimpsed when the second flare
streaked up from *Petrel*. He also saw flecks, wooden chips,
flying up around the figure, but then the PT boat swung
hard about, evading the Kalashnikov's fire, coming
straight for the Zodiac.

"Port!" Frank yelled to the seaman at the tiller and kept
the Kalashnikov firing at the cockpit. Its Plexiglas splintered but there was no one there. "Damn!" he shouted as
the Zodiac ran aft of the PT boat and he clipped another
magazine. In the break he saw a head reappear, look
about, then it was gone. The PT boat was coming around

again, once more trying to run them down, coming in very fast from twenty yards away; then suddenly it veered away.

"They're hightailing it!" said the seaman hopefully.

"No, they aren't," Frank said, dropping the Kalashnikov. "Bastards are trying to get out of our range." He and Saburov knew the Browning could outreach the Kalashnikov by much more than a hundred yards.

"Go after them!" Frank shouted. "Full speed!" He felt the surge in his stomach as the Zodiac's nose shot up, smacked the crest of a wave contemptuously, careening down the other side. The PT boat was a few waves ahead, its big drum of gasoline astern blocking any clear shot he might have had at the cockpit. Laying two of the bottles and the grenades between his knees like a jockey gripping the saddle, he held on to the safety rope looped around the inside of the Zodiac. In another two minutes the Zodiac, its outboards screaming, was gaining on *Sea Dart*, when suddenly the PT boat reduced speed, its bow wave collapsing in a long trough between waves. It turned, showing the Russian at the Browning. Its speeding away had been a trap to draw the Americans in close.

"Port! Quarter speed!" yelled Frank with all the power he had, and the Zodiac veered left as he threw two grenades. Neither hit the PT boat, but their explosions and shrapnel forced the two figures to duck in the cockpit. In those few seconds Frank threw both of the Molotov cocktails made for him by the oilers. One, the Torio bottle, missed; the other struck and broke on the PT's deck a foot from *Sea Dart*'s stern, but its pool of fire was disappointingly small, the size of a pie plate, most of its gasoline having been siphoned off by the wind.

"Full speed!" Frank called. Ten feet from the PT's stern he tossed the last grenade. The PT boat's extra gas drum blew and *Sea Dart*'s stern was a fireball, taking on the shape of a comet, its tail, fanned by the west wind, sweeping back on itself toward the cockpit, the two men aflame. But then, incredibly—at least to the seaman aboard the

Zodiac but not to Frank—one of them, the man in the military cap, reached for the Browning. Frank emptied his magazine in an unbroken burst and the figure was flung back into the sea, fiery arms outstretched, the Kalashnikov's bullets ripping out his chest. The other man lay sprawled on the foredeck consumed as in a funeral pyre.

As the Zodiac turned the sweetish smell of cooking was on the wind.

Frank and the seaman were quiet on their way back to *Petrel*. Jimmy was firing the flares and everyone on duty was searching for the clusters of floats so that they could send out a relief crew in the Zodiac to puncture them with the boat hooks, sending Saburov's sunflowers to the bottom. Tate let *Petrel* drift until dawn when, once all the floats were clearly visible and punctured, the ship could once again resume her homeward course. By then the radio static was normal, that is, still sounding like a sizzling steak but no longer solidly jammed, the Polish trawlers by now well away to the north. Soon Sparks's messages for all possible assistance were getting through. Four hours later, in the gray, sullen daylight—a daylight that seemed beautiful to those aboard *Petrel*—a big, bug-eyed copter, this time from the U.S. Coast Guard at Warrenton, the air station at Astoria, appeared, hovering overhead, to take up Scotty and Gloria in stretcher harness.

Epilogue

THREE DAYS LATER, Frank and Gloria were told that Scotty would "make it" but wouldn't be doing any sea duty for at least six months. The statement was wrong in one respect. Twelve weeks later Scotty said if he had to stay ashore for another month he'd go bonkers, complaining to Gloria and Frank in utter astonishment that, "D'ye ken they no have porridge in American hospitals? Savages!"

IN MOSCOW IT WAS REPORTED that Comrade Kornon, alternate member of the Politburo, would be unable to take up full membership "at the moment," due to the fact that he was about to undertake a "reorientation course" in Gorky.

THE SAME DAY in Zurich, the University Hospital on Ramistrasse was alerted to prepare its number-one operating theater for emergency surgery. Herr Klaus, head of the giant multinational Swiss Rhine Petrochemicals, had collapsed in his office after receiving a telephone call—someone said they thought it was a call from Moscow, others said America—and was hemorrhaging badly from a perforated ulcer. The receiving sister at the hospital tried to get some information from Herr Klaus regarding allergies to penicillin, et cetera, but not being able to make sense out of what he was saying, sought the help of the chief resident. He asked Herr Klaus the same questions while waiting for the medical file from Klaus's physician to arrive, but all the resident could get out of the semidelirious patient was a continued repetition of the German word, *Halle*, which means "hall" as in town hall or guild-hall.

To Frank and Gloria, who were by then seeing a lot of each other, and to the officers and crew of *Petrel*, grateful thanks were expressed by the United States government, but all involved were "requested" not to mention the "incident" at Eagle Island. The American government, it was explained to them, was engaged in what a State Department official described as "delicate, preliminary" arms negotiation talks with the Soviet Union, and the department was concerned that any "adverse publicity... at this time" would seriously jeopardize what might otherwise be an "extensive arms limitation treaty." Their informant was sure they all understood.

They understood perfectly.

**Cloaked behind a family curse
and Irish legend, a madman stalks
his final victim.**

BANSHEE

DAN
BARTON

When the body of a woman buried alive is discovered,
a doctor begins a desperate manhunt to prevent a psychotic killer, who is terrorizing a small canyon commu-
nity in California, from reaching his next victim!

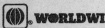